# *Healer's* APPRENTICE

# THE
# *Healer's*
# APPRENTICE

## Melanie Dickerson

**ZONDERVAN.com/**
**AUTHORTRACKER**
*follow your favorite authors*

ZONDERVAN

*The Healer's Apprentice*
Copyright © 2010 by Melanie Dickerson

This title is also available as a Zondervan ebook. Visit www.zondervan.com/ebooks.

Requests for information should be addressed to:
Zondervan, *Grand Rapids, Michigan* 49530

Library of Congress Cataloging-in-Publication Data

Dickerson, Melanie.
 The healer's apprentice / Melanie Dickerson.
   p. cm.
 Summary: Rosa
 Summary: In this story loosely based on the Sleeping Beauty fairy tale, seventeen-year-old Rose, a healer's apprentice, falls in love with the betrothed Lord Hamlin, who is seeking the sorcerer who cursed his future bride.
 ISBN 978-0-310-72143-7 (softcover)
 [1. Love—Fiction. 2. Middle Ages—Fiction. 3. Christian life—Fiction.] I. Title.
 PZ7.D5575He 2010
 [Fic]—dc22                                              2010021582

*Cover design: Mike Heath*
*Cover photography: Mike Heath*
*Interior design: Publication Services, Inc.*

*Printed in the United States of America*

10 11 12 13 14 /QG/ 20 19 18 17 16 15 14 13 12 11 10 9 8 7 6 5 4 3 2 1

To Joe, Grace, and Faith.

—M. D.

# Chapter

## 1

❦

*Spring, 1386. Hagenheim. The Harz Mountains, Lower Saxony.*

*The townspeople of Hagenheim craned their* necks as they peered down the cobblestone street, hoping to catch a glimpse of the Duke of Hagenheim's two handsome sons. The top-heavy, half-timbered houses hovered above the crowd as if they too were eager to get a peek at Lord Hamlin and Lord Rupert.

Rose shifted her basket from her left hip to her right and wrinkled her nose at the stale smell of sweat from the many bodies pressed close, mingled with the pungent scent of animal dung. Chickens and children skittered about, the clucking and squealing adding to the excited murmurs.

"I'll wait with you to the count of one hundred, Hildy, then I'm leaving." Rose couldn't let Frau Geruscha think her apprentice was a lazy dawdler.

"Are you not curious to see if they've changed?" Hildy asked, her green eyes glinting in the sun.

"No doubt the duke's sons have developed into humble scholars after two years at Heidelberg's university." Even as she spoke, she glanced up the street. In spite of wanting Hildy to think her indifferent to the young noblemen, Rose was glad she had a good view.

Rose's dog, Wolfie, began barking so zealously his front paws lifted off the ground.

*"Hist.* No barking." Rose leaned down and rubbed the ruff of fur at the back of his neck.

"Rose!"

Her heart leapt at the horrified tone in Hildy's voice, and she stood and faced her friend.

"You didn't even wear your best dress!"

Rose glanced down at her green woolen kirtle. "Oh, Hildy. As if it matters."

"At least your hair looks beautiful." Hildy ran her hand down Rose's loose mane of brown curls, only partially hidden by her linen coif. "How do you ever hope to get a husband if you don't pay more attention to your clothing?"

Rose scowled. "I don't hope."

How many times would she have to explain this to Hildy? When Rose was a little child, Frau Geruscha had taken a liking to her. Now that Rose was grown up, the town healer had chosen Rose to be her apprentice—an honorable life's work that would prevent Rose from being forced to marry. Frau Geruscha, having grown up in a convent, had not only taught Rose about medicinal herbs, but also how to read Latin—a skill Rose was very proud of. But it was a skill most men would hardly value in a wife.

"You don't fool me, Rose Roemer. Every girl wants to be married. Besides, look across the street at Mathias." Hildy pointed with her eyes. "He speaks to you every chance he gets, and he's quite handsome."

Rose harrumphed at Hildy's dreamy tone. "The blacksmith's son?" *With his lecherous grin?* "He only wants one thing from me, and it isn't marriage."

"How can you be so sure ..."

Hildy's voice trailed off at the crowd's whispered exclamations as six men on horseback came into view around the bend in the narrow street.

Hildy grabbed her thick blonde braid and draped it over her shoulder then chewed on her lips to redden them. "You should at least try to catch their eye."

Rose shook her head at Hildy. "You know Lord Hamlin is betrothed—as good as married—and Lord Rupert must marry an heiress." Rose took hold of her friend's arm. Someone had to be the voice of reason. "I hate to dampen your excitement, Hildy, but if either of the noble sons takes a single look at us, I'll be vastly astonished."

Hildy smirked. "I won't be."

The approaching clop-clop of hooves drew Hildy's gaze back to the street. "Shh. Here they come." She set her basket of beans, leeks, and onions on the ground behind her and smoothed her skirt.

The throng of people fell silent out of respect for their young lords.

The duke's elder son, Wilhelm, Earl of Hamlin, led the way down the street on his black horse. His younger brother, Lord Rupert, rode beside him. Two bearded knights on cinnamon-colored horses followed three lengths behind the young men, with two more bringing up the rear.

The knights were simply dressed, but the noble sons were covered from neck to toe in flowing robes. Rose stifled a snort. They were only returning home. Did they think they were on their way to the king's court?

Yet as he drew nearer, she saw that Lord Hamlin wore not a robe after all, but a plain cloak of dark wool. His bearing and the proud tilt of his head were what made him look so regal.

In contrast to his brother's outerwear, a fur-trimmed surcoat of lustrous sapphire silk hung over Lord Rupert's lean frame, with only the toes of his leather boots peeking out. The disparity between the brothers went beyond their clothing. Lord Rupert's light brown hair was long and curled at the ends, and a blue ribbon gathered it at the nape of his neck. A jaunty glint shone from his pale eyes. Lord Hamlin's black hair hung over his forehead, and he seemed oblivious to the crowd. He focused his gaze straight ahead, toward Hagenheim Castle, whose towers were visible over the tops of the town's tallest buildings.

No, she'd say they hadn't changed at all.

"*Willkommen!*" Hildy called out. "Welcome back, my lords!" She waved her hand high, as though hailing a messenger.

All eyes turned to Rose and Hildy. A spear of panic went through Rose. She wanted to hide, but it was too late. Lord Hamlin's eyes darted in their direction, alighted on Rose, and held. His expression changed and his features softened as he looked at her. Then his gaze swept down, taking in her basket and her dress. He quickly faced forward again.

*He realizes I'm nobody, a peasant girl.* Heat spread up Rose's neck and burned her cheeks.

Lord Rupert's huge blond warhorse walked toward Rose and Hildy as the crowd suddenly took up Hildy's cheer. "*Willkommen!* Welcome back!" The horse came within three feet of the girls and stopped, stamping his hooves on the cobblestone street and sending Wolfie into a wild fit of barking.

Rose threw her arms around Wolfie's neck to hold him back. Her temples pounded at the sight of the warhorse's powerful legs.

The younger nobleman swept off his plumed hat, bowing from his saddle. His eyes roved from Hildy to Rose, then he winked. "I thank you, ladies, for your kind welcome." He grinned and swung his hat back on his head, then spurred his horse into a trot and caught up with the others.

"Did you see that? Did you see it?" Hildy pounded on Rose's shoulder.

Wolfie calmed as the men rode into the distance. Rose let go of him and stood up, glaring at Hildy. "I can't believe you called out to them."

"Lord Rupert actually spoke to us. *To us.* And did you see how Lord Hamlin looked at you?" Hildy clutched her hands to her heart, gazing at the clouds. "Are they not the most handsome men you've ever seen? I could hardly breathe!" She turned and smiled at Rose. "I knew they'd like what they saw once they caught sight of you."

"Would you keep your voice down?" Rose urged Hildy to start walking toward the *Marktplatz*. She glanced around, afraid the towns-people would overhear their embarrassing conversation. She imagined the miller's skinny wife, who walked ahead of them, snorting in deri-sion at Hildy's compliment. The shoemaker's buxom daughter, striding down the other side of the street, would laugh out loud.

Hildy and her romantic notions of love. She was a candle-maker's daughter, dreaming about the local nobility as if she had any chance of inspiring a serious thought in them. As a woodcutter's daughter, Rose held no grand illusions about her own prospects.

Hildy's chatter faded into the background as Rose wondered at Lord Rupert's flirtatious wink. But what stuck in her mind was the way Lord Hamlin had looked at her. Thinking of that, her face began to burn once again. She'd encountered her share of leering men and their crude comments, but Lord Hamlin's look was different. It had made her feel pretty—until he noticed her clothing.

She should have worn her good dress, the crimson one with the bit of white silk at the neck and wrists that Frau Geruscha had given her. Hildy said it brought out the red tint in her chestnut hair. But how could she have known Hildy would draw the attention of both Lord Hamlin and Lord Rupert and that they would look straight at her?

Realizing her train of thought, she snorted. What difference did it make which dress she wore? Everyone knew Lord Hamlin was betrothed to the daughter of the Duke of Marienberg. But betrothed or not, he'd hardly be interested in her. And Lord Rupert, as the younger son, would inherit none of the family's wealth and so would need to find a rich heiress to marry.

If, as an apprentice, Rose could impress Frau Geruscha with her skill, she would become the next healer — needed, respected. She could avoid the indignity of marrying someone out of desperation.

So she'd never experience love. Most married people didn't, either.

Rose dipped her quill in the pot of ink and concentrated on scratching out the next sentence of the tale she was writing. Frau Geruscha encouraged her to write her stories, although she said it was probably best if she didn't tell anyone about them.

Shouts drifted through the open window of the healer's chambers. From her vantage point in the southwest tower of Hagenheim Castle, Rose peered out, seeking the source of the commotion.

"Make way!"

Two men hastened across the courtyard. They carried a boy between them, using their arms for a seat. A woman ran behind them.

Rose scrambled to hide her parchment, pen, and ink in the small trunk beside her desk. "Frau Geruscha! Someone's coming!" She snatched up a gray apron that lay nearby and slipped it over her head.

Wolfie adjusted his grip on his bone and growled low in his throat. "Wolfie, stay."

The dog's lips came together, sheathing his fangs, but he focused his eyes on the door.

Frau Geruscha entered the chamber from the storage room, her wimple bobbing like the wings of a great white bird.

The two men carrying the boy burst through the door, the woman following close behind. Rose recognized one man as a farmer who lived near her parents' home. The boy was his son, perhaps eight years old. He wore ragged brown hose and his torn shirt drooped on his thin frame. Bright red blood covered one of his sleeves. His lips were white, as if all the blood had drained out of his body.

Here was her chance to show Frau Geruscha she was a competent apprentice. She would strive to appear calm and ready to help. She was thankful she had already braided her hair that morning and covered it with a linen cloth, as her mistress had instructed her.

"Frau Geruscha!" Fear and panic lent a high pitch to the woman's voice. "Our son fell on the plow blade."

The healer's wise face wrinkled in concentration as her gaze swept the boy from head to toe. She pointed to a low straw bed against the wall, and the men laid the child on it.

Pain drew the boy's features tight. Rose longed to comfort him, but she didn't want to get in Frau Geruscha's way.

Frau Geruscha sat on the edge of the bed. She showed no emotion as she pulled back his sleeve, revealing the gaping wound.

"No!" The boy screamed and shrank away from her. He held his arm against his chest and drew his knees up like a shield.

Rose turned her head. *O God, don't let me get sick.* She had to prove herself.

Frau Geruscha glanced back at Rose. "Fetch me some water from the kettle and a roll of bandages."

Rose scurried to the fireplace and grabbed a pottery bowl. Using a cloth to hold the lip of the iron kettle, she tipped it to one side and poured hot water into the shallow vessel. She carried it back to Frau Geruscha then dashed to the storage room to get the bandages.

"Don't touch it!"

Rose tried to force the boy's terrified voice from her mind. When she returned, Frau Geruscha was washing the blood from the wound. Rose held out the roll of fabric.

Her hand shook. She had to get control of herself before her mistress noticed.

Frau Geruscha took a section of the clean linen and used it to soak up the blood and water around the wound. "Rose, get him some henbane and wormwood tea." She turned to the parents. "The herbs will help ease his pain."

Biting her lip, Rose ran into the adjoining storage room again. She should have guessed Frau Geruscha would want that tea. She should have already gone for it instead of standing there with her mouth open. So far she wasn't proving herself very competent.

Shelves of dried herbs lined the walls. She grabbed the flasks labeled *henbane* and *wormwood* and scooped a spoonful of each into a metal cup, then used a dipper to ladle in steaming water from the kettle.

She hurried back and placed the cup in the mother's outstretched hands. The woman held it to her son's lips.

Frau Geruscha made the sign of the cross and laid her hand on the boy's arm. She then closed her eyes. "In the name of the Father and of the Son and of the Holy Ghost, we ask you, God, to heal this boy's wound in the name of Jesus and by the power of his blood. Amen."

The smell of blood, warm and stifling, mingled with the odor of sweat. The bowl of water was now bright red, and Rose caught another whiff of the familiar, sickening smell.

Frau Geruscha opened her eyes and crossed herself again. She reached into her box of supplies and held up a needle. The tiny metal object glinted in the morning light.

The boy locked wide eyes on the needle and screamed, "No! No! No!" His father moved to hold him down.

Rose fled into the storeroom, her bare feet noiseless on the stone floor. She leaned against the wall and sucked in deep breaths. Her head seemed to float off her shoulders, as light as a fluff of wool, while her face tingled and spots danced before her eyes.

How childish. Rose pressed her face into her hands and stifled a groan. Had Frau Geruscha seen her flee the room? She must get back in there and overcome this squeamishness.

She drew in another deep breath. The earthy odor of the herbs that hung from the rafters was stuffy, but at least it didn't trouble her stomach like the smell of blood. Rose focused on the sights around her — the rushes strewn over the stone floor ... low shelves packed with flasks of dried herbs ... the rough stone wall poking her back. The screaming drifted away.

The tingling sensation gradually left her face and she breathed more normally.

She entered the room again, stepping carefully so as not to rustle the rushes on the floor and draw attention to herself. The boy's eyes were closed and his lips were the same ash gray as his face. He must have lost consciousness, since he didn't even wince as the needle pierced his skin.

Frau Geruscha quickly finished stitching the wound. After she tied the last knot and clipped the string of catgut, she wound the remainder of the bandage around his arm and tied a thin strip of cloth around it to hold it in place.

Finally, the people left, carrying the limp boy with them.

Rose hurried to clean up the water spills and the bloody linen.

Her stomach lurched at every whiff of the metallic odor, but she had to pretend it didn't bother her, to hope her mistress didn't notice how it affected her.

"Are you well?" Frau Geruscha's gray eyes narrowed, studying Rose. "You looked pale when you ran into the storage room."

So her mistress had noticed. "I am very well."

How could she be so pathetic? She had to find a way to prepare herself for the next time she must face the blood, screams, and smells.

Ravenous after his long journey from Heidelberg, Wilhelm attacked the roasted pheasant on his trencher. A page, a lad of less than ten years, leaned over his shoulder to refill his goblet. The boy lost his balance and teetered forward. Wilhelm grabbed him around his middle and righted him, but the goblet overturned onto the table.

The boy's face flushed red. "Lord Hamlin, forgive me. I—"

"No harm done." Wilhelm gave the boy an encouraging smile.

With a quick bow, the boy refilled Wilhelm's goblet and moved on to the next cup.

The Great Hall looked exactly as Wilhelm remembered it. Flags bearing the family colors of green, gold, and red jutted out from the gray stone walls on wooden poles, and several hung like banners on either side of the large mural painted on the wall. His father still spoke sternly, and his mother still clucked over him and his brother, continually admonishing Rupert to proper, gentlemanly behavior. At that moment she was reprimanding him for pinching the serving wench.

If she only knew. While they were supposed to be educating themselves in Heidelberg under the finest teachers in the Holy Roman Empire, Rupert had spent more time carousing than studying. And as Rupert misbehaved, Wilhelm had continued sending out spies in search of Moncore.

His younger sister, Osanna, smiled at him from across the table. Wilhelm smiled back and winked. She'd grown up in the two years he had been away. He missed the freckle-faced maiden who used to trail behind him, begging him to teach her to hunt or fish or shoot arrows.

His father sat at the head of the trestle table, on Wilhelm's left. He put down his knife and wiped his hands on the cloth across his lap. Then he took a drink from his goblet and turned to Wilhelm.

"So, son, you are still scouring the country for Moncore." He peered at him from beneath bushy eyebrows. "You'll get him."

Wilhelm remembered how his father had awed—and intimidated—him as a child. His greatest desire was to make his father proud of him. "Thank you, Father."

His brows lowered in a scowl. "You must."

"Yes, Father."

"Your responsibility is to your people and to your betrothed. You must not let them down."

Did his father say these things because he doubted him? He had worked hard to become mighty in strength and swordplay, believing that would please his father. But there was still one thing he had not been able to accomplish; one thing that would exalt him in the eyes of his father, as well as the entire region.

"Wilhelm." His father nudged him with his elbow, pointing toward the far end of the table. A man dressed in leather hunting clothes stood near the door of the Great Hall. He nodded at Wilhelm, tucked his chin to his chest, and backed out of the room.

"Pray excuse me." Wilhelm stood and stepped over the bench where he sat with his family and the guests who had come to welcome him home. He strode from the room.

"Lord Hamlin." The courier stood in a shadowed corner of the corridor outside. He handed a folded parchment to Wilhelm then bowed and slipped out the door.

Wilhelm glanced at the wax seal, confirmed it was from his spies, then ripped open the missive.

*Lord Hamlin, we have reason to believe Moncore is in our region. Be on your guard.*

Wilhelm crumpled the note in his fist. "Glory to God."

After Wilhelm's six years of failing to locate the evil conjurer, the fiend had come to him.

If he were able to capture Moncore, he could tell his future father-in-law, the Duke of Marienberg, to bring his daughter out of hiding. Wilhelm's betrothed would finally be safe.

But Moncore had eluded him before. The fact that one man had continued threatening Lady Salomea's safety, despite Wilhelm's best efforts, was a frustration like he'd never known, a splinter he couldn't gouge out no matter how hard he tried.

With long strides, Wilhelm headed back into the Great Hall. He'd find Georg and Christoff and discuss where to hunt for Moncore. They would ride out in less than an hour.

Morning sunlight winked through the narrow window as Rose moved about the southwest tower. The only sounds were the blows of the blacksmith's hammer ringing from the castle courtyard. She straightened jars of herbs, checked to see which of them needed to be replenished, and began sweeping up the old straw from the stone floor. Once finished, she would sprinkle new rushes and dried lilac over the chamber floors.

Rose so wanted to impress her mistress, but had failed miserably. Frau Geruscha never turned ashen at the sight of blood, never shrank from the bad smells, never grew squeamish when sewing up a wound.

*O God, make me like Frau Geruscha.*

Because one day she would be expected to take over her mistress's healing work, Rose grew increasingly more desperate to be a good healer. If she returned home a failure, her mother would torment her until she accepted one of her suitors—a desperate widower with nine children, an old man with no teeth, anyone with a little money.

A commotion in the courtyard cut her musings short. She put her broom away in case the noise was the result of someone in need, coming to the healer for help.

As the shouts drew closer, her stomach knotted. Frau Geruscha was away and might not be back for several hours. *Please, let them not be coming to see Frau Geruscha.* She stood in the middle of the room and held her breath as she stared at the door, waiting.

"Frau Geruscha!" a masculine voice boomed. Someone pounded on the door.

Rose rushed to unlatch the door. Three men stood at the threshold. The middle one's arms were draped over the shoulders of the other two. His head hung down so that she couldn't see his face. Sweat dripped from the dark hair clinging to his brow.

She recognized the men on either side as the two knights who yesterday had traveled alongside Lord Hamlin and Lord Rupert. That meant the one in the middle was—

Lord Hamlin lifted his head, his face pale. His eyes riveted her with a look of pain.

# *Chapter*
# 2

*Rose couldn't stand there gaping,* so she spurred her mind to action. "Lay him on the bed. Where is he hurt?"

The two knights eased him down. "Right leg," one of them said. "Wild boar gored him. Where's Frau Geruscha?"

Of course they wanted Frau Geruscha, the healer, not her lowly apprentice. "She's gone."

"Where?" The man with the dirty blond hair barked the word, tension showing in the wrinkles between his eyes. "Where did she go? We'll fetch her."

"I know not. The woods somewhere, gathering herbs and visiting the sick." She averted her eyes to Lord Hamlin's leg, lest the man's dismayed expression drain her of courage.

She sank to her knees beside Lord Hamlin. The dark stain on his hose indicated an injury on the outside of his calf. The boar's tusk had sliced through his leather boot, its jagged edges dangling open. "Help me get this boot off."

The knight nearest to her was twice her size, with red hair sticking straight up on top of his head. He bent over and tugged on the shoe.

"Ahhhg," Lord Hamlin groaned.

Rose glanced up. Lord Hamlin's eyes were closed and his features clenched in pain. Compassion squeezed her stomach like a fist.

Once the boot was off, blood dripped from his foot off the side of the bed. She grabbed a knife from a nearby shelf and half cut, half ripped the cloth away at his knee. The material stuck to his leg, held on by dried blood.

Running to the adjoining room, she fetched a bowl of water and a clean cloth. She dipped the cloth into the water and repeatedly soaked his leg until the water turned bright red.

She must not focus on the smell or sight of the blood, must not dwell on the fact that this was Lord Hamlin — the duke's eldest son — bleeding all over the floor.

Gently, Rose pulled the cloth away from the jagged wound, which extended the length of his calf and looked very deep. Fresh blood oozed from the gash. She used her thumb and fingers to push the two edges together while pressing a linen cloth against it with her other hand, angrily commanding herself the whole time not to get sick.

Lord Hamlin moaned low in his throat.

Thinking about his pain made her stomach twist. *Don't think about it. Be like Frau Geruscha. What would Frau Geruscha do?*

"You there." She glanced up at the redheaded knight, who squatted beside her. "Hold this."

The man dropped to his knees and pressed the bandage.

Rose stood and rushed into the storage room. She found the dried henbane and wormwood and put a spoonful of each into a cup, spilling some on the floor in her haste. A jar labeled *poppy* arrested her gaze. *It couldn't hurt.* Rose threw in a spoonful, ladled hot water from the kettle into the cup, and carried it to Lord Hamlin.

His eyes were still closed, but when she approached, they flickered open and fixed her with a heavy-lidded gaze.

"Here." She addressed the other knight, whose equally unkempt blond hair and beard were covered in dust. "Give him this tea."

The man helped Lord Hamlin into a sitting position.

Rose knelt beside the knight holding the bandage. "I thank you," she said.

The knight stood and she took his place. She held her breath and eased the cloth away from the wound. The bleeding had stopped.

The wound was ugly. She closed her eyes and tried not to think how much it must have hurt when the angry boar thrust its tusk into Lord Hamlin's leg. She hoped it wouldn't fester. The yellow pus that sometimes developed in wounds often led to death. *O merciful God, let Lord Hamlin's leg not develop that telltale sign.*

She would have to stitch up the wound. *God, I don't know if I can do it!*

She had to do it.

His lids hung so low over his eyes, she couldn't tell if he was looking at her or not. She swallowed past the dryness in her throat. "This is when Frau Geruscha would pray for you, if she were here."

"You pray for me, then."

She made the sign of the cross. Her stomach fluttered at the thought of touching him again. But determined to follow Frau Geruscha's example, she placed her hand on his bare leg. "In the name of the Father and of the Son and of the Holy Ghost, and by the blood of Jesus, heal Lord Hamlin's leg. Amen." *Please, God. And help me not make a mess of this.*

Opening her eyes, she saw the cup of tea still in his hand. He seemed to read her thoughts and took a gulp. Could he read the panic rising inside her?

She would give him some time to drink the tea before she attempted to sew up his wound, although she knew the tea would help very little. She hoped God would be merciful and he would pass out from the pain, as the little boy yesterday had done.

The prospect of what lay ahead forced Rose toward the window and she looked out, searching the only entrance into the castle. She willed Frau Geruscha to be there, straining her eyes, hoping, agonizing. But Frau Geruscha was nowhere in sight.

Lord Hamlin's men were talking. "We were closing in on him," the red haired one said. "He was hiding out in the cave."

"Had it not been for the boars, we would have caught him," the blond one answered.

"He must have sent demons into them, the way they came after us."

So Lord Hamlin had been injured while searching for the evil Moncore. But now was not the time to think about Lord Hamlin's valiance in trying to rescue his betrothed. Frau Geruscha was not coming. Rose was alone in caring for Lord Hamlin's leg wound.

Wilhelm held the cup to his lips and watched the healer's apprentice walk to the window, giving him a clear view of her profile. Her brown hair glowed in the sunlight that poured through the glass. Her nose and chin were small, her cheekbones high, and her lips full and perfect. He recognized her. She was the girl he'd seen on the street with the dog.

He knew about this girl. His father had recently approved Frau Geruscha's request to have the maiden as her apprentice. If he remembered correctly, her name was Rose. She was a beauty, a woodcutter's daughter who ordered his knights around as if they were lackeys. But he'd been betrothed since he was five years old, so he was used to guarding his heart. Besides, he wasn't likely to be tempted by a woodcutter's daughter—or a healer's apprentice—no matter how beautiful.

Her wolfish dog sat in the corner of the room and eyed Wilhelm's two knights, who were staring at Rose. The dog growled low in his throat, his forelegs pulled in tight, ready to spring at the men if the need arose.

Wilhelm studied Christoff and Georg. With a fair maiden in their midst, he knew his men too well to doubt their thoughts. He suddenly agreed with the dog. He didn't want them staring at her.

"Christoff, Georg, you may go now."

They tore their gaze away from Rose. "My lord?"

"Unless you want to watch her sew me up?" He raised his eyebrows.

The men seemed to realize what was coming and practically raced each other to the door. From outside, Christoff called, "We shall wait nearby."

Wilhelm grinned at their haste. He brought the tea to his lips and drank until he had swallowed some of the leaves and all of the liquid, the bitter taste lingering on his tongue.

The maiden turned from the window with dread in her face. He hoped the tea worked. The pain in his leg made him clench his teeth, but he bit back a hiss, since the girl looked as though she might cry herself at any moment.

He set the cup on the floor and lay flat, letting his head sink into the prickly, straw-filled pillow. She placed a low stool next to him then rummaged through a basket at the foot of the bed and withdrew black string and a needle.

"So what is that you're stitching me up with?" He forced his tone to sound calm, hoping to put them both at ease.

One side of her mouth went down as if she were avoiding his gaze. "Catgut, my lord."

She stared down at the needle and he watched her draw in another big breath. She closed her eyes as she made the sign of the cross. Her lips moved silently, then her long lashes swept up, revealing warm brown eyes that brimmed with determination.

His heart beat faster.

"When Frau Geruscha sews up a wound, she tells the person to think about something else, to imagine they are in a favored, peaceful place."

Wilhelm nodded and closed his eyes. He could do that. He wouldn't think about the needle, the catgut, or his leg.

Her soft fingers, gentle and tentative, touched his bare leg, near the wound. But he couldn't think about that, either. He'd think of a stream ... *Yes, with the sun glittering on it ... a nice grassy bank and a big tree. The leaves are moving with the breeze ... the grass is cool.*

There it was, the stab of the needle piercing his flesh. His leg tensed in spite of himself. He forced a moan to the back of his throat. The tea wasn't working.

*I'm floating above the stream, watching the water glide over the rocks. The breeze rustles the leaves ... birds are singing. The sun is bright and warm...*

His eyes watered. He wanted to groan against the fiery pain reopening in his leg. He tried to ignore it, but he couldn't see the stream or the tree or the grass anymore.

He opened his eyes. The maiden was bending low over his leg. Her hair fell like a curtain around her face, but she sat at an angle and so he had full view of her features. She bit her lower lip, and he thought he saw her chin quiver. Was that a tear glistening on her eyelashes?

The pain was intense, radiating from his leg to his whole body like flames of fire. He wanted to cry out, but he wouldn't do that to her. No, he wouldn't make a sound. Instead, he would concentrate on making her think he was asleep. He would relax each muscle in his body, starting with his legs ... going up to his stomach ... relaxing his arms ... now his face. Yes, he was on the stream bank again, watching the leaves of the tree, hearing the water rush along.

Time seemed to stand still as he fought to ignore the pain. Sweat slid from his forehead into his eyebrows, into the corner of his eyes and down his cheeks, but he didn't move to brush it away. At some point he stopped seeing the stream and tree and opened his eyes again. He saw Rose, her hair glowing in the sunlight, and heard her soothing voice.

"It's almost over now."

The pressure near the wound lifted as she removed her hands from his leg. He watched her disappear into the storage room.

Raising his head, he looked at the crisscross of black stitching. The whole area throbbed and burned, but he was relieved to see the wound closed.

Wilhelm collapsed back on the pillow, his thoughts filled with the maiden, Rose. He remembered the compassion emanating from her eyes. And that was the thing that had surprised him. Plenty of people were afraid of him, and he'd received many amorous looks from women, but he wasn't sure he had ever seen such raw compassion.

He closed his eyes and saw her again as she'd looked standing at the window, and a warm, pleasurable sensation flooded him.

*Must be the herbs.*

Out of sight of her patient, Rose sobbed silently into her hands. It was over now. She hadn't mishandled the stitching too badly — she hoped. Thanks be to God, Lord Hamlin must have sunk into unconsciousness halfway through.

She stopped crying and wiped her face with a cloth. She poured some water into a basin and washed her hands, rubbing her cuticles where Lord Hamlin's blood had dried black.

The sweat had poured off his brow while she worked on his leg. She should get a damp cloth to wipe his face. She poured cool water from the pitcher onto a clean bandage. Her hands shook and the water dribbled onto the floor.

As Rose emerged from the storage room and walked toward Lord Hamlin, she thought his eyelids flickered but hoped he was still unconscious. She hesitated beside his bed. Wipe the face of the duke's son? If she knew he wouldn't wake up she would gladly perform that small act of kindness.

His chest rose and fell beneath his fine white shirt and hip-length, sleeveless doublet. Her gaze shifted to his face. She couldn't pull her eyes away from his masculine features — strong chin, high cheekbones, thick lashes, and well-formed lips. The way his black hair curled and clung to his forehead gave him an endearing look. His arms and chest were well-muscled, possibly from his training in archery and sword-play. And now that she had seen him up close, her curiosity had been assuaged and she could tell Hildy — his eyes were blue, deeper and darker than a woodland pool.

Those eyes flicked open and fastened on her.

Rose inhaled sharply and thrust the cloth toward him.

He stared at it then reached and took it from her. "I thank you." He wiped the sweat from his face.

Heart pounding, cheeks burning, she scurried back toward the storage room. She prayed he didn't realize she'd been standing there visually examining him.

At least she hadn't wiped his face.

When she returned, he had pulled himself into a half-sitting position and regained the color in his cheeks. His bare leg looked vulnerable on the white sheet. The black stitches stood out against his skin. She cringed. They looked like the crooked stitches of a child just learning to sew.

Rose sat on the stool, holding a long strip of clean linen. She tried to ignore Lord Hamlin's steady gaze. *Saints be praised, this is almost over.*

She wrapped the bandage around the wound several times with one hand, awkwardly holding his leg up with the other. Finally, she tied a thin strip around it to hold it in place. Relief spread through her. It was done.

"May I get you some water?" She didn't have any wine to offer him.

"Yes, I thank you."

She filled a tankard from the pitcher in the storage room and carried it back in to him. As she returned, his eyes focused on her skirt.

"Forgive me. I've ruined your dress."

She looked down and saw a blood stain the size of an apple. She shook her head. "It's my fault. I forgot to put on my apron."

"The fault is mine. I'll see that it is replaced."

"I pray you not to trouble yourself."

"I shall have it replaced."

Her face grew hot. *I'm arguing with Lord Hamlin.* She curtsied. "As you wish, my lord."

Rose handed him the water and began cleaning up, relieved to have something to do. She picked up his cup of tea and the pan of bloody water and carried them into the storage room, emptying them in the refuse bucket. When she returned, he was drinking the last of the water from the tankard. He set it on the floor, his expression gentle.

"I am most indebted to you, Rose."

He knew her name.

She swallowed and shook her head. "I apologize that Frau Geruscha wasn't here. She's the experienced one." Her voice trailed off at the last sentence. She wasn't eager to let him know that his was the first wound she'd ever treated.

At times such as this Rose wondered why Frau Geruscha had chosen her to be her apprentice. Rose had always been a favorite with the healer, who had often visited Rose's family when Rose was a child, teaching her to read and write. But Rose suddenly wondered why she'd never thought to ask her parents why Frau Geruscha—obviously an influential woman at Hagenheim Castle, a woman educated in a convent—had paid so much attention to her, a poor woodcutter's daughter.

Lord Hamlin sat calmly studying her. She remembered the proud tilt of his head and the disdainful way he'd looked away from her the day he and his brother returned from Heidelberg. There was no evidence of that arrogance now. But as the son of the Duke of Hagenheim, he possessed more wealth and power than anyone else in the region. If truth be told, more than King Wenceslas himself.

She felt uncomfortable beneath his gaze. If the townspeople thought of her as lacking social status, how much more lowly would she appear to Lord Hamlin?

"You will want to return to your room." She jumped to her feet.

Lord Hamlin raised his eyebrows, but before he could reply, she bolted to the door. She spotted Sir Georg and Sir Christoff in front of the blacksmith shop in the castle courtyard and motioned them in. The two knights entered the room and advanced to where Lord Hamlin lay. They each hooked an arm around his shoulders, hoisted him up, and started for the door.

Lord Hamlin looked over his shoulder. His eyes locked on hers with an intensity that paralyzed her.

She should curtsy at least. She bobbed a quick one as he disappeared out the door.

The morning after tending Lord Hamlin's wound, Rose went to the kitchen to break her fast. When she returned, a stack of fabric lay on the desk by the window where she often sat. On top was a folded note with *Rose* written on the outside. She unfolded the parchment and read.

*Please accept these fabrics as a replacement for the dress I ruined. My sister, Lady Osanna, chose them for you.* It was signed, *Lord Hamlin.*

*Lord Hamlin wrote a note to me?* Hildy would die of raptures when she heard. But what did the gift truly mean? That he pitied her? That she was obviously in need? Her dress *was* ugly, the material coarse and plain. Rose's cheeks tingled in embarrassment.

She put the note aside, unable to resist examining the fabrics. One was a luxurious gold silk. Beneath it was a smaller amount of matching gold-and-red brocade. She let her fingertips glide over the smooth cloth and intricate stitching.

The next was a burgundy velvet, its texture soft and rich. These materials were very fine and would make the most exquisite dresses, by far, that Rose had ever owned. But when would she ever have need of such clothes?

The last one was a bolt of plain blue linen that would make the sort of dress more fitting for a working maiden like herself. At least she would get some use from *that*. The rest of the fabric was appropriate only for a lady — Lady Osanna, for example.

Her thoughts drifted to Lord Hamlin, his deep voice saying her name, his blue eyes and perfect teeth and lips as he glanced at her over his shoulder.

Abruptly, she turned away from the fabric. She folded the note and stuffed it into her apron pocket. *Dreaming about Lord Hamlin. I'm as bad as Hildy.*

The southwest tower window was before her. She watched dark clouds roll toward their walled town. The wind raced ahead of them, causing the people in the Marktplatz to gather their goods and pack them away into sacks and barrels before the rain came.

With his injured leg, Lord Hamlin and his knights would not be riding out today, as they'd done so often before Lord Hamlin went away two years ago, to hunt for the man who stood between him and his betrothed. If it were not for Moncore, Lord Hamlin would be married. The lady was of age by now. Rose was ashamed to admit, even to herself, that she felt a twinge of jealousy toward her.

That very morning Arnold Hintzen, a young farmer, had asked Rose — no, commanded her — to go with him to the May Day Festival next week. She had pitied him, but as he became more insistent, she found him increasingly repulsive. Were it not for Wolfie, she might have been afraid of him. But the dog was quick to warn away anyone who came too close to her, baring his fangs and sending chills down even Rose's spine with his snarls and ferocious barking.

She could see Arnold's face now, his watery green eyes and rotten teeth. When she became the town healer, surely neither he nor anyone else would dare to thrust such unwanted invitations on her.

Then there were the suitors her mother was constantly entreating her to marry.

Frau Geruscha entered the room and came to stand beside Rose. "Are you troubled, child?"

"My mother wants me to marry a widowed butcher with six children." Rose's voice sounded flat as she struggled to hide her feelings. "Two weeks ago it was an old spice merchant. She says if I marry a wealthy tradesman it will improve my brother's chances of being apprenticed to a good trade."

"What does your father say?"

"I don't know. But I don't want to marry an old man. All I want is to be a good healer."

Frau Geruscha squeezed Rose's shoulder. "If you need my help to convince your mother she shouldn't try to force you to marry, tell me, and I will speak to her." She was quiet for a moment as her concerned look slowly changed to a bemused half smile. "I have a confession to make to you, Rose."

"A confession?"

Frau Geruscha seemed to force her smile into a frown, deepening the wrinkles around her mouth. "I allowed Lord Hamlin to take one of your stories."

"You ... what?" Rose backed up a step, bumping into a bench, and sat heavily.

"He came in this morning while you were in the kitchen. Your story was lying open on the table, and when I walked in he was reading it."

Rose felt the blood drain from her face. "But, he — but I — no one was supposed to — "

"He said it was very good. He asked if he could take it to his family and read it to them. I couldn't say no."

"His family? Oh." She pressed her hands to her cheeks.

"I'm sorry, Rose." But with her smile, Frau Geruscha didn't look very sorry. "I didn't think you would mind. I realize I should have suggested that he request your permission. But he seemed so delighted with it."

The prospect of facing Lord Hamlin again, of him asking her permission for anything, almost made her grateful that Frau Geruscha had allowed him to take it.

Rose's face burned as she thought of the lord and his entire family—the duke and duchess, Lord Rupert, and Lady Osanna—reading her story.

"Don't be angry with me, Rose."

Rose pretended to examine her shoes. She shook her head. "I'm not angry." *Only dying from embarrassment, betrayed by my own mistress.* She could only hope she would be out of the room if and when Lord Hamlin came back to return it.

A week later, Rose was hanging herbs to dry when she recognized the peasant woman standing in the courtyard as a neighbor of her parents. She stepped out of Frau Geruscha's chambers and into the sunlight.

"Your mother bids you come home today." The woman bowed her head, glancing up from beneath lowered lids. "She has an important matter to discuss with you."

No doubt the "important matter" was another potential husband her mother wanted to foist on her. Although becoming an apprentice for the town healer improved Rose's status, it didn't benefit her family as would marriage to a wealthy burgher.

After asking Frau Geruscha's permission, Rose trudged along the path outside the town wall, delving a short way into the forest to her father's wattle-and-daub cottage. She opened the front door to the smell of peas and pork fat cooking over the fire.

"Rose!" her little sisters squealed. Before Rose's eyes could adjust to the dimness of the room, one pair of sooty arms wrapped around her waist, the other around her knees. Rose squeezed her sisters tight.

Her mother straightened from bending over the pot. The hole in the center of the ceiling of the one-room house didn't do much to draw out the smoke, and Rose's eyes watered and burned.

"Rose, you will be reasonable, for once, when you hear of the wool merchant who wants to marry you." Her mother fixed Rose with a hard look, her eyes narrowed and her jaw set.

"Who?"

"Peter Brunckhorst."

Rose's mouth fell open as she recalled the man, old enough to be her father, who had introduced himself to her one day in the street. He had stared at her face as if there were words stamped there that he was trying to read.

She spoke through clenched teeth. "I will not wed Peter Brunckhorst—"

"What?" Her mother clamped her fists on her hips, still gripping her ladle in one hand.

"—No matter how rich he is." He only wanted a wife with a good strong back to birth a swarm of children. Soon after, he'd die of some old person's disease—if she was fortunate.

"You ungrateful little wench! I ought to snatch every hair from your head." Her mother shook both fists at her, as though imagining doing exactly that. "This is the best offer you could ever hope to get!"

*The best offer I could ever hope to get.* She thought of Peter Brunckhorst, his greasy black-and-white hair plastered to his head. Why was *he* the best she could ever hope to get? Because she was stupid? Mean? Lazy? Unworthy of being loved?

No. Because she was poor.

"Watch your sisters and brother," her mother ordered, then stormed out of the house.

Rose spent the day with her six- and eight-year-old sisters and her brother, the baby of the family at five years old. "Rose, will you tell us a story?" Agathe asked. Rose stopped what she was doing, and her brother crawled into her lap while she told them a tale about twin princesses locked in a tower that was made entirely of sweets. They listened in rapt attention.

She hugged them and kissed their cheeks. She knew what it felt like to want attention and affection and not get it. She could remember trying to put her arms around her mother and being pushed aside.

"Get away," her mother would say, "and let me get my work done." Rose learned not to expect affection from her. Her father often patted her on the head and spoke a word or two of praise. But he became awkward with her when she turned thirteen and developed womanly curves.

Now that she was seventeen, she didn't need affection—at least, she'd better not. She knew a few maidens who had needed it and ended up with child—and without a husband.

Her mother returned in the late afternoon with her straw-colored hair freshly braided. She refused to look at Rose, addressing the younger children instead.

Rose slipped out the door and ran with Wolfie at her heels to her favorite spot beneath a large beech tree at the top of a hill. She threw herself down on the lush grass, propped her back against the tree, and stared across the empty meadow. She would never please her mother. The memory of her angry face made Rose's chest ache. But she rarely had to see her mother anymore, now that she spent most of her days and nights with Frau Geruscha at Hagenheim Castle.

Wolfie laid his head in her lap and gazed up at her with big, russet eyes. She rubbed behind his ears, finding the patch of extra-soft fur. Her heart swelled as she blinked back tears. At least Wolfie loved her.

Rose stepped out of the southwest tower the next morning into the courtyard, blinking at the bright sunlight. The plaintive strains of musical instruments playing in the distance sent a tingle of excitement through her. Her feet moved of their own accord toward the sound.

Hildy trotted toward her from the gatehouse, grinning and waving. They linked arms and hastened toward the Marktplatz for the May Day festivities, Hildy chattering about who they might see at the festival and whether there would be jugglers, dancing bears, and acrobats performing in the square.

When Rose and Hildy emerged from the gate into the large Marktplatz, they found themselves in a crowd of people—some buying, some selling, and some merely gawking. Rose's heart beat faster as the trill of flutes and clang of tambourines grew louder. To their left a tall, skinny man juggled three balls. The jongleur wore parti-colored hose—left leg was red, the right, blue. His shirt was the opposite—left sleeve, blue and the right, red. She smiled at the tiny bells that hung from his pointed hat and jingled merrily as he kept all three balls spinning in the air. The people gathered around him gasped as he added a fourth ball to his act.

She soon grew tired of watching the jongleur and tugged on Hildy's arm, urging her toward the music. Three musicians stood in the middle of a tight circle of people. Rose and Hildy nudged their way to the front. One man pulled a bow across the strings of a rebec, while another played a shawm, his fingers dancing over the holes. The third strummed a lute and sang about a knight and his lady love.

Rose's chest swelled with joy at the harmonious sounds of the instruments. Music was food for the spirit, and she closed her eyes to better feed upon it. She so seldom got the opportunity to hear music, she didn't want to miss a note.

Too soon Hildy was ready for something else. "Let's go see the miracle play." Rose allowed her friend to lead her several paces away from the troubadours, consoling herself that she would still be able to hear them.

The play was just beginning. Several performers stood on the flat bed of a wagon. A man wearing dirty rags, his face smeared with mud, cried out to a tall bearded man, "What have I to do with thee, Jesus, thou Son of the Most High God? Torment me not!"

The bearded man pointed his finger at him and said, "Come out of the man, you unclean spirit! What is thy name?"

The ragged man said, "My name is Legion, for we are many."

The voice sounded so unearthly, Rose had to remind herself it was only a play.

"I beseech thee, do not send us away from this region. Rather, send us into the swine."

"I give thee leave. Go!" The bearded Jesus turned his finger to six actors who crouched in a huddle on the ground.

The supposed possessed man convulsed violently, his body jerking in all directions. Finally, he threw himself down and lay still, his eyes closed.

The six actors on the ground began squealing like pigs. They scurried around on their hands and knees then fell over onto their backs and ceased their pig noises. Their hands and feet moved slowly forward and back, clawing the air.

The Jesus figure turned to the man lying at his feet. He held out his hand and commanded, "Stand up."

The man's eyelids fluttered open and he sat up, taking Jesus' hand. He stood, blinking and shading his eyes as though blinded by a bright light. The audience cheered and applauded. Rose clapped as well while Hildy turned to speak to the woman beside her, who was a friend of Hildy's mother.

At that moment, a hand clamped down on Rose's shoulder. Peter Brunckhorst towered over her.

"You have decided to disobey your mother and refuse to marry me?"

*Where was Wolfie?* "Take your hand off me."

Rose tried to shrug off his grip, but his fingers tightened on her shoulder. He bent down, bringing his sallow, sunken cheeks and pointy chin close to her face.

"I asked your mother if I could take you to the May Day festivities, but she said you haven't yet agreed to marry me. Methought

Hagenheim's maidens were more obedient to their parents' wishes." He exhaled a putrid breath in her face.

She turned her head and spoke through clenched teeth. "Pray excuse me, but I am not obliged to marry you."

Peter Brunckhorst's face stretched into an ugly grin, revealing a row of brown teeth. "Come now. You have no hope of wealth, and I can help your brother get an apprenticeship." He reached out his long, bony fingers and stroked Rose's cheek. She jerked back, but he leaned closer. His eyes were devoid of color and filled with darkness.

# Chapter
## 3

*"What's the meaning of this?" Hildy asked.* "You're frightening my friend."

The man glanced at Hildy. "I'm not trying to frighten anyone. You both mistake me." He fixed his eyes on Rose again. "But perhaps that is intentional."

Wolfie's deep-throated bark stunned the air one second before he bounded between Rose and Peter Brunckhorst, causing the man to take a step back. The dog snarled and bared his teeth at the merchant.

Rose rubbed her palm across her cheek, trying to brush away the feeling of Brunckhorst's fingers on her skin. As people gathered around them, murmuring, he curled his lip upward in what Rose presumed was meant to be a smile. "I have hope that you will yet come to accept me."

He stepped back. The Marktplatz was growing more crowded, and a group of people walked between Rose and the merchant. When they passed, Brunckhorst was gone.

Rose's legs turned to water. She sank to her knees and buried her face in Wolfie's neck. "Thank you, boy."

Wilhelm sat astride his horse near the entrance to the castle courtyard, at the north end of the Marktplatz. He patted Shadow's neck as his gaze swept over the various performers, sellers' booths, and people taking in the sights and sounds. Amid the crowd, someone caught his eye. A maiden stood in front of the musicians. Her eyes were closed and a blissful smile graced her lips.

Rose.

The back of his neck tingled. She looked beautiful, especially with that rapt expression on her face. *But I shouldn't be watching her.* He tore his eyes away. He was supposed to be making sure the May Day celebrations took place in an orderly fashion. And, as always, he was keeping an eye out for Moncore, though the evil conjurer was hardly likely to show himself so publicly. Wilhelm had lost days of searching due to his injury, and the man could be far away by now.

He'd read Rose's story to the rest of his family while he was laid up with his leg, and they were as impressed as he'd been. Now he felt strangely excited at the way she obviously appreciated music.

Perhaps some day he would get a chance to play for her.

Perhaps he should cease staring at her. She was fair of face and form, but it was crude of him to stare admiringly at someone so far beneath his station in life. He'd never been tempted to do so before. But it didn't mean anything—he was simply curious about the maiden who had taken care of his injury. Besides, he knew his duty, which was to wed the daughter of the Duke of Marienberg. Their grandfathers had quarreled and become enemies years before. As the eldest son, it was his responsibility to his people to marry his betrothed and solidify the alliance between their regions. He didn't want death and destruction on his head. War had come about under less serious circumstances than a broken betrothal.

Such had been his focus for years now. That, and capturing Moncore. The self-described conjurer and expert in pagan magic had been the personal advisor of the Duke of Marienberg, his betrothed's grandfather, enjoying the riches of the duke's fortune and the privilege of favored counselor. However, when the elderly duke died and his son took over, he cast Moncore out as an evil conjurer, banishing him from the region. Moncore swore he would get revenge through the duke's newborn daughter. He seemed to think his revenge would be more complete if he could prove his powers—by finding the duke's daughter and unleashing demons to torment her.

If Wilhelm could track down Moncore and stamp out the threat of his black magic, his betrothed's parents would be satisfied that she was safe. She could come out of hiding and they could marry.

Nearby, a performer played a recorder. Wilhelm watched as the man's trained bear hopped from one hind leg to the other, shaking his shaggy head from side to side. The sight did not long detract him, however, and within moments his gaze returned to the place where Rose stood. She was gone, having vacated her spot in front of the musicians.

A twinge of disappointment stung him, but he told himself it was for the best.

A shout rang out to his right. A boy ran toward him, dodging and pushing in his attempt to escape. A man jogged not far behind, yelling, "Thief! Stop!"

Wilhelm dismounted and limped two steps, catching the boy by his shoulder. "Whoa!"

The boy stared up at him, his face pinched in fear as his pursuer rushed up, gasping for breath. The man's ample stomach jiggled at his sudden stop. He bowed to Wilhelm and pointed a malevolent finger at the boy. "My lord ... that boy ... stole an apple ... from me."

The boy looked to be around seven years old, and his eyes were the only part of his face not covered with dust. The green apple in his hand was quite small. A person would have to be terribly hungry to steal such a thing.

"Give the man his apple," Wilhelm ordered the boy.

The child dropped it into the man's fleshy palm.

"Thank you, my lord." The man bowed again to Wilhelm. "Little beggar," he muttered as he walked away.

Wilhelm held on to the lad's arm. "What's your name?"

"Lukas, my lord."

"Go to the castle, Lukas, and find the kitchen."

The boy's mouth hung open as he stared up at him.

"Tell Cook that Lord Hamlin said to give you something to eat, and that you're to wait there for me."

"Yes, my lord, sir."

He let go and the boy shuffled his bare feet through the gate toward the castle. He turned back for a second, a wondering look in his face. Wilhelm winked at him.

If the boy was an orphan, perhaps he could put him to work in the stable. Lukas could sleep with the other stable hands and take his meals in the castle kitchen. At least he wouldn't have to steal food anymore.

He climbed back on his horse, throwing his bad leg over the saddle. Raising himself as high as possible, he scanned the crowd and caught sight of Rose again. She stood in front of the players, but she was not watching the play. Instead, a man was holding her by the shoulder. She backed away from him, but he pressed toward her. Now he was touching her face. She cringed and shrank away.

Wilhelm's face went hot with anger and his fists tightened on the reins. He thrust his heels into Shadow's sides. But so many people were milling between him and Rose that he had to jerk back on the reins to keep from trampling them. He could only inch forward, forced to wait for the crowd to part.

A deep, ferocious bark rang out, and he imagined rather than saw Wolfie charge to Rose's aid. The tall man backed away and lost himself in the crowd.

Wilhelm turned his horse in the direction he had gone. He hadn't seen the man's face, but he was sure he would recognize him by his clothing and his height. He searched the crowd, scanning the tops of heads, but the man seemed to have vanished.

The way the man had touched Rose made Wilhelm clench his teeth. How dare he? Remembering the fear and repulsion on her face, he maneuvered Shadow around the square, still forced to move slowly because of the crowd. Everywhere he turned, the people acknowledged him with a bow or curtsy, slowing him down even more. The man was certainly long gone now.

His muscles tensed with built-up energy. If only he could expend it on the brute who had dared to touch Rose. He would find a way to make sure this didn't happen to her again.

Rose couldn't help but smile at the cheerful red flowers in her arms. She hoped Frau Geruscha would be pleased, since red was her favorite color. She'd bought the ceramic pot with money from her new salary, and the geraniums came from a spot near her parents' home.

Hildy stood beside the town gate, her older brother beside her. As Rose called out to Hildy, he tipped his hat and walked away. He'd waited with Hildy because of the Church law that said women were not allowed to walk unaccompanied through town — though like most other Church laws, the edict was often disobeyed. Wolfie was Rose's usual escort, and she believed he was more than sufficient.

They started through town. Rose as usual found the view very impressive — the two- and three-story houses crisscrossed with heavy wooden beams, often decorated with carvings and brightly painted flowers and figures.

Beyond the town Marktplatz rose Hagenheim Castle's five towers. Its towers anchored it on all four corners, with the largest tower, the keep, rising up in the middle. The crenellations around the top were like stone fringe, perfectly straight and even, decorating the imposing structure.

"Lovely flowers." Hildy glanced at the red blossoms then fixed her eyes on Rose, her face aglow with excitement. "I have two things to tell you—very interesting things." Hildy raised her eyebrows, as though trying to look mysterious.

Rose gave her a bland look. "Very interesting things" assaulted Hildy's notice on a daily basis, things which Rose rarely found so thrilling. "That's what I love about you, Hildy. Everything is interesting to you."

"Don't say another word until you see this." Hildy practically dragged her forward.

Soon they were standing at the great bronze door to the Hagenheimer *Dom*—the town cathedral—where new decrees were often posted. A sheet of parchment was tacked to a large wooden placard next to the door. Rose read it aloud.

*"Nicolaus Gerstenberg, Duke of Hagenheim, hereby decrees that no man or youth beyond the age of accountability shall touch any woman or maiden who is not a relative or is not his betrothed. Touching a maiden is punishable by placement in the stocks. Death by hanging shall be the penalty if it is found that the woman's virginity has been compromised. Punishment shall be meted out according to the judgment of Nicolaus Gerstenberg, Duke of Hagenheim, or his son, Wilhelm Gerstenberg, Earl of Hamlin. May God be glorified in all things forever, and amen."*

Duke Nicolaus's seal was stamped in red wax at the bottom.

She stared. Could this decree have something to do with Peter Brunckhorst accosting her? But how could it?

Hildy leaned forward and peered at her. "Well? Don't you see what this means?"

"No." Rose shifted her pot of geraniums to her other arm, abruptly turning away from the decree.

"Rose! Lord Hamlin must have seen the way Peter Brunckhorst grabbed you."

Rose's breath stuck in her throat. She shook her head. "I hardly think it likely."

"Oh, Rose, I think it very likely! Everyone knows there's already a law that no man can molest a woman. Why would they make a new decree about it unless the duke—or his son—had seen something that aroused his ire and made him think the law wasn't being heeded?"

"I know not." Rose trudged toward the castle, wishing Hildy would talk about something else.

"You want to know what I think?"

"I think I know what you think." Rose looked heavenward.

"I think Lord Hamlin is smitten with you and wants to protect you—after what you did for him when he was wounded. It must have been so romantic."

"It wasn't romantic at all!" Rose drew her eyebrows together, incredulous.

"But I do have some bad news." Hildy's tone turned somber. They now stood in front of the castle gate. Hildy grabbed Rose's arm, making her stop and look at her.

"A lady is coming to stay with the duke's family. She's been boarding at Witten Abbey for the past ten years. Her father is a duke—or so it is supposed—from somewhere south of here, who spends most of his time with King Wenceslas." Hildy leaned closer and whispered, "She's eighteen. The same age Lord Hamlin's betrothed would be. Rumor has it that she *might be* his betrothed, Lady Salomea in hiding."

"I'm sure that cannot affect me." Rose said the words as much for her own benefit as for Hildy's.

"Well, it affects me." Hildy sniffed. "I was hoping his betrothed no longer existed, that she died or something, and he would fall in love with someone else—like you, Rose."

Rose couldn't help but smile. "That's sweet, Hildy, but not realistic." How could Hildy possibly even entertain such an idea?

With a sudden burst of drama, Rose tilted her head and squinted at the early morning sun. "I strive to wish everyone well, even Lord Hamlin's betrothed. As for me, I only hope that one day I shall be as independent as Frau Geruscha—no obligations except the ones I choose."

She was surprised that her words didn't elicit a laugh, or at least an amused smile from Hildy, as she had intended.

"There's probably no man worthy of you anyway." Hildy's voice was unusually quiet.

Rose felt a stab of regret. Was her cynicism finally taking a toll on Hildy's outlook? "That doesn't sound like my Hildy. After all, we're seventeen and in the prime of our beauty. Any day now two chivalrous men will sweep us onto their noble steeds and take us to their castles—or cottages, or whatever it may be—where we shall live happily forever after."

Hildy's shoulders drooped. "It's seeming less and less likely, even to me."

Rose stood on a stool while the Lady Osanna's own seamstress measured her for a new gown. Things had happened so fast over the last few days, she hadn't even had time to tell Hildy about all the new developments.

A lovely young lady had approached the entrance to Frau Geruscha's chambers the day before and asked if she could enter. Lady Osanna introduced herself, smiling with her lips and her eyes. Barely sixteen, she had recently grown taller and thinner, and Rose scarcely recognized her. The young noblewoman asked after her health, made a comment about the weather, then said, "I enjoyed your story, Rose. We all did. I do hope you are writing more."

Rose gaped at the duke's daughter, whose quiet grace she had always admired, and the praise washed over her heart like cream over strawberries.

"I wanted to ask you to please come to the feast we are giving for our new guest. Perhaps you have heard that Lady Anne, the daughter of Duke Alfred of Schweitzer, has come to us."

Rose forced herself not to stammer. "Yes, I heard she was arriving soon." Was Hildy's theory true? Was she only being passed off as Duke Alfred of Schweitzer's daughter? It would make sense that they would want to keep Lady Salomea at Hagenheim Castle, where she'd be safe.

"We want to invite you and Frau Geruscha. It's to be a week from tomorrow, with much music and dancing."

*A ball!* Rose couldn't possibly go. She had little idea of how to conduct herself at such an occasion. Several months before, as part of grooming Rose to be her apprentice, Frau Geruscha had made Rose take lessons to learn the dances of the nobility. But Rose wasn't sure she remembered them. Besides that, she could hardly expect to know a single soul there.

Lady Osanna added, "The scribes and their families are invited, as well as the guild presidents."

Which wouldn't include any of Rose's acquaintances. "That's very gracious, I'm sure," she murmured. How should she respond? She couldn't be impolite.

"I also wanted to thank you for what you did for my brother, Lord

Hamlin." Osanna smiled sweetly. "Our family is very grateful. His leg is healing well. Wilhelm was quite impressed with your skill."

Rose's face burned and she knew she was blushing. "I'm thankful I was able to help."

"I hope you like the fabrics I picked out for you. The gold silk would make a nice gown for the ball. Our seamstress, Cecily, could make it for you. I'll send her to take your measurements."

Rose opened her mouth to refuse, but she didn't know how.

"You must come. You'll be my personal guest."

Her mouth went dry as she heard herself say, "It would be my pleasure."

# Chapter
## 4

*Two days later Rose left Frau Geruscha's* chambers to take a walk and clear her head of thoughts of the coming dance. With Wolfie by her side, she exited the town gate. The bright sun warmed the top of her head, and her cheeks stung as the wind lashed her face with her hair. She breathed deeply, filling her lungs with the fresh spring air, and strode up the hill to her favorite spot between the stream and the big beech tree.

Wolfie dashed past her, barking and snapping at a butterfly. He stopped and paced with his nose to the ground, stalking something in the grass. Suddenly, a hare dashed out of its hiding place and leaped away. Wolfie jumped straight into the air before racing after it.

Rose laughed and the sound made its way around the nearby trees as it was snatched away by the wind.

She stood gazing at the tall tree's spreading branches. How much she had enjoyed climbing it as a child. A lovely view of the stream and surrounding meadow always rewarded her. If she were to climb it now she could see if everything looked the same.

It truly was the perfect climbing tree, with branches and crooks in just the right places. As she studied it, she tried to recall exactly where she could place her feet. Almost before she knew what she intended, she grasped a limb and hoisted herself up.

As a child, her skirts had been short — not as cumbersome as the voluminous, full-length ones she now wore. Rose stepped on her hem and then had to kick it aside while she searched for a crook in which to place her other foot. She held on with one hand while she shifted to a higher branch, reaching up with her free hand.

A sound like the snort of a horse came from below her. Her heart jumped. As she turned her head to see who was there, her foot slipped and her fingers lost their grip. She scrambled frantically, her fingertips scraping loose bark. Before she could even scream, she landed on her back on the ground.

Air forcibly escaped her lungs. Darkness shot through with tiny bursts of light filled her vision.

"Are you hurt?" A masculine voice, laden with concern, entered her consciousness a moment before his face came into view above her.

Lord Hamlin.

After the longest moment of her life, Rose drew in a gasping breath. Rolling to her side, she closed her eyes and tried to breathe deeply. *O God, let this be a dream.* But when she opened her eyes again, he was still there, kneeling beside her, worry creasing his brow.

"Are you hurt?" Lord Hamlin repeated.

"No."

He studied her face, as though trying to make sure she was telling the truth. Then he grasped her arm and pulled her into a sitting position. She leaned limply back against the tree.

He released her, and her arm tingled where his hands had touched her.

Her back ached and her chest had a painful, hollow feel, but she wanted to show him she was not injured. Instead of smiling in reassurance, however, she stared at her lap, too embarrassed to raise her eyes.

"Are you sure you're not hurt? I'll go fetch Frau Geruscha."

"No, no, I am well."

"Do you climb trees often?"

Rose couldn't help but peek at him. His eyes were wide, as if he was amazed at her.

"Why not?" She threw the question at him, feeling suddenly reckless.

He lifted an eyebrow. "I should think you'd stop climbing them after such a tumble."

"If you hadn't distracted me, I wouldn't have fallen."

She could hardly believe she said it. No one of her station should speak in such a way to Lord Hamlin. But there was something liberating in saying exactly what she thought, instead of making the humble, deferential replies expected of her.

"Forgive me," he said quietly. "I'm thankful you didn't injure yourself." A slight smile tugged at his mouth. "But perhaps I saved you from falling from an even greater height."

Rose folded her arms across her chest. "I could easily climb this tree. I've climbed it many times." She wanted to add, *when someone wasn't sneaking up on me*, but managed to muster a bit of self-possession.

Lord Hamlin ducked his head, but Rose saw the smile he was trying to hide.

"You don't believe me." She suddenly wanted to prove to him that she could do it. However, climbing a tree while wearing a dress, with a man below her, did not seem wise.

"No, no, I believe you. I of all people know that you are a maiden of many talents."

Wolfie ran up, barking wildly, and planted himself between Rose and Lord Hamlin's big black horse.

"Wolfie, stop that."

The horse began to graze, as if to show that the dog was beneath his notice.

Lord Hamlin reached out a hand to Wolfie. The dog sniffed him then allowed Lord Hamlin to rub his shaggy head. Rose held her breath, fearing Wolfie would bite him. Instead, Wolfie relaxed under his touch, moving closer to him.

Rose shook her head at her dog's unusual behavior. "He must like you. He doesn't let people get that close." *Especially men.*

Lord Hamlin stroked him behind the ears. Wolfie grinned up at him, saliva dripping from his tongue.

"I had a dog once," Lord Hamlin said. "A good one too. Unfortunately, he got trampled by a horse and died."

"Oh, I'm so sorry." And she truly was. How sad to lose a beloved dog.

Lord Hamlin looked up and their eyes locked as his features softened. His earthy, leathery smell drifted over her, warm and pleasant. Aware of his close proximity, Rose's heart beat erratically.

As though also conscious of their nearness to each other, he moved a couple of paces away. "My sister, Lady Osanna, told me you're coming to the ball next week." He sat down on the grass, one knee pointing toward the stream, and picked a tall weed. Staring at it, he twisted it between his fingers.

"Yes, although I'm sure I won't know anyone." Rose frowned, wondering if she should have revealed her insecurity.

"At least there will be music, and I know how much you like music."

"Yes." *How did he know that?* "I do love music."

He smiled and twisted his upper body to face her. His broad shoulders stretched the fabric of his white shirt as he propped one elbow across his knee. "Do you sing?" he asked.

"A little. Do you?" She couldn't believe she was asking personal questions of Lord Hamlin. Their whole conversation was unthinkable. Yet here he was, looking relaxed and quite interested in answering her questions.

Wolfie, on the other hand, must have grown bored, because he dashed off to chase a chipmunk.

"Osanna and my mother like my singing. I'm not sure anyone else could appreciate it, and I'm certain I don't sing as well as you tell stories. You have the gift of storytelling. It is remarkable that you know how to read and write. Did Frau Geruscha teach you?" He fixed his eyes on her face.

Rose didn't feel offended by his statement, as she knew it truly was remarkable. None of her friends knew how to read. "Yes. Frau Geruscha started teaching me when I was very young. She said she'd never seen anyone so eager to learn." Rose felt a bit smug and then laughed at herself.

She met his gaze. He was smiling at her. His deep blue eyes absorbed the sunlight and sparkled like gems. His dark curls shifted in the breeze and brushed against his forehead.

*Oh, but you are handsome.*

Rose drew in a quick breath, shocked at herself.

At that moment Lord Hamlin stood and pulled something from the leather pouch that hung behind his horse's saddle. It was a lute. He sat back down and smiled at her, the light dancing in his eyes.

"Will you sing for me if I play?"

Rose shook her head. "Oh, no, I couldn't."

She could hardly believe she was refusing a request from Lord Hamlin, even though she couldn't imagine actually singing for him. But it could hardly matter what he thought of her. She could never hope to be anything to him except a servant, a healer's apprentice working for him in his castle. Besides, he would never think twice about her when he had nobly born ladies around him like Lady Anne, who might even turn out to be his betrothed. Nonetheless, Rose was glad he didn't seem angry at her refusal to sing. He simply stared down at the stringed instrument.

Her heart fluttered at the strange honor of Lord Hamlin playing the lute for her.

He strummed his thumb across the strings and a familiar tune emerged, the song of a maiden, fair and gentle, who walked alone, waiting for her lover to come to her. Rose listened, enraptured by the melody—and the sight of Lord Hamlin. She watched his hands, sun-browned and strong, expertly evoking the song. And watched his face, his eyes half closed as he appeared to concentrate on his playing, sighing in spite of herself.

He looked up and caught her eye. Never had she felt so alive—alive to the sound of the music, alive to the sight of Lord Hamlin's beautiful eyes gazing at her as though her soul was visible to his.

Rose tried to quiet her heart. She should not be thinking about Lord Hamlin this way. But if she believed in the songs that spoke of love, or believed what his eyes seemed to be saying to her ... no, it was wrong to even think that she could be anything to Lord Hamlin, that he could find her in any way as interesting as she found him. It was simply the music playing tricks on her, making her feel strong emotions that didn't apply to the situation.

As the last note drifted away, she cleared her throat. She should speak of something, anything, to distract herself from her reaction to the music. "That was beautiful. I suppose you have to practice a lot to remember all the songs ... all the notes." She was babbling.

"I play for my family a lot."

Rose nodded, searching her mind for something to say. He was smiling at her in a way that made her even more nervous, so she picked up a chestnut from the ground and studied it.

"I noticed a new boy helping out at the stables."

"You mean Lukas. I found him in the Marktplatz stealing an apple, so I put him to work."

"Just for stealing an apple?" Rose heard the dismay in her voice. Part of her said to be quiet, but another part was indignant that he would punish a young child for such a minor offense.

"He seems to be an orphan. He says his mother is dead and he doesn't know what happened to his father."

"The poor thing."

"He'll make himself useful in the stable."

"But he's only a child. Will you force him to work with those rough men? Who will look after him, take care of him?" Rose knew she should hold her tongue, knew that boys often were put to work at a very young age, but she didn't like it. Where was the justice in forcing a child to do dirty, hard work, merely because he had no parents to take care of him?

Lord Hamlin said nothing for a long moment. He stared into the trees across the stream bank.

Rose's throat tightened. Perhaps he was angry at her ranting. Certainly she had spoken far beyond what her status allowed.

"You're right. I myself shall make sure he isn't worked too hard and has a few hours every day to romp with the town children. I'll assign one of our matrons to look out for him, and I'll make sure he has a comfortable, safe place to sleep with the women servants."

She let his words sink in.

"Does that satisfy?"

She examined his face but found no hint of resentment. A bubble of joy expanded in her chest. He had actually listened to her.

"Yes, my lord."

His expression was unreadable. "My father needs an advisor like you. The region would be a more compassionate place, I dare say."

Rose stifled a laugh at the absurdity of a female advisor and at the outrageous compliment. The tension between them dissolved.

Lord Hamlin tossed the weed on the ground and leaned back on one hand. "You must live near here."

"I stay at the castle, with Frau Geruscha in the southwest tower, but my family lives near here."

A shiver of horror ran down her back at the thought of him seeing the small hovel where the five members of her family lived. Desperate to keep him from asking where she lived, she stood abruptly. "I have to go ... help Frau Geruscha ... with something. Farewell, my lord."

She turned and walked quickly down the grassy hillock, escaping her second unlikely encounter with Lord Hamlin, the future Duke of Hagenheim.

"Farewell," he called after her.

# Chapter
## 5

*Several days later, one day before the ball,* Rose held up her skirt as she walked across the dusty courtyard toward Frau Geruscha's chambers. She was startled when Lord Rupert stepped from around the back of the castle, directly into her path.

He smiled and bowed low. "Beautiful weather today, is it not?"

His bowing to her seemed a ridiculous gesture. She was hardly more than a servant.

"Yes, my lord." Although she knew she shouldn't stare, Rose glanced at him, curious. He was dressed fashionably in a violet doublet and a bright white shirt with sleeves that puffed out from shoulder to elbow. His light brown hair curled against the back of his neck and he carried a bunch of red roses in one hand.

"May I ask your name?"

"Rose, if you please, my lord." She curtsied.

"My dear maiden!" He clutched at his chest with one hand while holding out the flowers with the other. "Why, just now I was in the garden and found these roses. I knew I was picking them for someone. Now I see they were meant for a maiden of the same name and beauty as the flowers." He stepped toward her. "I don't think I could have planned anything more appropriate."

Rose hesitated. She did not want to accept them, thinking it rather *in*appropriate. But it was also inappropriate to refuse the duke's son. She reached out and took the flowers, carefully avoiding touching his hand. "I thank you, my lord."

He stood smiling at her for so long that Rose broke the uncomfortable silence. "You must have many important duties to attend to. I bid you good day." She took a sliding step to one side to walk around him.

Rather than allow her to pass, he studied her, and she watched as his eyebrows shot up in recognition. "I know who you are. You're the author of that amusing tale my family was so enamored of."

He laughed out loud and Rose felt her cheeks turn pink, knowing he must be drawing the attention of every person in the castle courtyard.

"Not only that, but you are the maiden who sewed up my brother's leg." He grinned down at her. "This is indeed an honor."

His demeanor, the jauntiness in his voice, and the tilt of his head, made Rose surmise that he was not entirely sincere.

"I look forward to seeing you at our ball. You are coming, aren't you?" He fixed his light blue eyes on her.

"Yes, Frau Geruscha and I will be there."

"I shall count the hours." He bent forward, holding out his hand.

He was waiting for her to lift her hand so he could kiss it. Her heart jumped, but she stood motionless, her head slightly bowed. Finally, he let his hand drop.

"Until tomorrow night." He winked then turned and sauntered toward the castle.

Wilhelm sat in the Great Hall with the musicians. It was the last day to practice their songs for the ball, and he was anxious to learn this new one.

As he strummed the strings of his lute, his mother swept in, her skirts dragging behind her. She crossed her arms. He cringed inwardly and pretended not to see her.

With that lofty air of hers that he disliked, she said, "Son, may I have a word with you?"

"Of course."

The musicians started to rise from their stools, but Wilhelm motioned for them to remain seated. "I'll return in a moment."

He followed his mother into the hallway. *Here it comes.*

"Now, Wilhelm, I know you usually prefer not to dance. However, I love to see our guests having a good time, and there are sure to be several young ladies who shall need partners."

He opened his mouth to speak, but his mother rushed on. "And more important, this is only Lady Anne's second week here. I would like you to make her feel at home by dancing with her."

"I'll give you three reasons why I cannot." He forced himself not to smile at her dire expression. It would only provoke her. "I am betrothed. You and Father have warned me—more times than I can count—that I must guard my heart. Dancing is not conducive to that end."

"Yes, but—"

Wilhelm held up a finger. "Wait. I have two more reasons."

She crossed her arms and pursed her lips.

"I'm also helping to provide the music, which means I can entertain more of your guests by *not* dancing. Third, I'm injured, or had you forgotten? You wouldn't expect me to dance on this gashed-up leg, would you?"

"You hardly limp at all now. Our dances are not so vigorous that you couldn't attempt at least every other one, resting in between."

"Ah!" said a loud voice from behind Wilhelm.

Rupert strode toward them and clapped him hard on the back. "My brother wouldn't give a fig for dancing, would you, Wil? He loathes it. As for me"—Rupert inhaled audibly, pushing out his chest—"I am prepared to dance with every woman in the room, whether she be fair or not." He wrapped his arm around his mother's shoulders and drew her to his side. "Don't worry, Mother. I'll keep the whole room entertained, to the best of my ability."

"Of that I have no doubt, but I ask you to spare my nerves and contain yourself. No carousing."

Wilhelm glared at Rupert. *He'll carouse—if he gets drunk.* Wilhelm planned to have a talk with his brother.

Rupert had already shaken off his mother's plea and turned to Wilhelm. "I met our talented little storyteller-healer, Rose. The one who sewed you up."

"Yes." Wilhelm studied his brother warily.

"Well, she's a beauty, is what I say. Very well could be the fairest maiden at the ball tonight."

Wilhelm despised the eager look in his brother's eyes. It reminded him of an incident involving Rupert and a serving wench back in Heidelberg. The thought turned his stomach.

"Yes, the dear maiden," the duchess said affectionately. "I am anxious to meet her. But I hardly think you would be interested in her, Rupert. Her family can have neither money nor noble connections. In fact, I believe her father is a woodcutter. But perhaps I'm mistaken." She shook her head as though it were not possible.

"No, it is true, Mother." With effort, Wilhelm held his voice steady.

"We are grateful to her for what she did for you, Wilhelm, to be sure. But instead of our healer's apprentice, Rupert should have his eye on Lady Anne." The duchess lowered her voice, looking pointedly at her younger son. "Laws being what they are and you being the younger son, you must make prudent life choices."

"Lady Anne!" Rupert cried.

His mother put one finger over her lips and looked at him sternly.

"Lady Anne is spoken for, Mother, or have you not heard the rumors that she is Wilhelm's betrothed?" With a gleeful smile and a raised eyebrow, he turned on Wilhelm.

Wilhelm fought the urge to throttle his brother.

"I don't believe that." His mother's voice was hushed but firm. "I don't know where Wilhelm's betrothed is, but I know *who* she is. She is the daughter of Godehard, Duke of Marienberg, not the daughter of Duke Alfred of Schweitzer."

Rupert shrugged. "Rumors nearly always have at least an element of truth, Mother. You've said so yourself, many times."

The duchess frowned.

"But don't worry about me. I'm destined for the Church, remember? I think I've persuaded Father to make me the new bishop." He faced his brother. "Don't you think I'd make an ideal priest?"

"No. I think you should wed." Wilhelm didn't like this conversation. If he weren't still considering giving Rupert the pounding he deserved, he would escape back to the musicians and his lute.

Rupert chuckled. "Ah, my brother knows me too well, I suppose." He gave Wilhelm a friendly pat on the shoulder before starting down the hallway. "I'll see you both tonight."

*Rupert. Always happy when there's a party to go to or a woman to seduce.* But if he dared set his sights on Rose . . .

"As for you," the duchess said, turning her eye on Wilhelm, "I hope you will enjoy yourself tonight."

"Yes, Mother, I'm sure I will." He stared at the iron sconce on the stone wall of the corridor, hardly seeing it. Instead, he saw Rose, as she'd sat on the sunny, grassy hill several days ago. *"I'm sure I won't know anyone,"* she'd said. The wind blew a strand of chestnut hair across her cheek at that moment, giving her a vulnerable look.

Wilhelm blinked to clear the memory from his mind. "Mother."

He looked into her faded blue eyes. "Please be kind to Rose. Remember what she did for me. I fear the other guests may look down on her because of her father's occupation."

"Oh." His mother's mouth opened in surprise, as though it had never occurred to her to be concerned for someone who might feel out of place. Her own self-assurance made her oblivious to such feelings in others. "I think she will enjoy herself immensely, having never been invited to anything so grand." Her face took on a disdainful look. "She should feel honored."

Wilhelm made an effort to unclench his teeth. "I'm sure she will be appropriately grateful. Just don't slight her, that's all I ask."

"Of course not, son. You always were the thoughtful one." She smiled and patted his cheek in a way that made him frown. She sighed. "I promise I will treat her with courtesy, not that I wouldn't anyway. But I shall make an extra effort, since you are so concerned."

"Thank you, Mother."

Rose sat up straight on the low stool in her new dress. Hildy stood over her, piling Rose's curls on top of her head.

Outwardly, Rose was nearly ready, but every time she thought about entering the Great Hall and facing a room full of elegantly dressed people, her stomach threatened to heave its contents.

She'd thought she wouldn't know anyone at the ball. Ha! The maidens from town, especially the daughters of the guild presidents, were sure to single her out for ridicule. Then there was Osanna, Lord Hamlin's sweet sister. While she appeared to like Rose, Osanna couldn't possibly realize what a bumpkin Rose was, someone who fell out of trees and would probably look just as clumsy attempting the dances.

Lord Hamlin. He had talked to her as though she were his peer, but perhaps only because he had happened upon her outdoors—certainly an informal setting. Would he ignore her at the ball? She was beneath his station in life. She wouldn't blame him if he didn't even acknowledge her tonight.

And yet, if she had not panicked and run away from him that day under the beech tree, how long might they have talked? He was chivalrous in both the way he behaved and the way he looked at her, so different from other men. He seemed so honorable, she felt safe with him.

Besides, he was betrothed.

And then there was Lord Rupert. She had only glimpsed him a couple of times since he and Lord Hamlin arrived home three weeks ago—until the day before, when he'd given her flowers.

She wasn't sure what to make of him. Lord Rupert had the polished manner of a person from whom compliments were free-flowing, but she had to admit, it felt good to be called "beautiful" by the son of a duke.

"Stop fidgeting!"

She sat still and let Hildy finish her hair. She couldn't see herself, since Frau Geruscha didn't own a looking glass, but she felt like a peasant dressed up to look like someone else. The dress had turned out beautifully. The gold silk skimmed the floor and the brocade bodice was studded with tiny pearls. The enormous sleeves hung from her wrists to the floor and were lined and cuffed with a dark cinnamon-red fabric.

Frau Geruscha would escort her to the ball. Her mistress didn't seem the least bit intimidated by the prospect. Rose wondered again about Frau Geruscha's family. She hadn't yet summoned the courage to ask her about her background, but her family must have been wealthy, since she could read and write Latin and had lived in an abbey in preparation for becoming a nun. She wondered what had caused her to leave the abbey.

Frau Geruscha may not have felt intimidated by the nobles and prominent burghers who would attend the ball, but Rose did. She hoped she could find a hiding place in the Great Hall where she could listen to the music without being seen.

The thought of seeing the tradesmen's daughters, who considered themselves in a higher class than she, made the sick feeling in her stomach worse. She thought of meeting Lady Anne, the daughter of a duke, possibly Lord Hamlin's betrothed. Her stomach balked at that too, so she closed her eyes and tried to think of nothing. That didn't work, as Lord Hamlin's face immediately appeared in her mind.

"Oh, Hildy, I'm scared to death to go to this ball. You should go in my place."

"I only wish I *could* go. There!" Hildy took her hands away from Rose's hair, staring at Rose from head to toe. "You look absolutely beautiful."

As if on cue, Frau Geruscha entered the room. Rose turned to face her mistress and watched her gray eyes grow round. "Rose, you look truly ... like a princess." Frau Geruscha smiled.

Rose smiled back. "You look very elegant too." The rich green of her mistress's velvet gown shimmered in the firelight.

Frau Geruscha held out her hand. "Shall we go? I hear music."

Rose took a deep breath, turned to Hildy, and hugged her.

"Don't!" Hildy shrieked. "You'll wrinkle your gown."

"Thank you, Hildy, for doing my hair. You're the best friend any-one could have."

"So are you." Tears stood in Hildy's eyes.

Looking at Hildy, Rose vowed silently that if there were to be any more balls in her future, she would figure out a way for her friend to attend the next one.

But tonight she had to face the crowd without her. She walked toward Frau Geruscha and linked arms with her. *I can do this. I can do this.* She held her head high — she could hardly do otherwise, since her hair made her neck ache when she bent her head in any direction.

Breathing deeply, she willed herself to stay calm. She glanced at her mistress from the corner of her eye. So content and casual were her features, Frau Geruscha looked as though she were simply walking to the market to buy herbs. She must have been at least five and forty years old, but her skin was smooth, and she was a handsome woman.

As they walked slowly down the castle corridor toward the Great Hall, Rose whispered, "Frau Geruscha, I'm afraid. Promise me you won't leave my side."

"Be not afraid, child. All will be well."

Rose's heart pounded harder than ever. The blood pulsed at her temples and she took another deep breath. *I can do this. I can do this.*

As they approached the door of the Great Hall, she heard the band of musicians start to play another tune. Frau Geruscha patted her hand. "Just enjoy the music."

# Chapter
## 6

*Wilhelm glanced up just in time to see Rose* walk in. His jaw fell. Her hair, her dress, her face ... She made everyone else in the room look pale and lifeless.

He'd better close his mouth before someone saw him staring.

Her gaze turned in his direction and he smiled to let her know he approved.

He suddenly realized that he had stopped playing in the middle of the song. He looked down and tried to concentrate on his lute. But his mind was filled with her image.

A pang of guilt stabbed him. He must stop this nonsense. It was unwise to ... well, to even look at her.

He tried to concentrate on the music, but when he glanced up again, Rupert was striding from the other side of the room toward Rose. He reached her, bowed, and placed his hand over his heart. He must be asking her to dance. A knot tightened around Wilhelm's chest.

*So this is how jealousy feels.*

Though on the outside Rose managed to control her trembling, her insides were quaking. The Great Hall seemed to stretch on forever. She'd never seen a room so large. The musicians played, sitting on stools near the south wall. People stood talking in small groups all around the room.

Lord Hamlin's eyes found hers. She was a little surprised to see him with the musicians, but she forgot about that as her heart flipped at his gentle smile. At least she had one friend in the room, even if he couldn't come and talk to her.

She observed him for a moment while his deft fingertips strummed over the lute's strings. Watching him play comforted her, and some of her anxiety slipped away.

She pretended not to see Lord Rupert staring at her from across the room, walking toward her. He couldn't possibly be coming to her. But when she could no longer doubt that he intended to speak to her, she turned to face him.

He bowed first to Frau Geruscha. Then he bowed to Rose, one hand over his heart. "Rose, we are honored that you have come tonight. You are the most beautiful woman here."

"I thank you, my lord." She curtsied, her face tingling. Frau Geruscha's expression grew cold, almost angry.

Lord Rupert's eyes stayed locked on Rose. "Will you do me the honor of being my partner for the next dance?" His teeth were straight and perfect, just like his brother's, as he smiled at her. He leaned forward, as though hanging on her every word.

"Of course."

Lord Rupert excused himself, saying he'd be back when the next song started.

*O Lord, did he truly just ask me to dance? Let me not forget the steps of the dance, or trip, or step on his foot.*

Rose could hardly believe the son of the duke and territorial prince had asked her to dance. Most people attending this dance would not even be seen speaking with someone like her.

She looked uncertainly at Frau Geruscha. "Did I do the right thing, agreeing to dance with him?"

"Yes, my dear." The frosty look did not leave her mistress's face, and she raised her eyebrows at Rose. "Be careful, though. Young Lord Rupert has a reputation for debauchery. You aren't to leave this room with him, do you understand?"

Rose swallowed. "Yes, Frau Geruscha."

Frau Geruscha's shoulders relaxed. "I don't mean to frighten you, child. You're perfectly safe. Lord Rupert is sometimes careless with his attentions, and I simply want to put you on your guard. Go ahead and dance. Have a good time."

Rose drew courage from her mistress's smile. She glanced around the room and caught a wealthy yarn merchant's wife staring at her. The woman's eyes darted back to her companion, the wife of the butchers' guild president. They were probably discussing their wonder at Lord

Rupert coming to talk to her. What would they say when they saw them dancing together?

An older woman approached Frau Geruscha and began to talk about an ailment, something about a pain in her side. They moved away as the woman's voice grew low and confidential.

Rose watched the dancers twirling in time to the music. She caught glimpses of Lord Hamlin as the guests bobbed back and forth between her and the musicians. Some girls standing several feet away were staring at Rose. When she looked at them, they burst into giggles.

Her stomach twisted into a nervous knot. She continued to scan the room but saw no friendly face. She decided to focus on her surroundings and practice describing them to Hildy.

Colorful tapestries, as well as several banners and flags, hung above a wooden table and on the center of the wall opposite the door. Some of the flags were battle-scarred, others were bright and perfect. One displayed the Gerstenberg coat of arms. The others were variations on the family colors of red, gold, and green.

Rose was most intrigued by a scene painted on the stone wall, stretching the whole length of the room. She strolled closer to get a better look. Knights in armor sat astride sleek horses. Gray hunting dogs ran ahead of them. Some knights jousted while others knelt before ladies in pale, flowing gowns with voluminous pointed sleeves that hung to the ground. A stream and a lake, along with mountains and a forest, graced the background.

She was admiring the beautiful fresco when she saw Lord Rupert approach.

"This was commissioned by my great-grandfather, Bertolf," he said, coming to stand at her left elbow. He pointed to a man in the picture whose head was bared, his helmet by his feet. He had Lord Rupert's rather long chin. "That is he, Bertolf Gerstenberg. And this one here is my grandfather, Conrad." He pointed to a younger man standing nearby with a shield in one hand and a lance in the other.

Just then Lady Osanna joined them, standing beside her brother. Rose couldn't help admiring her sea-green gown trimmed in gold. Her eyes matched her dress, the cut of which enhanced her slim waist and delicate shoulders. Her light brown hair was tightly braided and wound into a bun at the back of her head, covered by a net of gold thread.

"It's good to see you again, Rose." Lady Osanna clasped Rose's hand. "You look beautiful."

"As do you."

"I see you've met my rogue brother." She shifted her eyes toward Rupert.

Lord Rupert feigned an indignant look. "Pay no attention to such flippant remarks."

Lady Osanna grinned as the song ended and the dancers began to arrange themselves into two lines. She inclined her head toward Lord Rupert. "I believe my brother wishes to dance with you, Rose. When you're finished, I shall introduce you to Lady Anne."

"It would be my pleasure." Rose said the words automatically then realized they weren't exactly true.

Lord Rupert held his hand out to Rose, looking impatient to be off to the dance. She placed her hand on his forearm and allowed him to lead her. They fell in line with the others, Rose beside the ladies and Lord Rupert beside the men, the two lines facing each other. She was surprised her knees weren't buckling underneath her as she prepared to dance the Carolingian Pavane with Lord Rupert.

The music and the dance began.

*I wish I were dancing with Lord Hamlin.*

The unbidden thought made her catch her breath. She tried to ignore it and concentrate on the steps.

Lord Rupert never once glanced away to look at his feet or at any of the other dancers, but kept his eyes focused on her face. If she didn't know better, she would think he was truly enamored of her.

They came to the part of the dance where the men had to kneel while their partners danced around them in a tight circle. Lord Rupert went down on one knee so quickly it startled Rose. His head tilted up to her, and he placed his hand over his heart. His eyes held hers.

Rose's heart skipped a beat at his flirtatious look. Of course, that's all it was. He was flirting with her, and after the dance was over he'd go dally with someone else. This was his way of enjoying himself at a party, no doubt.

Rose danced around Lord Rupert then took her place in front of him. Now it was his turn. She stood still as he began his slow dance around her.

Her insides were quaking again. Everyone was staring at them, the woodcutter's daughter and the only eligible son of the ruling prince of Hagenheim. She took a quick peek at the musicians. Lord Hamlin was looking down at his lute. He lifted his head and Rose quickly looked away, not wanting to see his reaction.

When the dance was over, Lord Rupert took her hand and bowed over it, gazing up into her eyes. "I thank you, dearest Rose, for dancing with me. You are a most ... delightful ... partner." He tucked her hand inside his elbow. "Come. Let me introduce you to my mother. She's anxious to meet you."

Rose resisted the urge to bolt for the door. Instead, she walked slowly, as Frau Geruscha had taught her, with her shoulders back and her chin high.

Heads turned as they walked by, but Rose looked straight ahead, too afraid of what she would see in the guests' faces. When she glanced up at Lord Rupert, he smiled.

The duchess stood conversing with Osanna and Lady Anne. They turned to face Lord Rupert and Rose as they approached.

"Mother," Lord Rupert said, "I would like to present Rose, our gifted healer and storyteller."

"I am delighted to meet you, Rose." The duchess took Rose's hand from Lord Rupert.

"Your Grace." Rose curtsied, her heart in her throat.

"I wish to thank you for your service to Lord Hamlin." There was a coldness in the woman's eyes that did not match the graciousness of her words.

"It is my pleasure to serve."

"Lady Anne, this is Rose. She is our healer's apprentice. Rose, this is Lady Anne, daughter of Alfred, Duke of Schweitzer."

"A healer's apprentice. That sounds like interesting work." Lady Anne was as tall as Rose, rather attractive, with delicate features. Her skin was so pale it was transparent, revealing bluish veins between her eyes and on her neck. A small cap hid most of her light brown hair, and little gold bells dangled from a belt around her waist.

Rose recalled Hildy telling her that bells were very much in fashion.

"I hope you will like it here at Hagenheim Castle," Rose said.

"I thank you." Lady Anne smiled back.

At least she wasn't cold or haughty, if she did turn out to be Lord Hamlin's betrothed in disguise.

"Rupert." The duchess's face brightened. "I insist you take Lady

Anne as your partner for the next dance. Go and be a good host to our guest."

Lord Rupert hesitated, glancing at Rose. She hoped he didn't anger his mother by slighting Lady Anne—especially on her account.

Finally, he held out his hand to Lady Anne.

Lady Anne smiled and took his hand. He looked back at Rose, but she avoided his gaze and focused on Lady Osanna and her mother. Lady Anne's bells jingled as she and Rupert crossed the room to join the dance.

Just then a young man in a fashionably cut doublet and enormous puffed sleeves approached Lady Osanna. "Will you honor me with this dance?"

"Yes, I thank you." Lady Osanna turned to Rose. "Pray excuse me, Rose." They hurried away as the music started.

The duchess folded her hands over her waist and faced Rose, boring into her with blue-gray eyes. "I trust you are enjoying yourself?"

"Yes, your grace. I enjoy music and dancing." Rose's head started to ache, whether from holding up her hair, or from the strain of trying not to say or do anything wrong in front of the duchess, she wasn't sure.

"Let me introduce you to some people." The duchess's glance settled on a red haired young man standing alone. She beckoned him with a slight "come hither" movement of her fingers.

The young man arrived with a bow. The pleasant smile on his freckled face put Rose at ease. "Your Grace."

"Gunther, I'd like you to meet Rose, Frau Geruscha's new apprentice. Rose, this is Gunther Schoff. His father is a scribe."

She said those last words so archly, Rose was sure she meant, "This young man is closer to your social status."

"How do you do?" Rose said.

"Most pleased." He bowed politely. "I've always been interested in the healing arts."

"I'm afraid I'm still new to the practice. Frau Geruscha is just beginning to teach me."

"I'm sure you already know quite a lot. But since I seem to be healthy today and have no medicinal needs, would you like to dance? I don't think it's too late to join."

Rose smiled at his gracious speech.

"Oh, no, it isn't too late." The duchess flicked her wrist. "Go on."

Gunther crooked his elbow and Rose took his arm. As they scurried away, Rose let out a deep breath at having escaped the duchess. Gratitude warmed her to Gunther.

The dance was the Black Almain. Gunther seemed to know it well, and his movements were smooth and graceful. Friendliness, as if absent of any ulterior motive, showed on his face. His chivalrous manner impressed Rose. She felt much more comfortable with him than with Lord Rupert.

She wondered if Hildy liked red hair. He was just the right height for Hildy too.

Lord Rupert and Anne danced several couples away, but Rose noticed out of the corner of her eye that Lord Rupert was looking at her. She ignored him and enjoyed the beauty and rhythm of the music. She wanted to glance at the musicians, but didn't.

When the dance was over, she and Gunther moved to a vacant spot near the wall while Lord Rupert and Lady Anne remained on the dance floor. They chatted about astronomy and mathematics, of which Gunther was very knowledgeable, having studied at a monastery for two years. He had also studied illumination, and Lord Hamlin had promised him a position illustrating the texts the duke's scribes were copying. He was polite and well-spoken, and Rose knew she had made a new friend. Perhaps this night would not be so bad after all.

She and Gunther watched Lord Rupert and Lady Anne, her bells making almost as much noise as the musicians' instruments, dance a branle known as Toss the Duchess. The dancers formed a large circle and frequently changed partners.

Gunther asked Rose about her apprenticeship, and their conversation turned to herbs and their benefits. She didn't notice that the dance had ended until Lord Rupert stood by her side.

"May I claim you, Rose, for the next dance?"

"Yes, of course." Rose tried not to show her astonishment at him asking her to dance a second time, especially after his mother's obvious disapproval.

Lord Rupert led her onto the dance floor for the Maltese Branle, a lively dance in which the dancers raised their hands high in the air and clapped three times before spinning and doubling back. She tried to forget that her partner was Duke Nicolaus's son and just lose herself in the activity. But he continued to stare at her, unnerving her with the look in his eyes, which did strange things to her heartbeat.

When the dance ended, instead of walking away to take a break,

Lord Rupert asked her to dance again. Rose agreed. She wasn't sure if she could say no.

"Did I tell you how lovely you look this evening?" Lord Rupert's hand rested lightly on her arm as he leaned down. His pale blue eyes sparkled in a flicker of torchlight.

"I thank you." Rose refused to take him too seriously, remembering Frau Geruscha's warning. She glanced away, and when she did, her eyes connected with Lord Hamlin's where he sat with the musicians. The corners of his mouth went up in a resigned expression. Sadness shone from his eyes.

*Lord Hamlin must think I'm flirting with Lord Rupert. But I'm not the one flirting—he is!* Rose blushed. Perhaps he disapproved of her dancing with his brother. Or perhaps he disapproved of her for the same reason his mother did, because any relationship between them was unseemly, as his family intended him to marry an heiress.

Suddenly, she didn't care about anything. Lord Hamlin was betrothed, the duchess was sending Lord Rupert disgusted looks, and all the young maidens at the dance were glaring at her. She would be oblivious to them all. A handsome man was paying attention to her, inviting her to dance, and she meant to enjoy it.

Rose flashed a smile at Lord Rupert as they got ready for the next dance. The music started and she recognized the Bassadanza, the slowest dance of all. Lord Rupert took Rose's hand and they stepped forward, passing and turning to face each other. Rose met his gaze with equal boldness now as they repeatedly brushed shoulders, dancing close, rising on their toes then backing away, only to step forward again.

Rose felt a sensation of power swell in her chest as Lord Rupert's eyes never left hers. He seemed to drown in her presence, as though they were the only two people in the room. Could he truly fall in love with her?

Perhaps a more pertinent question was, could Lord Rupert, son of a powerful prince of the Holy Roman Empire, wed anyone he pleased—even Rose? From his mother's reactions tonight, perhaps that was exactly what the duchess was afraid of. The only thing he stood to inherit was a manor house and farm within a half-day's ride from the castle. Rose, on the other hand, was as poor as—as a wood-cutter's daughter. How could he ever think of marrying her?

Marriage was surely the last thing on Lord Rupert's mind, but she didn't care. She would enjoy this moment. She refused to think about the probability that Lord Rupert wanted the selfsame thing the blacksmith's son wanted.

The dance ended, but Lord Rupert didn't let go of her hand. He didn't move, either, as he stared into her eyes. "I must have you sit with me at the feast."

She had not expected this. "I'm ... not sure that would be appropriate. Your mother—"

"I will arrange it with Mother. You will be my dinner partner."

The person in question was coming their way. Rose leaned away from Lord Rupert, pulling her hand free.

"Rose." The duchess's eyes pierced her then turned on Lord Rupert. She placed her hand on his arm. "Rupert, you must dance with more of our guests." She turned to Rose for a moment. "You understand, of course. He has obligations."

"Of course." Rose curtsied as the duchess led Lord Rupert away.

He looked back at her, and his expression said, "*I shall return.*"

Rose clasped her hands together, trying to squeeze out her nervousness as she remembered the duchess's cold stare and Lord Rupert's determination to have her sit with him. *How awkward.* Her heart fluttered. She took in the Great Hall in a sweeping glance, trying to get her mind off the conflict she was causing.

Everyone seemed small, swishing around the enormous hall in their colorful clothes. The torches reached upward with bright tongues of light, the flags were majestic, and the marble floor was as elegant and smooth as the silk garments floating above it. Rose stared again at the wall but didn't see it. She was thinking of the dances, the way her lungs had filled with air and her body floated as she'd executed the steps— correctly too, thank goodness. And she thought of Lord Rupert, his attentiveness, the look in his eyes.

"Rose?"

She turned. "Lord Hamlin." Her heart seemed to stick in her throat as she curtsied.

"I saw you dancing. I hope you're enjoying the ball."

She swallowed, trying to push her heart back down where it belonged. "Oh, yes, and the music is heavenly. I thank you. Please tell the other musicians that I think they are wonderful."

"I will. I'm sure they'll be pleased." He looked at her intently. His dark blue eyes seemed more brilliant than ever, and his suntanned face contrasted handsomely with his white shirt and sleeveless sapphire doublet. "Will you honor me with the next dance?"

*Me?* Rose swallowed. "Yes."

Her knees shook as they joined the dancers. The musicians began to play and the large human circle moved in unison. His hand was warm around hers, sending a tingle through her arm that spread additional warmth all through her. All thoughts of Lord Rupert disappeared from her head.

Since the song being played was a carol, all the dancers were expected to sing. She couldn't help but close her eyes for a moment in pleasure at hearing Lord Hamlin's voice, so deep, rich and masculine, and perfectly in tune.

They stepped to the left, then to the right, forward and then back. Rose was so aware of his hand holding hers, of his closeness, that she couldn't utter a sound. Lord Hamlin glanced at her, and his gentle look made her heart twist. She wished the dance would never end.

But it did, and Lord Hamlin turned to her, gently releasing her hand. To cover her nervousness, she gave her voice a teasing tone. "I thought you said you couldn't sing. In fact, you sing very well."

"I thank you." He smiled at her, and her legs seemed to melt. He had such an earnest, sincere expression on his face, and Rose couldn't imagine worrying that Lord Hamlin's intentions were immoral.

People were beginning to form two lines for another almain.

Lord Hamlin raised his eyebrows at her. "I suppose they can do without me for one more song. Would you dance with me again?"

"Yes." She didn't understand the strange emotions that were going through her. Lord Hamlin had proved himself to be her friend, but these feelings were not those she would feel for a friend.

They stood opposite each other, waiting for the music to begin. Rose felt she was the most blessed maiden in the world to be dancing with him. He projected such an air of responsibility and confidence. He towered over her, a conspicuous presence even in the large hall full of people.

The music began. He reached out and took her hands, and she lost herself in the rhythm and in his eyes. His feet moved deliberately but gracefully through the steps. She allowed herself to smile at him and enjoy this dance, trying to imprint it on her memory forever.

When the dance was over, he thanked her and quickly excused himself to rejoin the musicians. She bit her lip as she watched him go.

Gunther came over and talked with her during the next dance. He made her laugh at his jokes and anecdotes until she felt more at ease again.

Then Lord Rupert returned to her side to ask her for the last dance. She was so tired and content, she wanted nothing more than to leave while she was still sure she hadn't done anything embarrassing. She wondered if it would be impolite to depart before the feast began. But one look at Lord Rupert's face at the end of the dance told her that he wouldn't let her go so easily.

Once the trestle tables and benches were brought in for the feast, Rose searched for Frau Geruscha. But she found herself, per Lord Rupert's instructions, seated between him and Lady Osanna. All eyes turned to see the poor peasant sitting with the two young nobles. The situation was ridiculous, and Rose felt the absurdity of it as keenly as anyone. But thither she was forced to sit, at the high table with Duke Nicolaus and his family.

At least the duchess seemed to bear it well, forcing a smile the rest of the night.

Lady Anne sat beside Lord Hamlin, several people away from Rose, on the other side of the duke. The sight of the two of them sitting side by side gave her such a sinking feeling that she avoided looking that way. She tried to catch the sound of his voice, but the room was too noisy and he was too far away. She was certain he had forgotten all about her, with Lady Anne sitting beside him, but she hoped he didn't think she was trying to somehow entrap his brother. He must, at the very least, see the inappropriateness of her being seated beside Lord Rupert.

She finally spotted Frau Geruscha several seats away, at a lower table. She looked worried, even angry, but when Rose caught her eye, she smiled.

"Ah!" Lord Rupert drew her attention away from the other guests. He pointed to the huge platter being carried in by four servants. "My favorite dish."

A peacock perched on the platter, its plumage having been placed back on the roasted body. It did look beautiful, but as the servants lifted off the skin and feathers and began to carve the meat, Rose didn't feel very hungry.

The guests' raucous laughter died down to a murmur as they were served the roast fowl with gravy on their trenchers of stale bread.

Everyone dug into their food. After a few minutes of focused eating, Lord Rupert began regaling her with stories about the superiority of his horse and complaints about the appalling condition of the roads from Heidelberg, which had almost caused his horse to break a leg. When the conversation lagged, she asked what subjects he had studied at the university.

"Oh, mathematics, philosophy, and debate … the like."

He leaned over and whispered, "That's Bishop Albrecht." With his eyes he indicated the man sitting to his left. The bishop wore a white robe with elaborate gold embroidery and gold jewelry around his neck. "The wealthiest man in the room."

The man was surely the oldest as well. His pink skin sagged beneath his eyes, and he had a hump where his shoulder blades should have been. Rose had heard the gossip — that Lord Rupert wanted the duke to appoint him the next bishop, to take Bishop Albrecht's place after his death. But it could only be a rumor.

"How would you like to be that wealthy?" Lord Rupert asked, watching her face.

"I can't imagine it." She looked away, uncomfortable with the question.

"I should like it immensely."

Perhaps he did wish to be the next bishop. But try as she might, she couldn't form a picture in her mind of Lord Rupert as a chaste clergyman.

Between enjoying the many courses of the feast, Lord Rupert often focused his attention on other guests who approached him to make some comment or share a joke they had heard. Lady Osanna graciously began to talk to Rose, preventing her from thinking how awkward she felt. Rose was grateful for her kindness, especially when one glance in the other direction would bring the duchess into view, as well as the wealthy merchants' daughters, who were seated at a lower table.

The feast seemed to go on and on as more food was paraded around the tables than they could possibly eat.

During the fourth course, Lord Rupert gulped his spiced red wine, smiling his satisfaction. Rose took small sips. She wasn't used to drinking wine that wasn't watered down, and she was anxious to leave the feast before Lord Rupert and the other men should begin to get drunk.

He leaned toward her, and in a subdued voice, asked, "Are you enjoying your first feast?"

"Yes, I thank you."

"Did you enjoy the dances?"

"Very much."

"I'm told I'm an excellent dancer."

"I would have to agree."

"Which dances were your favorites?" He leaned even closer and his gaze settled on her lips.

Rose cleared her throat and glanced down at her plate. "The Carolingian Pavane and the Maltese Branle."

"And you danced those with me, if I recall correctly."

But tonight she had enjoyed the almain and the carol even more.

He looked away long enough to pick up his silver tankard and take another long drink. He set it back in its place and turned to her again. "I saw you dancing with my brother. He's quite taken with you."

His comment made her thoughts race. Taken with her? "That is an unfortunate thing for you to say." She looked away, pretending to ignore him.

"Now don't take that tone. I know you like me best." He grinned.

She didn't like the way he was behaving or this conversation. He'd obviously had too much to drink.

"Go riding with me tomorrow."

Affecting the same cool tone she'd used earlier, she said, "I cannot. It would be improper." Not to mention unwise. "Besides, I don't know how. I've never ridden a horse."

"I'll teach you."

"Not without a chaperone."

"Then I'll get a chaperone. One of Osanna's ladies will go with us."

The prospect left her feeling anxious, but what other excuse could she give? "Frau Geruscha may have something for me to do tomorrow. I would have to ask her first. I work for her, you know."

"And she works for my family, and therefore you must do as I say." His eyes teased her.

"As I said, I will ask Frau Geruscha tomorrow."

"Then I shall come for you in the morning, before the sun gets high."

Rose merely shook her head. Her mind was sluggish and she wasn't sure what to say. She would discuss it with Frau Geruscha. Her mistress should be able to provide her a good reason not to go.

After the fifth course, Rose saw a few people leave. Men began shouting crude jokes and dallying with the maidens who were helping serve the food and wine. Rose turned to Lady Osanna and whispered, "Would it be rude if I left now?"

"No, most of the ladies will leave soon. I enjoyed our conversation. I hope my brother wasn't too trying."

"Oh, no, it was a wonderful night." Rose glanced up to see Frau Geruscha standing just behind her.

"Let us go, Rose."

"You're not departing so soon, are you?" Lord Rupert grabbed Rose's hand as she stood. He affected a crestfallen expression.

"I'm afraid I must. I thank you for favoring me tonight." She extracted her hand from his.

He waved and called after her, "Farewell until tomorrow."

She cringed, wishing he had not said that so loudly. Lord Hamlin was getting to his feet at that moment, and his eye caught hers. With a serious expression, he nodded. She nodded back. What could he be thinking about her sitting with his brother?

And why did she care so much?

# *Chapter*
## 7

*Wilhelm headed out of his bedchamber and* down the corridor. As he passed Rupert's chamber, the door burst open and Rupert bumped into him.

Just the person he wanted to see. Wilhelm refused to move out of his brother's way, forcing him to look him in the eye. "I saw you dancing with Rose last night, making her sit beside you at the feast. What are your intentions toward her?"

The lighted candle on the wall sconce illuminated Rupert's face. "Intentions?" Rupert squinted at him.

"You had better not try anything dishonorable with her, Rupert. She's not—she's not the kind of maiden that—"

"Save your sermon, big brother." Rupert's teeth glowed in the dim corridor. "I'm not as big a louse as you think I am. I like Rose. In fact, I think she's just the maiden I've been looking for."

Wilhelm eyed his brother, his stomach tightening. "What do you mean by that?"

"I said what I meant."

"You know Rose has no wealth, no property." Wilhelm couldn't imagine his brother giving up the prospect of finding a rich heiress to make his fortune. And he knew Rupert's desire to become the bishop was connected to the clergyman's opulence.

"Why don't you go find your conjurer and stop trying to be my conscience?"

A prickly heat crept up Wilhelm's neck. If Rupert dared to hurt Rose ... "Just don't try what you did with the maid at the inn in Heidelberg."

Rupert's reply was strained. "Your advice is duly noted. I thank you." He turned his back on Wilhelm and strode down the hall.

Wilhelm resisted the urge to go after him, to spin him around and make him swear never to try any of his disarming tricks on Rose.

He would like to think Rupert's intentions were honorable and he was only angry because his older brother didn't trust him. But Wilhelm suspected Rupert's anger arose from the fact that he had come too close to the truth.

Certainly if Rupert chose a wife without a sizeable dowry, Wilhelm could, and would, make sure Rupert's life was comfortable. And if Rupert fell in love with a respectable maiden like Rose, perhaps he would be willing to settle down at the manor house that rightfully belonged to him and live a comfortable life in the country. At least, that was what Wilhelm had always hoped for him. Rupert certainly wasn't the right man to lead the Church.

Despite his hopes, he found it hard to imagine Rupert settling down. After all, he was only twenty-one years old. And hadn't he proven himself licentious and immature during the past two years while they were away in Heidelberg?

But Rupert's interest in Rose aroused Wilhelm's anger more than he dared explore. She was not one of the dissolute wenches Rupert frequently spent time with. Surely Rupert realized that. If he didn't, Wilhelm vowed he would impress the fact on his brother in terms he could not mistake.

He sighed and turned in the direction of the southwest tower. It was time to have his stitches taken out. And time for him to stop thinking about Rose. Past time. He should never have allowed himself to dwell on her beauty, her unaffected manners, her sweet but determined temperament...

Wilhelm shook his head. He was doing it again.

Rose turned the crank on the side of the stone well. Water sloshed in the bucket at the end of the rope. As it neared the top, the handle turned slower and she pulled harder. Finally, the full bucket came into view, and she unhooked it from the windlass. Wrapping both hands around the handle, she hefted it off the short stone wall of the well. She made her way across the castle courtyard toward the southwest tower, inching along and sloshing water on the ground around her feet.

A shadow crossed her path and she glanced up. Lord Hamlin stood three steps in front of her.

"May I?" He took the bucket from her, wrapping his big, sunbrowned hand around the handle.

"Thank you."

He started in the direction of the tower without looking at her, carrying the bucket easily with one hand.

Rose pushed the hair out of her eyes. She couldn't help but contrast the way she must have looked the night before—her curls elegantly piled on top of her head, her colorful silk dress gliding across the dance floor—with how she looked today. This morning her hair trailed over her shoulders and down her back in a disheveled mass, and she wore the same ugly green kirtle she'd worn the day she sewed up his leg. She had scrubbed the blood stain until it was so faint she didn't think anyone would notice.

"I was just on my way to Frau Geruscha's chamber to get my stitches out." Lord Hamlin stared straight ahead.

"Oh." *Today?*

"I was supposed to come yesterday."

"Frau Geruscha is here. It won't take her a moment." *Thank goodness I won't have to do it.*

They reached the door and Lord Hamlin stood back to let Rose go in first. Rose tried to take the bucket from him, but he pointed into the storage room. "Do you want this in there?"

"Yes, my lord."

Rose watched as he set the bucket on the floor, his shoulder muscles straining against his white linen shirt. He looked around. "You have a lot of herbs in here."

"Yes, Frau Geruscha knows everything about medicinal herbs."

Frau Geruscha must have heard their voices, because she called from the second floor, "I'll be down in a moment!"

Lord Hamlin and Rose wandered back into the main chamber.

"What is this?" Lord Hamlin strode over to the desk by the window.

"The Bible." Rose stopped in the middle of the room, several steps away. "It belongs to Frau Geruscha, but she lets me read it."

His face softened and his eyebrows quirked upward. "The Bible? That's my favorite book."

He did that thing with his eyes again, exchanging wordless

information with her own. He seemed to say, "*It pleases me to know you read it.*" An inexplicable happiness flowed through her.

*Uh-oh.* Her imagination was doing a Hildy again.

"Frau Geruscha taught you to read Latin as well as German?"

Rose nodded.

"Lord Hamlin." Frau Geruscha's voice caused Rose to jump. "You've come to have your stitches removed, I presume."

Frau Geruscha stepped into the room from the dark stairwell. Her starched wimple covered her graying hair. "Sit here on the bed and stretch your leg out so we can have a look."

Lord Hamlin sat down on the bed and pulled off his boot. He was wearing footless hose and pulled them up until they exposed his stitches.

"Oh, my." Frau Geruscha leaned over his leg. "You healed faster than I anticipated. Some of the stitches have become a touch embedded. But that's no matter. Come here, Rose."

Rose hurried to Frau Geruscha's side.

"Rose, I want you to remove the stitches."

Rose's heart sank. What could she do? If she refused, Lord Hamlin might realize how embarrassed she felt touching him, and Frau Geruscha would be disappointed in her. If she hoped to be a good healer, she couldn't shirk such a simple task.

Frau Geruscha stood to let Rose take her place. Rose swallowed her panic and sat down. She kept her eyes focused on Lord Hamlin's stitches.

"Here." Frau Geruscha handed her the small shears with sharp metal points.

Rose looked at them, then down at Lord Hamlin's white leg and the black stitches. She couldn't help glancing up at his face. He gave her a slight smile.

*Does he know I have no idea what I'm doing, that I'm embarrassed about touching him, and terrified of disappointing Frau Geruscha?*

She should project confidence, not fear and timidity. She had seen Frau Geruscha do this before. It was a simple thing to clip the stitches and pull them from the flesh. Yes. Simple, easy. She could do this.

Rose leaned down. She drew close to the skin with the shears, then straightened again. "Frau Geruscha, will you make sure I do this correctly, please?"

"Yes, Rose, of course. Go ahead."

She drew near again, pretending to work on a stranger's leg. *I simply have to get the stitches out . . . efficient, quick.*

But some of the stitches were embedded. She placed the points around the knot at the end, which had sunk into the skin. She pulled on the catgut with her fingers and tried to get between the knot and the skin with the points. Then she snipped. *Oh no.* Red blood seeped from the knick she'd inflicted.

Wilhelm let out a hiss of pain.

"Oh, I'm so sorry." She grabbed the cloth Frau Geruscha was holding out to her and dabbed at the blood. "Frau Geruscha, you had better do this." Leaping to her feet, she upset the stool, which clattered onto the floor. Her face burned.

"No, no, you're doing fine. There'll be a little blood. The stitches don't want to come out now that the skin is beginning to grow over them. You must just snip and then give them a little tug."

Rose knew that the blood had come from her pricking his leg with the shears and not from the embedded state of the stitches. Some healer she was!

Frau Geruscha addressed Lord Hamlin. "A little blood is to be expected."

He smiled as though amused. "Sorry I made that noise, Rose. Snip away. You won't hurt me."

With a slight tremor in her hand, she picked up the stool, righted it, and sat down. She bowed over his leg and concentrated. Carefully she slipped the end of the shears under the first stitch and clipped it with a soft snap. No blood. But now she had to pull out the embedded stitch.

First she would snip all the stitches and then remove them. She cut the next stitch and the next. Her eyes watered as she forced herself not to blink. But so far, no more blood.

Was it just her, or was it hot and stuffy in the room? A lock of hair tickled her forehead, and she took a swipe at it with the back of her hand.

"You're doing fine, Rose." Frau Geruscha stood near, watching.

Rose snipped again and again, finally reaching the last knot, which was so embedded, she had the same problem as with the first one. She pulled on it, hard, until it slipped from the skin. A little blood oozed out, and she dabbed at it with the cloth. "Sorry." She looked up at Lord Hamlin and winced.

He laughed. "It's my fault for not coming sooner to get them taken out."

He was only being kind. Nobles never took the blame for anything.

But Lord Hamlin was not an ordinary noble. She suddenly felt blessed by this chance to be so near him again, even if it meant dealing with his wound.

She pulled the rest of the stitches out one by one, but Lord Hamlin didn't complain or even flinch.

"I thank you, Rose." He gave her a smile as she finished.

"Shall I bandage it for you?"

"It is well. Hardly any blood—"

"Yes, you should," Frau Geruscha broke in. "A bandage may help prevent festering."

Lord Hamlin had started to rise but sat back down and lifted his leg onto the bed again.

Rose took a small bandage from the shelf and wrapped it twice around his leg before cutting it off and tying it in place. Frau Geruscha made small talk with him while Rose fiddled with the leftover bandages. She heard Lord Hamlin stand.

"I thank you again, Rose." He hesitated, as though considering his next words.

"Please excuse me, my lord." Frau Geruscha bowed to Lord Hamlin. "I must go back upstairs for a few minutes."

"Frau Geruscha." He nodded to her.

How extraordinary that Frau Geruscha would leave her alone with a man. But that man was Lord Hamlin, who radiated honor and goodness like the sun radiates warmth. And he was leaving anyway.

Except when he turned his eyes back to Rose, he didn't seem in any hurry to go. "We have a library in the castle. There are several books there you might be interested in. I should have offered the use of it to you before. You are most welcome to borrow any volume you wish to read."

Rose's smile broadened and she looked at the floor. "To be honest, my lord, I have been borrowing books from your library for half a year." She glanced up to see his surprised expression. "I hope you will forgive me, but I never take them out of the castle, only to Frau Geruscha's chambers, and I take great care of them."

"You know that books are very expensive. I'm afraid it's a serious offense to take a book without permission." He tightened his lips, as though displeased, but his eyes twinkled. Rose found it strangely hard to take a breath.

He laughed. "I'm glad you were able to be so ... resourceful."

She started to breathe again.

A figure darkened the doorway. "Ah, Wilhelm!"

Lord Rupert ducked his head to step inside the chamber and Rose inwardly cringed. She had forgotten to talk to Frau Geruscha about going riding with Lord Rupert.

"I came to see Rose, and I see you beat me here."

The two of them stood face-to-face, their arms tense by their sides, eyeing each other at three paces. Rose wanted to say something to break the tension but couldn't think of a single word.

"Rose, I trust you are well this morning." Lord Rupert turned away from Lord Hamlin and smiled, though his eyes did not mirror the emotion.

"Yes, I thank you."

Lord Rupert cut his eyes back to his brother. "Do you have business here?" His voice sounded tight.

"As a matter of fact, I was just leaving, but it's fortunate that I'm still here, since you should not be alone with an unmarried maiden."

"And yet you are here."

"I was just leaving." A muscle twitched in his jaw.

"No one's stopping you."

"I believe I'll stay." He crossed his arms in front of his chest.

Silence ensued, and neither man moved. Rose shifted from one foot to the other, her shoulders starting to ache with the tension. She had to say something. "I'm not sure if I can go riding today, Lord Rupert. I haven't asked Frau Geruscha yet."

"Riding?" Lord Hamlin raised his brows at Rupert again. "Not without a chaperone."

"I thank you for pointing out the obvious, brother. The fact is I have been unable to locate a suitable chaperone, which is what I came to tell Rose." Under his breath, he muttered, "Not that it's any business of yours."

At that moment they heard Frau Geruscha making her way down the steps to the first-floor chamber. When she appeared at the bottom, Lord Rupert brightened. "Good morning, Frau Geruscha."

"Good morning to you, Lord Rupert." Geruscha's eyes narrowed suspiciously. Could this get any more awkward?

"Frau Geruscha, I would like to take Rose riding, but we have no chaperone. Would you be able to come with us?"

Frau Geruscha looked from one face to another. "I could not be gone long, in case of any emergencies."

"Oh, I promise we shall return very soon, Frau Geruscha." Lord Rupert's voice rang with eagerness.

Her jaw hardened. "One hour. I can allow no more."

"Yes, I promise." He turned to Rose and leaned toward her, seeming to forget that anyone else was in the room. "I've picked out the gentlest mare in the stable for you. I shall have you riding like an experienced horsewoman in no time."

Frau Geruscha scowled.

Lord Hamlin's face darkened, and a muscle twitched in his jaw. He nodded at Rose. Then he turned and left.

# *Chapter*
## 8

*Lord Rupert held the reins of a gray mare,*
already saddled for Rose.

"She's beautiful." Rose rubbed the horse's neck, so big and warm, her short hair so different from Wolfie's long fur.

A stable hand led out Rupert's huge Belgian warhorse. His white mane and tail contrasted with his honey-colored coat. Another stable boy brought out a dappled mare for Frau Geruscha.

Rose's father had always been too poor to own a horse. That hadn't stopped her girlish fascination with them. Many times she had gazed into the big brown eyes of the wealthy burghers' horses. A favorite game was deciding if the animal was gentle and sweet, or strong-willed and wily, simply from the way he looked back at her.

Rose patted the mare's shoulder and then stroked her forehead. She crooned softly near the horse's ear, "What a fair lady you are, so strong and sleek."

"Ready?" Lord Rupert came over to her. His eyes were wide, reminding Rose of her little brother when he was excited about something.

Rose nodded.

"Put your foot into my hands and I'll give you a boost. Don't worry, I won't let you fall."

He looked so solicitous. It was ridiculous—almost as ridiculous as having her sit beside him at the high table during a feast.

"I'm ready."

He touched the pommel of the sidesaddle. "Put both hands here to help pull yourself up."

Rose grasped it and took a deep breath. Lord Rupert bent low, laced his fingers together, and held them, palms up, by her leg. Not believing she was doing this, Rose placed her leather-clad foot into his hands. He boosted her, and Rose felt herself leave the ground. The next moment she was sitting in the saddle, gazing down at Lord Rupert.

"I did it!" Exhilaration filled her and she laughed. She was actually sitting on a horse.

Lord Rupert beamed. "You executed that perfectly. *Horsewoman extraordinaire* will be your new title."

Rose's heart soared right out of her chest. Of course, it was daft of her, but his words of praise made her feel good.

A "humph" sounded from her other side and she turned to look. Frau Geruscha was mounting her own horse with the help of the groom.

Rupert gave Rose a few more instructions on how to guide the horse. "Whatever you do, hang on and don't fall off. We'll go at a slow walk until you grow accustomed."

Rose held on to both the reins and the saddle. She wished she could sit straddle, like a man. As it was, perched on her sidesaddle, she felt as though she would slide off at the slightest unexpected turn or jolt.

Lord Rupert sat much higher on his massive horse, Gregor, but he stayed very close to Rose, giving her instructions—and multiple compliments—as they slowly headed out through the gatehouse onto the cobblestone Marktplatz.

"That's it. You're doing wonderfully."

The horse obeyed her gentle nudges and one-word commands as they made their way through the town gate to the meadow where the shepherd boys grazed the sheep and cows. Rose couldn't help smiling, sitting high atop her horse. And Lord Rupert couldn't seem to keep his eyes off her. He taught her, in rapid succession, the command to turn the horse around, to go left, to go right, and to stand still.

"Are you ready to practice different gaits?" He hovered beside her.

Rose nodded.

First they went from a walk to a trot, surprising Rose with how much the slight increase in speed jolted her. When she grew somewhat accustomed to the rhythmic motion of the horse, he encouraged her to speed up to a canter. She did, gently pressing the mare's side with her heels. She liked the feel of the wind blowing her hair, but her heart stayed in her throat. One false move and she'd hit the ground with a painful thud.

"How do I slow down?"

"Why do you want to slow down? You're doing fine."

How would she stop? He hadn't taught her that either. She felt completely at his mercy.

Lord Rupert drew his horse even closer to hers. Eight powerful legs pounded beneath them. What if the legs got tangled up? They'd bring her, Rupert, and the two horses down in one mass. Her heart thumped hard against her chest.

"Lord Rupert, I want to stop."

He didn't speak, only reached over and grabbed her reins, pulling back gently. "Whoa."

Both horses slowed and halted.

Rose held on to the pommel with both hands. Her breath came in gasps and she marveled at how easily Lord Rupert had managed to slow the powerful beasts to a halt.

"I'm sorry if I frightened you." Rupert still held her mare's reins. He covered her hand where it rested on the saddle. "Forgive me."

Rose looked into his eyes. "Of course."

He was relentless with his flirting. She knew she should feel irritated, but instead, his words made her feel like cooked pottage—warm and weak. What a ridiculous romantic she was turning out to be—as bad as Hildy.

Lord Rupert removed his hand from hers and Rose blinked hard, trying to clear her mind. The sun bore down on them from high in the cloudless sky. She brushed a strand of hair back from her temple.

"Where's Frau Geruscha?" She turned and spotted her mistress behind them, the scowl on her face so threatening it made Rose's heart sink. "We'd better head back. I would not upset Frau Geruscha."

"As you wish, my lady." He turned his horse around.

Rose had trouble turning her horse. It took her three tries before the gray mare obeyed and followed behind Lord Rupert and his big mount. She was startled when he suddenly stopped his horse and slid off. He walked to the edge of the meadow and bent down.

He was picking flowers.

Lord Rupert came toward her, holding a handful of purple, pink, and white wildflowers. If he wanted to flatter her and make her feel special, he certainly knew what he was doing.

It was the second time in her life someone had given her flowers, and he was the giver both times.

"I thank you. They're beautiful."

"Not as beautiful as you." His voice was an octave lower. Even though she had reached out to take the flowers, he continued to hold them then let his thumb lightly stroke the back of her hand.

His touch irritated her, for she was afraid that Frau Geruscha would see him touching her. Her mistress was still several horse lengths away but getting closer.

She should not be letting him do this. What would he try next? Her face burned at the thought. Letting him touch her hand went beyond propriety's boundaries. Besides, she didn't like the way his touch made her feel—alarmed and out of control.

"Lord Rupert, I would not mislead you. You know my social position is not comparable to yours—"

"Rose, please." The hurt look on his face affected her much more than she wanted it to as she gazed down at him from atop her mare. "I know what you must be thinking, Rose, but I swear, I—"

"Lesson's over for today." Frau Geruscha had closed the gap between them, and her tone brooked no argument. "We thank you, my lord."

Rose noticed her stern look. She glanced down at Lord Rupert. His pained expression made her feel worse, as compassion for him suddenly welled up inside her.

She must harden her heart. He was like all men, merely wanting what he couldn't have.

*O God, help me.*

A week later, Rose sat beside Hildy on the bench in the southwest tower of Hagenheim Castle. Hildy's mother was minding their candle shop today, giving Hildy the day off and a chance to spend time with Rose. She'd brought some mending with her. Their needles moved in and out of the fabric on their laps while they talked, and when the conversation was at a lull, Hildy hummed while she sewed.

Rose's thoughts drifted to her family. She had gone, just that morning, to remove her few remaining possessions still at her family's cottage, since she was sleeping at the castle now. Her childhood memories had been stirred, and she remembered how her father came home each evening with his ax slung over his shoulder. No matter how tired he was from chopping wood, he always had a smile for her and her sisters and brother. Her mother, on the other hand, was always yelling and scolding, complaining bitterly about the work she had to do. Rose pitied her mother even as she longed to escape her. Her high-pitched voice, raised frequently in anger and frustration, filled Rose with an ache of desperation.

Now that she had escaped, the ache strangely remained, as though she'd escaped physically, outwardly, but inwardly she was still affected. She only hoped her little sisters and brother would not feel the brunt of her mother's sharp harshness. She had always been kinder to them than to Rose.

Rose was shaken back to the present by the sounds of Frau Geruscha, who was nearby in the storage room putting away some herbs and making a list of those she would need to replenish. Hildy then leaned over and whispered to Rose, "After all you've told me about Lord Rupert, I think he must be falling in love with you."

"That's silly, Hildy. Even if he is," Rose hissed back, "he wouldn't want to wed me."

"Why ever not? You're beautiful, and you have what every noble family wants—a body capable of bearing children."

Rose snorted and rolled her eyes heavenward. Leave it to Hildy to point out things Rose would rather not think about.

"Not *every*thing a noble family wants," Rose said. "Lord Rupert is accustomed to privilege and wealth, and yet he will not inherit any of it. You know the law. It all goes to the eldest son."

"So?"

"So he will need to marry an heiress. He wouldn't be happy with only the manor house his mother has entailed to him."

"How do you know that?"

"He told me at the feast that he should like to be as wealthy as Bishop Albrecht. He doesn't want to be poor, and he would gain nothing from marrying me. And besides, no one seems to trust him—not his brother, not Frau Geruscha. What does that indicate to you?"

"That the poor man is being treated unfairly. That motives are being attributed to him that are not his own."

"Oh, Hildy." Rose sighed and shook her head. She had no illusions about what men desired from women of her class or about the lengths to which they would sometimes go to get it.

She thought of Lord Rupert's face as he stood near her, of the flowers and of his words before he was interrupted by Frau Geruscha. *"I know what you must be thinking, Rose, but I swear, I—"* How would it feel to be loved by the son of Duke Nicolaus of Hagenheim? To be loved for herself, her thoughts, her values?

It would feel good ... very, very good.

She closed her eyes and the image of Lord Hamlin appeared, of his earnest expression. The thought never made it into words, but it was there, in her mind.

There was no comparison between the two brothers.

But she would not even allow herself to imagine how it would feel for Lord Hamlin to love her. He was betrothed.

Rose shook her head again. "I'm afraid it's more likely that Lord Rupert is hoping to use me for dishonorable purposes."

"Rose, I know you like to be realistic, but have a little faith in people. Besides, stranger things have happened."

"Name one."

Hildy frowned and fell silent for a moment. "What about the duke's nephew? He married that maiden who sold berries at the market."

"Only because she was pregnant with his child. And then he abandoned her, secured an annulment from the pope, and married a duke's daughter from Bavaria."

"Oh." Hildy's frown deepened. "I forgot about that."

Rose squeezed her eyes closed and rubbed her forehead.

A maiden caught giving away her virginity to someone other than her husband would be publicly humiliated, placed in the stocks in the Marktplatz for all to see and heckle—if the man was not in a position to marry her. But for Rose, something even more important was in jeopardy. If she allowed herself to be duped by Lord Rupert, if he pressured her and she gave in, she would disappoint her father, Frau Geruscha, and worst of all, God. The prospect was too horrible to contemplate. Rose shuddered.

"You're not getting a chill, are you, Rose?"

"No." She would heed Frau Geruscha's warning. She would stay away from Lord Rupert.

"I can imagine that Lord Rupert was a wonderful dancer. Did you enjoy dancing with him? Oh, tell me again what it was like."

Rose hadn't told her she'd also danced with Lord Hamlin. For some reason, she couldn't bear to tell Hildy about that. It would be like publicly showing off one's most treasured possession. Some things weren't meant to be shared.

"Dancing with Lord Rupert was very exciting."

"Did he kiss your hand?"

"No."

"Tell me again what he was wearing."

Frau Geruscha emerged from the storage room. "Rose, I'm going into town to look in on Adelheide Bulger. She had a high fever yesterday. I may not be back until nones."

Rose nodded and listened to her mistress's instructions until she left, closing the door behind her.

Rose regaled Hildy with more details of everyone's dress, from Lord Rupert to the duchess, to Lady Osanna and other girls who were there.

Hildy sighed deeply. "Oh, it would be heavenly to be able to dance and wear beautiful clothes and be admired."

Rose hoped that Hildy would get her chance some day.

Someone knocked at the door. Rose got up and opened it to find Gunther Schoff.

"Good morning, Rose." He smiled and bowed.

"Gunther! Come in, please." Feeling almost as giggly and excited as Hildy often looked, Rose pulled Gunther inside. "Gunther Schoff, I present to you Hildy, daughter of Hezilo the chandler."

"Good morning." A look of interest flickered in his pale blue eyes. His sandy red hair and freckles made him boyishly handsome. "I came to see Frau Geruscha about some herbs for my mother."

"She'll be back later." An idea came to Rose. She smiled and arched her eyebrows. "You have time to wait, don't you? I want to teach Hildy to dance. It would be hard without a man to serve as her partner. Would you ...?"

A smile spread across Gunther's face, and Hildy's cheeks turned pink.

Rose and Hildy set their sewing bundles in the corner. The chamber where Frau Geruscha and Rose tended the sick and injured was spacious. They pushed the benches against the wall, leaving plenty of room for a couple to dance.

Rose clapped to provide the rhythm while Gunther instructed Hildy in the dances, starting with the Maltese Branle. Rose watched with approval as Gunther gently guided his pupil, who caught on quickly to the order of the steps. The air was cool for May, and a breeze blew through the open windows and fanned the dancers' cheeks. Rose hoped Gunther noticed the alluring tendrils of blonde hair that had wriggled loose from Hildy's braid and fluttered at her temples.

As Hildy laughed at a misstep, someone moved into the open doorway. *Lord Hamlin.* Rose caught her breath and covered her mouth with her hand. Gunther and Hildy saw him too, and the dancing ceased.

"Good day." Lord Hamlin nodded first to Rose, then to Gunther and Hildy.

Hildy snatched her hand away from Gunther's and placed it behind her back. Though Rose and Hildy outnumbered Gunther two to one, they were all unmarried and, therefore, improperly chaperoned. Rose held her breath, waiting for Lord Hamlin's reaction.

She swallowed. "Good day, Lord Hamlin. We were just teaching Hildy some dances."

"I see."

All the blood had drained from Hildy's face. Her eyes had the look of a rabbit caught in a trap.

Finally, Lord Hamlin spoke. "I have my lute in my saddle bag. I could play for you."

They all exhaled at once. Rose almost giggled.

"That is most gracious of you, my lord," Gunther said.

Lord Hamlin disappeared from the doorway and returned moments later with the lute. "What dance were you practicing?"

"The Maltese Branle, my lord," Gunther said.

Lord Hamlin looked down, adjusted his fingers on the instrument, and began to play the melody for the dance. Rose perched on the stool by the window. She tried to keep her eyes on the dancers. They did provide a delightful scene, since by now Hildy had learned the dance well. But Rose's eyes were drawn over and over to Lord Hamlin. He stood against the wall, exuding easy confidence. She watched his hands move over the strings, his brow puckered in concentration. The music gave her an overwhelming feeling of joy. She told herself it had nothing to do with Lord Hamlin's presence.

He seemed careful to look only at his lute, with an occasional glance at the dancers. Part of her felt relieved not to have to return his penetrating gaze.

The two dancers had eyes only for each other.

She sighed. How different would Lord Hamlin behave were he the son of a scribe, like Gunther, instead of the betrothed son of a duke? If he were free to give his attention to whomever he wanted, would he give it to her?

She scolded herself for even having such a thought.

Lord Hamlin came to the end of the song he was playing and Gunther suggested they move on to a new dance, since Hildy had mastered this one. Gunther held out his hand to Rose. "Will you help me demonstrate the steps?"

Rose felt self-conscious dancing with Gunther, wondering if Lord Hamlin was watching her, but she dared not look at him. She couldn't help remembering how it had felt to dance with him and wondered if he was thinking the same thing. But no. He wouldn't be.

And so the afternoon went. They even attracted a small crowd of children who stood in the doorway and watched, wide-eyed, as the dance lesson continued.

After several songs had been played and different dances practiced, Frau Geruscha walked in. She looked around the chamber.

Lord Hamlin stopped playing. "Frau Geruscha, good afternoon."

"Good afternoon, Lord Hamlin." A bemused smile came over her face — the one she always seemed to wear when Lord Hamlin was around.

"A dance lesson. I hope you don't mind." He turned to Gunther. "I suppose we should put an end to our frivolity."

"Yes, my lord, quite so," Gunther replied.

Frau Geruscha shook her head. "I don't mind. How is your leg? Is it mending well?"

Gunther took advantage of Frau Geruscha's and Lord Hamlin's averted attention to whisper something to Hildy. Then, after grabbing the herbs for his mother, he took his leave of Rose and the healer and followed Lord Hamlin out the door to the courtyard.

Hildy's face flushed as she turned to Rose. She threw her arms around her, buried her face in her shoulder, and squealed.

Rose sat at her desk in Frau Geruscha's chamber, happily writing a new morality tale, a story about a man who cured his wife of her habit of complaining.

"Rose? Are you here?"

She looked up, her quill poised above the parchment, and smiled at the figure that appeared in the doorway. "Lady Osanna. Good morning."

Lord Rupert stood just behind, peeking over his sister's shoulder. Rose's smile faltered.

Lady Osanna lifted her skirt and stepped inside. "Since it's such a beautiful day, I thought you might go on a picnic with me. And Lord Rupert begged to come along. I hope you don't mind." She lifted her eyebrows hopefully. "Would you like to go?"

Lord Rupert waited beside her with an equally expectant expression.

Just then Frau Geruscha walked in from the storage room, wiping her hands on her apron.

"Frau Geruscha, good morning," Lady Osanna said. "Would you like to go on a picnic with us?"

Frau Geruscha stared at Lord Rupert, her brows lowering. "Good morning, Lady Osanna, Lord Rupert." She held the folds of her apron in her hands. After a long pause, she said, "I believe I shall not, today."

Rose placed her quill in its stand and stood, quickly taking off her apron and smoothing her skirt with her palms. She breathed a sigh of relief that she'd worn her crimson dress and had put on her apron earlier that morning to protect it while she helped Frau Geruscha bandage a woman's bad burn from a cooking fire. It wasn't as fine as Lady Osanna's damask gown, but it was one of her best.

She smiled. "It sounds like a lovely idea."

"Rose, wait," Frau Geruscha said.

They all turned to look at her.

"May I speak with you?"

Rose followed Frau Geruscha into the storage room and stood waiting.

"Rose, I—" Frau Geruscha stopped, took a deep breath, and held it for a moment. She then exhaled and lowered her face, pressing the inside corners of her eyes with her thumb and forefinger. She opened her mouth as if to speak, and closed it again.

"What is it, Frau Geruscha?"

Frau Geruscha looked at her with pain in her eyes and took hold of Rose's arm. "Lord Rupert is Duke Nicolaus's son, but that doesn't make him any different from other men. You have the option to say no to anything he asks, do you understand?"

Rose wondered why Frau Geruscha felt the need to remind her again of Lord Rupert's reputation.

"Yes, Frau, of course. I won't do anything foolish. I only want to be with Lady Osanna."

Frau Geruscha looked at her for another moment then patted her arm. "Go on, then."

# Chapter
## 9

*Rose and the noble sister and brother walked* to a section of the meadow on the north side of the castle, opposite from where Lord Rupert had taken her riding. A stone fence separated them from the grazing area, where a boy guided a group of sheep with a stick. Wildflowers in shades of blue and purple carpeted the ground, and beech trees loomed on two sides.

Lady Osanna and Rose spread the wool blanket on the grass, then spread a smaller linen cloth on which they placed the food. Sitting together as they were, Rose was unable to separate herself from Rupert by more than a couple of handbreadths. Wolfie lay on the grass right beside her, his paw touching her leg. He kept his eyes on Lord Rupert.

The basket contained chunks of cooked pork, chicken, and cheese, bread and pastries, as well as toasted walnuts, raisins, and apples cut in quarters. A flask of wine completed the repast, along with a pewter cup that they all shared.

As they began to eat, Rupert picked up a large piece of pork and held it out to Wolfie. The dog pulled his head up and back, eyeing him suspiciously.

"Here, boy, take it." Rupert tossed the chunk of meat at Wolfie's front paw. Wolfie sniffed then wrapped his jowls around it. He chewed twice and swallowed.

"That's right, see?" Lord Rupert said. "I'm your friend."

Wolfie licked his black lips. Rupert picked out another nice-sized bite. He held it out, this time waiting until Wolfie inched forward and took the meat from his hand.

"I knew you would learn to like me," Lord Rupert said with a satisfied grin, but his eyes settled on Rose when he said it.

They ate quietly. Rose didn't eat with much appetite, aware as she was of Lord Rupert's eyes on her. She was determined to act naturally, but Hildy's words about him kept repeating in her head. "*I think he's in love with you ... motives are being attributed to him which may not be his own ... You have what every noble family wants.*"

"Are you writing a new story, Rose?" Lady Osanna asked. "I saw you working on something in Frau Geruscha's chamber."

Rose turned to Lady Osanna. "Yes, a new one."

"Oh, do tell us about it."

Lord Rupert leaned in. "Do tell."

Rose smiled and tucked her hands underneath her, trying not to fidget. "Well ... it's about a farmer whose wife constantly complains. She complains when it rains, she complains when it doesn't. Either the chickens lay too many eggs, or not enough, and her bed is always too lumpy, until her husband decides to cure her of complaining."

Rose smiled at the way their eyes were focused on her. The meadow around them was quiet except for the rustle of the leaves as the wind blew over the nearby trees.

"So one night after she goes to bed and falls asleep, her husband wraps himself in a white sheet and drapes a veil over his face. He lights three candles and holds them just in front of his chin so that his face appears to be glowing. He calls her name to wake her up. She sits up, clutching her throat, her eyes wide. He tells her he is the angel Gabriel and God has sent him to rebuke her for all her complaining. She must never complain again, for when she does, she will fall down dead on the spot. Instead, she must be thankful for rain and sunshine, food to eat, and a bed to lie in."

"So what happens next?" Lady Osanna asked.

"The angel—her husband—commands her to lie down and go back to sleep. She falls onto her pillow and closes her eyes. The next morning is cloudy and misty. Her husband greets her with, 'Good morning, good wife. It's a lovely day, think ye?' She opens her mouth to speak, but closes it again. She says nothing for a long moment. Then she says, 'So it is.' She goes about her usual chores the entire day but doesn't speak another word. Finally, that night, when they go to bed, she speaks."

Rose paused again.

"What did she say?" Lord Rupert asked.

"She said, 'I hope that angel comes back tonight so I can ask him what I'm supposed to say to my husband now. I can't think of a single thing.'"

"Oh!" Lady Osanna clapped her hands.

Rose popped a shelled walnut into her mouth and looked down at her skirt, hoping she wasn't blushing noticeably.

Lord Rupert smiled then laughed. His eyes sparkled and his voice was rife with enthusiasm. "That's wonderful! You must finish writing it so I can read it to everyone."

Rose brushed a piece of grass off her skirt, embarrassed at his praise.

"You have a gift for stories," Lady Osanna said.

She shrugged. "It's a short one."

They continued eating while Lord Rupert and Lady Osanna discussed which of Rose's stories was their favorite. After a few minutes, Lady Osanna said, "Lady Anne is sick a lot. Perhaps Frau Geruscha could prepare something, a remedy for her, some kind of herbal concoction that would make her stronger."

"I'm sure she could."

"She is so often tired. But I'm very happy Wilhelm asked her to come and stay with us for a while."

"Wilhelm—I mean, Lord Hamlin—asked her to come?"

"He decided to send for her when I told him she was so lonely there at the abbey. Wilhelm handles a lot of decisions like that now. If something happens to Father, it will all fall on his shoulders anyway." Lady Osanna sighed. "Sometimes I pity him."

"Why?"

"He's so serious. He won't let himself forget his duties, even for a short while, and enjoy himself."

Rose could have argued the point with her, remembering the way he'd played his lute all afternoon so Gunther and Hildy could dance.

"He never does anything solely for himself. He has a heavy sense of his responsibility. Don't you think so, Rupert?"

"Yes, my brother's a prude, a priest in layman's clothing."

"That's not what I mean." Lady Osanna glared. She leaned back on her hands and stared thoughtfully at the sky. "He's ... determined. And he would never break his word or do anything unchivalrous."

"And he wants to make sure the rest of the family doesn't, either." Lord Rupert half closed his eyes and reached out to pet Wolfie, but the dog pulled back out of reach.

"True. He feels responsible for the family's honor."

What a heavy burden. But Lord Hamlin seemed capable of bearing it. Rose sensed he accepted his responsibilities almost with relish. Would they some day become cumbersome to him? She couldn't imagine it. Rupert, on the other hand, would chafe under such a load of responsibility.

"Well, he isn't responsible for me." Lord Rupert stood up. He walked a few steps away and began picking the red-orange poppies that grew nearby.

"He's always trying to find Moncore. He feels so accountable for his betrothed, for her safety. He's never even met her, but he fully intends to marry her. I worry about him being too serious," Lady Osanna said. "You understand my meaning, don't you, Rose?"

"I think I do."

"You're the oldest in your family, and you've been working with Frau Geruscha for a while now. Do you have that problem? Is it hard to throw off the mantle of responsibility every now and again?" She chewed absently on some raisins.

"Perhaps, but I don't have a region to rule like your brother will. I'm sure he is quite capable of bearing the mantle of responsibility. I believe it makes him happy to do his duty, for the good of his people."

"Yes, duty, that's it. And you're right. He'd never be happy if he shirked his duty, but …" Lady Osanna sighed. "I suppose he'll be happy enough some day, when he's married to Lady Salomea. It's only the strain of trying to capture Moncore that weighs so heavily on him, I suppose."

Rose was sure Osanna was right, but thinking of Lord Hamlin married to the unknown Lady Salomea cast a pall over her spirits. A dark cloud drifted over the sun, blocking its rays for the first time since they'd started on their little jaunt.

Lady Osanna watched Lord Rupert as he gathered a handful of flowers. "That's a good idea. I could pick some flowers to decorate the table tonight." Rising, she wandered away toward the assortment of pink, blue, and lavender wildflowers that covered the meadow.

Rose jumped up to help. As she leaned over, pinching off stems one by one, a leather boot came into view next to her. She straightened, tossing her hair over her shoulder and out of her eyes. Lord Rupert stood holding out a fistful of poppies, a big smile on his face.

"For you."

Rose hesitated. Out of the corner of her eye she saw Wolfie with his nose buried in the grass, probably trying to sniff out a partridge or hare. Lady Osanna was also several feet away. She had fetched the food basket and was stuffing flowers into it.

The look in Lord Rupert's eyes was so eager she couldn't disappoint him. She reached out and took the handful of red poppies. He then wrapped his hand around the multicolored wildflowers she had gathered in her other hand, letting his fingers rest against her own for a moment. His chest, covered by his sleeveless crimson doublet, was at eye level and much too close. She took a step back.

Lord Rupert turned and walked over to his sister, and Rose started to breathe again. He placed the flowers Rose had picked into his sister's basket, then strode straight back to Rose and reached out his hand. Before Rose knew what he was about to do, he pulled out a single red poppy from the bunch he had given her.

"May I?" His voice was low and gentle. He didn't wait for her answer, but placed the flower in her hair next to her temple. "Now it is even more beautiful."

Rose looked away from him. "I'd better go see if Lady Osanna has enough flowers."

"Wait." The smile left his face. "I know you don't trust me, Rose. I suppose that's wise of you." He looked at her with a pained expression, his brows creasing his forehead. "You aren't like other maidens, Rose. You're enchanting, clever, confident. I've never met anyone like you."

*Me? Confident?* Rose considered him with raised eyebrows.

"And you're the most beautiful—"

"Rose!" Lady Osanna called.

She jumped. "Yes?" Stepping around Rupert, she walked toward Lady Osanna.

"Oh, I didn't see you on the other side of my ox of a brother. Aren't those poppies lovely?"

Rose looked down at the bunch of flowers in her hand.

"Rupert picked those for you, didn't he?" Lady Osanna half frowned, half smiled, and shook her head. "He's such a trifler. Pay no heed to him."

Rose glanced up at Lord Rupert, who had walked up beside her. His expression turned dark at his sister's words.

"Why are you looking at me like that?" Osanna cocked her head and thrust her hand onto her hip.

With visible effort, he lightened his expression and turned his gaze on Rose. "My sister likes to malign me unfairly. It's her way of jesting. Humorous, isn't it?"

Lady Osanna shook her head. She hung the basket full of flowers over one arm and slipped her other hand through Rose's arm. "Shall we go?" They started back toward the castle, its five cylindrical towers of grey stone the only things visible above the surrounding wall.

"What about the blanket and food?"

"Oh, I'll send a servant to retrieve them."

Rose glanced over her shoulder and saw Lord Rupert still standing in the same spot, staring after them.

Wilhelm enlisted the help of Lukas to saddle Shadow. The boy was eager to learn all the steps to grooming and saddling a horse. Rose would be pleased at how happy the child seemed. He wished she could see the smile on his face now as Wilhelm praised him, how the boy's cheeks had filled out now that he was eating regularly. He would love to see the look on her face when she realized Wilhelm was taking good care of him.

But what was he doing, thinking about Rose, desiring her approval? He was treading on dangerous ground.

His father was conducting a large hunt to entertain himself and an earl who had come for a visit. As usual, it was a massive event. A crew of dog handlers, falconers, archers, and assistant huntsmen moved to and fro about the stable and courtyard. Rupert was striding toward them as well. His brother had always enjoyed the hunt as much as anyone. Rupert had felled many a stag, decorating the wall of the Great Hall with several big racks of antlers. A buck was a great prize, but Wilhelm usually let someone else do the killing. He didn't especially like destroying the noble creatures.

Someone was approaching him from behind and Wilhelm turned around as Rupert clapped him on the shoulder. "Ready for the chase?"

Rupert was smiling and friendly. He must want something.

"Georg, Christoff, and I are going wolf hunting and leaving you and Father to the deer." Wilhelm knew how much Rupert loved stag hunting—and despised hunting wolves. Wolf hunting was much less exciting, and usually less fruitful.

"Some sheep have gone missing." Wilhelm turned back to his

horse, yanking the saddle's girth. "We've heard reports of a wolf in the area, killing lambs and pigs."

After a short pause, Rupert said, "I'll go with you."

Wilhelm stopped and turned to study his brother. Rupert looked strangely earnest. What was he up to? "As you wish."

Duke Nicolaus entered the yard, followed by a servant carrying his bow and arrow. His presence infused the scene with instant energy as all the men scurried about, making sure they were ready the moment the duke mounted his horse.

A servant had prepared Gregor for Rupert, and he swung into the saddle. He hung back with Wilhelm and the two knights.

Two huntsmen on foot with several of the dogs were first to enter the forest. The duke and the other stag hunters started after them.

Remaining behind with Wilhelm and Rupert, Jakob, the assistant huntsman, held the leashes of a greyhound and two white alaunts—thin hunting dogs as tall as ponies—who would help them track the wolves. After the stag hunters and their dogs were almost out of earshot, Wilhelm and his party started off toward the east and the Harz Mountains.

"We'll head into the hills to search among the caves for the den," Wilhelm said over his shoulder.

Rupert's expression looked woeful. Why was he here, missing the chase for a stag? They were likely to be out all day, charging through the trees to hunt for a wolf they probably wouldn't even find. Rupert hated the terrain of the mountains, which was slow and tedious, not at all like crashing through the forest, ducking limbs, and following the shouts of the other hunters.

Wilhelm wondered again what his brother was up to.

When the sun had climbed high into the sky, they stopped to let the horses rest and take a drink from a stream that tumbled down a rocky slope. Wilhelm stood by his horse as he drank. Georg and Christoff were out of earshot, checking the stream bank for wolf tracks.

Rupert approached him. "Brother, I want you to know that I have the best intentions toward Rose."

Wilhelm's eyes narrowed as he looked at him. Finally, he turned away, staring into the beech trees across the bank. "I'm listening."

"I know you think I'm not to be trusted around women."

Wilhelm continued to look straight ahead. Maybe this was why

Rupert had come with him. But he had a bad feeling about what his brother was about to say.

"I suppose I deserve that reputation. But I've confessed my past sins. Perhaps you think me incapable of committing to only one woman."

Wilhelm glanced at Rupert. He was starting to sweat, and he looked uncomfortable, as though he was choosing his words carefully.

"You would be wrong to think that about me, Wilhelm. I know Rose is the maiden I want to commit to, and I swear I won't betray her." He wiped his face with his sleeve.

Wilhelm kept his head turned away, hoping Rupert couldn't read the thoughts racing through his mind. His throat suddenly felt thick and dry and he swallowed, hard. His brother sounded sincere, but that thought only made him remember all the shallow, selfish things Rupert had done in the past.

"Why are you telling me this?" Wilhelm turned suspicious eyes on him.

"Because Rose doesn't trust me, and you and Osanna are doing nothing to improve me in her eyes. If you aren't going to help my suit, you could at least not make me out to be a scoundrel."

There was a long pause as Wilhelm wrestled with memories, of both his brother and of Rose.

After a long pause, Rupert said, "I swear I'll be good to her. I know she's a favorite of yours."

What made him say that? Guilt soon gave way to anger, but Wilhelm strove to make his voice sound calm and even. "I think of her as a sister. That is all."

"She is the one for me. If she'll have me, I vow to love her only and to take care of her for the rest of her life. Please believe me."

"If that is true, then I wish you joy." He grabbed the reins of his horse. "Let us be off," he called to his men. He swung his leg over his horse's rump and guided them toward the wolf's trail.

The rest of the castle had long retired to sleep, but Wilhelm paced back and forth over his bedchamber floor, still clothed in his white shirt and hose. He never allowed his servant to undress him. He disdained the idea of allowing others to do things he could do himself.

Wilhelm liked to think of himself as competent, able to accomplish any task worth doing. But now ...

He was helpless against this ache in his chest—in his heart.

He would force himself to picture Rose with Rupert, imagine them married, holding hands, kissing. Even though it made him feel like retching. He would think of her as the future mother of his nieces and nephews. He must think of her this way, since he could never have her. If she married Rupert Gerstenberg she would at least be safe and well cared for. The name alone would protect her. No one could molest or harm her, and she would be able to live comfortably. It was the best thing that could happen to her.

But why did it feel like the worst thing that could happen to him?

He was betrothed. He had a future wife of his own. Never had he struggled with his thoughts for a woman. Not like this. Why did she affect him so much?

Because he cared for her.

If he were completely honest, he didn't want Rupert to marry her, because he wanted to marry her himself. It was a grievous sin indeed.

He would confess this sin in the morning to the chapel priest. But no. He couldn't wait until morning. He would confess it now, to God, in his own chamber. He fell to his knees in front of the slit of a window. The moon's light, void of any warmth, fell on his face as he clasped his hands.

"O God, I am a miserable wretch. I vowed to remain pure for my betrothed, but my feelings for Rose ..." He closed his eyes. "Forgive me. I will conquer this. I can't avoid her, but I will think of her only as a sister. I will, God. And she is blameless. It was I who looked at her too long, who chose to dance with her, who, like a fool, allowed my mind to dwell upon her. Forgive me, God. I will try not to think about her, and I will never touch her again. I will marry Lady Salomea. I cannot, now or ever, marry Rose."

He knew what he had to do. Rupert had asked Wilhelm for his help, and he knew it hadn't been easy for him. He would be glad Rupert had apparently given up his avaricious goal of becoming the next bishop. As surprising as it was, Rupert truly must want to marry Rose. And Wilhelm would help him convince Rose that Rupert's intentions toward her were good. Rupert hadn't used the word "marriage," but he said he wanted to commit to her, to love her and only her for the rest of his life. It was the best thing for Rose—and more than other maidens in her position in life could ever hope for.

The kindest thing he could do for Rose would be to convince her to marry Rupert.

But what if something else was preventing Rose from accepting Rupert's suit? What if she felt the same way about Wilhelm that he felt about her? He groaned deep in his throat, sinking his head into his hands. He never should have danced with her. It was a foolish, weak thing to do. Of course, she might not care for him at all. But if she did ... he needed to do something to turn her thoughts from him to Rupert.

What was it he had told himself more than once? That he would never be in danger of losing his heart to a mere woodcutter's daughter. He had been prideful to think that way, to believe the poorer classes were somehow less noble in character. Rose had shown him how wrong he had been. Maybe if he could prove to her that Rupert was not prideful ... He wasn't sure how he would do it, but he would find her tomorrow and convince her that Rupert was the one who could offer her a future. And that he, Wilhelm, could offer her nothing but pain.

As he tried to change his thoughts away from Rose, something more troubling entered his mind. He'd never stopped searching for Moncore, so why hadn't he found him yet? He knew Moncore was good at disguising himself. As much as he hated to admit it, the man did seem to have a certain amount of supernatural power, a demonic force that was keeping Wilhelm from finding him. But wasn't God on Wilhelm's side? Certainly God's power was greater.

"O God, I vowed I would find my betrothed's enemy, that accursed conjurer, Moncore. I've tried." He ran his fingers through his hair, tightening his hands into fists. "I've tried everything, traveled everywhere, searched out every rumor, sent out spies. I need to find him, and soon. I can't let him get to her. If I do, I'm an utter failure."

Wilhelm groaned. A trickle of sweat ran down his neck. He pressed his burning eyes with the heel of his hands. Never had he failed at anything. And this was so important.

*O God, why can't I find him?* He wasn't sure he'd ever asked God for help before. Perhaps that had been his mistake.

"Help me now, God. Help me."

# Chapter
# 10

*Frau Geruscha finished bandaging a cut on a* boy's hand and sent him on his way home. Rose cleaned up the room, getting down on her knees to scrub the floor clean of the boy's blood. As Rose finished up, a bearded man wearing the purple and gold livery of the Duke of Marienberg appeared in the doorway.

"Frau Geruscha?"

"Yes?" Frau Geruscha's expression changed from expectancy to shock as soon as she saw the man, and she hurried to the door.

The man held out a folded parchment. Frau Geruscha snatched it and held it against her apron, as though to hide the wax seal on the front. But Rose had already glimpsed the purple and gold ribbon hanging down from it — the colors of the Godehard family.

The back of Rose's neck prickled. *Why would Godehard, the Duke of Marienberg, send Frau Geruscha a message?*

Her mistress put her hand in her pocket and pulled out a coin. She pressed it into the man's hand.

"I will be back in an hour for frau's reply."

"Very good." Frau Geruscha nodded to dismiss him. The man turned and left.

"What is that, Frau Geruscha?"

"What?" Her head jerked up. "Oh, it's nothing, child. Nothing." Frau Geruscha slipped the letter into her apron pocket. "Why don't you take Wolfie and gather some liverwort and feverfew? We're almost out, and it's a beautiful day for a walk."

Rose was stunned by her mistress keeping a secret from her, and by her having a reason to correspond with the Duke of Marienberg.

Should she ask what was in the letter? But her mistress looked much too preoccupied to be patient with Rose's questions.

Rose walked toward the door and made a clicking sound with her tongue. Wolfie jumped up from his place in the corner and leapt out ahead of her. She gave Frau Geruscha one last backward glance before stepping out.

What could the letter be about? And why was Frau Geruscha trying to hide it from her?

Rose held up her skirts as she walked free of the town gate and headed out into the green grass beyond. She lifted her face and closed her eyes, the summer sunshine warming her shoulders. Passing the tree on the hill, she followed the stream into the shade of the forest. She ran her hand along the gray bark of the beech trees as Wolfie crashed through the bushes nearby.

After gathering herbs for some time, she came to a place where the stream waters pooled and then tumbled off the rocks into the stream bed below. Sinking onto the grass and pulling off her shoes, she dipped her bare feet in the pool of water at the base of the waterfall.

Her mind wandered over many events, puzzling first over Frau Geruscha's letter and her strange behavior, then over Lord Rupert's flirtations, then the budding relationship between Hildy and Gunther.

She placed her hands on the grass behind her and let her head hang back, closing her eyes and listening to the water splashing on the rocks and dribbling away downstream. Taking one deep breath after another, she let her thoughts wander—until she became aware of some noises across the stream, not far away. Probably Wolfie chasing a chipmunk. "Oh Wolfie, leave those poor animals alone."

She listened but heard no answering movement from Wolfie.

Rose's skin tingled along her arms with the sensation that someone was watching her. She opened her eyes.

Lord Hamlin stood beside his black horse on the other side of the stream, hardly five yards away. She jerked herself upright, snatching her feet out of the water.

"Forgive me. I didn't mean to startle you."

Rose threw her skirt over her ankles. Her heart fluttered at the way he was looking at her. "Oh, no. I was just sitting here ... with Wolfie." She looked around but didn't see the dog anywhere.

"You probably want some solitude. I can go." Lord Hamlin took a step backward, holding Shadow's reins.

"No, you don't have to go. If you don't want to." *Of course he didn't have to go. The whole region belonged to him.* "What brings you here?"

"Thought I would take one last ride through the woods before I go away. I won't see this place for a while."

Rose wanted to ask his destination, but was afraid to ask such a personal question. But he had volunteered the information that aroused her curiosity hadn't he? "Where are you going?"

He patted his horse, giving him permission to drink and graze, then sat down on the grassy bank across from Rose. He leaned back against a tree and rested his arm on his knee. "To a region north of here, in the Harz Mountains, to look for Moncore."

Rose nodded, struggling to hide how this news deflated her. She would miss him. "Do you have reason to believe he is there?"

"Duke Godehard's spies believe he may have gone there to rendezvous with his pagan friends. We know he likes to hide in that area." He leaned his head against the tree. "But sometimes I think he's making up these rumors himself to throw us off."

He looked tired, his shoulders slightly stooped, his eyelids low. The silence was broken only by the crunch of Shadow's teeth clipping and chewing the grass, the birds singing overhead, and the rush of the waterfall. Rose started thinking about Lord Hamlin's betrothed. Her parents had been so afraid of Moncore demonizing the child that they'd hidden her away.

"Do you believe Moncore has power to demonize your betrothed?" Rose blushed, realizing she had asked the question out loud.

Lord Hamlin sat forward. "I believe he will do something to hurt her, if he can find her."

"You believe in God and angels and miracles, don't you?"

"Yes. God still performs miracles, and the Bible says that angels are spirits sent to minister to us. I just don't agree that every failed crop, every illness, every accident is caused by a demon."

"And you don't believe they exist?"

"I've never seen one." Their eyes met and he smiled. "You aren't trying to get me excommunicated with all these questions, are you?"

Rose laughed. "I doubt I'm any safer from that than you."

"Oh? What damnable philosophies do you adhere to?" He lifted a brow at her as he smiled in amusement.

"I'm a woman who reads the Bible. Isn't that enough? It wouldn't be wise to confess the rest."

"A woman is entitled to her secrets." He stopped smiling and looked agitated, as if he suddenly remembered something. He was no longer looking at her. A muscle twitched in his jaw as he clenched his teeth and pursed his lips. She wished she knew what he was thinking.

He stood up and rubbed the back of his neck. When he spoke, he still didn't look at her. "Do you remember the boy I found stealing an apple in the Marktplatz on May Day?"

She nodded.

"I discovered who his parents are — or were. His father was a farmer, south of town, who fell to drinking and disappeared a year ago. The boy's mother died shortly thereafter of a fever. Lukas had been sleeping in a ditch, or in the forest, or in whatever shelter he could find."

"Oh, the poor thing!" Rose cried. Her heart constricted as she thought about the boy who now helped clean the stables and ate his meals with her and Frau Geruscha in the kitchen. He often asked to pet Wolfie. "I can't believe his father would leave him. So sad."

"It's not uncommon, especially among the lower classes."

Rose felt a hollow place open in the pit of her stomach. *The lower classes?* "What do you mean by that? That poor people are less virtuous?"

Lord Hamlin shrugged. "Most nobles believe so. Think of it this way. A wealthier family has more reason to uphold the family honor, more at stake. They're expected to look out for the interests of God and the Church. It's their duty. A poor family has no such duty."

"Every mortal soul has a duty to God. No person of nobility can take that from him."

"Forgive me if I offended you. It's a much-accepted theory."

"I'm not offended, merely sorry that you hold to such a theory." She clenched her teeth and tried to look cool and unaffected, but already she could feel the tears damming behind her eyes. She crossed her arms and struggled to contain the rush of emotions flooding her.

He didn't answer her.

She could hardly believe Lord Hamlin ... Of course, she knew this was the way the wealthier townspeople thought, always looking down on those who were poor. She had understood from childhood that people judged each other by their occupations, by their clothing, by their wealth or lack thereof. But Lord Hamlin? She had thought he was different.

"So my friend Hildy, because her father died and her mother struggles to feed her family, is not as virtuous as a merchant's child, who dresses in fine clothes and hurls insults at a beggar?" Her throat hurt from holding back the tears

He didn't answer, simply cleared his throat as though he was uncomfortable.

She blinked furiously. *These cursed tears!* She turned her back on him to keep him from seeing them. What was wrong with her? How could she embarrass herself this way? She rubbed the salty drops off her cheeks.

"But Rupert, he's different. He doesn't feel that way. He thinks everyone should be treated the same. He's always felt that way."

Rupert? Why was he talking about Lord Rupert now?

"I think I should go," she said, still with her back to him. She called Wolfie, her voice cracking.


"If anyone should go, it's me." Wilhelm hesitated, reluctant to leave, but waiting for her signal.

*What kind of boorish lout am I?* He had made Rose cry. He could tell by the way her shoulders shook and she kept wiping her face. It hadn't occurred to him that he might make her cry. He felt sick.

"Rose?"

She didn't answer.

*Please forgive me. You're the last person I would ever want to hurt, but I'm doing this for you.* It was probably a good thing they were separated by the stream. He was tempted to leap across it and try to comfort her. But he couldn't. He had to stay true to his betrothed, and the only way he could do that—and help Rose—was to convince her that his brother was a good person and that he wanted to marry her.

He cleared his throat. He might as well go through with the rest of his plan and get it over with. "I want to talk to you about Rupert."

Rose looked up in surprise. Her eyes looked red and puffy. Guilt stabbed him again, but he plunged into his prepared speech.

"I can understand why you would be wary of him, why Frau Geruscha may be a little suspicious of his attentions to you. But he isn't a bad fellow. Even though he's young, I believe he's made up his mind about who he wants to marry." He stopped and considered how to proceed. Absently, he rubbed his chest, trying to get at the pain there.

Rose stared. "Are you trying to warn me away from him? I know his mother must have an idea who she thinks he should marry—"

"No, no. I'm talking about you, Rose. He swears he will love no one else but you."

Rose's eyes widened, then she looked down again. He couldn't see her face, as a thick strand of hair fell across her cheek. She shook her head. "Why are you telling me this?"

*Yes, why am I?* He wasn't doing it to help his brother, even though he'd come to Wilhelm and asked for his help. He was doing it for Rose, to turn her heart toward Rupert. Rupert could protect her, love her. "I thought you would want to know. Rupert spoke to me yesterday and said he didn't think you trusted him." He closed his eyes, feeling like a fool. "But you must judge him yourself, of course. I simply wanted to let you know that I now believe his intentions to be honorable."

"Now?" Rose looked up at him, lifting her eyebrows.

He shrugged. "I know my brother well, and he hasn't always behaved as honorably as … I didn't intend to let him trifle with you." He looked down at his boots, scuffing a tuft of grass with his toe. In character Rose was far above his brother, but what did that matter when Rupert was her best hope for a husband who could take care of her and provide a better life for her?

He looked up and let his eyes meet hers.

He had come searching for her, and when he had found her sitting beside the waterfall with her eyes closed and looking so beautiful, he'd nearly decided to forget his plan. Her lips were parted and her hair fell in a golden brown cascade behind her, shimmering in the sunlight that filtered through the leaves. He'd had to remind himself of his prayer from the night before. He'd vowed to help Rupert win her over, and so perhaps God had led him here now so that he could speak these things to her.

"You said you were going to search for Moncore. How long will you be gone?" Her voice sounded muffled.

"A few weeks at least."

"I hope you find him. I'll pray for your success."

His breath caught in his throat. After he had hurt her with his callous, insensitive words, making her cry, she was still willing to pray for him. He had to swallow before he could speak. "I would appreciate your prayers very much." He was a louse.

Rose moved to a tree and sat, keeping her eyes down.

A memory flashed before him, the look on her face when she saw his gashed-up leg, the determination in her voice and actions. Her look of compassion and her heartfelt prayer. Another memory—the way his heart stopped beating and his knees went weak after he watched her fall out of that tree. And another—the touch of her hand as they danced together. Gazing at her now, he couldn't imagine her married to Rupert.

It was a good thing he was leaving. Perhaps he could contrive to stay away for quite some time.

Feeling the need to talk about Lady Salomea and his betrothal—that had been part of his plan, after all—he thought of the note that came an hour earlier. Mentioning that would at least turn his mind away from dangerous memories.

"Even if I don't find Moncore, it looks as though my betrothed, Lady Salomea, will be coming here in a few months."

"Oh?"

"I got a letter today from her father, Duke Godehard of Marienberg. He still intends to bring his daughter out of hiding on her nineteenth birthday, two weeks before Christmas. He's tired of waiting for Moncore to be caught." He cringed at his own words, that old feeling of failure rising inside him.

"I see. Will you be getting married soon after?"

"Yes. One week after." He wondered if Rose was thinking about the fact that he would only know his bride for one week before marrying her. He hoped she wouldn't ask him how he felt about that.

She frowned as she seemed to remember something. "It seems strange, but Frau Geruscha also got a letter today from Duke Godehard."

Wilhelm stared at her. "Frau Geruscha? Are you certain?"

"Yes. I saw the seal."

Wilhelm rubbed his jaw. *Why would the Duke of Marienberg be sending missives to Frau Geruscha?*

Wolfie crashed through the brush. He splashed across the stream and sat on his haunches in front of Wilhelm, who rubbed the dog's head.

"I should be going," Rose said, "before it gets dark."

"Let me walk with you, to make sure you get back safely."

"No, that's not necessary. I walk here a lot. You go and enjoy your last ride. Farewell." She turned and headed through the trees, not waiting for Wolfie.

He watched her go. The next time he saw her she could be married to Rupert. The pain in his chest grew so intense it took his breath away. *So this is what a broken heart feels like.*

# Chapter 11

*Rose burst out of the trees and into the* meadow near town. Wolfie came running by, finally catching up to her. Rose walked faster, anxious to get home.

She clenched her fists. Lord Hamlin was no different from other nobles. She should have known.

Perhaps Lord Rupert was the one who was different. Could he truly want to marry her? Lord Hamlin might be arrogant, but he wouldn't lie about such a thing. After all, he'd practically written a proclamation that all men should stay away from her. Now he was trying to convince her that Rupert loved her and wanted to marry her.

She took a deep breath, contemplating this. Was such a thing possible? Lord Rupert so in love with her that he was willing to give up wealth and prestige? He was handsome, and the way he looked at her and spoke to her made her feel beautiful. If he truly wished to marry her, if he truly loved her ... To be loved, truly loved, by the handsome son of a duke ... It didn't seem possible.

When Rose reached the town gate, she turned to look for Wolfie. There he was, walking beside Lord Hamlin.

So Lord Hamlin had followed her.

She expelled a burst of air. *I don't need you, Lord Holier-Than-Thou. Go marry your Lady Salomea, a woman you've never even seen.*

The ungracious thought brought on a pang of guilt. After all, he'd been a good friend to her, and she had promised to pray for him to find the conjurer. Well, she would stay angry at him for a little while, but she would get over it. Then she would pray for him.

Lord Hamlin went away. And for the two weeks preceding Midsummer's Eve, Rupert came to Frau Geruscha's chambers almost daily to speak to Rose. He even contrived to take her on another riding lesson, teaching her how to slow her horse gradually to a stop. Every time his face appeared in the doorway, her heart would trip excitedly. But Frau Geruscha didn't make it easy for her to enjoy his visits, with her glowering looks and unfriendly stares.

One day he found her alone, as Frau Geruscha had just left on an errand. Rose suspected he'd been watching the door, waiting for her mistress to leave.

He came inside and seized her hands, an excited glint in his eyes. "I have something for you." He reached inside a small purse that hung at his waist and pulled out something shiny and silver. Her heart thumped against her chest as he draped the chain around her wrist and fastened the clasp.

"It's beautiful," Rose breathed. The bracelet gave her arm a delicate, feminine look and felt cool and smooth against her skin. The beautifully crafted silver rings of the bracelet caught the light. Her first piece of jewelry.

"Do you like it?" he asked softly.

"I've never seen anything so lovely."

He still held her hands. His eyelids closed as he bowed low and pressed his lips against the bracelet. He then kissed the back of her hand. His lips lingered. Rose's heart skipped erratically.

She had never been kissed before, not even on her hand. She knew Rupert's actions were very inappropriate, but her face tingled and her mind registered how good and soft and warm his lips felt.

If Frau Geruscha should come in now and see them, Rose would be in deep trouble. She wasn't sure what her mistress would do, but it would certainly be unpleasant. Things had already changed between them. Frau Geruscha's manner had cooled toward her since Rose had not heeded her advice to tell Lord Rupert to stay away.

Rose took a step back, and Rupert looked up, still holding onto her hand. He drew her palm against his chest, pressing it over his heart. His eyelids drooped, darkening his light blue eyes. "Do you feel it? My heart beats for you, Rose."

Rose frowned at his drama, even as her cheeks burned. She gently pulled her hand away and retreated a couple of steps, trying to calm her racing heart.

Neither of them spoke or even moved. After several moments, Lord Rupert broke the silence. "Midsummer's Eve is tomorrow and I've planned a surprise for you."

"Please, sit down." She swept her hand toward a wooden chair in the corner. Perhaps if he was seated she could force him to keep his distance.

He picked up the chair and carried it to her desk, placing his chair next to hers.

She leaned away and tried to sound lighthearted. "So what is my surprise?"

"Oh, I can't tell you all of it. Just that you must sit with me at the feast tomorrow. Then you must go with me to the Marktplatz for the festival fires and dancing."

"Must?" Rose stared him down.

Lord Rupert placed his hand over his heart and sighed. "Will you please accompany me tomorrow"—he lowered his voice to a husky whisper—"my dearest, sweetest, most beautiful Rose?" An intense light glowed in his eyes.

"Yes." She gazed into his face until she realized she was staring at his lips and he was staring at hers.

"What's this?"

Rose jumped to her feet, a guilty, prickly sensation washing over her at seeing Frau Geruscha enter the room. She remembered the bracelet and stuck her hand behind her back.

"Frau Geruscha, good morning. How are you this fine day?"

Rose marveled at Lord Rupert's calm greeting. Frau Geruscha's disapproval never ruffled his cool demeanor.

"Well, I thank you." Her voice sounded icy.

Although both Lady Osanna and Lord Hamlin seemed to have changed their minds and now approved of Lord Rupert's attentions toward her, he certainly hadn't won Frau Geruscha over. Her arms full of yarrow root, she turned abruptly and disappeared into the storage room.

Lord Rupert leaned toward Rose and whispered, "I'll come for you at ten o'clock in the morning for the feast." He grabbed her hand and gave it a quick kiss. With a wink, he strode across the floor and out the door.

She slipped off the bracelet and dropped it into her apron pocket.

Rose woke early to attend the special St. John's Day service at the cathedral. Participating in the Midsummer Eve festivities always made her feel guilty unless she first went to church to celebrate John the Baptist.

She stared at the new dress hanging in her room, the one she'd had made, using the salary she was receiving as a healer's apprentice. It was damask, a beautiful shade of emerald green, trimmed with a wide band of gold silk at the hem. More gold silk formed a feminine collar that widened at the shoulders. The sleeves were fitted, as was the bodice, and the skirt contained so much material she had to hold it up to walk. She longed to wear the new dress, but she put on her old crimson one instead. She would change later, before attending the feast at the castle.

An hour later Rose entered the Hagenheim Cathedral and waited for her eyes to adjust to the dim interior. Gradually, the flickering candles illuminated the long, high-ceilinged hall. She crossed herself and genuflected, facing the crucifix. Rose found her family members, who were kneeling in their usual spot, and bowed her head in prayer.

A slight shuffling noise to her right caught her attention. She glanced up. Lord Rupert was coming toward her, quickly closing the gap between them. He knelt beside her, then winked.

What was he doing here? Rarely did any of the duke's family members come to the cathedral to worship. They attended their own chapel within the castle courtyard.

Lord Rupert seemed determined to make his feelings for her known. She couldn't help thinking that if Lord Hamlin had the misfortune to fall in love with a woodcutter's daughter, he would be too proud to publicize it. *No, he'd rather marry the daughter of a duke, someone of his own class.*

But why was she thinking about him? She mentally shoved him away.

Lord Rupert moved a fraction closer and Rose smiled. Could it be true, what Lord Hamlin said? Did Lord Rupert intend to marry her? From his behavior, how could she doubt it? But whether he was in love with her or not, she shouldn't have accepted the bracelet from him. Frau Geruscha would be shocked at such a lapse. Her conscience pricked her.

Rose tried to concentrate on the priest's words, but with Lord Rupert's tall frame looming so near, her mind wandered. What would his promised surprise be? She hoped whatever it was, it wouldn't upset Frau Geruscha.

Her mistress's behavior was unreasonable. After all, Lord Rupert had been respectful and chivalrous so far. Yet, witnessing the piercing looks Frau Geruscha gave when Rose was with him, she always felt as if he—and she—were doing something wrong. She was glad Frau Geruscha couldn't see him with her now.

When the service ended, Lord Rupert leaned closer to her. "Keep praying," he whispered.

Most of the worshipers made their way through the long sanctuary to the back of the church and exited the building. In a matter of moments they were alone, except for a few people who were lighting candles near the altar. Rose kept her head bowed. Perhaps she should leave. Surely it was a sin to pretend to pray in order to be alone with a man.

She glanced up at him. His gaze was so intent, his smile so knowing, she finally whispered, "What is it?"

"I simply love looking at you."

She tried without success to think of something to say. Instead she stood, and he also rose.

She opened her mouth to speak and he bent low, bringing his face to within a hand's breadth of hers. "I don't think you should come to Frau Geruscha's chambers for me," she said. "I'll meet you in the courtyard, at the well."

"As you wish. I'll meet you there at ten o'clock. But can't we stay here for a few minutes and talk?" He motioned toward a bench that stood against the wall.

"I don't think we should." Rose glanced around to see who might have already spotted them together. He stood so close that she cringed at the thought of the priest's glare should he spy them. And what would other people think? They would assume Lord Rupert and she were having a sinful liaison, so far apart were their social positions.

She gave him a smile and rushed out before he could protest.

"Ten o'clock," he called.

Rose turned just long enough to nod at him.

She'd left Wolfie at the castle, since she couldn't bring him into church. It felt strange to walk alone, without her constant companion. She made her way down the street, feeling the hard, uneven cobblestones through her thin slippers. Breathing deeply of the morning air, she realized she was smiling to herself. How good it had felt to look up and see Lord Rupert beside her. How good he had looked, in his white shirt, his smile warming her to her toes.

How good it felt to be loved.

Rose kept her eyes on the cobblestones, not really seeing the road at all. When a shadow fell across her path, she looked up. A man, tall and angular underneath his long black robe, stood in her path. His eyes raked her up and down.

Peter Brunckhorst.

She stopped short, but he stepped forward and grabbed her arm. He started to drag her toward a narrow alley between two shoemaker shops.

"Let go!" Rose started to scream, but he clamped his hand over her mouth, crushing her lips against her teeth, his fingertips digging into her face. Where was everyone? The street was deserted.

Rose stared into his small black eyes. She had to get away. Her heart pounded painfully against her chest. His rotten breath huffed on the back of her neck. She tried to turn her head but his grip was too strong.

Since he'd stopped just out of plain sight of the street, in the edge of the alley, she decided to bide her time and see what he planned to do. She could kick and claw him, but he was too strong. He would simply overpower her. And he might drag her down the alley where no one would be able to see or hear her struggling.

His hand continued to crush her face. She tasted blood from her teeth cutting the inside of her mouth. Desperation and a compulsion to fight back swelled inside her. She breathed through her nose in order to stay conscious while she calculated how she could hurt him the most.

"You think you're the darling of the duke's family now, do you?" He hissed in her ear. "Well, I've had my eye on you. Your pretty face gives you away." The corners of his mouth curled back in a sneer.

What was he talking about? He must be a lunatic. She started to feel dizzy as she struggled to breathe.

"You won't get away from me. And when you least expect it, I'll come for you. You can't escape the destiny I have planned for you." His sinister grin grew, and he turned her, pulling her against his chest, still holding her by her face. He let go of her arm with his other hand and pulled something out of his pocket. It looked like a small pouch. He started speaking in a strange tongue, chanting in a strained, hollow voice. He opened the pouch with his teeth and sprinkled a gray-green powder over her head.

He'd let go with one hand. This was her opportunity to act. She twisted her body as violently as she could, catching him off guard. Then she slammed her elbow into his throat.

His grip loosened. Rose jerked forward, freeing herself. She grabbed her skirt and ran out of the alley. Her heart beat so hard it hurt her chest but she didn't slow her pace. She tried to listen for footsteps behind her. But she could only hear the pounding of blood in her ears, keeping time with her feet on the cobblestones.

# Chapter
## 12

*She ran until she passed through the castle* gate, across the courtyard, and into the chambers of the southwest tower, slamming the heavy door behind her. Gasping for breath, she sank, trembling, onto a nearby bench, then to the floor, wrapping her arms around herself. She sucked in the stale air like someone who had just survived drowning.

"O God, thank you for saving me ... O Jesus ... O God."

"Rose?" Frau Geruscha's voice seemed dim and far away. "Rose, what in the world—"

She felt hands on her arms and looked up. Dazed, she concentrated on Frau Geruscha's face. "He grabbed me. But he didn't hurt me. I'm not hurt."

Frau Geruscha lifted her and helped her sit on the bench. "Who? Tell me everything. What happened?" Frau Geruscha's voice sounded tight.

Rose took a deep breath. "I was walking from the cathedral after the service and Peter Brunckhorst was standing in front of me."

"Peter Brunckhorst? Who is that?"

"The wool merchant my mother wants me to marry. He was standing in front of me and grabbed me." Rose's voice began to quiver. "He put his hand over my mouth and dragged me into the alley." A tear slid down her cheek and she wiped it away with the back of her hand. Her hands trembled like a butterfly's wings. "I hit him in the throat with my elbow and ran away."

"Oh, my dear." Frau Geruscha wrapped her arms around her. "You're safe now. We'll take care of this, don't you worry. The duke does not let incidents like this go unpunished." She said the last sentence with extra feeling and pulled away to look in Rose's face. "I'm so proud of you for getting away."

Rose blinked back tears. Her mistress was proud of her. "Thank God he didn't hurt me."

Frau Geruscha stared at her hard. "Where did he grab you? Was it here?" She touched Rose's face.

"Yes." She had a terrible thought. "There isn't a bruise, is there?"

"Three fingerprints." Frau Geruscha's face grew taut. Fury flashed from her eyes.

Accompanying Lord Rupert to the feast, sitting beside him with bruises on her face. How embarrassing.

"I could kill him with my bare hands."

Rose stared at Frau Geruscha in shock. If Frau Geruscha felt that way, how would Lord Rupert react? She would have to tell him, she supposed, to explain the bruises. Would the same look of fury come over his face? Did he care enough about her to be that upset?

She tested her jaw by opening her mouth, feeling the soreness, remembering for a moment the raw fear that had swept over her when the man grabbed her. The memory of his black eyes boring into her caused a shudder to pass through her. What had he wanted? His words hadn't made sense.

"I shall speak with Duke Nicolaus's bailiff this moment. And the duke himself, if possible." Frau Geruscha stood. She started toward the door, then looked back at Rose. "You stay here."

Rose waited anxiously for Frau Geruscha. It was nearing ten o'clock, but she couldn't leave to go meet Lord Rupert until her mistress came back. She rubbed her arms up and down and tried not to think about the man's face. But his cold eyes and twisted mouth appeared whenever she closed her eyes.

What would be done to him? A common punishment for violent crime was hanging. Could Peter Brunckhorst be hanged for what he had done to her? Probably not. Perhaps they would banish him from the region. She would never have to see him again.

Just as she began to pace the room, Frau Geruscha stepped in the door. "Well, that will be well taken care of, I have no doubt." She sighed and sank on the bench. "I spoke to Bailiff Eckehart. He doesn't know a Peter Brunckhorst, but he promised that he and his men would find him. They will imprison him in the dungeon until he can be sentenced by the duke." She crossed her arms with a satisfied look on her face.

"Thank you, Frau Geruscha." Rose hugged her.

"Now don't let this frighten you too much, Rose. You go ahead and attend the Midsummer's Eve festival tonight. I'm sure Hildy will be with you."

"Yes, she will." Rose hesitated for a moment. "And Lord Rupert has invited me to join his family for their St. John's Day feast."

Frau Geruscha gave her a sharp look. After a momentary silence, she said, "What do you think about Lord Rupert and his attentions to you, Rose?"

Rose thought carefully before speaking. "At first I didn't believe he was sincere. But now I think he is. He told Lord Hamlin that he loved me. Lord Hamlin believes his brother wants to marry me."

Frau Geruscha's mouth fell open and her brows came down in a way that made Rose's stomach twist into a knot. Frau Geruscha turned away and walked to the window. After standing there for several minutes, she began to shake her head back and forth.

"Oh, please don't disapprove of Lord Rupert, Frau Geruscha. Surely you see that he is the best thing that could ever happen to me. I'll be able to help my family if I marry him."

Frau Geruscha turned from the window and faced her. Was she angry — or sad? Rose couldn't tell.

"Oh, my precious Rose. Please believe me when I tell you that Lord Rupert is not part of your future happiness. I want to help you, but you must make wise decisions and not try to take matters into your own hands." She crossed the room and laid her hands on Rose's shoulders. "Promise me."

"Promise you?"

"Promise me that you won't make rash decisions when it comes to Lord Rupert, that you won't allow yourself to succumb to his persuasiveness to do something you might later be ashamed of. Ask God to lead you in this matter."

*Something I might be ashamed of?* Rose tried not to feel offended at Geruscha's insinuation. "I promise."

"All right, then." She let go of Rose's shoulders. "I hear the cathedral bells striking ten o'clock. Go on now and enjoy yourself."

Rose quickly changed into her new dress and hastened to the well.

She wished she weren't on her way to a feast, about to face a crowd of people. She smiled when she saw Lord Rupert approaching.

He looked distracted, glancing around the courtyard. He took in her new dress in one swift glance. "You look beautiful. Are you ready?"

"Yes."

He started to look away then his eyes snapped back and settled on her cheek. He frowned. "What happened to your face?"

Her smile disappeared. So it was noticeable. She hadn't wanted to tell him about it while standing in the castle courtyard where people might be watching.

He looked away, scanning the courtyard again.

No one was near, so Rose began, "Something happened after I left the cathedral this morning. A man—"

"Hey, Gebehart! Ludwig!" Lord Rupert shouted, staring past her. He motioned with his hand and two men started toward them. "Where are the rest?"

Lord Rupert took a couple of steps away from her to converse with the two men. He motioned toward the castle, and the men started off in that direction. He turned back to Rose.

"Now what did you say? Something happened?"

He reached a hand toward her face, but she pulled back, not willing to let him caress her cheek in public. "Can I tell you about this later?"

"Of course."

With a sinking feeling in her stomach, she followed him toward the door at the center of the castle. She wasn't sure what she had expected from him—perhaps some concern?

She took a deep breath. She would tell him later, when he wasn't distracted. After he had heard her story, he would be furious that someone had done such a thing to her. She imagined him overcome with emotion, vowing to keep her safe from this day forward.

The Great Hall was even more ornately decorated than it had been for the last feast. Colorful banners hung from the rafters, and flowers bloomed in every available space. The room buzzed with activity. Servants stood just inside the doorway holding the pitchers and bowls of herb-scented water for the guests to dip their hands into. Lukas, who apparently had been snatched from his stable duties to help with the feast, stood with a towel to dry their hands.

They took their places, Lord Rupert leading her to the seat beside him. As she watched the rest of the guests find their way to their places, she felt small. She almost wished she were in her bed, curled up under the covers. Peter Brunckhorst's horrible face kept thrusting itself into her thoughts. Maybe no one would talk to her. Or better yet, perhaps Lady Osanna would sit beside her again. Rose might even tell her what happened. Lady Osanna would be properly horrified and perhaps would say something comforting and sympathetic.

Rose's heart sank when Lady Anne sat beside her, separating her from Lady Osanna, who sat on Anne's other side. She forced herself to smile and greet her. Lady Anne responded in kind, then turned to Osanna. A glance in another direction showed Duchess Katheryn glowering at her. The duchess immediately looked away.

Serving girls filled their tankards with wine, and two servant boys carried in a large boar on a platter. The animal was complete with head and tusks, its skin decorated with designs painted in red dye. Spicy gravy was served with the meat, along with honeyed rice pudding. Other servants offered sliced chicken and pheasant and an assortment of cooked fruit in thick sauces. Rose accepted the food offered her, even though she wasn't sure she would be able to eat it. She was still feeling too nervous from her incident with Peter Brunckhorst.

Lord Rupert didn't seem to notice that she wasn't eating. He pointed to the boar. "I wonder if this is the beast who ripped into Wilhelm." He chuckled.

Rose felt weak at the thought. She wanted to rebuke him for the comment. Instead, she looked away.

"Oh, Rose, I was only jesting." He took a long drink of wine. "A note came from Wilhelm yesterday. He thinks he's on Moncore's trail, and he may be away for several more months, until the onset of winter."

Rose nodded, trying to look properly interested without showing too much concern. But the news made her feel even more like running away to be alone.

At the end of the first course, the servants brought out a subtlety in the shape of a castle. Everyone clapped and shouted their approval of the sculptor's skill. After it had been paraded around for all the guests to get a close look, Lord Rupert said, "I will get a piece for you."

"I don't like marzipan."

"Oh, come. Eat some. It's the festive thing to do."

The servant brought the marzipan castle—an exact replica of

Hagenheim Castle, perfectly proportioned, with its five towers—around to their table again. It seemed a shame to destroy something so intricate, but Lord Rupert took the knife and sliced off the biggest tower.

"For you."

Rose took it from his hand. He looked like Wolfie when he'd killed a rabbit and laid it at her feet. She smiled and took a bite to please him.

"Now you're ready for my surprise."

A group of men and women entered the minstrels' gallery at the opposite end of the hall. There must have been over a dozen people, each holding a musical instrument—a lute, harp, recorder, viol, drum, or hurdy-gurdy. The noisy conversation in the Great Hall ceased.

So this was her surprise—professional musicians performing for the guests. She recognized two of them as the men Lord Rupert had been talking to in the courtyard just before the feast.

He smiled down at her, so obviously proud of his gift to her.

She smiled back at him, genuinely impressed and pleased.

Lord Rupert leaned down, his lips close to her ear. "The first song I requested especially for you."

The song was a ballad, the music slow and sweet. The words were in Italian, of which she only understood a smattering.

Lord Rupert translated. "You see beauty and gentleness joined together," he whispered, his breath causing wisps of her hair to brush against her ear, "and adorned with virtuous manners."

He paused while they sang the next verse.

"She moves her eyes in a face that proves heaven exists."

Rose could feel his gaze fixed on her, but she locked hers on the musicians, a blush suffusing her cheeks. He continued with the next verse, his voice deeper.

"And makes me a faithful subject of love. I enjoy sweet
service more than freedom.
For when I come before her face I place all my desire
in pleasing her.
I feel all unworthiness perish in my heart and virtue awaken there."

Rose risked a peek at him. His expression was so intense it made her heart pound against her chest. He leaned very close. His gaze raked over her face, and Rose was glad the light was too dim in the Great Hall for him to notice again the bruises, or the blush infusing her cheeks.

She forced herself to turn away from him, with the thought that others were probably watching.

The song ended and everyone applauded. Rose felt a warm hand on her back and realized it was Lord Rupert's. She turned her eyes to his and gave a little shake of her head. Kissing her hand in private was bad enough, but touching her in public was too bold.

He took his hand away, but with a pitiful look.

The Meistersingers continued to play their instruments while the servants brought out the fish course, consisting of spiced lampreys, roasted salmon, eel, and fish pies.

Lord Rupert seemed to have lost his appetite. He passed over nearly every dish, and instead of eating, drank wine and spoke in low tones to Rose.

"I've arranged for the singers to accompany us to the square after the feast, where we can dance all afternoon." He gave her an arch look. "I know you like to dance."

They finished the fish course, and the servants carried the leftovers out to the poor who waited at the door, as was the custom.

The Meistersingers began another song, this time a lively tune in Latin.

"I requested this song also. Do you understand Latin?"

"Yes."

Lord Rupert smiled down at her. "You'll like it. It makes one want to dance."

The lead singer belted out the verses, then the deep, rich voices of the other singers answered him with the rollicking chorus.

Rose listened to the song as Lord Rupert conversed with the bishop.

When the music ended, the servants carried in a giant pie that was so large it required two young men to carry it. The servers set it at the high table in front of the duke as the cook followed them in. She took a long knife and sliced open the crust and several birds flew out. Women squealed as the birds fluttered up to the rafters. Everyone applauded, except Duke Nicolaus, who roared with laughter.

The next course featured venison with frumenty, but the liquid meat pudding was everyday fare for her and not very tempting. She ate some pears in syrup instead, and a bit of fruit pastry.

The Meistersingers sang another ballad, this one about a hunter who, with his greyhound and falcon, was caught in the rain and sheltered by a shepherdess. Lord Rupert translated part of it for Rose then was distracted by a friend.

Rose tried to look interested in the food, in the entertainers, jugglers, and acrobats. She sighed in relief when the feast came to an end.

Lord Rupert turned to her and placed his hand on her arm. "The Meistersingers shall play some dancing music for us in the Marktplatz." His grin grew wider. "And I have one more song I asked them to play just for you. Will you meet me in front of the *Rathous* at three o'clock?"

Rose smiled and nodded.

"And wear your bracelet?" The inflection of his voice made it a plea.

"I can't promise."

"It would mean so much to me."

"I'll try. You know, if Frau Geruscha found out you gave it to me, and that I accepted it —"

"She won't find out." He smiled, as though happy now that he realized Frau Geruscha was the reason she was resisting.

"I'll see you at nones."

# Chapter
## 13

*Hildy came to walk with Rose to the Markt-*
platz, since Frau Geruscha wouldn't allow her to go by herself. The
Marktplatz was alive with people milling about. The focal point of
the square was the three-story *Rathous*, or Town Hall, one of Rose's
favorite buildings. It wasn't ornately decorated like the Butchers' Guild
Hall on the opposite side, with its painted wooden carvings, but was
magnificent in its own way. Rose marveled at its size and its gray brick
façade, decorated with triplet Gothic-arched windows. Pointed stone
arches ran the length of the bottom floor, forming a canopy over the
sidewalk. She and Hildy waited for Lord Rupert there.

Rose ran her hand over the tight, smooth braid down her back,
drawing it over her shoulder. Hildy had come to visit her after the feast,
and her friend had braided Rose's hair in preparation for the dancing.
While Hildy tugged and worked Rose's strands of hair between her fingers, Rose described the awful incident with Peter Brunckhorst. Hildy
cried, "If only Lord Rupert had come and saved you! That would have
been so romantic."

She listened absentmindedly to Hildy's excited chatter. A lingering shiver of abhorrence ran through her at the thought of Peter
Brunckhorst's long fingers biting into her face and crushing her lips.
Was he still inside the walls of Hagenheim? If so, he could be nearby.
She looked about her but saw no one resembling the tall wool merchant. Besides, the duke's soldiers were out looking for him, and perhaps even had him locked in the dungeon at this moment.

Excitement about the Midsummer Eve festival filled the air
with extra noise and happier sounds than normal. The actual festival
wouldn't commence until twilight, when bonfires would be ignited all

around the countryside. In the Marktplatz, there would be a ring of candles, around which people would sit and sing and eat St. John's bread and destiny cakes. But first, Lord Rupert's impromptu music and dancing would entertain everyone.

"Rose."

She turned and saw Lord Rupert striding toward her.

Hildy squeezed her arm. "I will find you later." Her eyes twinkled before she turned and hurried away, across the wide Marktplatz.

Lord Rupert's face was lit by a broad smile. He stopped before her and lifted her left hand. His smile fled.

"You're not wearing it." His eyes narrowed. "Still afraid of Frau Geruscha?"

"I don't want to excite her ire unnecessarily."

"What about my ire?"

"Oh, I think I can manage yours."

"Is that so?" Lord Rupert backed her up against the inside wall of one of the arches of the Rathous. Shadows surrounded them as the wall mostly hid them from the people milling around the Marktplatz. He propped his elbow against the arch above her head. His eyes danced with a tender light.

Her heart quickened. If she were the wife of Lord Rupert Gerstenberg, wouldn't she be happy? How could she be otherwise? He was very handsome. Everyone thought he was quite a catch for any woman, rich or poor.

He leaned closer, his eyes already closing. If she simply stood still, he was going to kiss her in less time than it would take to say, "Halt. State your business."

Rose ducked her head and slipped under his arm. "I suppose you remember that I wanted to tell you about something." She turned around to face him. Trying to affect an innocent smile, she clasped her hands behind her back and stood on her toes.

He leaned back against the wall and crossed his arms with a frown of disappointment. His features, his hair, his clothes, seemed even more perfect in the dim light under the arches. He sighed. "I anxiously await the telling of it."

"There is a man named Peter Brunckhorst who has asked to marry me."

"Are you trying to tell me you're betrothed?" He uncrossed his arms and pushed himself off the wall.

"No, of course not." Rose frowned, ready to grab him by the throat and shake him if he wouldn't be quiet and let her finish. "I am trying to tell you that this man, Peter Brunckhorst, has twice accosted me. The second time was this morning after I left the cathedral. He grabbed me by the arm and put his hand over my mouth. That's how I got the bruises on my face."

"The surly—" Lord Rupert's features took on a threatening expression. "Our bailiff shall be notified at once. We'll have the lout whipped for that."

"Frau Geruscha has already informed the bailiff of the entire incident. He and several of his men have gone to find him."

"Very good." Lord Rupert cocked his head to one side, his shoulders relaxing. "Well, then, I'm glad I took care of that." He grinned, stepped toward her, and draped his arm across her shoulders. "Not frightened anymore, are you, my pet?"

She opened her mouth to say that there was more to the story. Instead, she shrugged off his arm and bristled at being called his pet. She wasn't sure why it bothered her. Perhaps it was because she was disappointed he hadn't shown more concern over what had happened.

"No. I suppose I'll simply strike him in the throat with my elbow again the next time he tries to wrench my face from the rest of my body."

"Did you truly do that?" Lord Rupert drew back, his eyes growing wide. "You're a maiden not to be trifled with, I see."

She tried to look smug. "I'm glad you realize that."

"Rose!" Hildy rushed toward her, Gunther following behind.

Gunther stepped forward, his lips pursed together in a very serious expression. "Hildy told me what happened. I'm only two houses away from the Marktplatz, Rose. Send for me any time of day or night. If that man ever comes near you again, I'll make him rue it."

Rose was surprised to find that Gunther's words made tears sting her eyes. She blinked. "Thank you, Gunther."

"It's fortunate that my brother is away." Lord Rupert joined the conversation. "He would personally have this man's head. Anyone who harms our Rose will have to face the wrath of the Earl of Hamlin." He winked at her.

Lord Rupert's words about Lord Hamlin, as well as Gunther's sincere offer of protection, made the heaviness over Rose's heart lift a little. She took a deep breath and decided to forget about Peter Brunckhorst.

The flat, expansive center of the Marktplatz was a perfect dance floor. Many couples, both young and not-so-young, took advantage of the rare treat of the Meistersingers. The dancers swirled, genuflected, raised their hands in the air, and generally kicked up their heels while the Meistersingers played and sang slow ballads, lively *saltarellos* and *istampitas*, and looked as if they were having as much fun as the townspeople.

She watched the carefree manner of the men and women singers. What would it be like to travel around the world? Rose had never been anywhere but Hagenheim. She studied the Meistersingers closely. Were the women each married to one of the men in the group? Rose imagined herself among them, making people happy, meeting people throughout the land. It must be an interesting life.

Seeing Gunther and Hildy together, dancing, laughing, and talking, sent a thrill of joy through her. Gunther obviously admired her friend. Hildy was properly demure, but Rose could imagine the raptures playing through Hildy's thoughts as she accepted Gunther's attentions.

Lord Rupert danced with no one but Rose, now that his mother wasn't there to force him to spread himself around.

The lead Meistersinger, Gebehart, suddenly looked at Lord Rupert with a quizzical lift of his eyebrows. Rupert gave the singer a nod. Gebehart nodded back.

Rupert turned to Rose and leaned in close to her ear. "Here is the song of my heart to you."

The drum began a deep, low rumble that vibrated Rose's breast bone and set the brisk tempo of the song. Rupert took her arm and they faced each other, forming two lines with the other couples. His eyes focused on hers. The other instruments joined the drum, which was like the beating of a giant heart.

The bass voice of the lead singer began with great enthusiasm,

"It is the joyful season—maidens and young men, rejoice!
*O! O! Totus floreo!*"

The other male and female voices joined in the chorus.

*"Iam amore virginali totus ardeo;*
My body's burning at the thought of first love;

*Novus, novus amor est, quo pereo!*
I have a new, new love, and it spells my death!"

Lord Rupert's look of palpable passion set her cheeks to stinging as they moved toward each other, brushing shoulders, then twirled away, only to pass each other again. She wished it was dark so that no one could see the way he was looking at her.

The song continued, and at the end of each new verse the bearded lead singer repeated the refrain with gusto, "*O! O! Totus floreo!*"

> "My love is a flower among virgins
> And a rose among roses.
> *O! O! Totus floreo!*
> Your consent comforts me,
> Your refusal exiles me.
> *O! O! Totus floreo!*"

Lord Rupert's appreciation was undisguised as his eyes roved over her. He circled her, dancing around her while she stood still. He ran his hand along her bare arm where the sleeve of her fashionable dress split.

> "In winter a man can control himself
> But in spring he's passionate.
> *O! O! Totus floreo!*"

He fell to one knee. While she danced around him, he placed his hand over his heart and patted his chest in time to the drum beats.

> "Come in gladness, little fraulein!
> Come, come, my beautiful love—now.
> *O! O! Totus floreo!*
> My body's burning at the thought of first love.
> I have a new, new love—and it spells my death."

The dance ended. Rose, a little out of breath, pushed back the stray strands of hair that had come loose from her braid and clung to her damp temples.

"Let me." He stood so close she had to lean back to keep his chest from brushing against her. He reached out and ran his finger along her hairline. In a gruff voice he said, "I feel as though I shall die if I don't kiss you right now."

Rose took a step back. "I assure you, you won't die." Her stomach flipped crazily and her heart jumped into her throat, but she attempted to look disdainful. In truth, she feared he would kiss her right there in the town square. His eyes were so bold and full of admiration for her. She already knew how warm and soft his lips felt on her hand. It was easy to imagine ...

Alarmed, Rose looked around for Hildy. *Don't panic. I'll simply stay here in the Marktplatz with all these people around.* Even Lord Rupert wouldn't be indecent enough to kiss her in front of everyone.

"I think I'll get some water." She turned and started toward the fountain in front of the Rathous. Lord Rupert was right beside her when she reached it. She got in line, as several others had had the same thought. But when they saw Lord Rupert standing with Rose, the line disintegrated. They all stepped back to allow him to go in front of them.

Lord Rupert bowed to them. "I am most grateful."

He walked forward, took a dipperful of water, and turned. His face lit with surprise to see her still standing at the back of the line. He motioned for her to come forward.

Rose's heart filled with dread. She began walking through the crowd. Her skin tingled as with a thousand tiny needle pricks, feeling every person's eyes on her, watching her make her way to Lord Rupert.

He handed her the dipper of water. She took it and drank a quick gulp, avoiding his gaze, handed it back, and hastened away without waiting for him.

Hildy appeared and Rose's breath went out of her in grateful relief. She glanced over her shoulder to make sure Lord Rupert wasn't close behind. "Talk to me, Hildy. I'm so bewildered. Is it too early to go home?"

"Go home? Why would you want to do that? Lord Rupert is looking at you like you're the Queen of the May, the Goddess of Love, his last chance at happiness."

"That's the problem! I don't know what to do."

"Don't you?"

Rose stared at her friend in frustration.

Hildy rolled her eyes. "All you need to do is smile and say a few encouraging words—and keep dancing. How hard is that?"

"But Hildy, everyone is watching, everyone is seeing just what you saw." Rose's eyes darted around, making sure no one was listening. She lowered her voice to a whisper. "They're probably all imagining immoral things about me. It's embarrassing!"

"Actually, they're probably all thinking how lucky you are."

"Lucky? I'm sure they don't believe he has any intention of marrying me."

"So?" Hildy shrugged her shoulders. "There's hardly a maiden over fourteen who wouldn't want to be in your place right now."

"You're not helping." Rose pressed the backs of her hands against her burning cheeks. Better to change the subject. "How are you and Gunther?"

"He went to buy something to eat. Do you want a chewet?"

A greasy fried pie didn't sound very good to her. "No, thank you."

"Well, I don't have to tell you, Gunther is wonderful." Hildy sighed dreamily. "But don't worry, I'm being coy — at least, I'm trying."

"Here you are." Gunther stepped up and handed Hildy the meat-filled pastry. "Rose, would you like one?"

"No, I thank you, Gunther. Are you enjoying the music?"

"Yes, I'm enjoying myself more than I ever have before, I do believe." His eyes caught and held Hildy's.

Rose looked down at the cobblestones and rubbed her forehead with the heel of her palm, trying to think of a plan of action before Lord Rupert confounded her to the point that she let him do something awful — like kiss her.

"There you are."

Rose looked up into Lord Rupert's face. "Oh, yes. Here I am." She tried to sound cheerful, but her smile wavered. *What was it Frau Geruscha told me to do?*

To pray and ask God to lead her, to ask God his will. She should have done that. Perhaps if she could slip away and be alone for a few minutes ...

"Excuse us." Rupert turned and bowed to Gunther and Hildy.

"Of course, my lord," Gunther and Hildy murmured.

He bent his head toward Rose and spoke softly, his voice taking on a meek tone. "The Meistersingers are taking a break now. Will you go with me somewhere so we can talk?"

Rose nodded and he placed his hand lightly on her elbow. She allowed him to lead her toward the Rathous, trying to think of a way to avoid being alone with him. Frau Geruscha had warned her that she could say no to him any time she wanted to.

Just as they came to the door, Rose stopped. "Why don't we stay outside? There's no one around. We can talk here, can't we?"

"There's a place inside where we can sit." He tilted his head and gave her an entreating look. "Rose, I promise I'm not trying to get you alone so I can ravish you. Is that what you're afraid of?"

"No, of course not." He had such an innocent look on his face, she decided to trust him. She followed him inside.

Their footsteps echoed through the empty building, everyone having gone outside to enjoy the music and sunshine. They sat down on a wooden bench against the wall, and he shifted so that he was facing her.

"Rose, I don't want to make you uncomfortable, believe me." He sighed. "But I have a feeling you are."

Rose's heart tripped as she thought about what to say. "Forgive me. I suppose I'm a little uncomfortable, wondering what people are thinking." *And there's the way you look at me sometimes, like I'm a stray lamb and you're a hungry wolf.*

"People are thinking what I'm thinking—that you're the most beautiful maiden they've ever seen."

"I doubt that."

"Rose, please listen to me. I know you like to dance, so I hired the Meistersingers for you. If I'm doing something that makes you sad, please tell me. Let me make you happy today. That's all I want ... to make you happy."

He leaned toward her, his hair curling around the sides of his neck. His unique smell, mixed with fresh air and the lilac his laundress folded inside his clean clothes, wafted to her. His eyes were the pale blue of a shallow stream. At the moment they looked wide and innocent and sincere.

"I want to believe you." Rose drew in a quick breath as she realized she'd let the words slip out. She bit her lip.

Rupert's features softened. He leaned closer and lifted her hand out of her lap. "Then believe me, Rose." He caressed the back of her hand with his thumb, drawing it to his heart, pressing it against his chest and sending tingles up her arm. "The truth is, I've fallen in love with you. I want to be with you ... forever."

He pulled her hand up to his lips and kissed it so tenderly, Rose's heart stopped beating for a moment.

"And I'm sorry I wasn't there to save you from that detestable cur. I would never let anyone hurt you."

He reached his other hand toward her cheek, and this time Rose did not pull away. He gently brushed his fingertips over the bruises. Rose closed her eyes and gave in to the warmth that flooded her from his touch. *O Lord, I'm in trouble.*

Rose opened her eyes as Lord Rupert took both her hands in his. He focused on her lips, and she knew he was preparing to kiss her. She bent her head and let him kiss her forehead instead. His lips were warm. "So beautiful," he whispered against her skin. He let go of her hands and his arms went around her back, pulling her close.

Rose ignored the warning bells ringing in her head and concentrated on how good it felt to be held, close and tender and warm. His hand caressed her back in smooth, slow circles. Her insides melted like butter. She laid her head against his shoulder and watched the faint, rhythmic pulse in his neck, then closed her eyes and savored the sensations washing over her.

He pulled away slightly. If she lifted her face, he would kiss her. Part of her wanted to let him, but she also felt as though his lip prints were already branded on her forehead.

She took a deep breath and placed her hands on his chest. Gently, she pushed out of his embrace and stood up.

Lord Rupert stood too and wrapped his hands around her upper arms. Rose was afraid that he would be displeased with the way she had avoided his kiss, but when she ventured a peek at him, his face held a strangely contented expression.

"I believe I hear the music again. Are you ready, *mein Liebling?*" The endearment sounded so good and sweet. She was "his dear."

Rose nodded and let him slip her hand through the crook of his arm and lead her out into the waning sunlight of late afternoon, back into the noisy Marktplatz.

# Chapter 14

*Rose fetched a bucket of water from the* courtyard well and came back inside the chamber, setting the water beside the fireplace. Frau Geruscha walked in, worry lines wrinkling her forehead. She crossed the floor to stand in front of Rose.

"I've just come from speaking with Bailiff Eckehart." She frowned. "Rose, they couldn't find Peter Brunckhorst. They don't believe there is any person by that name in Hagenheim."

Rose felt the blood drain from her face. "How can that be?"

"I know not." Frau Geruscha wrung her hands. She sat on a wooden bench and leaned forward, then straightened, then stood up again. "Rose." She fixed her eyes on her. "What did the man look like?"

"He was tall, with black and white hair."

"How tall?"

Rose raised her hand high. "About this tall."

"What else did he look like? Describe him."

"He doesn't have any distinguishing features to speak of. He has black eyes and bushy eyebrows, brown teeth, and a pointy chin." Rose shook her head and shrugged.

Frau Geruscha's expression grew even darker. "Who else knows him?"

Rose thought for a moment. "My mother. He came to her months ago, asking to marry me."

"Good. I'll go tell the bailiff." Frau Geruscha flew out the door.

But later that day, when the bailiff came to talk to Rose, he said that her mother had not been able to provide any helpful information, having no knowledge of where Brunckhorst came from or of his family. The man who called himself Peter Brunckhorst had met her on the street and mentioned an interest in Rose, so Rose's mother had invited him to her home, where he made an offer of marriage. Seeing his expensive clothes, she gave her consent and promised to try to procure her daughter's. She also admitted to his giving her a small bag of coins—a secret gift, he had said.

"I know nothing else about him either," Rose said.

Bailiff Eckehart looked puzzled. He abruptly ended their conversation and left.

Rose's heart took a long swim in the pit of her stomach for the rest of that rainy day. Not only had they not found Peter Brunckhorst, there *was* no Peter Brunckhorst. She sat by the window, listening to the steady fall of the raindrops.

But the man who had accosted her was real. And he'd filled her with a very real terror.

Rose imagined herself dressed in chain mail and heavy metal armor, like she had seen Lord Hamlin and his knights wear once during a tournament. She imagined the armor protecting her against Peter Brunckhorst and his schemes, keeping her safe, as she fought him off with her sword and shield.

It was a silly thought. Women never wore armor. She must think seriously. If Peter Brunckhorst tried to harm her again ... she had no control over what the man would do next. Perhaps she would be able to fight him off again. But what hope did she have against a grown man like him? He was stronger and bigger than she was. She'd been fortunate to have gotten away from him this time. She didn't think she would be so fortunate if there was a next time. *Please, God, protect me. Don't let him get me.*

She refused to think any more ugly thoughts. She let her mind wander to more pleasant memories, to the tender and respectful way Lord Rupert had behaved for the rest of Midsummer's Eve. At the end of the festivities in the Marktplatz, he had walked her back to the southwest tower. Rose had heard Wolfie scratching from the inside, letting out a bark and probably waking Frau Geruscha.

"Thank you for the Meistersingers, Lord Rupert. I enjoyed dancing with you."

Rupert brought her hand to his lips, then straightened. "You are welcome, my beautiful Rose."

"Good-bye." Rose put her hand on the door, inching away.

"Farewell, my love."

Rose went inside and bent down to rub her dog's head. She petted him and echoed Lord Rupert's words, "My love." She sighed. "Well, Wolfie, how would you like to move out to the country, to a manor house?"

The next morning, sitting in front of the window with the rain pouring down, Rose suddenly wondered if Lord Hamlin was safe and warm and if he had found and captured Moncore. She no longer felt angry at him, she realized, about the words he'd spoken that last day in the forest. He couldn't help his upbringing, after all, any more than she could help hers. So she decided to pray for him. Taking up the prayer beads that hung from her waist, she clasped her hands tightly in her concentration and prayed silently.

Someone touched her back and Rose jerked away. She turned and saw Frau Geruscha.

"I didn't mean to startle you, Rose. I have something to tell you."

"Yes?"

"I think it's best if you not leave the castle courtyard, at least for a while."

Rose stared. "Why? Wolfie always keeps me safe. I only left him here that day because I was going to church."

"I know." Frau Geruscha frowned, something she did quite often these days. "I've received permission for you to attend the chapel with me so you don't have to go to the cathedral. I want you to be safe. It's only for a few weeks. You don't mind so much, do you?"

"I suppose not." At least she would have a good excuse not to visit her mother, who still hadn't forgiven her for refusing to marry the supposedly wealthy wool merchant. She shuddered whenever she thought of Peter Brunckhorst — or whatever his name was — out there somewhere.

Rose now saw Lord Rupert every morning at prime, when she went with Frau Geruscha to the chapel for prayers. He also came to Frau Geruscha's chambers once a day, if only for a minute. He often brought Wolfie a bone he had pilfered from the kitchen, meat still clinging to it. He hadn't tried to kiss her hand since Midsummer's Eve, but if Rose read his looks correctly, his feelings for her had not waned.

Three weeks after Midsummer's Eve, a man stumbled into the healer's chambers clutching a cloth to his head. Thank the Lord of heaven, Frau Geruscha was there to tend to his injury. His ax head had slipped off its handle and grazed his temple. Frau Geruscha examined the wound and proclaimed the man quite blessed to still be alive. A little closer to the skull and he would be dead. As it was, the cut was shallow and would not require stitches. She reached for the roll of bandages in Rose's hand.

A timid voice called to her from the door. "Rose, are you busy?"

"Hildy."

"I don't need you right now, Rose, if you want to go talk to Hildy," Frau Geruscha said, not taking her eyes off her patient.

Rose stepped outside the door to where Hildy was standing. Her eyes were red and puffy, as though she had been crying. Rose's heart filled with dread, and Hildy's hands trembled as she reached out to her.

Rose squeezed Hildy's hands. "What's wrong?"

Hildy swallowed then whispered, "Can we go upstairs? I have to tell you something."

"Of course." Rose looped Hildy's arm through hers and walked to the stairs. Her heart tripped nervously as she wondered what could be the matter.

Once they were inside Rose's tiny room and she had shut the door behind them, Hildy began to cry — a soft, high-pitched sound.

"Arnold Hintzen tried to hurt me." She bent over, sobs shaking her whole body.

Rose pulled Hildy into her arms and let the horrifying words sink in. Arnold Hintzen was the young man who had always prodded her to go places with him. He'd always made her shudder, with his mean eyes and persistence. Rose patted Hildy's back and stroked her hair while she cried. Her blood boiled with anger, but she would stay calm, for Hildy.

"Will you tell me what happened?"

Hildy made an effort to stop crying and lifted her head off Rose's shoulder. She took several jerky breaths, wiping her face with her apron. "Last night I went to the privy." Her voice quavered with every word. "When I came out, someone stepped out of the dark and grabbed me." She started to cry again, but soon controlled herself enough to go on. "It was too dark to see, and I didn't know who it was. He pushed me down on the ground and told me if I screamed he would cut my throat. He flashed a knife in front of me."

Hildy trembled all over, even though Rose held her tight.

"He got on top of me and tore my dress. I told him that if he didn't stop I would tell Lord Hamlin and he would have him hanged. He said, 'You can't. You know not who I am.' And that was when I just suddenly knew. I suppose I recognized his voice. I said, 'Yes I do, Arnold Hintzen, and I will see you swinging from a noose.'"

Tears slid down both cheeks. She looked pale and weak.

"He slapped me and punched me in the stomach. Then he got up and left."

Rose felt hollow and sick. "Oh, Hildy. I'm so sorry. But thank God he left." Tears slid down her own cheeks as she closed her eyes and let the horror sweep over her at what her friend had suffered — and how much worse it could have been. It made her incident with Peter Brunckhorst seem mild.

"Have you told the bailiff?"

"Not yet."

"Do you want me to go with you?" She thought of the bailiff's expression the last time she'd seen him. What if he thought she had made up her incident with Peter Brunckhorst? Rose's heart sank. Bailiff Eckehart might not trust Rose anymore. How horrible for Hildy if he were to question her honesty after such a horrible event. "Or Frau Geruscha would go with you."

Voices echoed up the stairs, and Rose got up and opened the door.

"Rose!" Frau Geruscha's voice called her from the bottom of the stairs. "Can you come down?"

"Yes." She turned to Hildy. "I'll be back."

At the bottom of the stairs, Gunther stood waiting, his face flushed and his eyes flashing.

"Rose, may I speak with you?" he asked.

"Of course."

Gunther motioned for her to precede him, and they walked outside into the courtyard.

"Rose, have you seen Hildy today?"

"Yes, she's upstairs in my chamber."

Gunther's jaw went rigid as he stared across the courtyard. "From the way I see things, there's no need to tell the bailiff about this." He turned his eyes on Rose. "Hildy's brother and I will take care of it."

"What do you mean?" But Rose knew already.

"Tonight, we'll see that justice is done. There's no need to humiliate Hildy — again."

"Are you certain, Gunther? Perhaps it's best to allow the bailiff to handle this."

Gunther smiled a strange, cool smile, sending a chill up Rose's arms. "I am resolved. Don't mention this, not even to Frau Geruscha. There's no reason for anyone to know. David and I will take care of Arnold Hintzen." Gunther was silent. After a few moments, he looked her in the eye. "But you must promise me—not a word to anyone."

Rose took a deep, shaky breath. She glanced away then back again. "Are you certain, Gunther?"

"Yes." His shoulders relaxed and he looked like himself again. "Don't worry. Men have been taking care of their women for thousands of years. It's instinctual."

Rose shook her head. "Does it matter that I'm against it?"

"No." He smiled again. "Remember, no worrying. Tell Hildy she'll never have to give another thought to Arnold Hintzen."

"You won't kill him, will you?" Rose's eyes grew wide at the thought.

"No, just punish him a bit, give him a taste of what it feels like to be helpless."

"Please be careful."

"I will." Gunther turned and walked away. Rose went back inside to Hildy.

Hildy seemed pleased with the idea that Gunther intended to personally punish Arnold for her. Rose had to admit, the thought was somewhat satisfying to her as well. But after Hildy went home and Rose was alone with Frau Geruscha, she began to feel uneasy. Was it wrong, even dangerous, to keep Arnold Hintzen's attack a secret from the duke's bailiff? The thought of them taking the man's punishment into their own hands smacked of vengeance, and the Bible said vengeance belonged to God. It was tempting to speak to Frau Geruscha about it, but she ignored the urge.

# Chapter
## 15

*Lord Rupert came by the next afternoon* and diverted Rose's attention with a story of a mouse the servants had been trying all day to catch. It had led them on a merry chase, resulting in a broken stool, a sprained ankle, and the upset of a pot of frumenty.

When Frau Geruscha was out of earshot, he whispered, "Is the old woman treating you well?"

Rose squirmed at his referring to her mistress that way.

He had made other derogatory comments, accusing Frau Geruscha of trying to control Rose's thoughts. Although far from agreeing with his suggestions, Rose still couldn't help but wonder if perhaps Frau Geruscha's disapproval of Lord Rupert was ill-motivated.

A tiny sprout of resentment had sprung up within Rose. Whenever Frau Geruscha pursed her lips at seeing Lord Rupert, Rose felt an urge to defend him, loudly and firmly. But she could never be so bold with Frau Geruscha, who had always been so good to her, taking a special interest in her when she was a little girl, declaring that she was unusually intelligent, educating her, and finally, apprenticing her. If Frau Geruscha had not favored her so, Rose would still be living in her parents' hovel, working hard in the fields and the forest, or worse yet, married to someone she didn't love.

Even if Frau Geruscha's attitude toward Rupert was ill-motivated, Rose could never be disrespectful to her or believe that her mistress wished anything other than what was best for her apprentice.

Two days after Gunther told Rose about his plan to punish Arnold

Hintzen, Gunther came again to talk to Rose. He pulled a stool close to Rose's chair and said quietly, "David and I took care of Arnold Hintzen. He'll never come near Hildy again."

"You didn't kill him, did you?" Rose whispered.

"No, of course not. But we made him sorry. We became his missing conscience, I'd say. He'll think twice before hurting another woman."

He changed the subject and said he had been hired by Duke Nicolaus for his illumination skills. He would be illustrating the books the scribes were copying. "My first project will be a new Psalter for the duchess."

"Oh, that's wonderful, Gunther!"

"Now that I am employed, I'm looking for a house. When I find one — or build one — I'll be wanting a wife. Do you think Hildy would accept me?"

Rose smiled. "Yes, and I hope you won't make her wait too long."

"I'm a prize worth waiting for, don't you think?"

"Cocky now that you've defended your maiden's honor, aren't you?"

They both laughed, causing Frau Geruscha to peek around the doorway from the storage room.

"I'd better go." Gunther bowed to Frau Geruscha. He winked at Rose and departed.

Two days later, Hildy came in the door while Rose rubbed Wolfie's head.

"Oh, Hildy, it's so wonderful to see you." Rose jumped up and grabbed her friend's arm. "It will only take me a moment to put away these herbs. Then will you walk with me around the courtyard? I feel like a prisoner." She whispered the last few words to make sure Frau Geruscha didn't hear.

Rose asked Frau Geruscha if she could go for a walk with Hildy, just around the courtyard. Upon receiving Frau Geruscha's blessing the two of them, followed by Wolfie, strolled out into the sunshine.

"Tell me something exciting." Rose hooked her arm through Hildy's.

"I love Gunther." She giggled exultantly.

"Tell me something I don't know."

"Well, Arnold Hintzen is missing, or so says his mother."

"Good riddance. I suppose he was deservedly ashamed and ran away."

"Yes, but I don't want to talk about him. Have you heard anything about when Lord Hamlin is coming home?"

"Actually, I have." Rose sighed, remembering feeling an eager anticipation when she'd learned Lord Hamlin would be home in a few days. Her conscience smote her. Was she so inconstant? After all, she was falling in love with Lord Rupert, wasn't she? She wasn't supposed to be excited about his brother coming home—the arrogant, burdened-with-responsibility older brother.

"Well?"

"He's coming home. He didn't find Moncore, and his wedding is five months away."

"I feel sorry for him." Hildy shook her head. "He's tried so hard to protect his betrothed from that horrible conjurer, and he hasn't even been able to find him."

"Oh, I suppose he'll be able to protect her well enough once they're married. Perhaps he should be trying to find *her*, before Moncore does."

"Hmm. I wonder that he hasn't thought of that."

That afternoon, Hildy rushed into Frau Geruscha's chambers, her eyes red, her face pale and desperate. She latched onto Rose and began to sob.

Rose had the eerie sensation that she had been through this before.

"What is it? What's happened?" She grasped Hildy by the shoulders.

"It's Gunther," Hildy choked out. "The bailiff and his men have taken him to the dungeon. The duke has already sentenced him, Rose—to death!" Hildy blanched. Her eyelids fluttered and her eyes rolled back in her head.

"Frau Geruscha!" Rose held tight to Hildy, trying to support Hildy's weight as she went limp in her arms.

Frau Geruscha entered from the storage room. "Oh my!"

The two of them half carried, half dragged Hildy to the bed and laid her on her back.

"Is she sick?" Frau Geruscha asked.

"I know not, I know not." Rose pressed her hands to her face. "I wish she would wake up and tell me!" She wanted to cry, to relieve the hard knot in her chest, but that wouldn't help her find out what had happened—although she was afraid she knew why Gunther was sentenced to die.

Frau Geruscha made a few passes under Hildy's nose with a handful of pungent herbs and she began to rouse. She wrinkled her nose at the smell, weakly lifting her hand and swatting at the offensive odor.

"Hildy? Are you all right?" Rose took Hildy's hand in hers as she hovered over her.

Hildy opened her eyes and looked up at Rose. Her face wrinkled up again. Tears overflowed their banks and slid across her temples into her hairline.

"Oh, Rose. I can't bear it. It's too horrible."

"Don't cry. I know there is something we can do. Please tell me everything. We'll save Gunther. We will." Rose infused her words with raw determination, hoping to bolster Hildy's courage.

"They found Arnold Hintzen, Rose. He was dead. In the river. Someone said Gunther did it. When the bailiff asked him about it, I guess he must have said he did. I'm not sure, Rose. But I don't care if he did kill Arnold Hintzen. I love him. He can't die. I couldn't bear it."

Rose sat on the edge of the bed and pulled Hildy into her arms. She had never felt so helpless in her life. *O God, please, please do something. Don't let Gunther die. Surely he didn't kill him. Something else must have happened. O Lord, please help us.*

Rose tried to think. She had to find Gunther a way out of his sentence. But first she had to find out exactly what happened to Arnold Hintzen.

"Frau Geruscha, help me. Make Bailiff Eckehart take me to see Gunther."

"Child, he's in the dungeon. Are you sure you want to—"

"Yes! Frau Geruscha, please."

"Rose ... perhaps you should let his family try to help him. Besides, I don't think there will be anything that can be done."

"His mother has already tried," Hildy wailed. "The duke won't listen to her."

"I must try. Please help me." Rose was determined to help Gunther, since she felt partially responsible. And to help him she had to find out from him exactly what happened.

"Very well, then." Frau Geruscha's brows were knit together in wrinkles of worry. "Hildy, stay here. Don't try to get up. Will you be all right for a few minutes?"

Hildy nodded, looking like a frightened, lost child.

Rose bent and kissed her cheek. "Don't worry. God will help us."

# Chapter 16

*Wilhelm, Georg, and Christoff made it to the* little valley hamlet in the northern section of the Harz Mountains after riding for several days. A cold drizzle started falling. Wilhelm was anxious to find a stable for the horses and an inn with beds, preferably without lice, for himself and his men.

The first establishment they came to seemed promising for the former—less so for the latter. Two shutters hung awry, providing inferior protection from the cold rain. The front door boasted a deep groove in the middle of it about the size of an ax blade. Raucous laughter, obviously influenced by too much wine, drifted out.

The three men debated on whether they should go on in the rain to try to find a better place or stay where they were. Christoff and Georg suggested they stay. "The next place may be worse," Georg said, grunting, "in this God-forsaken …" His voice trailed off.

They saw to their horses first, making sure the stableman provided them some hay. Then Wilhelm and his knights slogged toward the inn after the stable hand assured him that at least one room was available.

They entered the smoky hovel, barely lit by a few stinking candles of pork grease. The patrons looked them up and down. Noting the three men's swords and confident postures, they quickly averted their glances.

Wilhelm fought his curiosity, thinking better of asking any questions until he'd had a night's sleep. The area was known for its soothsayers and self-described witches and conjurers, and the locals might not take to strangers on the hunt for one of their own kind. The bishop who ruled this section of the Harz turned a blind eye to the pagan beliefs and rituals espoused by his people. Wilhelm had gone to him to ask permission to seize Moncore, if he were found, and take him back to Hagenheim. The bishop had grudgingly granted his request but offered no help.

Wilhelm strode forward and asked the serving maid for a room. She left and came back with the proprietress, a nearly toothless woman with a rotund figure and a stronger than usual body odor.

"I have just the thing for you," she said, taking a candle and leading the way up the stairs.

She opened the door of the room and Wilhelm turned his head to avoid the smell that assaulted him.

"The last boarders enjoyed their incense. Burned a lot of sandalwood and such, they did."

Three straw mattresses lay on the wooden floor. Nothing else was visible in the room. Wilhelm didn't think what he smelled was sandalwood, but he decided not to argue the point.

"Stow your things and come down for some lamb stew."

Wilhelm hesitated but Georg and Christoff were already brushing past him and tossing their bags in the middle of the floor, where the barest light filtered in through the cracks in the shutters.

After eating his meal of lamb stew — flavored, so it seemed, with a few weeds and a sprinkling of dirt — in a dark corner table of the inn, Wilhelm wearily climbed the stairs again. He wished for a bath but knew better than to expect any facilities besides a nearby stream or lake. His large tub at home would be a welcome sight upon his return.

In the room, Wilhelm stared at his mattress. Fleas. He scowled with hatred for them and their vicious biting. He had traveled enough to suspect they infested every inn mattress in the Holy Roman Empire. He reached into his pocket and pulled out a handful of dried pennyroyal and sprinkled it on his mattress.

"Trying to keep away the little beasties?" Christoff asked. The two knights looked at each other and laughed.

"We'll see who's laughing in the morning."

He lay his sword beside his bed, and Georg and Christoff did the same. Then Wilhelm pulled his blanket from his saddle bag and wrapped it tightly around himself, fully clothed, before lying down. He lay on his back and looked straight up at the ceiling, since turning his head to the side brought the odor of stale sweat to his nostrils. Closing his eyes, he willed himself to sleep.

He was surprised to see bright fingers of sunlight highlighting the dust of the tiny room when he opened his eyes. Georg and Christoff were both stirring. Wilhelm saw Christoff scratching his chest, and Georg was scratching his neck.

"Fleas?"

The two grimaced and muttered under their breath. Wilhelm grinned.

They strapped on their swords and went downstairs. After they had drunk some warm ale, Wilhelm gave his knights a significant stare and inclined his head toward the door. They took the hint and exited. When the proprietress returned, he called her over. "Frau, do you know of any conjurers of pagan magic in the area?"

She narrowed her eyes suspiciously. "Who wants to know?"

"Someone who's very discreet." Wilhelm pushed a gold coin across the rough wooden table toward her.

She quickly covered the coin with her hand and slipped it into her apron pocket. "There are those who adhere to paganism what meets on yonder mountaintop." She hooked her thumb over her shoulder, indicating the ridge that towered over the little village. "I don't truckle with none of their kind, not I."

"You wouldn't happen to have heard of a man by the name of Moncore?"

"I see and hear nothing, and I say nothing."

Wilhelm laid down another coin on the table but kept his hand over it. "Are you sure you never heard of him?"

"Well, now." Her gaze shifted toward the door then made a pass around the room. When she seemed satisfied no one was listening, she leaned forward. "He was in town last winter. Haven't seen him since." She looked over her shoulder then went on. "He has a friend, one Dietmar, lives near the mill."

She stared pointedly at his hand, and Wilhelm lifted it. She snatched up the money.

He nodded to her. Only when she left the room did he allow himself to smile at this bit of information.

Rose marched out ahead of Frau Geruscha. When they arrived at the dungeon, Geruscha talked to Bailiff Eckehart and convinced him to allow Rose a few minutes with the prisoner. He led Rose to the wooden door at the top of the dungeon stairs and unlocked it with two huge metal keys. It creaked on its hinges as the bailiff pushed it open. The odor of unwashed bodies, excrement, and dead, decaying rats wafted out at them. Rose's hand flew to her nose, but she yanked it back down by her side.

She turned to Frau Geruscha. "There's no need for you to go too."

"I'll go back and check on Hildy. Bailiff Eckehart will take care of you."

The bailiff lit two torches and gave one to Rose. He placed a cloth over his nose and mouth then led the way down the uneven stone steps. Rose again fought the urge to cover her nose and instead raised her head. She would brave the smells and not let Gunther see her cowering at the odor.

The stones of the walls glistened with the damp, and far below she could hear water dripping. They continued their descent until Rose began to wonder if they would ever reach the bottom. She heard an occasional scuffling near her feet. Rats. Even with the two torches, she couldn't see farther than a couple of steps in any direction.

Finally, Bailiff Eckehart said, "Excuse me, Fraulein Rose. You stay here while I go make sure the prisoner is decent."

Rose hugged herself while waiting on the step. Her arm brushed the cold, wet wall, and she drew it back with a gasp. She didn't want to bring anything back upstairs with her.

After a moment, the bailiff and his torch came into view again. "You may proceed."

She stepped down carefully, as the last few steps were wet and slippery. The bailiff placed her torch in a sconce on the wall. He took the other and started back up the steps without a word.

Gunther sat slumped against the stone wall, his red-blond head bowed. His feet were anchored to the wall with thick metal chains around his ankles. His wrists were chained as well.

He lifted his head and his eyes met hers.

Her throat closed. She swallowed hard to force out her words. "Gunther? Are you all right?" Tears of pity stung her eyes, but she was determined not to let him see his own pitiable state reflected in her gaze.

He slowly raised himself to stand, his chains rattling—a sickening sound. "Rose. I'm sorry you have to see me like this." Dried blood plastered his hair to his head above one eye. What had they done to him?

She tried to sound cheerful. "But these are temporary surroundings."

"Very temporary, since I am to be hanged in three days." His voice sounded flat and unemotional.

"Gunther, tell me what happened." In her urgency Rose laid her hand on his shoulder.

Gunther looked her in the eye, pain clearly etched in the lines of his face. "I'm so sorry."

When he didn't go on, she asked, "What do you mean?"

"I suppose I did kill him. But I didn't intend to."

"How? What happened?"

"David and I found him the night after I talked to you. He was sitting on the riverbank, drinking. He didn't even put up much of a fight, he was so drunk. I beat him senseless and left him lying there, on the bank." Gunther shook his head. The chain on his wrist clanked as he put his hand over his face. "I think he must have rolled into the river and drowned."

Rose closed her eyes. "So is that what you told the bailiff?"

"Yes."

"And the duke still sentenced you to die?" Rose spoke the last word in a whisper and immediately wished she had not uttered it.

"Yes."

"But surely he understood you were simply defending Hildy. It was an accident. He was drunk. He fell in the river and drowned."

Gunther shook his head. "You were right. I should have gone to the bailiff with our complaint against Arnold Hintzen. The duke was furious that I took the law into my own hands." His voice trailed off absently, as if he'd forgotten anyone was listening. He held out his hands, palms up, pulling taut the noisy chains. He stared at his hands, his expression full of misery and anguish.

*And I should have tried to stop you.* The guilty thought stabbed Rose like a knife.

"I am responsible for his death, Rose," Gunther said, as though reading her thoughts. "Only I am to blame." He shifted his feet, clanging his leg irons. "I had a dream last night. I had been praying, asking God to forgive me. In my dream, an angel came to me here, in the dungeon, and said, 'God has heard your prayers and has forgiven you.'" He slowly shook his head as he looked her in the eye. "So don't cry for me, Rose. God has forgiven me."

A tear slipped off her chin and disappeared in the darkness. *No, I mustn't cry. I have to think.* She pressed her hand against her trembling lips. "Oh, Gunther, I promise I'll try to get you out. We have three days. There must be a way."

"Don't worry. My soul is at peace."

She grabbed Gunther's limp hand. "I haven't given up hope of saving your life, and you mustn't either."

He looked her in the eye. "Tell Hildy I'm sorry, and that I love her. I had hoped to make her my wife ... someday. Farewell, Rose. You're a good friend. Promise me that you will always be Hildy's."

"I promise." Rose stifled a sob and squeezed his hand. She tried to say, "Farewell," but her voice had left her, and she was only able to mouth the words. Lifting the torch from its stand, she shuffled toward the stairs.

As she climbed the steps, she tried to think of her options. What could she do to help Gunther? She couldn't let herself feel hopeless. There had to be something she could do.

She reached the top of the steps and knocked on the door. Her only thought was to find Lord Rupert. After all, he was the duke's own son. Perhaps he could help her win favor with the duke and plead Gunther's case.

Bailiff Eckehart's keys clinked against the lock and he opened the door to her. She handed him the torch and moved past him down the castle corridor.

The rain had not let up since the night before in the little northern hamlet. The streets—if such they could be called—had turned into a muddy soup. Wilhelm's boots slipped and sank into the sucking mire. Raindrops trickled down his neck, chilling him all over. But if Moncore was here, or if there was information of him to be had, Wilhelm would have it.

He, Georg, and Christoff had found another, cleaner inn on the other side of town and returned there to devise a plan.

"I'll disguise myself," Wilhelm said, "and go to Dietmar, asking for Moncore."

"No, my lord," Georg spoke up. "It's too dangerous. You might be recognized."

"Better that one of us should do it," Christoff said.

"I won't be recognized," Wilhelm said. "Nobody here has ever seen us before."

"Better that one of us should do it."

"Very well. Christoff, you go to Dietmar, and Georg and I will be nearby if you need us."

Morning was a slow time of day for the inn, and, due to the rain, the big downstairs room was empty. Wilhelm and Georg waited inside while Christoff started across the street to see what he could discover from Moncore's reported friend, Dietmar. After he was a good distance down the street, they started out behind him.

Wilhelm hunkered against the wall of a mill which faced Dietmar's little house. He took out his dagger, picked up a small tree limb from the ground, and began to whittle, glancing now and then at Dietmar's door. Georg was positioned on the other side of the street, under the overhanging roof of an abandoned hut.

Wilhelm whittled so long, he almost forgot where he was for a moment. His shoulders began to ache from the cold and wet and from hunching over. He straightened, flexing his shoulders. *Where was Christoff?* He couldn't imagine what he and Dietmar could be talking about at such length. But perhaps it only seemed like a long time because he was weary, in both mind and body. He hadn't been able to sleep well most nights of the trip for thinking about Rose.

The farther away he traveled from home, the more he thought about her. It was tiring to try to force her from his mind, to try to focus on something else. Again and again his thoughts went back to the moment in the forest when Rupert had sworn his commitment to her, saying, "*I vow to love her only and to take care of her for the rest of her life.*"

His face burned with shame even now as he remembered his reaction — he who was already betrothed, experiencing such pain at knowing someone else would marry Rose and love her. He was ashamed for envying his brother, and even more shameful was the resentment he felt toward his betrothed. He had thought himself above petty feelings like envy and resentment, but he saw now that he was a common sinner after all.

He shoved such thoughts away. *God will absolve my heart of these feelings.* He refused to let them gain a foothold. As long as he pushed any tender thoughts of Rose away each time they foisted themselves on him, as long as he tried to "take every thought captive," God would help him overcome. Besides, he had an important task to accomplish. He must keep his mind clear to find Moncore and free his betrothed. It would be a balm to his soul when he finally was able to capture the evil conjurer.

Wilhelm studied the house. A faint light shone out from the cracks around the windows, but there was no indication of what was happening inside. *O God, give Christoff success. Let us find the man this time.*

At that moment Christoff emerged from the door. Wilhelm's pulse quickened. He continued whittling but watched his knight make his way slowly along the street and pass by him. Georg left his place and started down the road behind Christoff. Wilhelm waited. Finally he sheathed his dagger and pocketed the stick of wood that had grown considerably smaller.

By the time Wilhelm reached the inn, he found his two knights already there, tugging off their muddy boots.

"Well?" Wilhelm stood waiting to hear what happened.

"He said Moncore left this region a month ago."

"Where did he go?"

"Hagenheim."

Wilhelm stared then rubbed his jaw. "We're leaving in five minutes."

"Five minutes!" Christoff and Georg set up a loud complaint, but Wilhelm wasn't listening as he gathered his things and stuffed them into his bag. He was frustrated and angry, as well as uneasy, about what Moncore might be doing in Hagenheim. And he was several days' ride away.

Rose made her way through the castle corridors and stopped the first servant she saw. She asked him if he knew Lord Rupert's whereabouts. He didn't. "Will you please go find him?"

Surprise flickered over the man's face, but he nodded and set off.

Rose leaned against the cold stone wall and closed her eyes. She covered her face with her hands and prayed.

The sound of footsteps broke her concentration. She looked up as Rupert came striding toward her.

"Rose! What's wrong?" He placed his hands on her shoulders.

"I need your help, my lord." Rose was surprised at how steady her voice sounded. "My friend, Gunther Schoff, has been sentenced to die for killing a man. I need you to convince your father that he didn't do it. You have to stop them from hanging him."

Rupert looked at her with a confused expression. "You say he has been sentenced?"

"Yes."

"Then there's nothing I can do, *mein Liebling.*" He shook his head and pulled her against his chest. "I'm so sorry about your friend."

"Please," she whispered. She pushed away enough to look into his face. "Please do something." *Please, God, let him see how urgent this is.*

Lord Rupert shook his head again. "I can't, Rose. There's nothing I can do. Once the duke has set the punishment, no one can change it, not even the duke himself."

"There has to be something. We can't let him die. It was an accident. Gunther's in love with my dearest friend, and if he dies it will tear her heart out." She looked into Lord Rupert's face again, searching, hoping to see some speck of compassion, of interest in saving Gunther.

He shook his head. "Nothing can be done, my pet."

Rose's throat and chest grew tight. She couldn't breathe, as though a thick blanket had been thrown over her head, suffocating her. Going to Lord Rupert for help had been her only plan. She had to think of something else.

But what if he was right?

Rupert pulled her close again and she didn't resist. She lay her head against his velvet doublet. He stroked her back with his hands, but she didn't feel comforted. He simply seemed to be taking advantage of the situation.

"I have to go check on Hildy." She pushed away and ran from him.

Rose passed the well in the courtyard and stopped. How could she go into Frau Geruscha's chambers and face Hildy with only bad news? She had to find some hope.

*There has to be a way!*

Lord Hamlin. He was coming home, wasn't he? He would know what to do. He was always so competent, ready to take charge of any situation. And besides that, he was the future leader. Surely he would be able to do something, even if he couldn't exactly reverse the sentence.

When was Lord Hamlin supposed to come back? *In a few days.* How many days ago was that? She wished she had asked Rupert when his brother was due back before she ran off. *O God, let him come back today! If he isn't back in three days, it'll be too late. Gunther will be hanged.*

Lady Osanna. She would know when Lord Hamlin would be home.

But Rose didn't know the whereabouts of Lady Osanna's chamber. She only knew it was on the opposite side of the castle from the men's bedchambers.

She found a maidservant and asked her to lead her to Lady Osanna's room. She took a deep breath and knocked.

"Who is it?"

"It is Rose, my lady." Rose waited. The door opened.

"Rose! Hello." Lady Osanna looked at her quizzically.

"I'm sorry to bother you, but I—" What should she say? *I need your brother, when is he coming home?*

Lady Osanna stepped aside and revealed Lady Anne standing behind her, staring at Rose as if she were an intruder.

"I'm so sorry to intrude on you, my lady, but I need help." Rose felt the tears prick her eyes as she spoke those last three words. Gunther was in the dungeon, chained to the wall, his only hope the hope of heaven when they hanged him in three days.

"What is the matter, Rose? What can I do?" Lady Osanna motioned for Rose to enter the room then shut the door behind her.

"I'm not sure anything can be done. I'm so sorry to intrude on you." Rose placed her hand over her chest, which felt so tight she could barely breathe.

"You're not intruding in the least."

Lady Osanna's voice was gentle and kind, which only made it harder for Rose to fight back her emotions. Staring at the ceiling, she went on. "My friend, Gunther Schoff, has been accused of killing a man. Duke Nicolaus has sentenced him to death by hanging in three days."

A look of repulsion twisted Lady Anne's face. Lady Osanna's expression was only slightly better—one of shock.

"But he's innocent. If Duke Nicolaus understands that he didn't kill the man, never intended to kill him, perhaps he will release him."

"Oh, Rose, it's so noble of you to want to save him, but I'm not sure there is anything that can be done. The duke's sentence is irreversible."

The tears came on stronger than ever. Rose tried to force them down, but one spilled out onto her cheek. Lady Osanna held out a handkerchief to her. Rose took it, wiping her face, then gained control of her voice again. "Can you tell me when Lord Hamlin is expected to return?" She couldn't look Lady Osanna in the eye, ashamed of what she must look like to her, her eyes red and her face splotchy.

"In three or four days. Perhaps he will get back in time and will know something that can be done."

Rose held the handkerchief to her eyes and nodded. "Yes, thank you. I thank you for wanting to help. Please excuse me." Rose turned to leave, wanting to run out of the room.

"I'm sorry, Rose."

Rose nodded again and rushed out the door.

When Hildy finally stopped crying, her pale face wore a lost, hopeless expression. Rose and Wolfie walked her home to her mother, who met them at the door of their little candle shop.

Rose went out to the castle stable. She found Lukas and told him she would pay him if he would run and tell her as soon as Lord Hamlin came home. There seemed to be nothing left to do except wait and pray. And Rose did pray, like she'd never prayed before. She prayed all the rest of the day and most of the night.

The next morning was torture. She knew she should go and sit with Hildy, but she couldn't bear to see her without any good news to cheer her. Instead, she waited until after nones, then ran out to the stable to inquire whether Lord Hamlin had returned. Perhaps Lukas had missed him. But he had not returned, and no one had had any word from him.

Rose went back to Frau Geruscha's chambers. She felt like crying, but her tears wouldn't save Gunther. She had to do something. Hoping Lord Hamlin would return in time seemed too little, too late. He might not be any more help than Lady Osanna or Lord Rupert had been. In the meantime, she had no choice but to go to the duke and beg him to show mercy to Gunther.

The thought sent a stab of fear through her. The big, blustery man and his booming voice terrified her. But she would do it. For Gunther and Hildy.

Rose turned and went back to the main castle. She found Bailiff Eckehart sitting on a stool outside the dungeon, cleaning his fingernails with his knife.

"My lord Bailiff, sir."

He looked up.

"If you please, sir, I would like to speak with His Grace, the duke. Would you ask him if he would speak with me?"

"Certainly, fraulein." His gray brows lowered. "What would you speak to him about?"

Rose swallowed. "About Gunther Schoff, sir."

"Very well." He stood slowly, putting his knife away in its sheath before starting off down the corridor.

She waited near the door to the dungeon. What would she say to the duke? He would look at her with those scary eyes, his bushy eyebrows lowered and threatening, grunting his disapproval of her. She would not cower but would humbly beg him to forgive Gunther, to reduce his sentence to something less harsh, due to the accidental nature of the death. She would tell him what a good man Gunther was, kind and gentle. Surely the duke wasn't completely hardhearted.

The bailiff's footsteps echoed through the hall. Rose braced herself as he approached.

He shook his head. "I'm sorry. The duke says he cannot see you today."

Rose's heart sank. *Today.* "Will he see me tomorrow?"

"He says he cannot change the sentence and he has no wish to discuss it further."

"I'll come back tomorrow." Rose clenched her teeth. She would not give up on whatever slim chance there might be.

She turned and walked down the corridor until she was out of sight of the bailiff.

What if the duke refused to see her? What else could she do to free Gunther? Tomorrow was Gunther's last day before the execution.

Wilhelm knelt on the stream bank to refill his leather water flasks.

"Will we bed down here for the night?"

Sir Georg and Sir Christoff stared, their shoulders limp, their eyebrows raised hopefully. All three of them were covered with the dust of travel. But Wilhelm shook his head.

"Let's go on a little farther." He needed to be home again, to rid himself of this urgency, and to get back to looking for Moncore. This trip had yielded them nothing—a chasing of the wind.

Georg shrugged and Christoff sighed. They turned to their horses and retrieved their water flasks.

He couldn't explain to them the strange sense of urgency he felt about getting home. Leaving Hagenheim had seemed like a good idea, to look for Moncore in one of his hideouts, and to get away from Rose — and Rupert. But now this vague-but-desperate feeling nagged at him every time they stopped to rest the horses or to bed down for the night, as if something were happening at home and he needed to be there.

That was foolish. He didn't believe in premonitions. There could be nothing at Hagenheim that his father couldn't handle. But then his imagination had conjured up all kinds of possibilities. Perhaps his father was ill, or his mother or sister. Or perhaps Moncore was in Hagenheim, stirring up some kind of trouble. It was probably none of those things, but the desire to get home became irresistible, driving him forward.

*O God, please give us a miracle.*

The last day before Gunther's execution, and Rose had come up with no new ideas.

Time to find out if Duke Nicolaus would see her today.

Was that a frown on the bailiff's face? Just the sight of her seemed to ruin his mood. But he nodded in her direction.

Swallowing and sucking in a shallow breath, she asked, "May I trouble you again to petition His Grace to allow me to speak with him today?"

"I'll see what he says."

Rose sat on the bailiff's vacated stool to wait. She consoled herself with Scripture. The unjust judge in the parable of the persistent widow in the Bible had thought to himself, "*Though I fear not God, nor regard man; yet because this widow troubleth me, I will avenge her, lest by her continual coming she weary me.*"

The fact that she had suddenly remembered this verse might mean that God was making the duke see her. Perhaps her persistence was working and was swaying him in her favor, as the unjust judge had been swayed in Jesus' parable.

Bailiff Eckehart appeared around the bend in the corridor. Rose jumped to her feet.

"His Grace will see you. Follow me."

Rose's heart thumped wildly in her chest. She could hardly breathe past the lump in her throat as she followed the bailiff into the deepest bowels of the castle. Finally, he stopped before a narrow wooden door and pushed it open for her. Rose stepped through the door and the bailiff closed it behind her.

Duke Nicolaus sat at the opposite end of the room, his head bent low as he scratched furiously with a quill. He paused to dip the quill in the ink pot.

He raised his eyes to Rose. "Well? Come forth."

His deep voice boomed, seeming to fill the small room with gruffness and impatience. Rose crossed the room on wobbly legs.

"Your Grace, may I speak?"

"That's why you're here, isn't it?"

"Yes, Your Grace. Forgive me for disturbing you, but I wish to plead for the life of my friend, Gunther Schoff." To keep him from interrupting her, she rushed on, pushing the words out of her mouth as fast as she could. "The death of Arnold Hintzen was not intentional. He fell into the river and drowned. It was an accident. Surely you wouldn't put a man to death for causing an accident."

"Pure speculation," the duke roared. His ponderous gray eyebrows hung dangerously low. "Were you a witness to any of it?"

"No, Your Grace. Please forgive my boldness." Rose's heart fluttered, but she clenched her hands into fists to steady herself. "I know Gunther would never kill anyone. He wanted to protect Hildy, who was viciously attacked by this Arnold Hintzen. He only wanted to defend her."

The duke stared at her with light blue eyes. "So the man thinks we have no order here? That I have no power nor inclination to defend the helpless or punish the wicked? He had to do that himself? No!"

He pushed himself up, sending his chair into the wall behind him with a crash. Rose drew in a quick breath and forced herself to stand her ground, her heart beating wildly again.

"I will not abide my people trying to enforce their own justice. I'm the law here. Your friend made a serious mistake, and now he must pay for it with his life. That is all I have to say. I do not wish to discuss it any further." He slammed his fist on the desk and took in a wheezing breath, then began coughing, a deep, chest-rattling spasm. He motioned with his hand for her to leave.

With a humble bow of her head, Rose turned and left the room.

*I've failed. O God, what can I do now?* There was no one she could turn to, no one left to help her. A weight descended onto her shoulders.

Since Rose was out of ideas, she should go see Hildy, to offer what comfort she could.

Hildy lay across her bed, but sat up when Rose came in the door. Her face was puffy, with red blotches over her cheeks. "Any news?"

Rose shook her head. The way Hildy's face fell sent a pain through her heart. "But there's still time. Lord Hamlin will surely come back today." Surely God would come through for them ... somehow.

"I hope I die of a broken heart. I can't go on living if Gunther dies—because of me!" Hildy burst into sobs, sinking down into the bed and burying her face in her pillow.

Rose sat on the edge of the bed and put her hand on her friend's head. "It's not your fault, Hildy. Gunther certainly doesn't blame you."

Hildy lifted her face and stared at Rose through tear-brightened eyes. Her usually tight braid was frayed, with strands of hair hanging loose about her face. "I went to see him today, in the dungeon. I had to see him. He said he wanted to ask me to marry him, would have asked me in a few more weeks." Hildy sniffed, a look of complete despair in her glazed-over eyes. "I wish they would hang me too."

Rose patted Hildy's back while she prayed silently, her throat aching. *Please, God, please. Please help us.*

Finally, with a vague expression of hope that Lord Hamlin would return before the morning, Rose left and went back to Frau Geruscha's to wait.

But as the sun drew nearer the horizon, the heavy, sick feeling in her stomach increased.

Night fell. Rose tried to comfort herself in the fact that Gunther would be in heaven, where there was no pain, no parting, no night, only endless, perfect day in the light of the Heavenly Lord. Surprisingly, a measure of peace and even joy for Gunther came over her, but it was fleeting and limited at best. What about Hildy? How could Hildy ever forget Gunther? Her heart would be decimated.

Rose lay on the bed and covered her head with her hands. "O God, I can't bear this. If you will not rescue Gunther, then give us all the grace to see something good in it."

But what good could there possibly be?

Rose cried until the soothing darkness of sleep closed over her.

When Rose awoke the next morning, it only took a moment for her to remember that it was Gunther's execution day.

She rolled over to face the tiny window, where the pale sunrise glowed yellow. Her whole body seemed made of lead, as though the weight in her heart had spread into her arms and legs and head. She rose slowly and put on her dress. Her fingers were so stiff and clumsy she could hardly tie the laces.

She opened the door of her bedroom and felt the tears begin again. She grabbed a handkerchief then plodded down the steps. Frau Geruscha waited for her with a sad, solemn look on her face. They walked to the castle kitchen together to take their breakfast, though Rose was sure she wouldn't be able to eat.

The two sat on a wooden bench with several servants who were also breaking their fast. Rose looked around at them. Some were talking. A couple of maidservants broke into loud guffaws. Others seemed oblivious to their surroundings, intent only on their food.

Rose looked down at the fruit pastry Frau Geruscha had retrieved for her. How could she possibly eat? How could these people act so jolly, as if life was the same today as every day? Hadn't they heard the workers' hammering as they built the scaffolding in the Marktplatz? Didn't they realize her friend would be executed in two hours?

Two hours. She wanted to curl into a ball and disappear.

"Fraulein?"

Lukas stood behind her, staring at her with wide eyes.

"I'm sorry I couldn't come to you last night, but Lord Hamlin, he came home. It was too late for me to be about—"

Rose jumped to her feet. "He's here?"

"Yes, fraulein."

"Oh, thank you, Lukas. You're a good boy." Rose grabbed him by the arm. "Come. I need you."

She ran from the kitchen and made sure Lukas kept up as she took a shortcut across the courtyard then entered the door nearest the Great Hall, between the north and south wings of the castle. She stopped just inside.

"Lukas. Do you know where Lord Hamlin's chamber is?"

"I think so."

"Run and knock on his door. Tell him that Rose needs to talk to him. It's urgent. I'll be right here."

Lukas turned, but Rose caught him by the arm.

"Here." She put two marks in his hand. "I'll give you more if you fetch Lord Hamlin as quickly as possible."

Lukas's eyes widened. He took off at a canter.

Rose clasped her hands, prayed, and waited.

# Chapter
## 17

⁂

*Rose heard footsteps coming, too loud to be* the footsteps of a little boy. She stared into the barely lit corridor, straining her eyes, her hands clasped in front of her. She forced herself not to hurry toward the sound of the heavy boots.

*Lord Hamlin!* She exhaled in relief. Tears stung her eyes—oh, he was a beautiful sight! Impulsively, she wanted to leap forward and hug him and tell him how grateful she was to see him. Instead, she clasped her hands tighter and pressed them to her chest.

He strode briskly toward her down the long corridor. "Rose." He must have dressed quickly, as he wore only a white linen shirt and hose, no doublet. His dark hair was wet and clung to his forehead, and he had not shaved in days.

Rose almost forgot to curtsy. "Lord Hamlin, please forgive me, but I need your help."

"What is the matter? Tell me." Even in the dim light she could see how intensely he was looking at her. And even with several days' stubble on his face, he was still so familiar, so handsome. There was such an earnest expression on his face, she believed he could—and would—help her. Gratitude swelled inside her, almost taking her breath away.

"It's Gunther Schoff."

"The young illuminator."

"Yes, well—" Rose hesitated, but she had to tell him the entire story, and quickly. "My friend Hildy was attacked. Gunther learned of it. Rather than make her report the incident to the duke's bailiff, he decided to punish the man himself." Rose drew in a shaky breath then pressed her hand against her mouth so that Lord Hamlin wouldn't see her lips tremble. She fought to keep her voice steady. "He found the man by the river. Hildy's attacker was drunk, and Gunther beat him. He knows it was wrong, but he did it for Hildy."

His eyes were riveted on her, his brows drawn together. Thank God, he was still giving his rapt attention to her half-rambling story.

"Gunther left him there. Three days later someone found him in the river. Gunther was accused of murder, and your father sentenced him to death." *Please sympathize. Please help us. Please save him.* "You're his only hope." Her voice broke. Anxiety twisted around her heart as she tried to read his expression.

Lord Hamlin rubbed his stubbly jaw. "I suppose you know that the duke's ruling cannot be changed."

His words did not cast her down, because she could see by the look on his face that he was trying to think of something they could do. Just knowing he hadn't given up gave her hope. *Oh please, God, help him save Gunther.*

"There is a way." His face was suddenly alight.

She held her breath as she waited for his next words.

"How quickly can you get your friend Hildy to the Marktplatz?"

---

Wilhelm sat astride Shadow at the back of the crowd. He frowned at the number of people who had gathered in the Marktplatz to watch the hanging. Scanning the heads, he saw neither Rose nor her friend. She had left at least an hour ago. Had she been unable to locate Hildy?

From the castle courtyard, the drum began its steady, slow tempo, beating out the last minutes of the prisoner's life.

Soon the procession came into view, making its way through the castle gate. A collective "Oh" issued from the spectators, who then fell silent.

The sight of the prisoner increased the sick feeling in the pit of Wilhelm's stomach. Young Gunther Schoff's hands and feet were bound as he followed behind Bailiff Eckehart. Wilhelm recognized Gunther's mother and sisters huddled together, weeping openly as he entered the Marktplatz.

Wilhelm searched the crowd again but saw no sign of Rose or Hildy.

Gunther's shoulders were stooped as he shuffled his feet toward the ominous platform. A rope dangled in the middle. Gunther's eyes, too, darted through the crowd as he walked. Apparently not finding who he was looking for, he bowed his head again.

*Make haste, Rose.* She had to come quickly or he would have to figure out some way to delay the proceedings. He rubbed his sweaty palms on his thighs.

Gunther reached the scaffold. He stumbled on the first step but caught himself. He continued slowly up to the platform.

The bailiff climbed up behind him and declared, "This man, Gunther Schoff, was accused, judged guilty by Duke Nicolaus, and has been sentenced to die for the murder of the man Arnold Hintzen. May God have mercy on his soul."

Wilhelm's heartbeat quickened. *No, it's happening too fast.* Where were Rose and Hildy?

Bailiff Eckehart slipped the noose around Gunther's neck and tightened it. He turned back toward the crowd. Wilhelm nudged his horse forward a step and opened his mouth to speak as someone called out.

"Wait! You must wait!"

Rose. She was pushing her way through the crowd, her chestnut hair glowing in the morning sun. Hildy followed as the press of people parted to allow them to get through.

Rose reached the front of the crowd, two feet from the platform. She turned and let Hildy pass. Even from across the square he saw the determination on Rose's face. Hildy was deathly pale, and she swayed on her feet. *O God, don't let her faint now.* Gunther might be dead by the time she came to.

"If it please you, sir, may I speak?" The crowd was so quiet, Hildy's soft voice carried even to Wilhelm.

Gunther lifted his head. A pained look of love infused his features, as though he had both dreaded and expected this moment.

"What is it, maiden?" The bailiff stared down at her from the platform, curiosity as well as a bit of annoyance in his tone.

She raised her voice, as though her courage had returned. "I wish to invoke the ordinance of redemption—to wed the accused to save his life."

Murmurs erupted from the spectators.

Confusion creased Gunther's face as a look of surprise crossed the middle-aged bailiff's. He wrinkled his forehead and cleared his throat, either waiting for the crowd to quiet down or trying to figure out what to say.

"The ordinance of redemption? No one has spoken of that ordinance in years. I'm not certain ... that is, perhaps we should consult His Grace, the duke—"

"That won't be necessary." Wilhelm tapped Shadow with his heels to start him forward. Wilhelm stared straight at Bailiff Eckehart as the crowd parted.

The bailiff's jaw went slack, as though he was relieved to see him.

Wilhelm avoided looking at either Gunther or Hildy. He was careful not to look at Rose, either. "Bailiff Eckehart, you are familiar with the ordinance of redemption, are you not?"

"Yes, my lord. I have never seen it invoked. That is ... yes, my lord."

"The law states that any unmarried woman of marriageable age may invoke the ordinance to save a condemned man. Please proceed." Wilhelm gave the man an intense stare.

"Yes, my lord." The bailiff reached out his hand to Hildy. "Come here where everyone can see you."

Hildy took his hand and climbed the steps. Her eyes were fixed on Gunther's. For the first time, the hopelessness left his face.

Bailiff Eckehart asked, "What is your name?"

"Hildegund, daughter of Hezilo the chandler, now deceased."

"Very well. Do you now, of your own free will, offer yourself in marriage to redeem this man, Gunther Schoff?"

"I do." Hildy's eyes glistened with tears.

The bailiff turned to Gunther. "Do you, Gunther Schoff, accept Hildegund, daughter of Hezilo, as your wife?"

"With all my heart."

Bailiff Eckehart lifted the noose from Gunther's neck. Next, he pulled a dagger from his belt and sawed at the thick rope around Gunther's hands until they broke free. Then he did the same at his feet. He straightened to his full height and sheathed his knife.

Facing Gunther, he said, "I charge you now to take this maiden to the priest forthwith and make her your wife."

Several cheers erupted from the crowd.

Wilhelm let out a pent-up breath. Thank God he had remembered the old ordinance, put into place centuries before. If he had not, how different this scene would have been. Instead of watching Gunther sweep Hildy up in his arms and kiss her—much to the delight and enthusiasm of the crowd—Gunther would be strangling to death.

He finally stole a glance at Rose. Joy radiated from her face, her eyes seemingly as wide as her smile. His heart raced and he had to swallow the lump that was caught in his throat. She waved to him, and her eyes shone with tears just before the crowd closed around her and blocked her from his view.

*Thank you, God, for getting me here in time.* How close he had come to being too late. But he had made it, and Gunther was safe. *Thank you, God.*

The joy of making Rose happy, of saving Gunther, of saving Rose's friend Hildy from heartbreak and pain, welled up inside him. He turned away from the crowd as they talked over the event in astonished tones.

After thinking it would be his last day on earth, that he would die in disgrace, instead Gunther would marry the woman he loved today. And Wilhelm had to admit, he envied Gunther at this moment. His mourning had turned to dancing and his hopeless waiting had turned to joyful anticipation. But Wilhelm's waiting had not ended, as one week before Christmas he would marry a woman he'd never met. Meanwhile he was a failure, having failed to accomplish the task that would ensure her safety. And Rose ... she would marry his brother.

He hoped no one could guess his thoughts and feelings. Better that everyone think he was indifferent to the people involved, that he was only doing his duty in reminding the bailiff of the ancient ordinance. Let them think that he wasn't particularly happy for Gunther and Hildy, and that, at the same time, his heart wasn't aching with emptiness and loss. Because he'd rather they didn't know that for the first time in his life, he wished he was an ordinary man instead of Wilhelm Gerstenberg, Earl of Hamlin, the future duke of Hagenheim.

With the vague realization that she was dreaming, Rose continued picking flowers in the misty meadow near the castle. But they kept slipping through her hands and disappearing, so that no matter how many she gathered, she never had more than two or three nestled in the crook of her elbow.

Stepping high through the tall, wet grass, she made her way to a thick stand of pink gladioli. But when she reached them, only one remained—skinny, dried up, and brown.

She raised her head. Someone was walking toward her from the other side of the meadow. Lord Rupert smiled and held out his arms to her. She wanted to run to meet him but her legs turned to stone, so heavy she had to pick her leg up with both hands to make a step.

When Lord Rupert finally stood before her, she held out her arms to him. But he wasn't Lord Rupert at all. He was Lord Hamlin, and instead of smiling, his dark blue eyes gazed intently into hers. She fell into his arms, allowing him to pull her against his chest. He felt so solid and warm against her cheek as she listened to his steady, beating heart.

Rose woke with a start and gasped. The dream had seemed so real. She could still feel the sensation of being held, the hardness of his chest against her cheek.

She pulled the sheet up to her chin and squeezed her eyes shut. Why had she dreamed about Lord Hamlin? *O God, forgive me. I didn't mean it. I should love Lord Rupert, not his brother …*

*Oh no. It is true.* In her heart, Lord Hamlin was the one who inspired her admiration and respect. When she saw Lord Hamlin for the first time in weeks, she'd felt elation. And when he saved Gunther from being hanged … she had looked at him and loved him.

*But that's wrong, God. He's as good as married.* It was Lord Rupert who loved her, and she should love him. If Lord Rupert married her, he would help her family. Her brother and sisters would have a better future.

*Lord Hamlin will marry his betrothed in a few months, and I will be happy for him, and happy for her too. I promise I will, God. I must.*

Rose rolled the clean cloth between her fingers as she and Frau Geruscha made bandages for future use. Rose didn't mind the boring work. She was so restless these days, it suited her to keep her hands busy while her thoughts were free to wander.

"Good morning."

Rose's heart leapt into her throat. Lord Hamlin stood in the doorway with his usual serious expression.

"Good morning, Lord Hamlin," Frau Geruscha answered. "Please come in."

Rose stood and curtsied, her thoughts going involuntarily to the dream she'd had a few hours ago.

"Our bailiff has spoken with me about the man who accosted Rose while I was away, and I just wanted to hear the facts from Rose, to try and plan our next course of action."

His eyes focused on Rose. She fidgeted with the roll of bandages. She would scold herself if she thought it would stop her heart from pounding.

"Tell me what you know about this man." He fixed his eyes on hers, and she strove to mirror his businesslike expression.

"Not very much. He approached my mother after he said he saw me in the Marktplatz. He said his name was Peter Brunckhorst and he wanted to marry me."

Lord Hamlin swept his hand toward her chair, indicating she should be seated. He dragged the wooden bench in front of her and sat facing her. Rose glanced at Frau Geruscha, who continued rolling the bandages, but her eyes darted back and forth between Rose and Lord Hamlin.

"Had this man bothered you before? Was he the one who grabbed you in the Marktplatz at the May Day festival?"

"How did you know about that?"

"I saw him and tried to help, but Wolfie got there first." He turned and looked at Wolfie, who took it as an invitation and lay down at Lord Hamlin's feet. Lord Hamlin rubbed him behind the ears.

"Yes. He told my mother he was a wool merchant. But no one in town has ever heard of Peter Brunckhorst." Rose frowned at the strangeness of it.

"Describe him to me, everything you can remember." He leaned forward, propping his arms on his knees.

"He's tall, about your height, very thin, and he has black hair with streaks of white in it. He has a pointed chin and rotten teeth."

"Is there anything else?"

"His eyes were very black, as if something evil was staring out of them." Rose shrugged. "I suppose that sounds silly."

Lord Hamlin shook his head. "Not at all." He stared at the floor. The silence dragged on as he sat motionless.

Finally, Rose spoke up. "Were you able to get closer to finding Moncore on your trip?"

Lord Hamlin sighed then clenched his jaw. "No." He shook his head. "Every time I go looking for him, I hear he's in our region again."

"What does he looks like?"

"I've only seen him once. He's tall, with black … hair, mixed with white … and black eyes."

Lord Hamlin and Rose stared at each other.

Frau Geruscha gave a startled little squeak.

"You don't suppose …?" Rose didn't finish her sentence.

Wilhelm knew what she was thinking, of course. But if Peter Brunck-horst and Moncore were the same person, why would he be after Rose?

He stood and began pacing the floor. "This Peter Brunckhorst is playing at some sort of deception. Why else would no one know him by that name? Perhaps he and Moncore are one and the same." He turned to Rose. "What did he say to you when he grabbed you?"

Rose looked like she was thinking hard. "It didn't make sense. I'm not sure I can remember. Something about me being the darling of the duke's family, and about my face giving me away. Just nonsense. He said I wouldn't get away from him. Then he pulled out a small pouch of powder." Rose shuddered and wrapped her hands around her arms.

A thought hit him like a fist between the eyes. *What if Rose is Lady Salomea?* He turned away from her, covering his eyes so he could think, but his thoughts were racing in a mad circle. He grabbed one and held on. *Why else would Moncore want to harm Rose?* It made perfect sense. If this Peter Brunckhorst was Moncore, then Rose must be his betrothed.

There was one way to find out. He and his mother were just discussing this a few days ago. Lady Salomea was eighteen. On her nineteenth birthday, two weeks before Christmas, the Duke of Marienberg planned to take her out of hiding and bring her to Hagenheim for their wedding.

He spun around to face her. She looked wide-eyed at him. He didn't doubt that at that moment he probably looked like a wild man.

He grabbed her arm. "Rose, when is your birthday? How old are you?" His heart stood still while he waited.

She stammered, "Five weeks before Christmas. I-I'm seventeen."

He felt as if he'd just been punched in the stomach. He let go of her arm and stumbled back.

He should have known. It had been a foolish thought. But now he was reeling from the disappointment. He turned away again so Rose and Frau Geruscha couldn't watch him as he tried to recover his composure. He leaned his elbow against the stone wall and covered his face with his hand.

For a moment he'd been the happiest man in the world.

"Lord Hamlin? Are you all right?"

Rose peeked around his left side. He looked a bit like he had the day he came in to get his leg sewed up. Why had he asked her how old she was? Was he thinking that she might be his betrothed? Rose would have to think about that later, because he finally opened his eyes.

His features softened as he held her gaze. He heaved a great sigh. "I'm sorry, Rose," he whispered. "I wish someone had been there to protect you."

"I did reasonably well for myself, I think."

He gave her a sad smile. "Yes, you did."

There it was again, that something that passed between them when he locked eyes with her. Rose hoped Frau Geruscha didn't notice it. She immediately thought of Lord Rupert and felt a stab of guilt.

"I ... I'd better go." Lord Hamlin pushed himself off the wall and stood, towering over her. He seemed taller than his brother, perhaps because he was broader in the shoulders and thicker in the chest. He had a protective, chivalrous aura about him, and Rose wanted to enjoy it, if only for a moment. He had thought, for a moment, that she was his betrothed. She was sure of it. *And had been disappointed that she was not.* That meant he cared for her, perhaps even *loved* her. It was such an amazing thought that Rose felt dizzy, and for a moment her vision blurred.

He surprised her by taking her hand in his. "I'm glad you're all right." He said the words softly, almost whispering. Her whole arm tingled at his gentle squeeze.

"Thank you." Rose got lost in his dark blue eyes.

He was getting married soon. She'd *have* to forget about him then. They couldn't stare longingly into each other's eyes anymore. This was the last time. Ever.

He let go of her hand and walked out the door.

Why did Frau Geruscha have to be so hard on Lord Rupert?

Rose stood by while Frau Geruscha bandaged the hand of a young woman who had spilled boiling broth on herself. As Frau Geruscha explained to her how to change the bandage and check for festering, Rose's mind wandered to Lord Rupert's visit earlier.

He had come to see her that morning after prayers, all polite graciousness, smiling and asking after Frau Geruscha's health. But the frau had glared at him and answered with a monosyllable.

Was there something her mistress wasn't telling her about Lord Rupert? She knew he'd done some unprincipled things in his past, but he was very good natured to allow Frau Geruscha to treat him so coldly. After all, he was the son of the duke. He couldn't be used to that kind of behavior.

But if Lord Hamlin trusted his brother and believed Lord Rupert wanted to marry her, why wasn't that good enough for Frau Geruscha?

She only wished Rupert would ask her to marry him. Surely that would cure Frau Geruscha's sour attitude toward him. And Rose had decided to accept his offer of marriage, if and when he made it. She had thought she didn't want to marry, but now she knew that wasn't true. She wanted to love and be loved, and if Lord Hamlin couldn't marry her — the very idea he could was absurd — then she would marry Lord Rupert. Lord Rupert loved her, and she was sure she would have little trouble loving him back. As Hildy had told her before, he was everything a woman could want. He was handsome, cheerful, and affectionate. Rose would be happy with him — and Lord Hamlin would be happy too, married to Lady Salomea. Intelligent, mature adults could choose to love the person they were married to, whoever it was. Didn't the Bible command wives and husbands to love each other? If it was a command, then it was possible. Besides, she was afraid she would never be very good at healing. She wasn't like Frau Geruscha.

If he did ask her to marry him, Rose would become Lady Rupert Gerstenberg. Frau Geruscha would be forced to address her as "Lady Rupert." Was that why Frau Geruscha seemed so determined to convince her that Lord Rupert's intentions were not honorable? Because she didn't like the idea of her apprentice taking social precedence over her?

Rose shook her head. Although it seemed a reasonable explanation, Frau Geruscha had never been prone to such petty feelings. Then why was she so hostile to Lord Rupert's attentions to her? Shouldn't Frau Geruscha be happy for Rose and want her to marry him?

But perhaps Frau Geruscha didn't believe Lord Rupert intended to marry her. Rose still had moments of disbelief herself, when she doubted his sincerity. But if Lord Hamlin believed it, it must be so. Mustn't it?

Her head hurt.

The next day Lord Rupert met Rose at the well when she went to draw water. He grabbed her hand, turned her toward him, and whispered, "Come away with me, to the orchard. I have something to tell you."

"I can't." Surely he understood that she could not do such a thing.

"Please, Rose." He bent over her hand and planted a kiss on her wrist so hot it seemed to burn her skin.

"Rupert! Oh, I mean, my lord—Lord Rupert—you mustn't. People may be watching."

"Then meet me somewhere they won't be watching."

"I cannot. What if Frau Geruscha found out?"

"Frau Geruscha! I want to exile her to Byzantium! Is she jealous because someone loves you? Does she want you to be miserable like her?"

"Please, Lord Rupert, you should not say such things."

"Then meet me in the orchard."

"But why?"

He stared down at her, his jaw tightening.

"All right." Rose was so confused. If she didn't go with him, he would be angry with her. If she went and was caught, Frau Geruscha would be angry with her. "I'll go. But I can only stay for a few minutes."

"When?"

"Now. In two minutes."

"Don't disappoint me."

"I'll be there."

Rose's hand shook as she hooked the water bucket to the windlass and turned the handle to fill it. She tried to hurry across the courtyard, sloshing water and marking her path all the way.

*Oh, let Frau Geruscha not be here so I don't have to explain.* But the healer met her at the door.

"There you are. Thank you for getting the water, Rose. I'm on my way out to visit the shoemaker's wife, the one who fell and broke her leg. I'll be back soon."

Holding back the relieved smile that started to curl her lips, Rose said, "Yes, Frau Geruscha."

Rose went inside but then stuck her head out and watched Frau Geruscha make her way across the courtyard. Once she was out of sight, Rose took off her apron, smoothed back her hair, and, as an afterthought, took Lord Rupert's bracelet out of her pocket. She put it on her wrist and fastened the clasp.

She ran out the door and headed for the orchard, with Wolfie at her heels.

# Chapter
## 18

*Rose approached the apple orchard that nes-*tled in a small valley overshadowed by the castle.

Lord Rupert stepped out of the trees with a huge smile on his face. "I wondered if you would leave me waiting here."

"I said I would come."

He stepped toward her and took her hand. He was dressed impeccably in a white linen shirt, a purple velvet doublet embroidered with white flowers, and black hose. His hair was pulled back and tied with a purple ribbon at the nape of his neck. She certainly couldn't fault his physical appearance.

Rose followed him between the apple trees. She breathed in deeply the apple-scented air.

Finally, Lord Rupert stopped at a fallen tree and motioned for her to sit. He sat next to her on the large trunk, still holding her hand in his. He looked into her face, his eyes wide and expectant. "Rose, tell me your plans for the future. What do you foresee yourself doing for the rest of your life?"

Rose had not expected him to ask her this, or anything else of such a serious nature. She tried to think. She couldn't very well tell him the truth — that she hoped to marry him and live in the country.

"I suppose everyone expects that I will continue to be Frau Geruscha's apprentice. Then, when she decides I'm capable of doing the healing work on my own, I will take over her work of helping the people of Hagenheim." Even as she spoke the words, she didn't truly believe them. For some time now she had been wondering if she'd ever be able to overcome her squeamishness and be a good healer. *O God, help me.*

"Is that what you want?" Lord Rupert leaned forward, holding her hand between both of his.

Rose shook her head in confusion. "I know not. What is it you want me to say?"

He stroked her hand with his thumb then lifted it to his lips, pressing a kiss into her palm.

A pleasurable, and at the same time uncomfortable, sensation spread all through her, but she had to keep her mind clear.

"I want you to say you love me, that you want to be with me."

Rose pulled her hand out of his grasp, her heart thumping.

"I think you already know that I love you," he said. "Do you love me, Rose?"

Rose looked into his eyes again, wishing she could read his heart there. Her own heart swelled with emotion. She didn't want to hurt his feelings, but she wasn't sure she could truthfully say she loved him. "I care for you, and I want to believe you love me."

Lord Rupert smiled in a pleased, boyish way.

"So you brought me here to question me, to make me say things that are improper? What else did you want to ask me? I should think you know everything about me."

"Oh, there's a lot I don't know about you, Fraulein Rose Roemer. I know you are the most beautiful maiden in the region of Hagenheim, but I'm curious about your mind, what you think."

Her eyes widened. No one had ever said such a thing to her before. No one, that is, except Lord Hamlin. He'd even suggested she'd make a good advisor to his father. But she shouldn't be thinking about him.

Lord Rupert stood and moved away from her. He wandered over to a tree and leaned his back against it, facing Rose. "What do you think of the Church? Many claim it is corrupt and needs reform. Do you agree?"

Rose sat straighter. Such a strange question. "I—I would never presume to say such a thing, my lord."

"Some say reforms are inevitable, that the pope will be forced to allow priests to marry. What do you think? Do you think priests should marry?" He fixed her with such an intense look, it startled Rose. She had never seen this side of him before.

Rose drew her brows together in confusion and a little fear. Such conversations could bring dire consequences upon a person. What did he want her to say? "Why are you asking me this?"

"I truly would like to know what you think, Rose. You're an intelligent woman. I know you must have an opinion."

"I admit," she said slowly, choosing her words carefully, "there are a few doctrines of the Church that I don't understand." She decided it best not to tell him she had read the Holy Scriptures. "But certainly I consider myself a loyal member of the Church." They gazed at each other for a long moment. "Why? What do you believe?"

"I believe priests should be allowed to marry."

Rose nodded. "I can understand why you would believe so."

"You do?" Lord Rupert pushed himself off the tree. His excited expression made her a little nervous.

"Well, yes. But I'm afraid the pope does not allow it. He does not see the issue as you do."

"This is true. But don't you feel that most people in Hagenheim believe priests should marry and have families, that it's unnatural for a man to be celibate?"

How strange that he should be pressing so hard on such a controversial issue. She couldn't imagine what he was getting at. She shook her head and focused her eyes on a large gray mushroom pushing its way through the decomposing leaves. "I have no idea what most people believe. But you certainly seem to feel very strongly about it."

"Let us talk of something else." He smiled again, seeming to shake free from his seriousness. "I don't want to waste our precious time together. It's enough for me to know that you care for me." He strolled over and held his hands out to her. "I told you I had something to tell you, remember?" As he sat, he took her hand in his again, his expression smug. "I have arranged for your family to move from their little house in the forest to a much better one, inside Hagenheim. The old Bernward house. They'll love it, Rose. It has three stories and seven rooms and a large fireplace, much better than that smoky one-room cottage."

Rose's heart thumped erratically again. She knew the house he meant, the home of a wealthy bachelor who'd died without an heir. Suspicion stiffened her spine and she snatched her hands away. "And if you give my family this house, what am I supposed to give you in return?" Her cheeks burned.

Lord Rupert threw his arms outward. "Nothing. Why, Rose, do you doubt me so readily? Do you think me a villain who only wants to take advantage of you?" He raised his brows triumphantly. "To prove

to you how much I respect you, that I don't expect what you've insinu-
ated, I've given them the house already. I sent servants there early this
morning to help them move their things."

He grabbed her hand and held it more firmly, preventing her from
pulling away.

She pressed her lips together so hard it hurt. That didn't prove
anything. She tried to read his face, waiting for an explanation.

"Rose, please don't doubt me anymore. I only wanted to please
you. I wanted to do something for your family, simply because they are
your family. Is that so wrong?"

She wanted to believe his words. "So, without questioning, my
parents simply moved from the cottage my father built in the glen to
a fine house in town that he had no part in building or paying for?"

"They did."

Rose found it hard to breathe as she considered what her parents
must think. She was sure they'd heard the rumors about her and Lord
Rupert, about the inordinate attention he'd been paying her. This unlikely "gift" must have all but confirmed that she was Lord Rupert's
mistress. Tears stung her eyes. "Are you trying to shred my reputation,
because you must be able to imagine what people will say —"

"I care not what people will say."

"You should care." Rose stood suddenly and yanked her hand
from his grasp before he had time to react. "You should care about my
reputation, at least." Her arms and legs felt weak from the emotion that
raged through her.

Lord Rupert stood too. "Rose, please. I meant no harm. I only did it
to help. Please forgive me for being thoughtless. I didn't think about how
it would look to all the mean, petty people who want to think ill of us."

He seemed more angry than contrite. Confusion scattered her
thoughts as she watched him.

"It was simply an act of kindness. Why should we care what people
think? Isn't it more important that your family is safer and more comfortable in their new home?"

Rose found it hard to argue with that.

"Rose, please don't fight me. I love you and I'm working on a way
we can be together." He held out his hands to her, a pleading look in
his eyes.

"I don't know." Was it possible her family was already moved in?
That they were living in a fine house, much finer than anything they

could have imagined affording on her father's meager living? In her wildest dreams, she had imagined such a thing for her family, but she never believed it possible. Shouldn't she be thankful? Or should she be angry? Surely if Lord Rupert intended to take advantage of her, he would have already made those intentions known.

No, she would believe the best about him. After all, he said he loved her. Still, it was all terribly shocking, as well as confusing. She'd have to try to sort it out later. "It is very generous of you. Thank you. I should probably be going now."

Something seemed to have arrested Lord Rupert's attention. "What is this?" He stared at her bracelet, twisting her wrist to the left and the right. His smile broadened. Slowly, he leaned down and kissed her forehead. His hands slid up her arms and came to rest on her shoulders as he pulled her closer and whispered, "I don't intend to let you spend your life tending to sick people, having to deal with blood and broken body parts all the time. You're too good for that, Rose."

She let herself slip her arms around his waist, resting her hands on his back. She sighed, and the exquisite feeling of being held flowed through her.

After a few moments, Rose pulled back to look up at him. "I'm sorry to go, but I need to return to the castle."

"Why must you?"

"I don't want Frau Geruscha to come back and find me gone."

"Frau Geruscha. I'll be happy when you are no longer under her thumb. She doesn't have your best interests at heart, Rose. You're beginning to realize that, aren't you?"

Rose found herself staring at his chest. "I truly wish you two could be friends, for my sake."

Lord Rupert sighed. "For you, Rose, I can be friends with anyone."

"Thank you." Rose smiled up at him, relishing the way he looked at her. Impulsively, she wrapped her arms around him again in a tight hug. "Farewell." She pulled away and started off quickly toward the castle before he could protest.

"Let me walk with you," he called.

"No. I don't want anyone to see us returning together."

He sent her a pouty glower, but Rose simply waved, running up the hill ahead of him.

"Oh, Rose, marriage is wonderful." Hildy's face was the picture of bliss as she raised her arms over her head, smiling up at the sky.

"It certainly looks good on you." A week had passed since Gunther's expected execution day—which had become their wedding day instead. Rose strolled along between Hildy and Wolfie as they walked to Rose's parents' grand new house. It would be Rose's first visit there.

Hildy proceeded to tell her of the joys to expect when she was married.

"Hildy, I'm not sure you should be telling me this."

"Of course I should! You'll want me to tell you all this and more when Lord Rupert asks you to marry him—which shall be any day now." Hildy smirked. "Then we'll both be married. Oh, Rose, isn't it wonderful?"

"I hope so." The truth was, she did expect him to ask her and thought it would be soon. She was too embarrassed to admit it to Hildy, but she looked forward to being able to enjoy Lord Rupert's caresses and kisses. What she did not look forward to was his mother's disapproval. The duchess was certain to be disappointed in her younger son's choice. She might even try to prevent their marriage.

They reached the clearing in front of her family's front door and stopped. Hildy faced her. "I predict you shall shortly join the ranks of us old married people." She gave her a quick hug and hurried away.

Rose pushed the door open and Wolfie poked his nose in. Rose could hear her mother's hushed voice. Standing in the doorway, Rose blinked until her eyes became accustomed to the dimness of the room. Then she saw her mother in the far corner with her father. Rose heard her name and held her breath, listening.

"She doesn't intend to marry," her mother said in a harsh whisper. "She's said that often enough. Now she's dallying with Lord Rupert and you know what people are saying about her and about us. She has no respect for us, the people who took her in and raised her. It makes me want to shake her by the neck to think that she's not even our own child, but after all we've done for her she refuses to do as we ask."

Rose concentrated on the words. Surely she had heard incorrectly. Not their child? She listened as her father's voice answered.

"Don't speak so. Rose has a right to choose her own husband. It's the law of the Church. Without her consent, the marriage can be annulled."

"Don't you think I know that? She could and should consent, but if I know her stubbornness and pride, she won't, just as she refused Peter Brunckhorst."

"For which we should be grateful, as it turns out."

"We don't know how it turned out. He disappeared. Perhaps if she had accepted him—"

Rose couldn't listen to any more. She turned around, not caring if her parents—if such they were—heard her, went out the door, and began to run. Her stomach burned as if she'd swallowed a lit torch. Her vision misted over as she struggled to take in the revelation.

Apparently her mother had found another marriage prospect for her and was angry at the thought that Rose would probably not accept him. Well, she was right about that. But now Rose understood her mother's long-time resentment of her. Her mother had not given her birth, had not even wanted her.

Wolfie galloped by her side as she ran toward the castle. When she arrived, she found Frau Geruscha refilling some flasks with herbs. Rose crossed her arms, standing in the doorway of the storage room. Her breath came hard and fast and her heart pounded uncomfortably against her chest.

"Did you know that I am not Thomas Roemer's daughter?"

The leather flask slipped from Frau Geruscha's fingers and fell to the floor, spilling the dried leaves in a wide arc around her feet. Slowly she turned. Her face looked as if it were made of stone.

"What makes you say that?"

"I overheard my mother saying—" Rose's voice cracked. Neither of them spoke as Rose's mind raced through all the times in her life that she had felt like an outsider in her own home. She didn't look like anyone else in the family. No one ever compared her to an aunt or cousin as they did her younger sisters. Why had Rose never thought of it before? She didn't belong to them—and her mother didn't want her and resented everything she had ever done for her.

"Did you know?" Rose demanded.

"How could I know? What did you hear?"

Was it Rose's imagination, or had Frau Geruscha's face grown ashen?

"My mother said I wasn't their daughter." Rose stared at the stone floor. "She doesn't love me ... never loved me."

Frau Geruscha said nothing.

Rose rubbed angrily at the tears in her eyes. If she was not Thomas

Roemer's daughter, then who was she? The illegitimate child of a prostitute? The orphan of someone who had succumbed to the Great Pestilence? It must have been an indigent family, since she had been pushed off on a poor woodcutter. *And they didn't want me, either.*

Rose ran up to her room.

For four days Rose thought constantly about her mother's words. Her father wasn't her father, her siblings weren't her siblings, and her mother wasn't her mother and had never wanted her. She felt unloved, a castoff, an orphan. Even as a baby, had she been so unworthy of love? She couldn't bear the questions inside her, and she decided to confront her father with what she had learned.

Rose headed out with Wolfie into the forest. She inquired about her father's whereabouts from another woodcutter and his son. She found him not far away, chopping steadily at a large beech tree.

"Father? May I speak with you?"

He looked up. "Of course, Rose." He placed the ax head on the ground and leaned on the handle. "Your mother sent you a message four nights ago saying she wanted to talk to you. Have you been well? We haven't heard from you."

Rose took a deep breath. "Father, I know I'm not your daughter. I want to know who my parents are and how you came to raise me. And why did you never tell me?"

A flicker of pain had crossed his face as Rose spoke. When she finished, he sighed. "I didn't tell you because I didn't want you to know. I wanted you to always be my daughter. And you are my daughter, just as much as my other children."

"But Mother doesn't feel that way, does she?"

He gave her a disapproving look. As always, certain topics were forbidden. One shouldn't even think about them, and to talk about them was worse.

Rose felt the tears gathering behind her eyes. But she didn't care. She was determined to say what she had come to say, even if she had to choke the words out.

"I know what my mother wants. She wants me to marry a man who will improve *her* children's status and prospects." Angry tears spilled down her cheeks. "But you can tell her I'm not interested in anyone she tries to foist me off on."

"Now, Rose, that's disrespectful and you know it. She raised you from a baby—"

"Who were my real mother and father? I think I have a right to know that, at least."

Thomas shook his head. "I know not." Rose waited, but he said nothing more.

"Why don't you know? Did you find me on the road? In the woods? Under a chicken coop?"

He gave Rose another severe look. "No, but it doesn't matter, Rose. You needed a home and I was happy to take you in. Your mother and I both were. We thought she was barren."

"So when she discovered she was with child, she began to wish she hadn't taken me." The tears came faster.

"Rose!"

The emotion in her chest rose higher and higher. If she had to listen to one more of his unsatisfying answers, to his scolding tone and see his disapproving look, she would explode. She had to be alone, to sob out the huge weight in her chest. She turned to go.

"Rose, wait."

Rose shook her head and ran.

A few mornings later, in Frau Geruscha's chambers, Lord Rupert stopped talking and looked annoyed. "What's the matter, Rose? Are you ill?"

"No." Rose gave him a smile. "I'm sorry. Only having a little trouble with my mother. It's nothing. Go ahead and tell me about your hunting trip."

"There is something else I need to discuss with you." He lowered his voice. A glimmer of excitement shone in his eyes, and something she'd never seen before. Was it nervousness? She hadn't known he was capable of the emotion.

"Rose, you know by now that I love you," he whispered. He leaned close to her ear, keeping an eye on the storage room where Frau Geruscha was working. "I need to talk to you. Can you meet me later?"

"Later?"

"Please, Rose. Something has been decided. I don't want to talk about it here. I need to ask you something very important. Your answer," he said slowly and deliberately, "will determine my future joy."

The solemn expression of his eyes fascinated her. "Where do you want to meet?"

"In the rose garden."

"I'll try to meet you this evening, a few minutes before vespers."

Lord Rupert smiled. He leaned down slowly, covered one side of her face with his hand, and Rose knew he meant to kiss her. She didn't move. He closed his eyes and pressed his lips against hers.

The thrill of her first real kiss sent a tingle all the way down to her toes. Her heart tripped at the thought of Geruscha suddenly coming in and seeing them.

Lord Rupert pulled away, a tender gleam in his eye. He leaned in and kissed her again, then ran his fingertips along her cheekbone.

"Until this evening." He stood and left.

Rose lifted her hand to her face, cherishing the lingering sensation of his touch. She closed her eyes. What could Lord Rupert possibly have to ask her? What, except those much-longed-for words— *Will you marry me?*

Unbidden, Lord Hamlin's face appeared before her eyes.

What was wrong with her? She had to forget about him, stop wondering what he was doing every day, stop wishing to tell him every time something good or bad happened to her. Anyway, he would be married, to his precious Lady Salomea, in a few months.

She closed her eyes and imagined marrying Lord Rupert. She had a few misgivings about his attitude toward certain things—responsibility, for instance—but if what Hildy had said about marriage was true, she would be able to overlook all of his faults.

# Chapter
# 19

*Rose anxiously waited for six o'clock to* draw near. In order to get away without raising Frau Geruscha's suspicions, she planned to make an excuse about having to visit her parents. Their new home was very near the castle gatehouse, and she would visit her parents, but only to leave Wolfie with her sisters. She thought Lord Rupert would appreciate being completely alone with her when he asked her to marry him. After he asked her, she would go back to her parents' to fetch Wolfie and tell them the happy news, that she would soon marry the most coveted man in the region of Hagenheim.

Maybe her mother—the only mother she had ever known—would finally be proud of her.

Frau Geruscha approached her. "Rose, I've wanted to talk to you about what you said about your parents."

*Not now.* She needed to leave soon. "Yes, Frau Geruscha?"

"Rose, sit down." They both sat on the bench. "I know it must have been devastating to learn that you were not born to your father and mother. But that fact doesn't mean they don't love you."

Rose stared out the window at some clouds and patches of blue sky. "I understand that."

"You are a wonderful maiden, with excellent qualities, virtues, and talents."

*So you've told me before.*

"It doesn't matter who your parents are. That doesn't determine your worth, Rose."

"According to the wisdom of the world, it does."

"But not according to God's wisdom."

Rose spoke softly. "I know that." *Do we have to talk about this now?*

"Your father loves you very much, and you have always been a blessing to him. You owe your parents love and respect, but you don't owe it to your mother to marry a rich husband. You don't have to marry anyone, Rose. You can stay here with me, helping me with my work."

Rose looked into her eyes. Would Frau Geruscha be hurt if Rose said she wanted to marry instead of becoming the next healer? "I know you don't want me to marry ..."

"It isn't that, my dear. I do want you to marry—to marry the person you love, who loves you in return."

Could she mean Lord Rupert? She sighed in happy relief. "Thank you for saying that."

Frau Geruscha patted her hand and smiled. "All right, child."

"May I go for a visit now, to my parents' home?"

Frau Geruscha looked surprised. "Of course."

"Thank you, Frau Geruscha. I'll be back in a couple of hours." Rose ran toward the door, and Wolfie jumped up and followed her.

"Be careful, Rose."

Rose's sisters, Agathe and Dorothye, met her when she opened the door. "Rose! Wolfie!" they squealed, throwing their arms first around Rose's neck, then around the dog's.

"Listen. Can you keep Wolfie here for a little while? I'll be back to fetch him before bedtime."

They nodded, their words tumbling over one another. "Come back, I have something to show you." "Me too." "Hurry back, Rose!"

Rose gave them each a kiss on the cheek and scurried away. She paused in the street just long enough to pull her bracelet from her pocket and fasten it onto her wrist.

The iron gate to the rose garden hung ajar. Shadows stretched long as the sun hung low in the west. Her heart fluttered. She opened the gate and walked in, shutting it behind her.

Lord Rupert stood in front of a huge red rose bush, the vines of which covered the wall behind him, studding the gray wall with dark red roses. His eyes glinted. A jaunty smile on his face, he stepped forward, took her hands, and led her to the iron bench.

He spoke with fervor, gazing into her eyes. "Rose, I love you. I want to spend the rest of my life with you."

Her heart jumped inside her. His ice-blue eyes held her prisoner in the glimmer of twilight.

"You see," he said, turning her hand over and playing with her fingers, "the Bishop of Hagenheim died two days ago."

"Oh?" *What does that have to do with us?*

Lord Rupert stared down at her fingers. "My father has granted me what I've always wanted, Rose." He looked up. His pale blue eyes pleaded with her, giving Rose a strange feeling of foreboding.

"Is something wrong?"

"I'm asking you to become my wife, Rose, in spirit, because we won't be allowed a legal wedding. My father has appointed me to be the new bishop."

*In spirit?* Rose instantly understood his meaning. The breath rushed out of her. She jerked her hands out of his grasp.

He spoke quickly, his voice taking on an authoritative tone. "But we will be no less married, Rose. You know as well as I do that the Church's doctrine against priests marrying is unfair and unbiblical. Rose—"

She recoiled from him, leaning back against the armrest of the bench. Her stomach twisted in horror. It was as though a curtain had been pulled and she now saw him as a vile, traitorous snake instead of the tender lover of mere moments before.

"Rose, truly, no one will think of you as anything other than my wife. You will be respected—"

"Stop it." Rose's voice came out raspy and foreign, even to her own ears. "I will not be your mistress. Never." She stood, clenching her fists in defiance. "I will not be anyone's mistress, do you hear me?"

"Rose, listen to me!" He stood toe to toe with her, grasping her arms hard in his hands. "I'll make you happy. You shall have all the music, all the beautiful clothes, everything you could want. You can run the household, read books—"

"Let go of me." Her body went rigid. She could barely see. Tears of rage blurred Lord Rupert's image. She glanced down and her eyes focused on the bracelet he had given her, glinting on her arm. Her face burned as she grasped it and ripped it off. She threw it at his feet. "You think I'm a nobody, nothing. How dare you ask me to live in sin?"

"Stop saying that and listen to me! It isn't like that, Rose!"

"It is! It is! And you know it is." Rose suddenly hated him, hated his detestable fingers gripping her arms. She had to get away from his voice. She couldn't bear to listen to another word out of his mouth.

Rose violently twisted her upper body and wrenched herself out of his grasp, throwing herself backward. He made a wild grab and caught her sleeve. She heard the fabric rip as she landed on the ground on her left hip. Cool air brushed her shoulder. Her right sleeve was torn and hung awry across her upper arm. She grabbed it and held it up in a feeble attempt to cover her exposed shoulder as she scrambled to her feet, ignoring the hand he offered her.

"You're being unreasonable —"

"You stay away from me." Rose gave him her fiercest look, determined to scratch his eyes out if he touched her. "Don't ever come near me again. Do you hear me?"

She turned and ran out of the rose garden, leaving the gate swinging on its hinges. She skirted behind the castle, across the courtyard, and through the castle gate, keeping her head down as she made her way out of town and then ran across the meadow toward the forest.

She ran as fast as she could, until her chest burned as though her heart were on fire. She reached the beech trees and turned to make sure Lord Rupert wasn't following her. Then she plunged into the evening shadows of the forest.

Tears coursed down her face and she panted for breath. Not caring where she was going, she kept running, only wanting to get far away. She came out on the other side of the trees, into the waning sunlight, and started toward the beech tree at the top of the grassy hillock.

Her shoulders shook with her sobs. She could barely see where she was going as she stumbled up the hill and sank to the ground under the tree.

She leaned against the tree's gray trunk and wrapped her arms around it. Her heart throbbed, hurting more with each heaving breath she took. Her throat ached and her eyes burned, but the pain inside was the worst. How could she have ever thought Lord Rupert, son of the Duke of Hagenheim, could possibly marry her? Frau Geruscha had been right all along. She never should have trusted him. He never intended to marry her. Humiliation pierced her and forced out the tears, doing nothing to relieve the ache in her heart.

Rose heard only her racking sobs as they wrenched her whole body. Then, suddenly, horse's hooves were pounding up the hill toward her. The animal was nearly upon her when she tore herself away from the tree to face the rider.

# Chapter
## 20

❧

*Wilhelm held Shadow's reins loosely as they* walked back to the castle through the dense brush and trees. A faint noise toward the west stopped him. He listened but couldn't identify the sound. Urging Shadow forward, he followed it.

They emerged from the forest. Someone lay crumpled at the base of the beech tree on the hill. His breath caught in his throat as he realized it was Rose, weeping.

He grasped the reins and catapulted onto Shadow's back, urging him into a canter up the incline. They closed the distance in a few seconds. Wilhelm dismounted before the agile beast had even come to a stop.

Rose lifted her face and jumped at his sudden approach.

"What is it?" His heart constricted painfully at her anguished look. He reached out to her, but she shrank back, staring at his hand as though he'd suddenly grown claws.

He drew back, startled at her reaction, taking in her ripped dress and tear-stained face.

"Dear Lord of heaven, what's happened to you?" He sank to one knee before her.

He longed to put his arms around her and comfort her but he remembered the way she had cringed when he had reached out to her.

"Who did this to you?" The impulse to tear her attacker apart set his muscles on edge.

Rose shook her head as fresh tears slid from her eyes and down her cheeks. "No, no." Tears seemed to choke off any other words she might have spoken.

"Tell me, Rose. Who did this?" On his knees a mere two feet from her, he had to restrain himself again from pulling her into his arms.

She shook her head. "I — can't — t-tell you."

"Yes! You can tell me, Rose. Please. You can tell me. I vow before God I will never let him hurt you again. Was it Peter Brunckhorst? I'll find him and make sure he never bothers you again." Pain strangled him at the emptiness of his promise. *You've been looking for one man for seven years and haven't found him yet.*

She shook her head again, and he yearned to smooth back the strands of hair that clung to her wet cheeks.

His heart pounded so hard it seemed to shake his whole body. He stared at her and felt the rage growing inside him. He had to know. "Rose, you have to tell me who did this. Tell me."

"I can't tell you!" She looked up at him, her eyes glinting.

He took a deep breath. "Why?" He softened his voice as he pleaded. "Please tell me, Rose. I don't understand why you can't tell me."

"If I tell you, you'll hate me." Her face crumpled. Fresh sobs shook her as she covered her face with her hands.

"How could I hate you? Especially for something someone else did to you?" He yearned to pull her hands away from her face and kiss her until she stopped crying. An irresponsible, nearly irresistible thought.

"Because. Because you won't believe me, and you'll hate me."

"Of course I'll believe you, Rose. I only want to take care of you. I won't be angry. Tell me." A hard edge crept into his voice.

A muscle writhed in her jaw. Anger flashed from her eyes. "All right, I'll tell you. It was your brother, Lord Rupert. He told me your father was appointing him the next bishop and he asked me to be his mistress."

Her fury seemed to rush out of her with the last word. Her chin quivered and she bit her lip.

Wilhelm closed his eyes as he grasped her declaration. His whole body sank under the weight of it. *Oh, Rose, what have I done?* He fell to the ground, his face in his hands.

Rose drew in a breath as Lord Hamlin collapsed in front of her. *Why did you make me tell you?* Now he would hate her forever. He would never turn against his own brother, yet he'd vowed to punish whoever did this to her.

Now that she had actually spoken the words out loud, the flood of tears subsided, but she was horrified at Lord Hamlin remaining in so undignified a posture. "He didn't hurt me, Lord Hamlin."

Still he didn't move.

"The rip in my dress was my fault." Heaven forbid that Lord Hamlin should get the idea that Lord Rupert had assaulted her.

But what did it matter? She was a lowly nobody to him and his privileged brother. With all his talk of love, Lord Rupert hadn't cared about her, had no respect for her. She wondered why she had ever found his face handsome or his pale blue eyes kind. Now he seemed cold, almost inhuman.

Lord Hamlin still lay prostrate, his face to the ground, motionless. What was he thinking? Was he embarrassed that he had thought Lord Rupert was going to ask her to marry him? Was he sorry for her hurt feelings and broken heart, or merely sorry he was to blame for making her think Rupert wanted to marry her? For causing her to trust him?

She hugged herself and shivered as a night breeze brought out chills along her arms. She wished she had not shrunk back when he reached out to her. At this moment his strong arms could be holding, warming, comforting her.

She closed her eyes. Of course he wouldn't have put his arms around her. This was the man who had issued a proclamation saying that no man could touch a woman who wasn't his wife or sister — and it seemed impossible now that she would ever be either to him.

Slowly, he raised himself and sat back on his heels. His eyes glistened as he locked his gaze on her.

"I'm so sorry." His voice was low and hoarse. Anguish creased his forehead. "Please forgive me. Forgive me for my arrogance. Forgive me for telling you I thought—Oh, Rose. Rupert is a scurrilous knave. You didn't deserve this ... Will you forgive me?"

Her heart pricked at the pain and tension etched on his face. She shook her head. "You didn't do anything wrong."

"I was arrogant, so pharisaical to believe that you would be better off marrying Rupert just because my family ..."

He stared out at the sunset. His face glowed in the pale orange light, which played up his strong, square jaw and his prominent brows and deep-set eyes. "I was wrong, obviously. You are the virtuous one, Rose. You are the one with honor and pure love. It emanates from you.

How my brother could have ever thought you would go along with such a plan ..."

"He didn't think it was wrong, doesn't see it as a sin," Rose said quietly.

Lord Hamlin scowled, his jaw clenching. "He knows better than that. He was only trying to make you believe it. He's a manipulator, a rogue, a—"

"It's all right. Please." Rose shook her head. "Nothing's hurt except my pride." *And my heart.*

She pondered that thought. Pain filled her heart, yes, but she was surprised to detect a little relief hiding there too, relief that she wouldn't be marrying Lord Rupert after all. She hadn't trusted him. She hadn't truly loved him. Did she even know her own heart? She obviously was a poor judge of other people's.

"I was wrong too, for thinking Rupert was selfless enough to give up wealth and power for love. I never dreamed my father would actually give him the bishopric. Please forgive me for trying to convince you it was best that you marry him. You were always too good for him."

"Please, Lord Hamlin, you don't have to defend me this way. I'm under no illusion about my status or prospects."

He looked at her a moment, as if about to speak. Then he stood abruptly and turned away. Gripping the pommel of his saddle, he leaned his head against his horse's neck.

She hugged her legs to her chest, making sure her skirt covered her feet. She laid her cheek against her knees, tired from all her crying, and marveled at the cool, self-possessed Lord Hamlin leaning against his horse as though for support. How could the two men even be brothers? She couldn't imagine Lord Rupert ever feeling so deeply sorry for anything. Would he ask forgiveness for arrogance? Would he care about a maiden's wounded sensibilities? Would he cry over a brother's lack of virtue?

It seemed so clear now. Lord Rupert was a self-seeking lout. He would have broken her heart a million times had he actually been man enough to give up prestige and power to marry her. With Lord Rupert as a husband, how many nights would she have cried herself to sleep? She had been caught up in the attention he showed her. She had to admit, it had made her feel good. He was handsome and he was desirable, in a worldly sort of way. And she had allowed herself to trust him. She'd even let him kiss her. Her stomach roiled at the remembrance.

*What a fool I am.*

But then, he had fooled Lord Hamlin too. But she was the biggest fool. She hadn't listened to Frau Geruscha, hadn't even listened to her own doubts.

The sun's light quickly faded, leaving them with only a slight glow in the sky. The tiny crescent moon wouldn't be much help, especially with clouds rolling in. Rose remembered hearing howls as a child, lying in bed at night in her father's cottage. She shuddered, imagining the wolves and bears emerging from their dens now, as night fell, to roam the forest.

Of course, she was safe with Lord Hamlin near. She glanced at the sword that hung from his belt.

She should get up and go back to town, before curfew began and they locked the city gates. Even now it might be too late to make it back. Lord Hamlin would have no problem convincing the guard to let him in, if indeed the gates were locked when they returned. But if she allowed him to walk her back and accompany her into the city after dark, people were sure to hear of it. What little of her reputation was still intact would be shredded before noon prayers.

What was it Lord Hamlin had said about her being virtuous and emanating God's love? She'd have to remember that when people were whispering that the brothers were sharing their trollop.

Determined to hurry home alone, Rose stood. Her head throbbed, as though all the blood in her body was pulsing through her brain, no doubt the product of all her crying. She'd missed supper too, after only eating a piece of bread for her midday meal. She'd been too excited about Lord Rupert's proposal to eat.

*Some proposal.*

She stood still, her eyes closed, waiting to see if the top of her head would shoot into the sky. When the pain subsided a little, she opened her eyes and found Lord Hamlin turning to look at her.

Blinking and ignoring the pain, she said, "Excuse me, Lord Hamlin, but I must get back before curfew."

"I'll take you back."

"I mean no offense, but I don't want to be seen sneaking in the city gate after dark with you. If indeed I still have a reputation, it would certainly be ruined."

He shook his head. "You won't make curfew anyway on foot."

"I might if I hurry." Rose raised her brows, hoping he would get the hint and end their conversation, which was costing her precious seconds.

The cathedral bells started to ring, announcing curfew. Her breath hissed out. She was too late. Yet again, tears sprang to her eyes, frustrating her further, and she crossed her arms. "Then I'll spend the night at my father's house in the forest. It isn't far from here."

He shook his head. "When was the last time you were there? Wild animals may have begun to sleep there. It isn't safe."

Rose hated his confident, firm tone. "I'll find a tree limb to bar the door."

"You can't, Rose." His voice softened, which only made the tears spill over. She stood with her arms still folded, knowing that if she reached up to wipe away the betraying drops he would know she was crying again. She wished he would look away, but he continued to watch her. She held her breath, trying to hold back the tears, but more spilled out and dripped to the ground.

Lord Hamlin took Shadow's reins and walked toward her. He pulled something from his pocket and held it out to her.

Rose took the handkerchief without looking up and wiped her face. *O God, haven't I been humiliated enough for one day?*

He took off his long black cloak. He wrapped the garment around her shoulders, pulling it down around her neck.

She instantly felt warmer—and relieved that her exposed shoulder was covered.

Lord Hamlin's masculine scent of leather and horses enveloped her along with the cloak. His nearness made her skin tingle. She longed to lay her head against his chest. If she only leaned toward him he might put his arms around her.

No, it was a selfish, imprudent thought. But at least it seemed to make the tears dry up.

She gazed up into Lord Hamlin's shadowed countenance. His dark eyes were beautiful and mysterious. What was he thinking, standing so close to her for so long? Finally, he spoke.

"I'll put you on Shadow so you won't have to walk."

"I don't think you should."

"Why not?"

Didn't he understand? "I don't want to be seen riding your horse through the town gate after curfew."

"You don't have to worry about that."

Rose looked at him doubtfully, trying to think of a clever, sarcastic reply.

"I have an alternate way of getting into the castle."

"Oh." Rose let this information sink in. Whatever this "alternate way" was, it had to be less public than the town gate. "Thank you, but I don't mind walking."

"I insist."

Rose only stared at him, trying to make out his expression in the dark.

"There's no reason both of us should walk. Come." He bent over, clasped his hands, and waited for her to place her foot in his makeshift stirrup.

"But you don't have a sidesaddle."

"It's dark. No one will see you. Merely throw your leg over."

"I can't do that." Rose was horrified at the thought. "Perhaps I can sit sideways and hook my right leg around the pommel."

"All right." He still stood patiently holding out his hands, reminding Rose of her first riding lesson with Lord Rupert—*that deceiver*. Rose had no trouble pushing his memory away with Lord Hamlin so near.

She placed her foot in his hand, praying she wouldn't fall. She grabbed the pommel and he boosted her up neatly into the saddle. Rose wrapped her leg, modestly covered by her skirt, around the pommel.

"Ready?"

"Yes, thank you."

She held on as he took the reins and led Shadow through the darkness and down the hill. She thought about all the things she would like to say to him. *Thank you for wanting to defend me. Thank you for thinking Rupert is a rogue. Thank you for being a man of integrity. Oh, Lord Hamlin, if you were mine, I'd make you so happy.*

Rose stifled a laugh at the stupid, outrageous thought.

As he led Shadow down the hill and into the quiet darkness of the trees between them and the castle, Wilhelm told himself to keep an eye out for wolves, but his mind was completely wrapped up in the maiden who so often made his heart ache. He smiled at how she had proposed to sleep in her father's empty house to keep from being seen with him. She didn't deserve the whispered judgments of the townspeople, who would have seen and heard of Lord Rupert's public attentions to her, and would soon notice the sudden cessation of those attentions, drawing the obvious conclusion—that he had used her and then cast her aside. His chest burned at the injustice of such a thing.

Bushes snatched at his legs as the vegetation thickened. He ignored them, glancing up at Rose. Her head and shoulders drooped. She must be tired. He had not asked her how her dress had gotten torn. While she'd claimed it was her doing, Rupert no doubt was at fault there as well. Anger bubbled up inside him so strong that he clenched his fist and silently promised his brother that he would pay for his boorish behavior.

They emerged from the trees into the meadow next to the castle. He ventured another quick look at Rose. He admired her spirit and intelligence, her compassion and character, but God help him, he also found her beautiful. When he'd seen the hurt on her face and her torn dress, then found out what Rupert had said to her, it almost ripped out his heart. He had assured himself that Rose and Rupert would marry, that all her needs would be taken care of, that she would have the protection of the Gerstenberg name. Now that wasn't possible. Who would marry her and take care of her?

*O God, let it be me.*

His chest ached with the fervor of his desire—and his impossible request.

Impossible. Impossible. Impossible. The word haunted his mind.

*For with God nothing shall be impossible.*

The Bible verse entered his thoughts, as though whispered to his spirit.

*Don't taunt me, God. You know I want to do the right thing. What do you mean, nothing is impossible?*

A slight breeze brushed his cheek and sifted through his hair, as though God's Spirit was brushing by him. He listened carefully, straining his ears, but no other words came to him.

They were close enough now to the castle wall that Wilhelm saw it looming in front of them in the moonlight. He led Shadow to the right, toward a small stand of trees that grew to within fifty feet of the city wall.

"I don't mean to be impertinent," Rose said, "but where are we going?"

"I'm going to show you something you must never reveal to another soul—not even Frau Geruscha, and especially not Hildy."

"Of course." A moment of silence passed. "Is it a secret entrance to the castle?"

The note of excitement in her voice made him smile. "Yes." They plunged into the trees nearest the wall. He frowned and muttered, "An ill-conceived secret entrance, begun by my irresponsible brother, allowed by my overindulgent father."

Wilhelm found the tree he was looking for, stood with his back against it, and took two paces forward. He bent to the ground, lifted a dead tree limb, and tossed it to the side. Then he felt around until he found the handle. He pulled it up, got his shoulder underneath the enormous wooden door, and flipped it all the way open.

"A tunnel?"

Rose had dismounted and was bending down to look into the gaping hole.

"Yes. Stay here for a moment." He jumped down into the hole and set up the wooden ramp that lay nearby, ready for service. Next he felt along the wall for the torch. The pair of flints that were supposed to be in the sconce alongside the torch were missing. Wilhelm winced and walked back up the ramp.

"No torch. But Shadow and I have gone through it in the dark before."

A band of moonlight filtered between the leaves overhead and shone on Rose's face, allowing him to see her look of apprehension.

"Or we can go around to the town gate and get the guard to let us in. Whatever you decide." He half-expected her to be outraged at his suggestion that she walk through the pitch-black tunnel, but apparently she was considering it.

"Are you afraid to walk through the tunnel?" she asked.

"No. I don't think any animals of significant size could have gotten inside."

"You don't think? Does that mean you're not sure?"

"I'm reasonably sure. But we can always go through the main gate."

"No, no, I can do this."

He grabbed Shadow's reins. "Wait here until I get Shadow in." He led the horse down the shallow ramp into the tunnel. Inside, the tunnel was only a little wider than the opening and just tall enough for a large horse. Shadow whinnied and snuffled his dislike of the earthen passageway as his hooves clomped on the wooden ramp.

"All right, boy, it's all right." He tried to make his voice soothing and low as he patted the horse's jaw.

He turned and looked over his shoulder. Rose started gingerly down the ramp.

"What do I do? Is there anything in here I might stumble over, any twists and turns I should know about?"

"There's a fork at which we'll have to go to the left." He turned his head. "But don't worry. It will help you keep your bearings if you put one hand on Shadow and your other hand on the wall as you walk."

He could only see her outline against the trees outside. With his big cloak draped around her shoulders, she looked small next to Shadow.

"I have to close the door." The tunnel was barely wide enough for two people, or one person and a horse. Wilhelm started to squeeze by her, and Rose moved back to let him pass, keeping one hand on Shadow's rump. His arm lightly brushed her shoulder when he passed. His heart skipped.

He climbed up the ramp and closed the trap door, blotting out what little light they had.

"Lord Hamlin?" came her voice in the dark.

"Yes?" Their arms brushed again.

"Can you keep talking?"

"Don't worry, I'm just ahead of you. Put your hand on the wall. Do you feel it?"

"Yes."

"We're starting to move."

He tugged lightly on Shadow's reins and the horse started forward.

# Chapter
# 21

*Blackness consumed her. Rose had never be-*fore experienced darkness so complete that she couldn't see her hand in front of her face. Mold and wet dirt invaded her nostrils, and she scrunched her face at the unpleasant odor. She kept one hand on the dirt wall and the other on Shadow's back, as Lord Hamlin instructed, willing her legs not to tremble. She didn't want to transfer her nervousness to the horse.

"Are you all right back there?"

"I'm not sure I've ever had so much fun."

"Who says I don't know how to have a good time?"

Rose imagined him smiling, his dark eyes sparkling in amusement. How she cherished the memory of the way he had looked at her earlier this evening, his features soft and his voice warm and kind.

*Why, God? Why couldn't you have given me Lord Hamlin?*

*Never mind. Don't answer that.*

A tiny drop of something cold plopped on top of Rose's head. *O Lord, let this tunnel not collapse on us.*

Just then, something cool and smooth slid across the top of her foot. Rose screamed. She covered her mouth, too late to stifle it.

"What is it?" Wilhelm said in the darkness ahead.

Shadow snorted and drummed his hooves on the dirt floor.

"Something slithered across my foot!" Rose shivered violently, afraid to move. She tried to find Shadow again with her hand, groping forward in the darkness, but grasped only air. She was alone in a dark hole. Her insides were a boiling mush.

"Probably a harmless garden snake. Stay there for a moment to give it time to get away." After a slight pause he said, "Reach out your hand to me."

Rose reached out and touched his fingers. He immediately covered her hand in a firm grasp. His warm fingers entwined with hers and made her heart beat erratically. The snake had nearly scared her to death, but his touch and his presence overwhelmed her with comfort and safety. The darkness gave her a feeling of intimacy with him. They could hold each other's hand and no one could see. She liked it—so very much.

She shouldn't allow herself the feeling that washed over her at being in this dark tunnel alone with him, clutching his hand. This whole adventure was simply a kindness, an act of chivalry on his part, taking her through the tunnel instead of making her walk with him through town after curfew. It was wrong—and slightly ridiculous—for her to enjoy it this much, her stomach going all warm and her heart beating a new, joyous beat.

"Here we are at the fork." His voice sounded gruff. "We have to veer to the left and we'll come out next to the stable. It's not much farther now."

Rose felt a little lightheaded. Her knees were still shaking as they had been ever since the snake wriggled across her foot.

Lord Hamlin led her to the left and the tunnel became a hill to climb.

"I thank you, Lord Hamlin." Rose's voice shook. She swallowed. "For being so kind as to take me this way."

"Of course."

Did he squeeze her hand, or did she imagine it?

"I would do much more for you, Rose. If you ever need anything, send for me."

Rose's heart skipped like a young calf. She wanted to remember every word of this conversation. Taking a deep breath, she was surrounded by his smell, which emanated from his cloak, still wrapped around her. She wished this moment might never end.

"I'm sorry I screamed and frightened Shadow."

"He's all right. I only regret that the snake had such bad manners."

A sliver of light came into view and she felt deflated that their journey was almost over. At the same time, after being engulfed in complete darkness, it was a relief to have somewhere to focus her eyes.

"We're here." Lord Hamlin loosened his grip on her hand and Rose let go. "As soon as I get these steps in place and raise the door, you can come out."

"Lead Shadow out first. It's amazing how well he behaves. He must trust you completely."

Her hand felt bereft and cold without his warmth, but it still tingled pleasantly. She resisted the urge to press it against her lips and cheek.

"Shadow's the best horse I know." Lord Hamlin worked to get the wooden steps in place, then walked halfway up and pushed open the trapdoor with his forearm and shoulder. The horse stepped carefully up and out of the dark, dank tunnel, snorting and nodding his head, obviously happy to be above ground again.

"Your turn." Lord Hamlin held out his hand from where he stood halfway up the steps.

"Thank you." Rose placed her hand in his. His grip was strong and confident as he led her up the steps and onto the grass.

The moon bathed them in its pale light as they stood facing each other.

He still held her hand in his. When he lifted his other hand toward her face, her heart stopped. She didn't move as he brushed her cheek with his fingertips, sending a pleasant tingling warmth through her.

"Dirt—from the tunnel."

"Oh." Rose reached up and rubbed the spot where his fingers had touched. Her hand shook.

His dark blue eyes shimmered strangely as he fixed her with an intense stare. "If there's ever anything you need, will you tell me?"

"Yes."

"You'd better go." Gruffness infused his voice again. "Frau Geruscha will be worried about you." But he continued to hold her hand.

She was enthralled with the look on his face and with the way he had come to her rescue tonight. She waited with a strange anticipation—for what, she didn't know. She wondered when he would let go of her hand and let her leave.

Instead of letting her go, he lifted her hand to his lips, his eyelids closing, and slowly kissed the backs of her fingers. She held her breath at the rush of pleasure his lips created as they brushed softly over her skin. A tiny sigh escaped her.

*I shouldn't let him do this.*

"Good night." She could barely squeeze the words past the knot in her throat.

He released her hand.

Rose swayed ever so slightly, feeling cold and shaky. She forced her legs to hold her up and her eyes not to look at him. She clutched his cloak under her chin and walked toward the tower and Frau Geruscha's chambers.

Once inside, she leaned against the door and pulled the cloak higher, burying her face in the lining and breathing deeply. *Forgive me, God. Only let me have this one pleasure.* And she took another deep breath, letting Lord Hamlin's manly, leather-and-horses smell envelop her in a sweet cocoon of warmth, before she took it off and hung it by the door.

She stared at it. No, she would not take it to her room. She would leave it right there.

Wilhelm watched her go, his heart aching. His conscience smote him for kissing her fingers, as well as for the thoughts he'd just entertained. *God, forgive me.*

So much for his promise to never touch her again.

How he had wanted to forget who he was for one moment, forget his duty and everything else, to pull her into his arms and kiss her with every ounce of his passion.

He rubbed the back of his hand across his brow, wiping the sweat that had beaded there. Then he remembered Shadow and grabbed his reins, leading him toward the stable.

His thoughts turned to Rupert as he systematically unsaddled his faithful horse, brushed him down, and forked some fresh hay into the stall. When he finished, he hastened into the castle, hoping to find his brother still at supper in the Great Hall.

The servants were cleaning up when he entered and reported that Rupert had left a few minutes earlier, taking a full tankard of wine with him.

Wilhelm stalked down the corridor in search of Rupert. He met him coming from the direction of the privy. Striding up to him, Wilhelm drew his fist back and landed a clean blow to Rupert's jaw.

Rupert reeled, and after two wobbly backward steps, hit the floor on his backside. He raised a hand to his face.

"Feel better?"

"No. Get up so I can hit you again."

"I think I've had enough, thank you." Rupert flexed his jaw, dabbing his bloody lip with the back of his hand.

Wilhelm stared down at him with a burning urge to expend a lot more energy on his brother than one single blow. His fists were tight and ready, but his louse of a brother seemed unwilling to get off the floor.

*Fine. Stay there.* He spun on his heel and strode down the hall. He went inside his bedchamber and closed the door.

# Chapter
## 22

*"Rose? What's wrong?"*

Three weeks had passed since Lord Rupert's odious proposal. Rose knew she'd been quieter than normal, and Frau Geruscha had to have noticed that he wasn't visiting her anymore. Her mistress hadn't questioned her about it, and Rose had tried not to raise her suspicions that something was wrong. Obviously, she was failing.

Rose shook her head. "Nothing."

But Frau Geruscha's brows lowered even more, telling her she didn't believe her.

"It's probably the weather, so cloudy of late . . ." Rose stopped, not wishing to tell a lie. How could she explain that her future looked as bleak as it ever had? Even bleaker, now that the whole region thought of her as the spurned former mistress of Lord Rupert. At least Lord Hamlin knew the truth. But she tried hard not to think about Lord Hamlin—and failed constantly.

Rose shrugged and turned to throw some more wood on the fire. She tried again. "Hildy rarely visits me anymore." Gunther had been given the job as the duke's illuminator that he'd been promised, his murder sentence having been forgiven and forgotten, apparently. "She spends her time making sure the house and meals are perfect for him. As she should."

Now she sounded self-pitying. Rose grabbed the fire poker and viciously jabbed it into the red hot embers in the fireplace, sending up a torrent of sparks.

Frau Geruscha stepped closer. She placed her hand on Rose's shoulder. "Some day you'll be married too."

Rose whirled around, dislodging her mistress's hand. The surprised look on Frau Geruscha's face only increased Rose's wrung-out feeling. "How can you say that? How do you know? No one would marry me. I'm your apprentice. Who wants to marry the next town healer?"

Why had she said that?

"I'm sorry. Please forgive me." Thank goodness Frau Geruscha didn't seem offended. "I suppose I'm only dreading winter. People get sick and die when it starts to get cold." The thought of winter was a heavy weight in her chest. Winter meant sickness and death, bad smells, groans, and the tolling of cathedral bells for someone else who had succumbed to cold weather's cruelty. She would be by Frau Geruscha's side, witnessing the diseases that would steal the life from the human victims of Hagenheim. Always she and the rest of the world feared the Great Pestilence that had decimated towns and countryside alike a few years before Rose was born. Hardly a family had been spared, and only God knew how many would die if it came again. A milder outbreak had happened when Rose was a child. She shuddered, remembering the hideous black buboes under the sick people's arms—the sign that death was imminent.

Rose's stomach twisted at being only a whisper away from admitting . . . she wasn't sure she would ever be a good healer.

"I pray I will become like you, Frau Geruscha."

"You don't have to be like me, Rose. God makes us all different, with our own talents."

"Then what's my talent?" *I don't have one.* Rose bit her lip. Why couldn't she just be quiet? The last thing she wanted was for her mistress to send her away.

"You have many talents. I know winter can be hard, especially when people die, but God will bring our town through another year. He always does."

Frau Geruscha was mature and unaffected by her own pity for the victims. Rose wanted to believe she could shrug off the deaths she would face this winter, but she dreaded her own compassion, the way it tightened around her insides like a giant hand, squeezing and paralyzing her.

Her mistress patted her on the back. "You'll feel better when you have more confidence in your abilities."

Rose tried to smile back. She nodded, hoping Frau Geruscha would believe she had been placated. Then Rose went into the storeroom to sort some dried herbs. Anything to keep busy.

It wasn't only winter and her lack of confidence that had been weighing on Rose, of course. Lord Hamlin's wedding was coming soon, just before Christmas, to Lady Salomea. What was she like? Was she warm or haughty? Kind or ruthless? Would their personalities be well-suited to each other, or would she make him miserable? Lord Hamlin would have to marry her no matter what she was like. It was his duty, and he would never shirk it. The people of the region respected him for that, even were dependent on it. After all, the marriage would go far toward assuring their safety.

Now instead of seeing Lord Rupert nearly every morning in the chapel at prime, she saw Lord Hamlin. She found herself living for the sight of him, packing all her memories of him carefully away to be revisited later. He knelt near the altar at the front of the chapel, the stained-glass window painting him in reds and blues and golden yellows. Often she stayed after everyone had left to ask forgiveness for having her attention on Lord Hamlin rather than the Lord of heaven.

The first weeks of autumn came and went. In spite of himself, Wilhelm looked forward every morning to going to the chapel for morning prayers. While Rupert had started attending devotions and mass at the town cathedral — whether to avoid Rose and his brother or to be near his future "flock," he wasn't sure — Wilhelm nearly always saw Rose at the chapel, kneeling near the back.

Most days he barely caught a glimpse of her, as he entered the chapel through the second-story entrance, directly from the castle. But sometimes he exited through the main door. When he did, he always searched for her. He would nod and smile just to see her smile in return. He often asked God to take away his love for her. But a part of him still believed in the message he had heard in the woods the night he took Rose through the tunnel. Hope had taken hold of his heart, hope that God would make a way for them to be together.

"I'm a silly, insipid, pathetic creature," Rose told Hildy. They were alone in Frau Geruscha's chamber, the frau having become less vigilant since Lord Rupert stopped coming to see her. "I can't get Lord Hamlin out of my mind. It sounds ridiculous, but I see us together in my dreams. I know it could never be. He's a man of honor and would never break his betrothal."

"Well, he is handsome. You can hardly help looking at him, and he isn't married yet."

"You want to know what I sometimes think about doing?" Rose rested her cheek against the cold, hard window casing. "Sometimes I wish I could run away with the Meistersingers and travel all over, singing. I'm sure they need someone who can write stories, and I could start writing songs too, and they would let me join them."

"Oh, Rose, you wouldn't truly do that, would you?" Hildy's face fell and she grabbed Rose's hand.

"Why not? I suppose Frau Geruscha would disapprove."

"What about your parents?"

Rose took a deep breath. She might as well tell someone. Hildy's shock would assuage some of her pain. "Two months ago I found out that Thomas and Enid Roemer are not my mother and father."

"What do you mean?" Hildy's eyes opened wide.

"They took me in when I was a baby. My father says he doesn't know who my parents were. He won't tell me the whole story, how I came to live with them. He said that he and my mother thought she was barren."

A slow smile spread over Hildy's face and her eyes brightened. "Rose, that's amazing. You know what I'm about to say, don't you?"

"Yes, I'm afraid so." Rose frowned.

"You could be Lord Hamlin's betrothed!"

"No, Hildy, I couldn't. His betrothed turns nineteen — *nineteen* — two weeks before Christmas. I will only be eighteen five weeks before Christmas. You know that."

Hildy sat musing, leaning her head on her hand. "I still think it's possible."

"Besides, what duke would leave his daughter to be raised by a woodcutter?"

"What's wrong with a woodcutter, Rose? Thomas Roemer is a good man."

"I know, but why would the duke leave his daughter with a stranger in another region and never make contact with her?"

"Because of the evil conjurer Moncore. To keep you safe from him."

"Oh, please, Hildy. Don't let crazy ideas in your head. It's simply impossible."

The cold autumn wind puffed down the chimney and into the fireplace, threatening to extinguish the fire Rose was trying to feed with more wood. She carefully placed small limbs over the flame until they caught and burned higher, then put down the poker and rubbed her hands.

The door banged open. A man and woman rushed in, carrying a small child about three years old. The child was flushed with fever. The parents — a baker and his wife — described a convulsion the child had suffered on their way to Frau Geruscha's chambers. Her pale blonde curls clung to her temples.

Rose drew some cold water from the well and dipped a cloth in it to wipe the little girl's face and neck. She was unconscious, but the mother had been able to make out the child's complaints earlier in the day. Her head and neck hurt.

For two days Rose and Frau Geruscha tended to the child, who made little murmurs in her sleep. Frau Geruscha stayed up with her that first night.

Rose stayed beside her the second night to let Frau Geruscha rest. She wiped down the child's small body many times and did her best to pour feverfew tea into her mouth. The child whimpered a few times but didn't open her eyes.

The next morning Rose spoke soothingly to her. "Sleep and get well. Your mother will be here to see you any moment now."

Rose gently squeezed the child's hand, but it was cold, much colder than it should have been. She held her breath as she watched the child's chest, praying to see it rise and fall. But there was no perceptible movement.

A tentacle of fear tightened around her. "O God, please don't let her be dead." She put her ear close to the child's mouth, desperately hoping to feel her breath on her cheek, but there was nothing. She touched her hand again, but it felt even colder and was growing stiff.

The door opened and someone walked in. Rose turned to face the mother and watched the woman's features crumple as she read Rose's expression. She flew to the child's side and picked her up, holding her against her chest and cradling her head.

The father stood near the door, motionless. "Our only comfort," he said quietly, his face stony, "is that the priest spoke the sacred rites over her yesterday."

Rose began to shake all over. She turned and walked up to her room, passing Frau Geruscha on the stairs. Rose didn't say a word, simply closed the door to her room and sank to the floor by the bed.

*Why? I prayed for her, Frau Geruscha prayed for her. I didn't want her to die. Why, God? Did you do it so that she wouldn't have to endure future hardships and pain? I don't understand.*

Rose stayed in her room all day and night and refused to eat what Frau Geruscha brought her. The next morning she came down and told Frau Geruscha, "I've decided to join the Meistersingers."

Frau Geruscha merely stared. Finally, she said, "Come, let's go eat something."

Rose ate a hearty meal of eggs, fried pork, and bread.

When they returned to Frau Geruscha's chambers, Rose stopped her just inside the door. "So you don't object to me joining the Meistersingers? They'll be here at Christmas. I plan to ask to join them then."

Frau Geruscha's top lip twitched. "Rose, that's no life for a respectable maiden like you. You'll see. God's plan for you isn't traveling the countryside with vagabonds."

"They're not vagabonds." Anger crept into Rose's voice, and she suddenly knew how a caged animal felt. Words and feelings expanded inside her, determined to find release. "You don't understand. I can't stay here, Frau Geruscha. I can't. I can't stand another winter of sickness and death. I'm not like you. I'm no good at helping people. I hate the sight of blood, I get sick when I see it gushing out of people's heads or oozing from some gashed-up body part. I asked God to change me, but he didn't. I can't do it. If I stay here another year I'll either die or go insane." Tears streamed down her face and sobs shook her. She covered her face with her hands.

Frau Geruscha's arms wrapped around Rose and she patted her on the back. "Now, now, everything will be well, my dear."

"Everything won't be well." Rose pulled out of her embrace and faced her. "I'm not like you. I'll never be able to do this."

"You're just upset. Come and sit down." Frau Geruscha took her arm and led her to a chair. "Now listen to me, Rose."

Rose struggled to control her sobbing.

"I want to suggest something. You think you want to meet up with the Meistersingers in a few weeks when they come to perform for Christmas. Well, you shall."

Rose wiped her face with her apron.

"When they come, I'll arrange it. You can talk to them and decide if that's what you want to do. Can you wait that long, Rose?"

Rose nodded. Only two and a half more months. Since Lord Hamlin's betrothed was supposed to come out of hiding and be presented to him and his family two weeks before Christmas, she wouldn't be able to avoid that dreaded event. But as long as she knew she would soon be getting away—away from him and his wedded bliss, and away from sickness, blood, and death—she could stand it. But for today, she didn't want to stay around Frau Geruscha's chambers, sensing her pity, and even amusement, at her wanting to run away with the Meistersingers.

"Can I take Wolfie and go for a walk?"

Frau Geruscha hesitated. "I don't think you should."

Rose felt her composure crumbling again.

Frau Geruscha must have seen her distress, because she quickly added, "It isn't safe for you, since they haven't captured Peter Brunckhorst yet, and Lord Hamlin is still searching for Moncore, who may be nearby." Now Frau Geruscha looked distressed.

"Wolfie will keep me safe. You know he would never let anyone hurt me. And I promise not to be gone long."

Frau Geruscha didn't say anything for a long moment. Finally she sighed. "All right. You may go. But don't wander far and be back before nones."

"Thank you." Rose wiped her nose, feeling some measure of hope. She longed to fill her lungs with fresh air. That would make her feel even better.

Wolfie followed her out the door. It was the warmest day they'd had since early September. She hastened through the castle gatehouse and down the street to the town gate. She drew in a deep breath of crisp autumn air then sighed in relief at being alone in the open meadow, heading for the woods and the stream.

Her head was starting to ache, probably because of her fit of crying. The thought of splashing some water from the stream on her face made her quicken her pace.

By the time Rose topped the hill, her headache was worse and her neck had begun to feel stiff and sore. Should she turn back? First she would make it to the stream for a drink. Wolfie bounded far ahead of her. She lost sight of him before she entered the forest.

She sank to her knees by the stream bank and dipped her hand in, drawing the water to her lips. When she swayed and nearly fell face first into the trickling brook, she sat back on her heels, rubbing her forehead with her wet hand.

Something was wrong.

"Wolfie!" she called. She slowly got to her feet. Her head ached worse than ever, and she put her hands against her temples. When she tried to turn her head to look for the dog, she gasped in pain.

Confusion threw a fog over her thoughts as she turned in a circle. Was she looking for Wolfie? She couldn't remember. She wanted to go home but wasn't sure if she lived in town or in the forest.

Wolfie broke through the underbrush and tromped toward her.

"Wolfie, we have to go home." Rose started off through the trees. She stretched her arms out in her effort to not look down or move her head.

Soon she came to the small clearing where her parents' cottage stood. The door hung open. She wandered inside. Perhaps her mother had some soup she could sip. Her throat was feeling sore.

"Mama?"

She looked around. No one was there. Leaves swirled around the dirt floor, and no fire burned.

"Mama? Agathe? Dorothye?" Where was everyone? Where was her bed? It wasn't very cold today but still, there should have been a cook fire.

A vague memory stirred in her foggy mind, of a castle, and of a house in town. *O God, there's something wrong with my head. I can't think.* She sank down on the dirt floor. Unable to hold up her head another minute, she lay full length, moaning at the pain in her neck.

Wolfie licked her cheek. Rose weakly brushed him away. The dog stretched out beside her, whimpering in his high-pitched dog's voice.

"It's all right, Wolfie. I'll lie here until I feel better."

Rose shut her eyes and darkness closed over her.

Wilhelm stared out the window of the Great Hall that faced the court-yard. The sky had been darkening all afternoon. Though the morning had been warm, a frigid wind had moved in around noon, bringing colder air and even freezing rain. Ice now covered the ground, turning it silver. He didn't envy anyone caught out in this weather.

"Lord Hamlin."

He turned and was surprised to see Frau Geruscha hurrying toward him. Her forehead was creased with anxiety and desperation shaded her eyes.

"Yes, Frau Geruscha?"

"It's Rose."

His body tensed as he waited for her to catch her breath.

"I don't know where she is. She left this morning to go for a walk and hasn't returned."

Fear stabbed his heart. His gaze darted to the window. "Do you have any idea where she might be?"

"No." Frau Geruscha clasped her hands together. "And now it's sleeting. I sent a messenger to her parents' home, but they haven't seen her. I'm so worried. She was upset this morning, but I don't think she would run away. You don't suppose Peter Brunckhorst—or Moncore …?"

"I'll find her." He spun around and barked to a servant, "Get Christoff and Georg. Bring them to the stable and tell them to wait for me." He turned back to Geruscha. The fear in her eyes sent a wave of blood pulsing through his body. "I have an idea where to look. If she isn't there, I'll come back for my knights and we'll search for her until we find her."

He took time only to grab two woolen cloaks then ran to the stable.

Instead of waiting for the stable boy to help him saddle Shadow, he grabbed the gear himself and readied his horse to ride. He threw one of the cloaks around his shoulders and tucked the other one under his arm. Swinging himself into the saddle, he set out, urging Shadow into his fastest gallop. He prayed for protection for Shadow's legs. *Don't let him slip on the ice.*

His heart pounded in rhythm with the horse's hooves. *O God, please help me find her. Please keep her safe. Show me where to look.* If Peter Brunckhorst or Moncore had her … He couldn't let himself think about that yet. He had a feeling he knew where she was, almost as if God had whispered it in his ear.

The icy rain pelted his face and hands like a thousand tiny pinpricks. His body heat warmed the extra cloak that was tucked against his side. He hoped he would soon be able to wrap it around Rose.

He guided Shadow first toward Rose's tree on the hill, then to her favored spot in the woods beside the waterfall. Not seeing her at either of those places, he began searching for her father's old house. He had to find it soon, before night fell and it grew even darker.

He pushed Shadow down the narrow path that he believed led to the woodcutter's cottage. Shadow responded nimbly to his commands as Wilhelm guided him off the path time and again, searching the woods for the cottage. It was so dark in the dense forest, with the thick clouds darkening the sky, he couldn't see far. "God, help me!" Wilhelm cried out. Every moment counted. With the fading light, the evening air grew colder and colder. If Rose did happen to be in the little cottage, she would be freezing by now. "God, help me find it!"

Wolfie's warning bark and growls came to him from his right. He turned Shadow toward the sound. Soon he spotted the dark square of the house. "Thank you, God." He leapt off Shadow's back. *Hold on, Rose. I'm coming.*

# Chapter
## 23

*"It's me, Wolfie. That's a good boy."*

The dog stood in the open doorway. Wilhelm slowed his steps and held out his hand to him, waiting for him to catch his scent and remember that he was a friend. The dog sniffed and then whimpered, moving aside. Wilhelm strode quickly into the house.

"Rose?" A dark form lay on the floor. He crossed the floor and dropped to his knees beside her.

"Thirsty."

Rose was lying on her side. Wilhelm laid his hand on her forehead. Burning hot.

She shivered. He whipped out the woolen cloak he'd kept against his side and spread it over her. "Everything is all right. I'm here."

He jumped up and whirled around, searching for something that would hold water. Spotting a metal dipper with a broken handle on a shelf, he grabbed it and ran outside to the stream behind the house. He dipped it into the icy water and hastened back inside.

Wilhelm sat on the floor beside her and slipped his arm underneath her. He lifted her head and shoulders and propped her against his chest. She grimaced, but still didn't open her eyes. "Drink this." He placed the cup to her lips.

Some water dribbled down her chin then she parted her lips and drank. She opened her eyes and looked at him.

"Rose. I'm here. I'm taking you home." He smoothed back the strand of hair that had fallen across her cheek. "Drink some more." He held the cup to her lips again.

"Thank you."

Her voice was raspy and weak, but it gave him hope.

"I don't think I can walk," she said.

"No, you don't have to walk."

Wilhelm pulled the hood of the cloak over her head and lifted her into his arms. She moaned.

"Are you in pain? Where?"

Her eyes were closed as she spoke. "My neck. But I think I'm merely tired." Her voice trailed off.

Wilhelm carried her outside where Shadow stood waiting. He lifted Rose's limp body and held her in the saddle while he mounted up behind her. He opened his cloak and pulled her against him, wrapping the material around her, protecting her from the rain and sleet that was still falling. Her head lay against his chest, just below his chin. He pulled her hood low over her face, seized the reins, and urged Shadow forward.

Rose moaned and Wilhelm slowed Shadow's pace. He pressed his lips against the top of her head. "Everything's all right now. I'm taking you home." The heat of her feverish cheek burned through his clothing.

*God, heal her. Don't let her die.* The words of his prayer repeated over and over to the rhythm of Shadow's hooves.

Her body shuddered and she snuggled closer to him. She placed one hand against his chest and slipped her other hand around to his back. She mumbled something, but he couldn't make out the words.

His temples pounded with his urgency to get Rose to Frau Geruscha. But he tried not to let Shadow move at too quick a pace. Finally, after making Shadow walk the whole way to keep from causing her pain, they neared the town gate. The guard recognized Wilhelm and let them in. He guided Shadow toward the southwest tower of the castle.

"We're here, Rose. I have you." He slid off the horse, pulling her off after him while supporting her head and neck. He cradled her in his arms as he carried her into Frau Geruscha's chamber.

"You found her!" Frau Geruscha hurried toward them. Her relieved tone and expression immediately turned to alarm. "Is she hurt?"

"She's burning up with fever." Wilhelm lowered her carefully onto the bed and she moaned again, her face scrunching up in pain. "Her neck hurts and she's confused."

Wilhelm watched the color drain from Frau Geruscha's face.

"What? What is it?" Wilhelm demanded.

She didn't say anything.

"Tell me." Wilhelm took a step toward her.

"She must have what the baker's daughter had."

"The baker's daughter? What happened to her?"

Frau Geruscha would not look up. "She died."

Wilhelm's heart stopped.

"But that doesn't mean ... Rose is older and stronger."

Wilhelm fixed his eyes on Frau Geruscha. "Pray for her. Now."

She knelt by the bed and Wilhelm fell to his knees beside her and made the sign of the cross. Frau Geruscha placed her hands on Rose, one on her shoulder, the other on her head. Wilhelm laid his hands on her lower leg.

Her quiet voice began, "Merciful God, heal your child, Rose. Make her well. Take away her fever and her pain. In the name of Jesus."

Wilhelm stared at Rose's face. Frau Geruscha stood. He took her place, kneeling beside Rose, and touched her forehead. Just as hot as before. A shard of disappointment pierced his chest. He lifted her hand. It was ice cold and he rubbed it with both hands, trying to restore the warmth. "Rose? Rose, can you hear me?"

Rose's eyelids flickered open and her feverish eyes focused on Wilhelm's face.

"Get well," he whispered.

Rose swallowed and a little smile tugged at the corners of her mouth. "I love you." And she closed her eyes again.

Wilhelm stared, his breath caught in his chest.

"I need you to go now, Lord Hamlin." Frau Geruscha touched his shoulder.

Still dazed by Rose's statement, Wilhelm stood. He laid Rose's hand gently by her side on the bed and looked at Frau Geruscha. "Let me stay. I can help. Let me do something."

Frau Geruscha shook her head. "You shouldn't be here. Do you want to get sick too?"

He couldn't keep his eyes off Rose. Her chestnut hair splayed around her head, her cheeks glowed red with fever, and her black lashes feathered against her skin.

*She loves me.*

Frau Geruscha tried pushing him toward the door, but he didn't budge. "Here." She bent over to pick up a water bucket. "Take this. Find a servant boy to get me some water from the well. I need cold water to bathe her, to get the fever down. Then get someone to guard my door. I don't want anyone coming in this room and spreading this sickness."

He stood staring at her. How could she be so calm?

"Pray. That's what she needs from you."

Wilhelm grabbed the bucket and strode out the door. He quickly filled it and brought it back. He watched as Frau Geruscha dipped a cloth into the icy cold water and wiped Rose's face.

"Please go now." Frau Geruscha didn't look at him.

He turned and stumbled back outside, slumping against the closed door. He was glad for the darkness of night and the freezing rain which kept everyone else inside. He was cold and wet, but somehow he barely felt it. He kept remembering Rose snuggled against his chest, the feel of her body in his arms. He closed his eyes as he recalled the way she had looked at him, the way she said "*I love you*."

Oh, he knew she was sick and delirious or she wouldn't have said it, but he also knew it was true. There had always been something between them. They understood each other. She needed him. She loved him.

*O God. I can't bear to lose her. Please let her live.*

But if she did live, he would lose her anyway, when he married his betrothed.

Wilhelm clutched his chest, at the pain inside his heart. He turned his feet toward the chapel. *I can't lose her, God. There has to be a way.*

Rose slipped in and out of the darkness. Sometimes she fought to open her eyes and understand what was happening. Other times she simply prayed for relief from the pain and feverish discomfort.

She was finally able to open her eyes enough to see the faint light of morning peeking in the window on the other side of the room. She blinked, trying to remember how she had gotten back to Frau Geruscha's chamber after falling asleep in the old cottage in the forest.

A knock sounded at the door, reverberating in her head. She closed her eyes again, hearing Frau Geruscha's soft footsteps scurrying across the floor. Then voices. One of them sounded like Lord Hamlin. She wanted to concentrate, to comprehend what they were saying, but she felt her hold on consciousness slipping away. The darkness closed her off from the world again.

"Is she better?" Wilhelm tried to look around Frau Geruscha into the room, and he caught a glimpse of Rose, lying where he had laid her the night before.

Frau Geruscha stood in the doorway and shook her head. "No."

Wilhelm's arms went weak at the anxious look on her face and the bags under her bloodshot eyes. He forced the air back into his lungs. "She's not worse, is she?"

"The same. Please keep praying."

"Isn't there anything else I can do?"

"Thank you, but no. I'll send for you if she gets worse." Tears welled up in her eyes and she closed the door.

"God, save her." He pressed his fist against the door. "Don't let her die."

Rose awoke and opened her eyes. Now the sun shone much brighter through the window. She tried to swallow, but her throat was dry. "Frau Geruscha," she rasped.

In a moment her mistress was by her side. "What is it, child?"

"May I have some water?"

"Of course." She went away and came back with a cup. She held Rose up with her arm.

Rose drank two gulps and lay back. Her head was spinning and she wondered if the water was about to come back up.

"Are you feeling better?"

"A little." She tried to stay awake, but already her hold on reality was slipping away.

"Rose?"

She tried to respond, but her mouth wouldn't obey her. Her heavy eyelids closed and she saw and heard no more.

How much time had passed while she slept? She looked around the room. Frau Geruscha was putting another log on the fire. Rose sighed, feeling a bit less feverish, hoping the worst of her sickness was gone. She studied the sunlight coming through the window. What time of day was it?

"Rose?" Frau Geruscha turned. "You're awake, child." She hurried to her with a cup of water. "Drink."

Rose propped herself up on her elbow and drank the water. She lay back down, feeling exhausted merely from that slight exertion. Again she tried to remember something about how she had gotten back to Frau Geruscha's chambers. She had a faint memory of being on a horse.

"Rose? How do you feel?" Frau Geruscha laid her hand on her forehead. "Oh, thank God! The Lord of heaven be praised, you feel much cooler."

"I think I'm better. I feel better." Rose closed her eyes, wanting to pursue the memory of what had happened to her the first day of her sickness. Slipping back to the darkness and pain of that evening, she smelled a familiar, masculine scent with a hint of leather—Lord Hamlin.

She was on the floor of her father's old cottage. Lord Hamlin held a cup of water to her lips. She felt his arms around her, lifting her up, holding her against his chest. His velvet doublet was soft against her cheek, and his voice was soothing and low. "I'm here. I'm taking you home." He held her on his horse all the way here, then carried her in and laid her on the bed.

Her heart began to beat faster, compounding her lightheadedness. Had that truly happened? Or was it a product of her sickness, along with the other hazy, delirious thoughts she'd been having?

"Frau Geruscha, how did I get back here?"

Frau Geruscha simply smiled.

"Did Lord Hamlin bring me back?"

"I told him you were missing. You were gone all day. He went looking for you and brought you home." Frau Geruscha averted her eyes.

Rose suddenly remembered something that made her cheeks burn. She swallowed. "I didn't—I mean, did I ... say something embarrassing to Lord Hamlin?"

"Embarrassing?"

Rose couldn't bring herself to repeat the words. "Did I say anything after he brought me in?"

"Oh, well, you may have said something. You were sick, out of your head." Frau Geruscha smiled and turned away again, as though trying to hide her amusement.

Rose closed her eyes in mortification. *What must he think of me?*

Frau Geruscha kept her back to Rose, tending the fire.

Even through the horror of her realization, Rose was baffled that Frau Geruscha had smiled. Would she smile about Rose saying she loved Lord Rupert? No, she would scowl and scold. It was probably because Frau Geruscha believed Lord Hamlin incapable of improper behavior toward her. Wouldn't she be shocked if she had seen the way Lord Hamlin had kissed her hand the night he brought her through the tunnel.

*Oh, how could I have said I loved him? I'm forever humiliating myself.* She covered her face with her hands.

"Now don't be upsetting yourself. You need to rest and get well. I'll be back." Frau Geruscha took down her cloak from a hook beside the door.

"Where are you going?"

"I want to let Lord Hamlin know you're better. He was anxious for you."

A rush of cold air blew in before she closed the door behind her.

He was anxious for her. Exhausted, Rose closed her eyes and tried to steady her breathing. But she couldn't help wondering what the repercussions would be to her stupidly declaring her love for a betrothed man.

Someone knocked at the door. After two days of improvement, Frau Geruscha had just sent word to Lord Hamlin that he could come and visit. But Rose hadn't expected him to come so ... immediately.

Frau Geruscha hurried to open the door, and Lord Hamlin stepped in.

How could she look him in the eye after what she had said? Rose blushed and glanced down at the blanket covering her.

She couldn't help but take a peek. He was so handsome, with his unruly black hair curling against his neck and over his forehead. The memory of him holding her in his arms a few days ago had become more vivid as the sickness continued to subside. She could still feel his rock-hard arms, his broad chest, remember him comforting and assuring her that he would take care of her. Her heart skipped around like a scared rabbit.

*O God, please let me not act like a lovesick fool.*

Lord Hamlin looked serious as he pulled a chair up beside her. "I'm so happy you're getting well."

"Thank you. Frau Geruscha said you brought me back from my ill-fated walk." *Maybe if I pretend I don't remember anything* … "I am grateful to you."

"I'm thankful to God that he led me to you." His voice was low and thick. "I don't believe you would have survived the night in the cold."

Rose fidgeted with the edge of her blanket, rolling it between her fingers. *Where is Frau Geruscha?* Lord Rupert comes and she hovers. Lord Hamlin comes and she disappears.

A muscle in Lord Hamlin's jaw jumped, and he looked away. He stood and walked to the window and stared out, rubbing his palms on his thighs. Then he came back and sat down beside her.

Why did he seem so agitated? Rose thought of her declaration and felt her cheeks flush again.

"I suppose you'll be fully recovered in a few days."

"Yes, if God wills it."

"I should go. But I'm happy to see you're better."

"Thank you."

He turned and put his cloak back on, nodding to her as he left.

He'd had so little to say, yet he'd been so anxious to see her. Such odd behavior, as if he was as nervous about seeing her again as she was about seeing him.

A week later, Frau Geruscha was summoned to Duke Nicolaus's bed-chamber. He was sick with fever and a bad cough. Rose was glad Frau Geruscha didn't ask her to go. The duke could pierce a person through with one look from underneath his bushy black eyebrows, as she well knew. But Frau Geruscha had insisted more than once that he was a good man.

Frau Geruscha gave him herbs for his cough and fever, but by the next day he was worse. He was having chest pain and chills and couldn't seem to catch his breath. Frau Geruscha came back from her visit to him with worry lines creasing her forehead.

Wilhelm prayed, attending the chapel prayers every three hours, but still his father worsened. He knelt before the altar as the howling winter wind rattled the windows. Winter was a cursed time of sickness and death. Every year at least one household servant, or someone who worked within the confines of the castle courtyard, died because of the unyielding breath of winter.

*God, unless you give us a miracle, my father will die. Please save him.* But perhaps he had no right to ask God to save his father too, after He had saved Rose.

He stood, bowed, and crossed himself, then left the chapel to visit his father.

When he reached the duke's chamber, his mother was standing beside his bed crying. She looked up and said, "Run fetch the priest. Make haste."

Wilhelm ran out into the hall. He found Georg and Christoff and sent them to get the priest. He sent a servant to summon Osanna and Rupert then waited with his mother. They watched helplessly as his father drew one weak, shuddering breath after another, obviously unconscious. The chapel priest arrived, with Osanna and Rupert on his heels. As soon as last rites were recited, his father breathed his last, one week after he had taken ill.

Wilhelm numbly put his arms around his mother and sister while they cried on his shoulders.

He was now the duke and ruling prince of Hagenheim.

# Chapter
## 24

*Rose stood beside Frau Geruscha and* watched the coffin pass through the castle courtyard. The cart carrying Duke Nicolaus's body was flanked by six knights as it made its way to the Hagenheim cathedral for the funeral. Following behind on foot came Duchess Katheryn, Lady Osanna, Lord Rupert, and Lord Hamlin, although he was no longer Lord Hamlin. Now she would have to call him "Your Grace." If she ever had occasion to speak to him again.

A veil covered the duchess's face, but Rose could still see her expression, stoic but drawn and sad.

Lady Osanna slipped her hand underneath her veil and wiped her eyes. Lord Rupert looked meek and quiet for once, his hands clasped in front of him. But Rose only had a glance for them. Her focus was on Lord Hamlin — or Duke Wilhelm, as he would now be known, the region's new leader.

Her heart ached with compassion for him. He held his shoulders up and his head high, but Rose saw the weight of responsibility and grief in his eyes. She longed to throw her arms around him and comfort him. But she could never do that, especially now.

He looked up and caught her eye. Rose's heart went out to him. She did her best to make her eyes convey that she was sorry, sorry for the burden of grief she knew he was carrying. He gave her a lopsided smile as he passed.

Frau Geruscha put her arm around her shoulders as she quietly wept. She was ashamed to realize that she wasn't only weeping for Wilhelm, his father, or the rest of his family. She was a seventeen-year-old who didn't belong anywhere, to anyone. In a few weeks she would lose the man she loved to another woman. And she was a failure at the only job she had ever tried to do.

"Rupert, I need to speak to you alone." Wilhelm looked at him from beneath lowered eyelids, daring him to refuse.

Rupert's lip curled. "Whatever you say, Your Grace."

Wilhelm led the way into the library and shut the door behind them. He turned to face Rupert. "Father had not yet signed the proclamation making you the bishop of Hagenheim. You will not be bishop. I'm bestowing the position on the cathedral priest." He crossed his arms.

"I see."

"But I have a proposition for you." Wilhelm said a quick prayer and let his arms fall to his sides. "I want to marry Rose."

Rupert blinked.

"I propose that the two of us change places. I will abdicate all my rights as the oldest son to you. You will be duke, and Duke Godehard's daughter, Lady Salomea, will then be betrothed to you. I will inherit only the land, tenantry, and house that were formerly entailed to you."

Neither of them spoke while Rupert stared wonderingly at him. He lifted his eyebrows. Then he put his hand to his chin and stared at the wall.

Wilhelm's face grew hot as he waited for Rupert to speak.

Finally Rupert looked at him and asked, "Are you sure this is what you want?"

"Yes."

"Then I agree." Rupert's eyes glittered as he smiled.

"Very well. But I must first make the offer to Rose."

"Very well." Rupert's look was triumphant.

"Listen to what I heard from Margrite, one of the serving maids at the castle."

Rose sat at Hildy's kitchen table, having convinced Frau Geruscha to allow her and Wolfie a visit to town. She didn't feel much interest in the gossip, but she was glad to be with Hildy and away from her own life in the southwest tower.

"Margrite said that Lord Hamlin—I mean, Duke Wilhelm—told Lord Rupert he couldn't be bishop. His father had not yet made it official, and Lord Hamlin—the duke—would not go along with it." Hildy arched her eyebrows. "Furthermore, I heard Lord Rupert was after Lady Anne. They were seen having a private tête-à-tête in the apple orchard several days ago."

"That sounds like the Lord Rupert I know."

"But at least you know he preferred you to her."

"Not exactly. He knew a duke's daughter would never consent to becoming his mistress, but he believed a woodcutter's daughter would jump at the chance." Rose tapped her fingernails on the wooden table. "Don't worry, Hildy. It doesn't upset me. I realize that power and wealth mean more to him than love. He only wanted me when he thought he could have it all. And frankly, I'm glad I'm not Lady Anne, because I wouldn't want to be married to Lord Rupert."

"Wouldn't you?"

"No. He would only break my heart until I grew to hate him. He's a selfish, self-centered man."

Hildy stared.

"I'm sorry, Hildy, but it's true. I don't love Lord Rupert, and I don't think I ever did. Frau Geruscha was right. I should have asked God his will for me. But instead I let my emotions control me, for all the wrong reasons."

Rose hoped Hildy would understand.

Hildy slowly nodded her head. "Lord Hamlin is the one you love, isn't he?"

"Oh, let's not talk any more about it, please, Hildy. I've thrown myself on God's mercy and I'll just have to see what he does for me."

It was five weeks before Christmas, three weeks since Lord Hamlin's father had died, making him His Grace the Duke of Hagenheim, or Duke Wilhelm, as his equals would call him. In three more weeks Duke Wilhelm's betrothed would be brought out of hiding and presented to him at Hagenheim Castle. A week after that, they would be wed.

Rose didn't want to think about it, tried to tell herself it didn't matter to her, and that if God was merciful, she would be leaving town after Christmas anyway.

Today was also Rose's birthday. Frau Geruscha gave her a new pair of gloves and had the cook bake her an apple cake. Her father came to wish her a joyful day before heading out to his work in the forest.

"Thank you, Father." She gave him a quick kiss on the cheek, and he smiled.

A pang went through her at her father's attempt to act as though everything was normal between them. She should have already gone to him and thanked him for taking her in, should tell him she appreciated him, and that he was a good father. But she hesitated and the opportunity was gone.

In the afternoon someone knocked at Frau Geruscha's door. Rose opened it to find Duke Wilhelm standing before her.

"Good afternoon, Rose."

She recovered her composure, curtsied, and stepped back to let him enter. "Your Grace."

Duke Wilhelm winced, then gave her his one-sided grin. "How are you, Rose?"

"I am well." Rose tried not to betray her nervousness, but she seemed to have lost all grace herself as she jerked the door closed and fidgeted with the beads hanging from her waist. She wasn't sure why she felt so breathless. He was the same man, except for the fact that he was now the duke.

She finally remembered the appropriate words for the situation. "I want you to know how grieved I am about your father's death. May God rest his soul." Rose solemnly bowed and crossed herself.

"Thank you. Will you sit with me?" He swept his hand toward the wooden bench against the wall.

Rose sat and Duke Wilhelm took the space beside her. He looked away then brought his gaze back to her face. He shook his head and said softly, "You're so beautiful."

Rose felt turned to stone. What did he mean? How could he say such an improper thing?

"Good afternoon, Your Grace."

Rose jumped. Frau Geruscha appeared from the storage room and smiled warmly at Duke Wilhelm.

*Good. She didn't hear him.*

"Good afternoon, Frau Geruscha." He stood and nodded to her but did not move away from Rose, even though his nearness to her should have drawn a frown at least from Frau Geruscha. Surely she wasn't afraid of offending "the duke."

"Let me say that I'm so sorry about your father," Frau Geruscha said. "Is your mother well?"

"Yes, I thank you, as well as can be expected."

She motioned with her hand. "Rose will take your cloak for you."

Rose jumped up so quickly she bumped the bench and almost knocked it over. Duke Wilhelm unfastened his wool cloak and swept it off his shoulders, revealing a purple doublet over matching hose. His sleeves were white with intricate gold embroidery—clothes fit for a duke. He let Rose take his cloak and hang it on a peg on the wall.

"Well, I have a lot of work to do upstairs. I'll be back down in half an hour."

Rose stared after Frau Geruscha. What work could she have to do upstairs? And why was she leaving Rose alone with Duke Wilhelm, announcing to them that they had a full half hour of privacy? The woman was clearly going daft.

She turned to Duke Wilhelm. Remembering his last words to her, she blushed, trying to think why he would say such a thing.

"I need to speak with you, Rose. Will you sit with me?" he asked again.

Alarm welled up inside her. Could he mean to make some horrific proposal similar to Lord Rupert's? Rose swallowed, trying to control her rising panic. But what choice did she have but to sit and listen? No one ever refused the duke anything. So she sat back down, clasping her hands together until her knuckles turned white.

He sat beside her and leaned forward, his forehead creasing as though in concentration. Then he clenched his fist on his knee and stood up, pacing the room. Even Wolfie lifted his head and stared with one ear cocked.

What was the matter with him? She opened her mouth to break the silence but he spoke first.

"Rose, do you remember when you took care of my leg, when I was gored by the wild boar?" He came closer then sat down again beside her.

"Yes, of course."

"Well, I must confess to you that ever since that day ... I've been struggling ... with myself." He suddenly stood again and strode across the floor, his hands clasped behind his back.

Rose hardly dared to breathe as she waited to hear what he would say next.

He glanced at her from the other side of the room then paced some more. "You've always talked to me as if I were a real human being and not the son of a duke. You're genuine, gentle, and good." He stopped and stared out the window. "I tried not to think about you. I even told God I would never touch you again after the ball when we danced together." He turned his head to look at her. "But I couldn't stop thinking about you. I wanted to watch over you and protect you. I hated to think about you with Rupert, but I thought at least he would take care of you. But now——" He crossed the floor and knelt in front of her, taking her hands in his.

Rose's spine stiffened in surprise. Her heart raced at the fervor in his eyes.

"I love you, Rose, and I've figured out a way for us to be wed."

Strange inklings of dread mingled with a surge of hope. She stared at him, wondering if she was dreaming again. She'd dreamed about marrying him so many times.

"In three weeks my betrothed is coming here, to the castle. But Rose, I can't marry her. I tried to believe that I could love her, and I'm sure I could have had I not met you. But knowing you, Rose, loving you as I do, I can't possibly marry someone else. So I came up with a plan." He took a deep breath, still clutching her hands between his. "I will abdicate all my rights as the eldest son to Rupert, and he will marry Lady Salomea. We will switch places as it were, and I will inherit his manor and he will be ruler of Hagenheim."

Rose took in his eager, expectant look, which softened to one of heart-rending tenderness. He bowed over her hands and began kissing her fingers, one by one.

"No." Rose shook her head slowly.

Duke Wilhelm stopped. He raised his head and stared, waiting, looking painfully patient.

"We can't." Rose's chest felt hollow, her heart dead and still. Her shoulders became almost too heavy to hold up. She shook her head again. "You can't."

His eyes grew big. "Everyone will say I'm insane, but I don't care, Rose. Is it insane to marry the girl I love? A girl with golden brown hair, with gifts of beauty and goodness and storytelling?"

"No." She shook her head again. "I can't let you do it." Unable to bear the betrayed look in his eyes, she looked away. "You would regret it ... regret me." Pain welled up inside her as she listened to her own words. *Please don't hate me.*

"No, Rose, no." He sounded angry.

"You are the responsible one. Your brother is not half the leader you are. You know that. You would begin to realize you had made a mistake, and you would resent me." She met his gaze. "I couldn't bear that."

"I could never resent you."

Rose spoke softly. "One day you will be glad you took your rightful place and married Lady Salomea to protect your people. Duty is important to you, as it should be, and God will bless you for your sacrifices."

"Rose, please." He bowed his head and squeezed her hands.

*O God, help me.* The pain twisted inside her like a knife. Her heart was wrenched from her chest. Was Lord Hamlin hurting like this? *I don't want to hurt him.* But it would hurt him more, in the grand scheme of his life, if she accepted his proposal now.

He slowly raised his head and looked into her eyes. "Do you love me, Rose?"

Rose squeezed her eyes shut against the raw hope in his gaze. "Please don't ask me that."

"Tell me you don't love me and I'll walk away."

She bit her lip. "I can't."

He pulled on her hands, as though to make her open her eyes and look at him again. "Tell me the truth, then. Say you love me."

She couldn't lie to him, staring into his beautiful dark eyes, but it wasn't right to tell him she loved him when he was going to marry someone else.

"Can you truthfully say you don't love me?" He squeezed her hands so hard it hurt. "Rose! Answer me."

She choked back a sob. "All right. I love you. I never loved Rupert. Only, always you."

He smiled, his eyes brightening. He bowed his head again, pressing his lips against her knuckles.

Her heart leapt, coming alive again at the tender touch of his lips. "But I can't let you give up your birthright for me." The words ached in her throat as she said them, and tears slipped down her face. "It would be wrong."

He lifted his head. "What's so wrong about it?" His brows lowered. "Rose, listen to me. Trust me. Our love will make everything right."

The pleading tone in his voice intensified the ache in her heart. "You love honor. You need respect and a sense of pride in fulfilling your duty toward your people. If you gave that up for me ... I want you to fulfill your duty and be happy."

"Can't you let me be the judge of what I love and need—of what will make me happy?" He reached up with one hand and gently wiped the tears from her cheeks.

His tender touch broke her heart. She could let him convince her, accept what he was saying and ignore what her head was telling her. She would fall into a haven of bliss if she only let herself tell him *Yes.* He would hold her and kiss her and smile. She could make him happy.

She looked down and tried to ignore the way he was looking at her, the feel of his fingers on her cheek. *O God, help me. Help me.*

She thought of her mother, the pain her resentment and lack of love had caused her. All her life Rose had longed for someone to love her, striven to earn her mother's approval. What had it gained her besides pain and disappointment? No, she couldn't let her desire for Wilhelm's love cause her—and him—so much pain.

"Your resentment would hurt me too much." She stared down at him, kneeling in front of her. How would it feel to run her fingers through his dark hair? Would it be soft or coarse? Would he gaze at her with passion in his eyes? Would he kiss her? She would not find out.

She forced herself to continue. "If God wants us to be together, then he will make a way for us. I don't want to go against his will, not again. I tried to force my will on God once, thinking I knew what was best for me. But it seems to be God's will that you marry your betrothed. If we try to force something else to happen, God will not bless it. Even now God has the power to change our future, and if your marriage to Lady Salomea is not to be, then God will prevent it."

Duke Wilhelm bowed his head. He was still and silent for a long time. What was he thinking? Her chest felt hollow and empty. How she wanted to comfort him. Why didn't he speak?

Finally, his grip on her hands loosened. He released her and stood up, avoiding her eyes. "I'll try to stop loving you, Rose, but I'll always be your friend ... if you should ever need me."

"It's better if I go away." Rose whispered the words then wished she had kept the information to herself.

"Go? Go where?"

"I know not." She shook her head and decided not to tell him her plan to go with the Meistersingers. He might try to stop her. And it wasn't a lie. If she went with them, she didn't know where she would be going.

"Please don't go, not because of me. Stay here with Frau Geruscha. Please."

Tears stung Rose's eyes again. She wanted to beg him to understand what a failure she was at her work with Frau Geruscha. She had to leave. And her leaving would spare him pain. He could learn to love his new wife without her around. But she saw the tears glistening in his eyes and stopped herself.

He leaned over her. "I vow I will never do anything again to … Only please don't go."

Rose clasped her hands and stared into his eyes, loving him, drinking in his love for her, for the last time.

"If you change your mind, you know where to find me. Farewell, Rose. God be with you." He strode to the door and retrieved his cloak. He walked out without looking back.

The pain in her chest was so intense, she wondered if she was dying. She bent over, pressing her hands to her throat, which ached from holding back tears. She could still feel his lips on her fingers.

*He loves me.* A castoff foundling raised by a woodcutter. *He was willing to give up everything for me, and what did I tell him? No.*

She sank to her knees on the floor. "O God, what have I done? I've broken my heart and his too. I'm so unsure now."

Maybe she should run after him. Surely their love would be enough. How did she know he would resent her? That was just her fear making her think that. Wilhelm was too good a person to resent her. He loved her. Hadn't he proved it, being willing to give up his title and responsibilities to his brother?

She could catch up to him before he got far. She would throw her arms around him and wipe that half-angry, pained expression off his face with a kiss. She would tell him she'd changed her mind. That she loved him too much to give him up, that she'd always wanted his love, that she couldn't live without it. His eyes would light up with joy and he'd sweep her into his arms.

"God, help me. Don't make me give him up. I need him." She began to sob, the stone floor digging into her knees. Her chest throbbed with pain.

She couldn't give him up, not after everything he was willing to give up for her. She needed his love. And he needed her too. What if his betrothed was a cruel, heartless woman who wouldn't love him and who'd treat him badly?

"O God, I want him. Please don't take him away from me."

Maybe God wanted her to go after him, find him, and tell him she'd made a mistake, but no. The thought gave her a terrible sinking feeling in the pit of her stomach.

She had done the right thing. She had released him to do his duty, the thing that would bring him honor and peace of mind.

She rested her forehead against the cold stone floor. "O God, did I do the right thing?"

*Yes.*

Rose couldn't exactly say she'd *heard* the word, but it was there, in her mind. Had she imagined it? Was it from God? She remembered someone in the Bible asking for a sign.

"God, if it's you, and if I did the right thing, then give me a sign." Tears streamed down her cheeks. She pulled herself up and walked to the window of the chamber. She squeezed her eyes closed. "Give me a sign, God, please."

She held her breath and opened her eyes, searching through the open window.

A line of sunbeams in the shape of a perfect arc broke through a thin cover of clouds, pink and yellow rays stretching from heaven to earth.

Rose stared. She had never seen anything quite like it. The tears stilled on her cheeks. A peace beyond her comprehension overwhelmed her senses.

Her heart still ached, thinking of what she could have had. But God would take care of her. Somehow, God would make a way for her to keep on living, to serve him and not be completely miserable. God was with her.

*O God, please give him the same assurance. Please take away his pain. I don't want him to hurt.*

"My precious Wilhelm." The sobs came again. She heard Frau Geruscha coming down the stairs and forced herself to take a deep breath. She couldn't let her mistress see her this way. The last thing she wanted to do was tell her what had just happened.

She looked out the window again. The perfect arc was still there, pointing to heaven.

# Chapter
## 25

*Moncore watched the door of the southwest* tower from his hiding place behind the blacksmith's stall in the courtyard. He felt his blood pulsing through his body, throbbing in his neck, as he watched Rose and her dog leave the castle and pass through the gatehouse into town. *My perfect opportunity at last.* He had seen Frau Geruscha leave several minutes earlier. He would finally begin the process of making Duke Godehard of Marienberg pay for his crimes against him, for taking away the income he'd enjoyed under Godehard's father and expelling him from the region. How he hated him, and how sweet would be his revenge when Duke Godehard learned his only daughter had been driven mad by demons.

For a while he hadn't been sure if Rose was the one he sought. But once he'd finally discovered Frau Geruscha's whereabouts, as Hagenheim's town healer, it had been almost obvious that her new apprentice was Lady Salomea. Besides, when he finally got a good look at the girl they called Rose, she looked so much like her mother the duchess that he had been certain she was the one.

After his failed attempt to pour the ash over her head and say the incantation, which would have begun her torments, he knew it was no longer safe for him to stalk her openly. Since then, he'd never seen her alone. If no one else was with her, it was her dog, that cursed animal, by her side. And dogs seemed to have a special sense. They hated him and knew when he planned to hurt their owners. Loyal beasts, dogs were, and they would fight to the death to protect someone they loved.

So he had waited patiently, thinking his revenge would be all the sweeter if he waited until just before Lady Salomea's wedding to the young Duke Wilhelm. If he timed his attack just right, Duke Godehard would reach Hagenheim just as it was too late to help his daughter. He'd be furious that Geruscha and Duke Wilhelm hadn't been able to protect her, with her right under their noses all the time. And if he got a good opportunity, he would kill all three of them — Godehard, Geruscha, and Wilhelm. As for Lady Salomea ... once she was completely under demonic possession, she would be at his mercy.

Moncore pulled the cowl of his coarse brown monk's tunic over his face. He tucked his hands inside the folds of his garment and bowed his head, careful to walk at a normal pace so as not to attract attention.

He had to stifle a gasp as he pushed open the door. It wasn't locked. Without pausing to look around, he casually entered, flipped off his hood, and rushed across the room and up the stairs to the tiny bed-chamber that had to be Rose's. He pulled a flask from an inside pocket and sprinkled black ash all over the floor around her bed. He chanted an incantation in Gaelic, rotating slowly around until he had made a complete circle in the ash with his foot. He grinned at the thought of the nightmares she would have because of the demonic spirits he had just unleashed in her bedchamber. Just a small hint of what he planned to cast into her soon.

If only he could stay and watch that insipid Geruscha's face when she realized her failure to protect her precious charge.

He hastened down the steps then threw his hood back over his head as he closed the door behind him.

Rose went to her room to get ready for bed. Barely enough moon-light filtered through the window to help her find her night clothes. She began to undress. The hair on the back of her neck prickled, as if someone was behind her, watching her. She spun around, but no one was there. She quickly donned her nightgown and slipped into bed, her breath coming fast and shallow. She scolded herself for her foolishness, but she couldn't shake the feeling of an evil presence filling the room.

She clutched the blankets up to her chin and prayed, *O God, please be with me. Jesus, protect me.* As her fear had not subsided, she decided to pray out loud. "Lord Jesus, save me. O God, I am your child. Protect me."

Her eyes darted around the room, searching for anything moving or lurking in the darkness, but she saw nothing. "Yea, though I walk through the valley of the shadow of death, I will fear no evil: for thou art with me; thy rod and thy staff they comfort me." *I will not fear, I will not fear . . . What is wrong with me?* There was nothing there to be afraid of.

Rose took a deep breath. No one was in the room but herself, and God was with her. She closed her eyes and refused to open them again.

Rose awoke with a start, her heart pounding and her breath short. She sat up and opened her eyes wide, trying to see something, anything, in the dark room. *I was only dreaming.* But her heart wouldn't calm down. In her dream an evil spirit hovered over her, a blackness with orange eyes and a green mouth, then wrapped around her body and squeezed, taunting, "You'll never get away."

Rose shuddered, sinking down again into her bed. At first she believed it had been a demon, come to her in her sleep. But then she told herself it was only her imagination that had caused the dream, a product of becoming frightened when she was getting ready for bed.

She huddled under the covers, her eyes searching every dark corner of her chamber. She wanted to run into Frau Geruscha's room but was too afraid to get out of bed. Instead, she lay shivering and praying, "God, help me. Jesus, help me. Holy Spirit, help me."

"Did you sleep well?" Frau Geruscha asked as they walked to the kitchen to break their fast.

Rose turned to look at her. She didn't normally ask her if she slept well. "No, I didn't. I had a horrible nightmare. You didn't hear anything, did you?"

"Hear anything?"

"Or know of anyone entering my room lately?"

"No. Why do you ask?" Frau Geruscha stopped, making Rose pause on the path to the kitchen.

"There is something strange on my floor. It looks like ashes, as if someone had drawn a circle and made some strange markings."

Frau Geruscha's face went white. She grabbed Rose's arm as if to steady herself.

"What is it?"

"Probably nothing, but I'd like to see this. Let's go back now and look at it."

Why was Frau Geruscha so concerned? The back of her neck prickled as it had the night before.

Frau Geruscha examined Rose's floor. The ashes were strewn about from Rose's walking across them, but though indistinct, the crude circle was still visible.

Frau Geruscha, after bending down and staring at the floor, searched about the room, itself in the shape of a semicircle as part of the cylindrical southwest tower. Then she got on her hands and knees and looked under Rose's bed.

She got up slowly, taking Rose's arm to help pull herself up from the floor. "Someone must have come into your chamber." Her eyes were dark and her brows were pulled down. With a quick, deliberate motion, she used her foot to smear the ashes around, messing up the circle and any other markings that might have been there. "We need to start barricading our door, Rose. I'll ask Bailiff Eckehart to have a crossbar placed on our door. You haven't seen anyone around—that Peter Brunckhorst or anyone suspicious looking, have you?"

"No. What do the ashes and the circle mean?"

"I'm not certain. But don't worry about it. Some servant probably spilled them there unintentionally." Frau Geruscha's voice seemed falsely cheery. "Let's go on and have some food. Then I'll go ask the bailiff for that lock."

She watched Frau Geruscha's face until she turned away and went down the stairs ahead of her. A shiver passed over Rose's shoulders. Frau Geruscha knew more than she was telling her. *How strange.*


Wilhelm needed some activity. He wandered out to the stable to saddle Shadow for a ride. He had hardly said two words to anyone in the last week, since he asked Rose to marry him and she refused him. He hated to admit it, but she had hurt his pride, and anger mingled with the pain of his heart shattering into thousands of tiny pieces.

His knights, Sir Georg and Sir Christoff, insisted on coming with him on his ride. They said his new status as Duke demanded that he be escorted wherever he went. But Wilhelm refused. He even sent the groomsman and stable boy out on errands while he tended to Shadow's brushing himself. He started with the horse's black mane.

Rose was right. He did love honor and duty and the respect of his people. Heaven above, she had seen through him and into his very soul. She might have even been right about him coming to resent her. His heart twisted painfully at the thought. He remembered Paul's words. *O wretched man that I am! Who shall deliver me from the body of this death?*

A mean, dirty trick life had played on him, forcing him to choose between his duty to his people and his love for Rose. But hadn't he chosen her for all the right reasons? Yes, he loved her for her beauty, but he also loved her for her mind and her heart, her compassion, and her ability to see people as equal. Even as God did. And he wanted Rose to be safe and happy and protected.

But his love for her was selfish too. He loved her because she would make a good wife. He just plain wanted her, and he had been willing to sell his people short so that he could have what he wanted.

But God obviously wanted him to marry his betrothed. Anger welled up inside him. Anger at God? That must be the worst sin there was.

Shadow whinnied, and Wilhelm realized he'd been brushing the poor horse's back over and over in the same spot. He moved to Shadow's other side.

Rose was nobler than either Wilhelm or his brother. She didn't want to be responsible for turning the region over to Rupert, for taking Wilhelm away from his duty and causing him to break his oath of betrothal.

But he had let her down. She loved him, and yet he couldn't make a way for them to be together. And he'd betrayed his betrothed by wanting to be rid of her. He couldn't even save her from Moncore, the man who wished to destroy her. In addition, he'd let his father down by not capturing Moncore in time.

*O God, I'm an utter failure.* He threw down the brush and clenched his fists, pressing them into his eye sockets until he saw only white light. Not only could he not protect Rose as she deserved, but he couldn't protect his betrothed either.

What did it matter now? He would be forced to marry Lady Salomea whether or not he found Moncore. And perhaps now Moncore would come to him.

Try as he might, he couldn't imagine marrying the Duke of Marienberg's daughter in three weeks. When he pictured the wedding, he saw Rose in the bridal gown, standing with him before the priest with her beautiful golden-brown hair flowing down her back. He tried to block her out, to picture someone else, someone with black hair, or blonde, or red, to think of a different face, with a different smile. But when he was able to force Rose out of his mind, he saw nothing but an empty veil.

*God, where is your help in all of this?*

He turned and began to saddle his horse. Clenching his teeth, he focused his concentration on Shadow and wrenched it away from the vicious circle of pain to which his mind kept returning. The crisp air nipped at his bare hands, reminding him that he had forgotten his gloves. He grasped Shadow's reins and hauled himself into the saddle. He steered his horse through the edge of the courtyard toward the gatehouse.

The hair stood up on the back of his neck. Was he imagining it, or was that Moncore standing two feet from the castle gate?

Wilhelm's pulse thumped in his ears as he spurred Shadow on, leaning forward in the saddle. The man turned and ran, disappearing around the gatehouse.

Wilhelm urged his horse into an all-out gallop, then turned him sharply to the left where he'd seen the man run. But upon rounding the corner, all Wilhelm saw was the empty side street behind the Rathous.

He jumped off his horse and drew his sword, running toward the alley behind the buildings that bordered the Marktplatz. He pushed himself to run faster. No one was in the narrow street, but perhaps he could overtake him down the next one, between the guild hall and the Rathous.

He splashed through the sludge and filth that stood ankle deep in the narrow passageway. He came to the back corner of the guild hall, not even pausing to look before streaking around into the alley between the two buildings.

*There.* He caught a glimpse of him at the end of the street just before he disappeared around the next corner to the left.

Wilhelm poured every ounce of his strength into moving his legs faster, never taking his eyes off the end of the alley.

He burst into the light of the Marktplatz and looked all around. Moncore must have gone inside the Rathous. Wilhelm darted into the gray building.

The light was dim inside the town hall, but Wilhelm's eyes adjusted. *O God, don't let him get away!*

He had to make a decision. Either he searched the ground floor or he headed up the steps to the second or third floor. He chose to search where he was, hoping Moncore couldn't get past him, since there was only one door leading out.

Holding his sword in front of his body, he moved toward the back of the large hall, trying to make his footfalls as quiet as possible.

He threw open a door, thrusting his sword into the chamber as he entered. No one was there. In the same way, he went through each room on the bottom floor but found no one.

He made haste to mount the steps to the second floor, taking them two at a time. He searched the rooms there, snatching open several creaking doors but finding nothing.

He bounded up to the third floor. If Moncore wasn't here, he'd gotten away. If only he could split himself up and look in two places at once! There were more chambers on the third floor than the other two. He snatched the doors open, looking into every room, but still found no trace of him.

Wilhelm let out a roar of anger and gritted his teeth. The villain had escaped.

He ran back down the steps and into the streets. The townspeople stared curiously as he ran past them. He reached the town gate and seized the guard's attention with his look of urgency. "Has anyone gone out of this gate in the last five minutes?"

"No, Your Grace. No one." The burly, bearded guard was all attention, his back straight and stiff as he waited for his master's instructions.

"Close the gate. Don't let anyone out until I tell you otherwise."

"Yes, Your Grace." The man put his shoulder against the heavy door and pushed it closed then slammed down the huge crossbeam.

Wilhelm stalked back to the castle to retrieve Shadow and to organize every available knight and soldier at his disposal into searching the town for Moncore.

<hr />

Rose screamed. She sat up in the bed, jerking her head first to the right, then to the left. *Was it still in the room?*

Frau Geruscha burst in. "What is it?"

"Do you see it?" Rose's terror was so strong she could taste bitterness in the back of her throat. "It was just here. Did you see it?"

"What, Rose? See what?"

"Something was here, right here by my bed. I saw it!"

"What did it look like?"

Rose shuddered. "It was a small, white man, and I could see right through him. It was here. It looked me straight in the eye."

"Were you dreaming? Because nothing is here now." Frau Geruscha searched the room as she spoke. "And your door was closed."

A dry sob escaped her. "I know not. I only know I was terrified. Oh, I'm so tired of these nightmares."

"It's time we took some stronger action." Frau Geruscha narrowed her eyes, looking ready to do battle. "Hold my hand and say these words with me. 'In the name of Jesus, I command all evil spirits to leave this room and never return.'"

Rose took her hand and repeated the words with Frau Geruscha. After saying them, she felt a measure of peace. She told herself that Jesus was more powerful than any demon. But her skin still crawled at the thought of being alone in her room again. "Can I sleep with you, in your bed tonight?"

"Yes, my dear. In fact, tomorrow I'll find a servant boy to come and move your bed into my room."

"Oh, thank you."

Moncore waited in his dark, dank cellar for night to fall. He cursed and gnashed his teeth at the voices in his head. Now that he had been seen, his plans would have to be moved up. He couldn't wait. Lady Salomea would be brought out of hiding in two weeks. He had to act sooner, before he was found out and captured.

*You're a failure if you don't get this right.*

Sometimes he hated the voices. But they were always there for him, always supporting him in his goal of revenge.

*No one respects you. If you don't want to be a blighted failure, you must kill Duke Wilhelm.*

Moncore didn't argue with the voices, as he knew they were right. After all, the spirits of darkness were in a position to know everything, weren't they?

He remembered the monk, Gustav, who had befriended him and given him a place to sleep when Moncore was a boy. Gustav told Moncore that his voices were lies, of the Devil. But Moncore felt the voices had chosen him, an orphan with few prospects for the future.

They helped him learn to place curses, to enforce his will on those he didn't like. They gave him power. So he gave himself over to them. In turn, they helped him ascend to a level of respect in the household of the Duke of Marienberg when the old man was still alive. But his son piously cast Moncore out.

*It was that Geruscha's fault. She convinced him my services were evil.*

But finally revenge was in sight. He'd located Duke Godehard's only daughter, had even fooled that simpleton family she'd been living with into leading him straight to her. Very soon, he would send powerful demons to possess her and completely destroy her sanity. Then he would kill Geruscha and Wilhelm, taking special pleasure in exterminating the annoying man who had kept him on the run and hiding these last seventeen years, interfering with his work as a conjurer to the rich nobility.

The bells began to toll, announcing curfew. Moncore waited, to make sure no one in the house was likely to hear or see him emerge from the tiny cellar. Finally, he crept up the steps.

A spider's web caught him across the mouth. He angrily clawed it away, cursing the spider under his breath. He moved silently, bending down to keep from bumping his head on the low ceiling as he crossed the floor toward the front of the house. He peeked out the window that faced the street and immediately saw two guards. They looked to the right and left of them, peering down the alley between the buildings across the street. One of them rested his hand on the handle of the sword at his hip.

Moncore ducked away from the window as they came closer. He smiled maliciously. He could wait a few days, until the watchfulness of the guards began to slacken. Then he would make his move, and no one in either the Duke of Hagenheim's family, or the Duke of Marienberg's, would ever feel safe again.

# Chapter
## 26

*Rose picked up the bucket and opened the* door, hunching her shoulders and bracing herself against the cold wind. Wolfie jumped up from his corner and followed her out. He seemed exhilarated by the bitter cold, standing with his face to the wind then running around in circles, jumping and barking. The cold had the opposite effect on Rose. Most days, after taking her noon meal in the kitchen, she longed to curl up with a blanket and take a nap. Sleep was the only friend that could temporarily take away the pain of losing Wilhelm's love.

She was still sleeping in Frau Geruscha's room, only going inside her own chamber in the light of day to get her clothes. Even walking past the door made her shiver as she remembered the horrible night she had seen the demonic creature by her bed. Whether it was merely a dream or not, she wasn't sure. She only knew she never wanted to see it again.

She reached the well, let the bucket down, and drew it up again, dripping with ice-cold water. She pulled it off the side of the stone wall and it tilted more than she had intended, spilling a big splash onto her shoe. The icy water immediately soaked through to her foot.

Rose sucked in a quick breath as the aching cold bit into her toes.

Wolfie barked, as though to encourage her. She lugged the heavy bucket back to the tower.

"Oh, child." Frau Geruscha emerged from the storage room. "You didn't have to get the water. Let me find a stable boy to do that chore for us, now that it's winter."

Rose shrugged. "Why shouldn't I? I have nothing else to do." She pulled off her wet shoe and rubbed her half-frozen foot.

"Why don't you write another story? You could give it to Lady Osanna, and it would cheer her. She's been so low since her father's death. Laughter is what she needs now. The Proverbs say, 'A merry heart doeth good like medicine.'"

"Yes, but the Proverbs also say, 'Even in laughter the heart is sorrowful; and the end of that mirth is heaviness.'"

"Oh, Rose, you love to best me with the Scriptures." Frau Geruscha smiled and shook her head.

Rose felt a prick of guilt. "Do I do that?"

Her mistress laughed good-naturedly. "No, child. I mind it not. The Word of God has an answer for everything, and you have a fine head for remembering it."

Why was Frau Geruscha always in such an infernal good mood lately?

Moncore hid in a cart that had stopped in the Marktplatz, as he'd overheard its owner say that his destination was the castle. The guard recognized the owner and waved him on through. Once inside the gate, Moncore slipped out unnoticed. He stood watching Rose fetch water from the well, and he cursed her faithful dog. If it weren't for that animal, he would dash in now and wreak his havoc on her world. Well, he'd simply have to find a way to separate dog from girl.

He couldn't wait. He wanted to hurt her, to hurt them all, and he was ready to do it now.

It had been a week since Wilhelm had chased the man who looked like Moncore, and no sightings of him had been made since. Perhaps he had found a way to escape over the town wall. Wilhelm himself had, every day, stood at either the castle gate or the town gate watching the guards check every person coming in and going out, but the effort so far had been fruitless.

Wilhelm, Sir Georg, and Sir Christoff strode to the stable where they would get on their horses and go patrol the town. As he passed the window in the Great Hall, Wilhelm's eyes darted to Frau Geruscha's chamber door. He stopped short when Rose appeared with Wolfie and her bucket. He watched her turn the windlass and then struggle with the full bucket of water. An urge pressed him to go to her and carry her load for her, but he held back. It would make for an awkward moment for both of them. They hadn't spoken since his proposal. And besides, by the time he reached her she would be almost to her door.

He couldn't help recalling another time when he had taken the bucket from her, when he had gone to get his stitches out. He wished he could injure himself again just so he'd have another excuse to be with her.

He let out a sigh of disgust. He had to stop thinking about Rose. He was getting married in two weeks, meeting his bride in seven days, and he didn't want adultery—lusting after Rose in his heart—to be his first sin against the wife God was giving him.

Rose disappeared inside the chamber.

"Your Grace?"

Wilhelm turned. Georg and Christoff stood behind him.

"Ready to set out?" Sir Georg asked.

Wilhelm nodded and led the way.

Moncore's joints stiffened as he crouched behind the blacksmith's stall. His extremities felt nearly frozen. The voices in his head attacked and mocked him. He had to get his revenge now—*now*—or it would be too late.

A potter with his cart stopped in the middle of the courtyard and called out to the guard. He decided it was as much distraction as he could hope for. He had to act, to stop the voices.

He stood and began walking at a normal pace toward the southwest tower. He reached the door without anyone acknowledging him. He opened it barely a crack and peeked in.

Good. He didn't see anyone inside except the dog. He leered at the animal, hoping it would take the bait and come to him.

The dog laid his ears back and growled low in his throat. Moncore taunted him with a menacing stare. Finally, the shaggy animal stood and crept toward him, crouching low and growling quietly as he went.

*That's it. Just a little farther.*

When the dog was almost to the door, Moncore jumped back. The dog leapt out the door, lunging for Moncore's throat. Moncore sidestepped the animal then jumped inside, closing the door in the dog's snarling face. He bolted it from the inside, the ferocious barking muffled on the other side.

Moncore was in. The dog was out. But the voices intensified. He breathed hard, a gasp of laughter escaping his throat.

He whirled around and saw Rose, standing across the room, her mouth open. He leapt toward her. She turned to flee but he caught her by her long hair and yanked her head back.

She screamed.

He jerked her against his chest and clamped his hand over her mouth while he fished out a vial of poison. He spoke the ancient incantation, then jerked the cork out with his teeth. Hooking his arm around her shoulder, he pinched her nose with one hand and poked the vial into her mouth with the other. He poured its contents down her throat.

She gagged, choked, and clawed at his hand. But he held her fast against him, covering her nose with one hand and pinning her arms with the other.

The voices in his head screamed with laughter.

Her thrashing and twisting grew weaker until she collapsed into a faint. When he let go, her body slumped to the floor.

Geruscha came hurrying down the steps and burst into the room. When she saw Moncore she shrieked and came running at him, her fists up. He had to laugh at the picture she made, a small woman, barely as high as his chest, her wimple bobbing up and down, her fists flailing. As if she could stop him. He caught her hands and pushed, sending her sprawling to the floor with an *Oof.*

"What did you do to her?" she said hoarsely, staring at the girl.

At that moment a loud pounding came from behind him, someone beating at the door, shouting and demanding entrance.

Curse that dog. His barks had brought the ever watchful Duke Wilhelm, no doubt.

*Trapped, trapped, trapped.* The voices taunted him. *Don't let them take you alive. Fight and live, or fight and die!*

The pounding on the door was so mighty, it shook the whole tower. Only a battering ram could do such violence. They would soon break the crossbar.

He turned and seized Geruscha by the neck and under her arm, hauling her to her feet. He pulled his dagger from its sheath and held it to the woman's throat, dragging her to the door, yanking her when her feet slipped. He flipped up the crossbar and stepped aside. Duke Wilhelm and two of his men crashed through.

He held Frau Geruscha in front of him like a shield, pressing the blade of his dagger against her throat. Exultation rose up inside him. He smiled.

Wilhelm drew his sword the minute the door flew open.

Moncore stood with a knife to Frau Geruscha's throat. But where was Rose?

"Welcome, Duke Wilhelm. As you can see, you're too late. I've just made sure that your precious maiden will have demons to keep her company for the rest of her life. She'll never be any use to anyone — unless you want a mad woman for a wife." He laughed as if crazed.

Wilhelm stepped farther into the room and saw Rose crumpled on the floor behind Moncore. His blood ran cold as a calm presence of mind overtook him. "What did you do to her?"

"I demonized her, precisely as I promised I would." He leered with an evil grin. "You see, I have powerful friends in the spirit world, dark forces much more powerful than you, and certainly more powerful than the impotent Duke of Marienberg. I swore I would avenge myself on him, and I have succeeded. And now I curse you, Wilhelm Gerstenberg, I curse you! May your house be left to you desolate!"

It took all Wilhelm's willpower not to lunge forward and slice into him. But he couldn't risk Geruscha's life. His mind raced through all the possibilities while he held his sword poised and ready.

"I will be leaving you now to tend your pathetic future wife." Moncore jerked Frau Geruscha forward as he started toward the door. "Stand aside and order your men to do so as well."

The evil man's voice shook, and so did the hand in which he held the dagger. Wilhelm nodded to his men and they moved aside, their faces twisted in ruthless glares.

Moncore slowly dragged Frau Geruscha out the door. Frau Geruscha's expression was defiant.

Wilhelm wouldn't let him hurt her, and he wouldn't let him get away, either. He would kill him for what he had done to Rose, whatever he had done.

Surely God would heal her. But he couldn't think about that now.

As Moncore slowly backed through the courtyard with Frau Geruscha, Wilhelm came after him, matching him step for step, Georg at his left, Christoff at his right.

"Get back, I say!" The fiend pressed the knife against Frau Geruscha's throat, forcing her head back. "Let me leave the city now or I'll kill her."

Wilhelm kept moving forward.

"Get back!"

Wilhelm's eyes locked with Frau Geruscha's. She pressed her lips together. Her whole body sank straight down in one swift movement, startling Moncore. He grabbed for her and missed.

The knife cut her neck when she went down. Blood appeared under her chin and dripped onto her dress. She darted to her left and Wilhelm lunged forward, taking Moncore's attention away from Frau Geruscha, allowing her to run out of his reach.

"Give up!" Wilhelm yelled.

"You will have to kill me!"

He guessed what Moncore was about to do—launch a dagger at his heart. As it flew through the air, Wilhelm leapt to his right, and the dagger sliced through his shirt sleeve. He landed hard on his hip. He felt the cut on his arm but ignored it.

Georg and Christoff drove forward with their drawn swords. But instead of running away as expected, Moncore stood his ground. Wilhelm watched as the conjurer began babbling, "Fight and live or fight and die. Fight and live or fight and die." As he spoke, he reached inside his cloak, surely reaching for another weapon.

Christoff reached the evil man first, his sword poised for the kill. Moncore, eyes wild, drew out a flask and flung powder in Christoff's face. Christoff lunged forward blindly, striking the conjurer in the chest.

Moncore sank to his knees, gurgling and coughing. He fell to his side, clutching the sword, which stuck out through his chest and back. "They're coming for me!" he cried. "No, no, don't take me!" Blood gushed out of his nose and mouth. He held his hands up before his face, as though to ward off an attacker.

Wilhelm and his knights stared in silence at the man dying before them. They all crossed themselves at the same time.

A strange mist began swirling above Moncore as he lay on the hard-packed dirt of the courtyard. The mist congealed into several ethereal heads, shoulders and arms, all reaching out toward the bleeding, gasping man. Wilhelm raised his sword. He focused his eyes on the evil spirits, for that was all he could think to call them. Their faces contorted, they looked only at Moncore. They seemed to claw at him while he screamed. Wilhelm held his breath, chills racing over his arms and down his back as he watched, half-disbelieving his own eyes.

Moncore continued to scream as the demons hovered above him. Finally, his voice gave out. His head fell back, his eyes closed. And the spirits disappeared.

Wilhelm shot a look at his men. They glanced back at him, their faces as gray and sickly as newly shorn sheep.

"Holy Jesus, save us," Georg whispered hoarsely.

Christoff's throat bobbed convulsively, and both knights crossed themselves again.

*Rose.* Wilhelm sheathed his sword and ran back to the healer's chamber.

When he entered the room, Geruscha was kneeling at Rose's side, supporting her head. Black liquid dribbled out of the corner of her mouth.

*O God, let her not be dead.*

Wilhelm crossed the floor and dropped to his knees by her side. "What did he do to her?"

"Some kind of potion." She swept her finger over Rose's tongue, continuing to remove any of the poison that had not gone down her throat.

Rose moaned. Then her arms and legs began to thrash around weakly.

"Rose." Wilhelm leaned over her. *Please don't die. Please open your eyes.*

"Get her up on the bed," Geruscha said. The cut under the healer's chin looked like it had stopped bleeding, although red drops stained her dress front.

Wilhelm picked Rose up and placed her on the bed. He gently brushed back the long strands of hair that had fallen across her face. She stopped moving.

Frau Geruscha went into the storage room and came back with an empty bucket and a cup of some liquid. "Lift her up."

He slid his arm beneath her and held her in a sitting position. Her head lolled on his shoulder. Frau Geruscha tried to get her to drink the cup of liquid, but most of it spilled out of her mouth and onto her chest. Finally, Rose moaned softly and parted her lips. She took a big gulp. As soon as she did, she leaned over and vomited. Frau Geruscha was ready with the bucket.

Rose's eyes were wide open now, but she didn't seem to see either Frau Geruscha or Wilhelm as Geruscha wiped her face with a wet cloth. Instead, her eyes were wild and searching, darting from one end of the room to the other, her mouth twisted in a look of absolute terror and horror.

"Rose, what's wrong?" Wilhelm asked.

She began babbling incoherently, cringing and staring at something over Wilhelm's shoulder. "What?" He turned and tried to see what she was looking at, but he saw nothing out of the ordinary. Certainly they were the only three people in the room. So what was she staring at?

Wilhelm leaned over her. "Rose? Look at me! What is it? Do you see something?"

She took no notice of him, but shrank back on the bed, as though something monstrous was coming at her. She screamed, throwing her hands over her face.

Wilhelm's heart raced and the hair on the back of his neck tingled, sending a crawling sensation across his shoulders. He turned to Geruscha. "What is it?" Had Moncore done as he'd boasted? Had he driven her mad with his potion? Had he sent demons to torment her?

Frau Geruscha's face was stricken and pale. She put her face so close that Rose couldn't avoid seeing her. "Rose. What is it? What's wrong? Rose, look at me. Rose." Frau Geruscha persisted. "Do you see me?"

Rose half-gasped, half-sobbed as she finally made eye contact with Frau Geruscha. Then she seemed to try to talk, opening her mouth. Nothing came out at first, then a few sounds that could have passed for words—if they had made any sense.

What could be terrifying her? It was as though she were having a nightmare, but her eyes were wide open. She saw something that Wilhelm and Geruscha could not see. But what?

Wilhelm leaned toward Frau Geruscha, his brain bursting with anxiety. "Don't you have some herb, some remedy to help her?"

Rose screamed again. Dear God, he couldn't bear it! There had to be something he could do besides stand around helpless, watching her suffer, hearing her scream.

Frau Geruscha turned suddenly and grabbed Wilhelm's arm. Her eyes grew wide. "Demons. That fiend said he would demonize her. There must be demons in the room."

"Why can't we see them?"

"Perhaps she can see them because of the poison Moncore gave her."

He drew nearer to Rose. She shuddered and shrank back, her face full of horror. He grabbed her shoulders and forced her to look at him. "It's me. Rose, don't look at me like that. I won't let them hurt you."

He looked around the room and shook his fists. He glanced back at Geruscha. "How do I fight demons?"

"You must cast them out."

"How?"

"The name of Jesus. He gave us authority over the demons. Command them in the name of Jesus to leave."

Wilhelm searched the room again, trying to follow Rose's gaze, to see the evil spirits that were tormenting her. But he saw nothing, only felt an eerie presence that made his skin crawl as if covered with a thousand spiders.

Clasping Rose's hand, he said, "In the name of Jesus, I command you demonic spirits to get away from this maiden, now." His voice echoed through the room.

Rose's breath rasped in her throat. Her expression seemed calmer, but her eyes continued darting around the room. She suddenly fixed her gaze on a back corner of the chamber and pointed, shrinking back.

*Dear God!* They were still there. Wilhelm scanned the room. "Show yourselves!" He shook his fists at them. But he had no power against them. Except of course the power of Jesus' name. He was a child of God, so that gave him the power and protection of Jesus, didn't it? Perhaps the demons couldn't really hurt her, they could only scare her. He then remembered a verse from the Bible, which spoke of a believer's ability to cast out any demon in his name. He had commanded the demons to leave her alone. Maybe he just needed to *cast them out of the entire region.*

"In the name of Jesus, I cast you out, demons! I command you by the power of Jesus to leave this room, this castle, and this region forever." His flesh still crawled but he felt suddenly invincible. And he knew. In the name of Jesus was more power than Moncore could ever dream of.

He turned his attention on Rose. Her eyes swept the room again, but she looked peaceful. She slumped back onto the pillow and closed her eyes, her face pale.

Frau Geruscha leaned her head down until her ear almost touched Rose's mouth. Her eyes met Wilhelm's. "She's sleeping." Geruscha picked up the cup.

He sank to the floor on his knees and held Rose up while the frau gave her water. This time she swallowed without retching. She drank without opening her eyes, and Wilhelm placed her back on the pillow.

He watched the ever-so-slight rise and fall of her chest. He wanted to pick her up and never let her go. *God, I pray that the potion will not hurt her any more. Help her wake up, God.*

He glanced up at Frau Geruscha. "Will she live?"

The frau sighed. "I hope so. She expelled a lot of the poison, so that is good. We shall have to wait and see if she awakens."

He let out a deep, calming breath, then clasped his hands tightly in front of his chest. He bowed his head and closed his eyes. "O God, you are mighty. We are witnesses of your great power. Oh, Jesus, thank you. Your name has cast out the demons from this place." He paused, unable to go on for a moment. A dry sob escaped him. "Please don't let her die. Block the poison from hurting her. Don't let her die, God. Save her from this poison."

He wasn't sure how long he knelt there. He tried to grasp all that had happened. Moncore was dead—that was for certain—and could never harm her again. But ... *why would Moncore want to harm Rose?*

Wilhelm fastened his eyes on Frau Geruscha, who stood behind him, watching Rose. He slowly got to his feet and faced Frau Geruscha, forcing her to look up at him.

"Is Rose my betrothed?"

Her lips parted as she stared back at him.

"Is she? Is she the daughter of the Duke of Marienberg?"

"How ... how would I know?"

He wrapped his hands around her frail shoulders, willing himself not to shake her. "Tell me the truth. Do you know who my betrothed is?"

Distress deepened the creases around her eyes and forehead. She shook her head. "I cannot tell you," she whispered desperately. "I swore an oath."

"Then it is Rose."

"Please, Your Grace. Have mercy on me." A tear slipped down her cheek.

Wilhelm let go. He turned to look at Rose. His heart seemed ready to leap out of his chest. Could it be? Rose? His Rose. It was too good to be true.

He knelt by her side, watching her breathe, watching her chest rise and fall. Frau Geruscha knelt beside him and, with her shears, she cut his sleeve at the rip.

"Leave it. It's nothing."

"It must be tended to, my lord. Your whole sleeve is soaked in blood."

Wilhelm looked at his arm for the first time and saw she was right. "You're cut too." He had to bend down to look at her neck. The blood had dried in a thin line under her chin.

"Merely a scratch." She smiled as though she had just been in a fist fight and won.

Frau Geruscha probed his cut with her fingers. The pain in his arm suddenly intensified.

"Take off your shirt." Geruscha stood and walked to the shelf where her bandages were stored. "I'll need to tend to your wound."

"What about Rose?"

Geruscha went into the storage room and came back with a bowl of water. "I will keep giving her water, which should help the poison move out of her body. But it is good that she sleeps. We must pray and hope ... Now take off your shirt."

He didn't move from his spot by Rose's bed, but removed his doublet and pulled his shirt over his head, wincing with the movement.

Frau Geruscha cleaned the cut on his upper arm. "It's deep enough that I'll need to close the wound. Do you want to lie down while I sew it up?"

"No." As Geruscha stitched up his arm, he held Rose's hand, stroking her fingers and gazing at her face, which helped take his mind off the pain.

Frau Geruscha finished stitching up his wound. As he was putting his shirt back on, he heard someone at the door, which was dangling open on its broken hinges, letting in the freezing air.

"I have a message for His Grace, the Duke of Hagenheim."

A man dressed in the purple and gold livery of the Duke of Marienberg stood in the doorway.

Reluctantly, he got up from Rose's bedside and faced him. "I am he."

The messenger bowed. "Your Grace. A message from the Duke of Marienberg." He stepped forward and handed him the folded piece of parchment. Wilhelm broke the wax seals and quickly scanned the message.

The duke was less than a day's ride from Hagenheim. He had decided to come early, not having heard any word about his upcoming introduction and subsequent wedding of his daughter, Lady Salomea.

*Not now. Why now?* Wilhelm closed his eyes. He had forgotten to write to the duke. That's why he was angry and coming a week early, practically unannounced.

Not wishing to portray any negative feelings in front of the duke's servant, but still trying to think what to do, Wilhelm looked up and said, "Pray, give my heartiest welcome to the duke. I shall ... prepare a feast for his arrival. Convey my sincere wish to find him in good health and spirits." He frowned. Unwise to trust the servant to remember his message word for word. "Wait."

He glanced again at Rose. She lay still, her eyes closed.

"Frau Geruscha, may I trouble you for some parchment and a quill?"

"Yes, Your Grace." She hurried into the storage and came back with both, as well as a pot of ink.

He sat down at Rose's desk then asked over his shoulder, "Do you have any beeswax?"

He dashed off the note as fast as he could write. In his haste, he splattered two spots of ink. He quickly blotted them with the heel of his hand, waved the letter in the air a few times to make sure it was relatively dry, and folded it. He held the beeswax candle in the fire for a few seconds and then pressed it against the parchment to seal the letter closed. Wrenching his father's signet ring from his finger, he pushed it into the soft wax.

He handed the letter to the messenger. "Take this to the duke. I thank you."

The man took the letter and was off.

Wilhelm had been so distracted lately, so disturbed at having to marry someone besides Rose, he had forgotten to send an official invitation to the duke. The wedding was supposed to take place in two weeks.

His head spun with all the things he would have to do—and at such short notice it was nearly impossible. He would have to warn the kitchen staff, who would be hard-pressed to prepare enough food for the duke and all his retinue before their arrival. Extra beds and chambers would have to be made ready. His mother should know what else would be required.

He stepped to the door and called out to a servant passing by. "Tell Duchess Katheryn that Duke Godehard is coming today. He will be here in a few hours. She will know what instructions to give for the meal and such. Go now and tell her."

He came back inside, clenching his fists at the duke's bad timing. But at least he would find out whether Rose was his betrothed — today.

*Could it be?* After all, Moncore was a crazed lunatic. Could a woodcutter's daughter and healer's apprentice be Lady Salomea, the daughter of the Duke of Marienberg?

He fastened his eyes on her and again knelt by her side. She looked so pale. "Please God," he prayed aloud, "please help her wake up. Please let her be well. Please heal her." Tears dimmed his eyes but he blinked them back. She was so lovely. If she was not his betrothed, if Moncore had insanely believed her to be someone she was not, he might never get this close to her again. He might never again have the pleasure of touching her.

He stared at her perfect lips. "God, if you have made a way for us to be together," he whispered, "then let me awaken her with this kiss of true love." Slowly, he leaned toward her, closed his eyes, and pressed his lips to hers.

Her eyes fluttered open. She smiled softly then reached up and touched his cheek.

He covered her hand with his. "You are well?"

"Yes." Her voice was breathy. "Thank you. But if it's all right, I think I will sleep a bit more."

"Thank you, God." He watched her face relax as she drifted into sleep again. She had awakened and spoke. He believed it was a sign from God that he had answered his prayer. She would be healed of the poison's effects.

He watched her sleep, knowing Duke Godehard would arrive very soon. His mother would need his help. He would need to gather some knights to ride out and meet his guest, to try to repair the damage caused by his negligence to the Duke of Marienberg. There was much to do and little time.

Releasing Rose's hand and stumbling to his feet, Wilhelm turned and forced himself to put one foot in front of the other and walk out.

# Chapter 27

*Rose slowly emerged from a heavy fog of* sleep. She lifted her head and propped herself on her elbows. "Did they capture Peter Brunckhorst? He didn't get away, did he?"

Frau Geruscha came over and patted her shoulder. "No, child, he didn't get away. You won't have to worry about him anymore."

"Truly?"

"Aye. He's dead."

"Oh." She thought for a moment, staring into her lap. She remembered the poison the man had forced her to drink, remembered the demons. She had been so terrified. Then Wilhelm had commanded them to leave in Jesus' name. And they vanished.

*Thank you, Jesus, for saving me from Brunckhorst and from the demons.* She was safe. Jesus had delivered her. She remembered Duke Wilhelm standing in the middle of the room, his fists clenched, commanding the demons to leave.

Frau Geruscha brought her a cup of water. "Drink this."

Rose sat up and obeyed, watching her mistress from over the rim of her cup. She let her gaze drop down to her lap as she handed it back, remembering something else. "Duke Wilhelm kissed me, didn't he? I must leave here." Her voice was a ragged whisper. "I can't stay and be a temptation to him, with his bride coming in a few days."

Frau Geruscha sat beside her on the bed and took Rose's hands in hers. "Don't cry, my dear. His bride is already here."

It had to be Rose.

Wilhelm paced the Great Hall. The Duke and Duchess of

Marienberg, after feasting for what seemed like days instead of an hour, had retired to a large chamber on the second floor. There they would meet their daughter in private.

During the feast, Wilhelm had turned to Duke Godehard and asked if he could be presented to his betrothed immediately.

"Tonight?" the duke roared, drawing his shoulders back and glaring at Wilhelm.

"Yes, sir, if you have no objection." Wilhelm stared back, daring him to object.

The man rubbed his enormous, stubbly jowls and squinted at Wilhelm. He broke into a grin and clapped Wilhelm on the shoulder. "Why not? You've waited long enough to see her."

Wilhelm's hope was bolstered when he noticed that the Duchess of Marienberg was a handsome woman. Did he only imagine a resemblance to Rose? If only he could see the color of her hair, but it was completely covered by a wimple and jeweled circlet.

Now here he waited, alone in the Great Hall, all the food having been cleared away and the trestle tables removed by the weary servants. They'd toiled hard all day, ever since the announcement of the Duke of Marienberg's unexpected arrival. He'd reward them with several days off at Christmas.

He'd sat through the interminable feast. Now he had to wait for her parents to talk to her first. Parents who had been too weak, too afraid, or too indifferent to protect their child themselves, having sent her away as a baby.

A cold feeling oozed through his stomach.

He could burst into the room and let them know he was tired of waiting. What could they do?

The clock chimed the hour—ten o'clock. He tried to pray, to calm his nerves, but the only thing he could say was, "O God, let it be Rose."

He heard footsteps coming down the corridor toward him. It was probably only a servant, but he couldn't resist going to the doorway and peering out.

It was Frau Geruscha. She curtsied to him.

"Your betrothed is in the library. You may go to her now."

He brushed past her, striding briskly down the corridor.

His heart thundered against his chest. He reached out his hand and pushed open the library door. He stepped inside.

Four large candelabras lit the windowless room. A woman stood with her back to the door, wearing a dress he didn't recognize. Her hair was gathered up on the back of her head and covered by a gold caul.

He took a step toward her. She turned around, a tentative smile on her face.

His beautiful Rose.

He sank to his knees and raised his hands over his face. "Thank you, God. You're so good to me."

# Chapter
## 28

*Rose's heart fluttered when her eyes met* Duke Wilhelm's. She waited for him to come closer, to say something. Then he sank to his knees and covered his face.

Should she go to him? She ventured closer, trying to make out what he was saying.

"Thank you, God, thank you. My Rose ... God is good ... God is so good."

He slowly lowered his arms. The look on his face reached out and wrapped her in a warm embrace of love. He got to his feet and held out his hand.

She closed the gap between them and buried her face in his chest. His arms enfolded her.

"Thank God, it's you." His voice was ragged, and his chest rose and fell with each breath.

"I love you." It felt so good to say the words. How warm and comfortable she felt, pressed close to him. She could hardly believe she was standing here, in Duke Wilhelm's arms.

His hands touched her hair. One of Lady Osanna's maids had twisted it into a bun on the back of her head. He lifted the wire net off the back of her head, dropping it on the floor with a clatter, which was soon accompanied by the *plink-plink* of metal hair pins hitting the stone tiles. He unwound her hair and sank his fingers in it as it spilled down her back. Gathering the long tresses up to his face, he breathed deeply.

He opened his eyes, and they shimmered in the candlelight. She gazed into them, and a dozen scenes seemed reflected in their depths, especially her last hazy memory of him bending over her and pressing his lips to hers. His every feature was highlighted by the flickering candles.

"You are the most beautiful sight," he whispered. He leaned down and kissed her forehead.

She leaned into him, her whole body melting.

His lips moved to her temple, then her cheek. Finally, they slipped down and found her mouth. He kissed her slowly, reverently, his hands resting on the sides of her head, his thumbs lightly touching her cheekbones.

His kiss intensified, sending warmth through her whole body. She slipped her arms around his neck and held on as though she were falling. Her legs turned to mush but she didn't want him to stop. She kissed him back and he responded, taking her breath away.

He finally ended the kiss, pulling her closer. "Oh, Rose. God is so merciful to me."

His deep voice sent a warm shiver down her back. His lips caressed her temple. Then they traveled across her cheekbone to her mouth again.

Rose's knees were so weak, she was afraid she would sink to the floor. "I need to sit down."

With one swift motion, he slipped his arm beneath her knees and picked her up.

Rose giggled. "You didn't have to do that."

"I wanted to."

She laid her head on his shoulder. He carried her to a cushioned chair as big as a throne in the corner of the room. He sat down, holding her on his lap.

She laid one hand on his chest, over his heart, and sighed.

"Are you tired? You don't have to do anything but rest for the next week, until we're wed."

*Until we're wed.* "That sounds so good." She closed her eyes, unable to suppress her smile.

"What did you think of your parents, the Duke and Duchess of Marienberg?"

Rose sighed again, but not from contentment this time. "I suppose they are fine, elegant people."

"Weren't they kind to you?"

She fingered the velvet mantle at his neck. Leaning her head back to look at him, she noticed the lock of dark hair that always fell across his forehead. She reached up to touch it, running her fingers through it.

She saw the passionate look in his eyes and pressed her face into his neck, a stab of guilt going through her for the way her body was reacting. "I don't think we should kiss any more tonight."

Rose could feel his pulse against her face. She inhaled his scent, masculine and warm, with a hint of cinnamon from the spiced drink he'd had at the feast. Did he notice that she was avoiding his question?

"So when did you find out," he asked, his voice gruff and deep, "that you were my betrothed?"

"This afternoon. When I woke up I remembered you kissing me—and I started to cry."

He hugged her tighter and kissed the top of her head.

"Then Frau Geruscha told me. She knew I was your betrothed all along and had sworn an oath not to tell me until the day my parents came to reunite with me. I don't know how she kept such a secret all these years. No wonder she didn't like Lord Rupert coming around." She shook her head. "My father, the duke, entrusted Frau Geruscha to come here to Hagenheim and find some unobtrusive family to take care of me and raise me as their own. The two dukes had even arranged to have Geruscha become the town healer so she could watch over me. No one else knew my whereabouts. Only your father was aware that Frau Geruscha knew. If something happened to Geruscha, there was a letter in your father's strongbox that would have explained about me. Frau Geruscha said it made her very nervous when Duke Nicolaus died. No one else knew about the letter."

"You were right here, right where I could see you, and fall in love with you, all along. But you broke my heart when you refused to marry me." His eyelids hung low over his eyes as he squeezed her waist. "I was very angry with you."

"But aren't you glad I didn't accept your marriage proposal?" she teased. "If you'd abdicated, I'd be betrothed to your brother right now."

He growled and poked her ribs just hard enough to make her laugh. But then she remembered the pain of that day and nestled closer to him. "I'm so glad we're together now."

Neither of them spoke as he caressed her cheek. "It must have been a shock for you to find out you had two sets of parents."

"I found out by accident a few months ago. I overheard my mother talking. But I never suspected that I was your betrothed, because my birthday—or so I thought—was five weeks before Christmas and the Lady Salomea's was eleven months earlier. I was a year too young. But Frau Geruscha told me that my parents began counting my birthday from the day I came to live with them—when I was eleven months old." Tears sprang up at the thought of her birth parents sending her away as a baby to live with strangers, with a mother who may have never loved her.

"So they didn't know who you were?"

"No. Frau Geruscha brought me to them and said it was best they didn't know. I'm surprised they never wondered. But then, my parents are never ones to question. They do as they're told and don't ask why."

After a pause, Duke Wilhelm asked again, "The duke and duchess—they weren't unkind to you, were they?"

Rose was quiet, trying to sort out her feelings. Finally, she shook her head. "No. But it was an uncomfortable meeting. I'm their daughter, they're my mother and father, but I don't know them and they don't know me. They sent Geruscha here to watch over me and make sure I was safe, but ..." She didn't want to think any painful thoughts, not now. "I'm happy that they're my parents, because it means I'll marry you, Wilhelm." She straightened and looked up at him when she said his name, letting it linger on her tongue, relishing how good it sounded.

"I suppose I shall have to start calling you Salomea." He smiled teasingly.

"I hate that name." She surprised herself at the vehemence in her voice.

"Then you'll always be Rose to me," he said firmly. He kissed her forehead. "If you wish it, no one shall ever call you Salomea."

Rose shook her head as the tears ran down her face. "It isn't the name." She tried to choke back the sobs, but it was no use. She pressed her face into his shoulder and wept, her shoulders shaking.

He gently stroked her back, speaking soothingly next to her ear.

She finally was able to control herself. "It's merely that ... they gave me away. They couldn't have loved me."

He tightened his arms around her, stroking her shoulder. "I vow to you, Rose, that I will love you so tenderly, you will never feel unloved again."

Rose closed her eyes and let the words soak in. She listened to his heart beating, rhythmic and steady beneath her cheek. She had grown up as a woodcutter's daughter, a nobody. Only Geruscha—and God—had known the truth, and God had made it so her whole world knew her to be Duke Wilhelm's betrothed—someone, someone who had a rightful place in the castle, in the ruling family. It was as if she'd been transformed in the blink of an eye. No, not transformed. She'd been the daughter of a ruler, a princess all along. She just didn't realize it.

A sudden knock at the door made Rose jerk herself upright. Frau Geruscha walked in. Rose tried to stand but Wilhelm held her firmly about the waist, preventing her. Rose's face heated at the picture they must present to her mistress.

Frau Geruscha smiled. "I will take Lady Rose to her new chamber," she paused, "when she is ready."

His hand resting possessively around Rose's waist, Wilhelm said, "One more moment, if you please, Frau Geruscha."

Frau Geruscha bowed and left the room.

She sank back against his chest and sighed. "You are the best thing that could have happened to me."

"And you are the best thing that could have happened to me."

Rose breathed a prayer of thanks for the beautiful sunshine streaming through her window on her wedding day.

She tried not to move as Hildy and several of Duchess Godehard's maids helped her dress. Of the many fine gowns the duke and duchess had brought her, Rose picked out a lovely pale blue velvet one with elaborately embroidered gold-silk borders at the neckline, down the front, and along the hem. Tiny pearls shimmered in the fitted bodice. Over this gown the maids fastened a velvet robe of royal blue. They left her hair hanging loose, as was the custom for brides, brushing her chestnut waves until they seemed to glow with a light of their own. Then they placed a gold circlet on her head, entwined with white and pink flowers.

They started to apply paint to her face.

"What are you doing? What is that?" Rose baulked at the white powdery paint. Wilhelm had never seen her wearing cosmetics, and why should he be shocked today? She consented only to a little lip color.

Next, they dabbed her with perfume, which smelled pleasant enough, a mixture of flower oils and spices from the Holy Land, they told her. Lastly, for good luck and prosperity, they tied a band of blue ribbon around her wrist.

She ran down the stairs, happy to be free from so many ministering hands, and entered the Great Hall. Wilhelm stood near the door, his lips pursed, as though impatient with waiting. When he saw her, his expression changed.

He crossed the room in long strides and took her hand. "You are so beautiful," he murmured, and kissed her fingers. He pulled her close to his side and gazed at her face as though he couldn't tear his eyes away.

The joyous procession of family members—most she barely knew—led her and Duke Wilhelm from the Great Hall of Hagenheim Castle through the courtyard and into the cobblestone streets that wound toward Hagenheim Cathedral, where they were joined by throngs of townspeople.

The girls preceding Rose and Wilhelm wore and carried ribbons of all colors. The rainbow of ribbons danced merrily with their movements as the giddy maidens bounced and skipped their way to the church.

Walking beside her soon-to-be husband, her hand warm in his, Rose hardly noticed the cold air on her cheeks. She couldn't stop smiling. Wilhelm smiled too, but she noted the tension in the squint of his eyes and knew he'd be glad when the merrymaking was over. The thought made her laugh, remembering what Osanna and Rupert had once said about him not being able to relax and enjoy himself.

Wilhelm squeezed her hand and eyed her suspiciously. "What's so amusing?"

"You could smile a bit more. You don't look half as happy as your family and guests."

He leaned toward her until his forehead touched her temple. "No teasing. Or I'll stop the procession right here and kiss you into submission."

And wouldn't this crowd love that? She knew how weddings were. Should the couple actually kiss in front of them, the people would cheer and shout lewd suggestions, hoping to persuade them to kiss some more. Wilhelm was bluffing.

She laughed again. Then she gave him a coy half-grin. "You could try. But I'd rather you waited until no one else was around."

He squeezed her hand hard, but the way he smiled showed he was pleased—and that he looked forward to doing just that.

Soon they reached the door of the cathedral. The priest stood waiting for them. The merrymakers in front of them melted away and Rose and Wilhelm stood together before the huge stone church.

Rose's eyes swam as she stared at the priest, the man who would declare them wed. His expression was solemn and his voice commanding. He asked, "Does anyone present know of any impediments to this marriage?"

His ominous words dried her tears immediately. She held her breath. What if it was all a mistake? What if she wasn't really Lady Salomea, Wilhelm's betrothed? What if the real Lady Salomea suddenly came forward and declared Rose an imposter?

Silence reigned. The priest cleared his throat, preparing to speak.

"Do you, Duke Wilhelm Gerstenberg, agree to take this woman, Lady Salomea Godehard as your wife?" Rose began to breathe again. She forced her mind to concentrate on his words.

"I do," Wilhelm said.

"And do you, Lady Salomea, accept this man, Duke Wilhelm, as your husband?"

More tears flooded her eyes but she quickly blinked them back, glancing at Wilhelm. "I do." How perfect he looked in his white, gold-embroidered sleeves and blue doublet, which deepened the blue of his eyes.

"I now bless this union by the authority of God and in the presence of these witnesses." He looked pointedly at Wilhelm. "You may present her the ring."

Wilhelm turned to her and reached for her hand. She held it out and he slid the shining silver band onto her finger.

It was done. They were married. Wilhelm clasped her hands.

In a daze, Rose allowed him to pull her along behind the priest. They entered the church.

After celebrating mass, the whole procession headed back the way they came, as lively as they were before, obviously anticipating the feast and celebration awaiting them in the Great Hall.

Once they were seated at the tables and the feast began, Rose was able to see her parents—Thomas and Enid Roemer—and her sisters and brother sitting nearby. Tears of joy again filled her eyes as she realized she would be able to provide for their needs, to improve their lives, all of their days. Rose also caught a glimpse of Hildy and Gunther, and her friends looked almost as happy as Rose felt.

And Lord Rupert sat a few seats away with Lady Anne. They were smiling at each other. Only last night Lady Anne's father had given his consent for them to be married. Rose sighed, thankful that everything had happened as it should have. She prayed they would be happy together, and that Lady Osanna would also be happily wed some day. And of course Duchess Katheryn was beaming. Her older son was marrying his betrothed and her younger one was marrying a wealthy duke's daughter. She even seemed to have completely forgotten that Rose had been raised by a woodcutter.

Rose's birth parents, the duke and duchess, sat talking with Duchess Katheryn, Rupert, Lady Anne, and Osanna. They all looked happy.

The entertainment included minstrels, jugglers, acrobats, and contortionists, but Rose hardly noticed any of it. So many people came forward to offer their well wishes and expressions of joy on their marriage that Rose hardly had a thought for anything except the guests.

But the men continued to drink and began to grow rowdy. Wilhelm nudged her elbow. He leaned down until his lips were almost touching her ear. "Shall we sneak away?"

Her stomach flipped excitedly. "A wonderful idea."

While a group of acrobats performed in the center of the tables, raising cheers and shouts of astonishment from the crowd, Wilhelm and Rose slipped out a side door. Hand in hand they hurried toward the stairs and the life that had been planned for them since before they were born.

# Dear Reader,

I've always loved the medieval time period. When I think of the Middle Ages, my mind is flooded with colorful images of flowing dresses, heroic knights in armor, castles decorated with banners and shields, forbidden love, betrothals, secret identities, and, of course, true love's kiss. But since I want my stories to be historically accurate, I did my best to thoroughly research the fourteenth century and the Holy Roman Empire, or Germany, where this story takes place.

One of the things I learned is that most people could not read, especially women, and that most books, including the Bible, were only written in Latin. Only those who were highly educated were able to read the Bible. Since Frau Geruscha had come from a wealthy family and had been educated in a convent, she was able to teach her protégé, Rose, to understand and read Latin. Since I do not know Latin, and readers may not either, I used the King James Version when quoting Bible verses in this story. I know this translation was not in existence in the time of this story, but it is the closest I could find.

Something else that might give the reader pause is the fact that, as a younger son of a duke, Lord Rupert is known by his first name, and as the oldest son, Lord Hamlin, is known by a place name, as his title is the Earl of Hamlin until he becomes the duke. These were the social rules of the time, and also meant that the oldest son would not be called by his first name except by close family members. I considered bending the rules and letting him be known as Lord Wilhelm but decided against it, since this "rule" is fairly well-known among readers of historical fiction.

I am blessed to know some wonderful researchers in the European historical writers' loop I'm a part of, and I asked them lots of questions in an effort to ensure I didn't make any glaring mistakes, although there certainly may be some things that I missed. One problem I've run into is that there are so many contradictions in what historians believe about the Middle Ages. One so-called expert's fact might be fiercely contested by another expert. New evidence has come to light in the last sixty years or so, refuting some earlier historians' assertions. Besides that, there is little concrete evidence that has survived the period. Few writings, especially from the lower classes, have survived, and few articles from everyday life are available to us now; therefore much that is written about medieval times is actually just speculation. In spite of this, I tried my best to gather the most accurate information I could, and I pray to be given leniency by any medievalists reading this work of fiction.

Blessings,
Melanie Dickerson

# Acknowledgements

*I first want to thank the original three writers* who helped critique this story from its very first draft, those Writin' Chicks Jamie Driggers, Caren Fullerton, and April Erwin. Jamie, I'll never forget what you said when you read chapter one. Thank you, my friend. All of you said encouraging things that I needed to hear and needed to carry with me for the next four and a half years. You guys are the best.

I am very grateful to my spiritual family at Weatherly for so much encouragement. You are one accepting, loving, encouraging bunch of people, and I love you for it!

Thanks to every judge who ever commented on it in the numerous contests I entered, back when it was titled "The Woodcutter's Daughter." And thanks to everyone who offered to read or critique parts of it, including Julie Lessman and my erstwhile crit group from the Hearts Through History Romance Writers. Thanks to all who helped me with research, including Diana Cosby, numerous ACFW'ers, those European-history-loving people from Therese Stenzel's His Writers loop, and the wonderful librarians at the Monrovia Library, Katherine and Katie.

And blessings on my "first readers," Denita and Victoria Black. Thanks for the tunnel idea, Victoria. I hope you get your car.

I want to thank my instructor, Cindy Savage, who gave me the encouragement I needed when I was just starting to write again.

A special thank you to Lloyd Porter. Without your help, I don't think I would have had the confidence to write word one.

My wonderful mentors, The Seekers—Mary, Julie, Janet, Debby, Missy, Tina, Audra, Ruth, Pam, Myra, Sandra, Glynna, Cara, Camy, and Cheryl—I hope you don't mind if I claim you all. Mary Connealy was the first to befriend me. Blame her. Thanks for being so real, so fun, and so generous with your time and love.

I want to thank my agent, Mary Beth Chappell, for being excited about this book and taking a chance on it. Thank you for keeping my hope alive at a time when nobody else wanted anything to do with this book.

I must thank Jacque Alberta for championing a medieval romance by an unknown author. Without Jacque, you would not be holding this book. She is a dream-come-true, truly talented editor who has strengthened both the story and the writing. She has blessed me over and over. Thank you, Jacque. I owe you so much.

The *Marktplatz* in the fictional town of Hagenheim was inspired by the town of Hildesheim, Germany, where I spent six weeks in 1992. That is where I fell in love with medieval architecture.

Growing up in rural south Alabama, I had to have a good imagination to imagine becoming a published author. But the fact that Harper Lee grew up thirty miles away from my hometown of McKenzie gave me hope that if she could do it, maybe I could too. I wrote constantly, but after high school, for about fifteen years, I stopped writing or even reading fiction. Then God gave my dream back to me. Thank you, God, for making my dreams come true and for helping your children, Rose and me included, fulfill our destinies.

*More to the Story*

### THE
# *Healer's*
## APPRENTICE

Author interview

Discussion guide

# INTERVIEW WITH
# MELANIE DICKERSON

**When did you decide to be a writer, and what did you do before you started writing?**

I wanted to be a writer when I was very young. I even wrote two novels when I was still in high school, but then I stopped writing when I started college. For fifteen years, I completely shoved my writing out the window while I graduated college, worked as a special education teacher, lived in Ukraine for a year, got married, and had two kids. Then I started writing again.

**What kind of activities do you like to do that help you relax and step away from your deadlines for a bit?**

I used to scrapbook, but when I started writing again, that hobby fell by the wayside. I like to watch movies with my husband, and I like to cook—to make recipes I've never tried before. I like to go to the gym (okay, I don't like to go, but I like that I've been) and I like taking my kids places they love, like skating or going to the zoo or a museum. I love the ladies' Bible studies at my church. We have some wonderful times.

**Where did you get your inspiration for *The Healer's Apprentice*?**

I already had the beginning of an idea—I pictured a teen girl and her older woman mentor. At the time, my two girls were very young and they watched a lot of popular movies based on fairy tales. One day they were watching *Sleeping Beauty*, and I thought the prince's reaction to meeting Rose was very unrealistic. Most men value other people's respect, and I started thinking, *What if someone wrote this story and made it more realistic? What if the prince believed strongly in duty and carrying out his responsibilities? What if he fell in love with a peasant girl when he was already betrothed? How would he deal with that?* I decided it would be really fun to take the basic storyline of *Sleeping Beauty* and rewrite it and flesh it out. Of course, I added a lot of characters who weren't in the original story or the popular movies, such as Rose's best friend,

Hildy, and Lord Hamlin's brother, Rupert. I also made up a lot of plot twists and subplots and changed the story quite a bit.

I was also inspired by the town of Hildesheim, Germany. I spent six weeks in this town, which dates back from the 1100s. Many medieval buildings are still there, or were rebuilt after World War II, including the entire town square, or Marktplatz. So I put together my love of fairy tales, my love for the medieval time period, and my love for medieval German architecture for *The Healer's Apprentice*.

**Did you know how *The Healer's Apprentice* would turn out? Were you surprised by any of the plot twists or characters?**

I always knew the ending, but there were several plot twists that surprised me! One was the subplot involving Gunther and Hildy. When I started the story, I had no idea any of that was going to happen! The climax of their story came directly from research, an actual law from medieval times.

**What is the main thing you hope readers remember from this story?**

That God had a good plan for Rose all along, and she only needed to trust God. I believe the same is true for all of us.

**Do you have any parting words of advice?**

Don't let anyone convince you to give up on your dreams. God is the God of the impossible. You can do anything He strengthens you to do.

# THE HEALER'S APPRENTICE DISCUSSION QUESTIONS

1. At the beginning of the story, Rose expresses concern over not finding a man to marry. In the medieval time period, women had little choice other than to find a man to marry to take care of them financially. Do you think women today are under a similar type of pressure to get married? If so, where does this pressure stem from?

2. Despite being the healer's apprentice, Rose often becomes squeamish at the sight of blood. Did you ever have to overcome a fear or an aversion in order to do a job? How did you do it?

3. Lord Hamlin makes a comment that many believe the lower class is less virtuous than nobility because the nobles have "more reason to uphold the family honor" and they are "expected to look out for the interests of God and the Church." In the context of this novel, do you agree with this statement? Do you think this is true of certain groups or classes today?

4. The author mentions several times in the novel that as the daughter of a woodcutter, Rose is not from the same social class as the duke's sons and their family, thus making a marriage between her and either son socially unacceptable. Do you think such social limitations exist today?

5. When it comes to love, are you more idealistic and optimistic like Hildy? Or do you try to be more practical and level-headed, like Rose?

6. When Gunther attacks Arnold Hintzen, he claims he does it to protect Hildy's honor. Do you think Gunther was right in taking the law into his own hands?

7. Do you think Rose makes the right choice in keeping Gunther's secret to herself? Would you have told someone? Why or why not?

8.  When Gunther is sentenced to death, Rose knows she can go to Lord Hamlin for help. When you get into tough situations, do you have someone you seek out first because you know they'll have the answers?

9.  Why, despite his rogue reputation, does Hildy think a match between Lord Rupert and Rose is so ideal?

10. Rose often worries about her reputation. Why is what people think so important to her? Have you ever worried about your reputation and what other people think?

11. At what moment did you realize Rose was Lord Hamlin's betrothed? Were you surprised like Rose when she learned who she was, once the duke and duchess of Marienberg arrived? Did you wonder like Lord Hamlin, who guessed she might be his future bride, but not entirely sure? Did you know all along like Frau Geruscha? Or were you somewhere in between?

12. Lord Rupert has a questionable reputation, as his brother often likes to point out. While he is courting Rose, however, his behavior toward her suggests his intentions are honorable. What do you think of Rupert's character? Is he capable of committing to one person? Do you think his marriage to Lady Anne will last?

13. What do you think Moncore represents? Does his character symbolize something greater than simply a corrupt man?

14. Throughout the book the main characters try to control their own fates, but learn God had a better plan all along. Do you ever struggle with trusting God has a plan for your life?

15. What have you learned about the time period while reading *The Healer's Apprentice*?

# Talk It Up!

*Want free books?*
*First looks at the best new fiction?*
*Awesome exclusive merchandise?*

We want to hear from you!

Give us your opinions on titles, covers, and stories.
Join the Z Street Team.

Email us at zstreetteam@zondervan.com
to sign up today!

Also—Friend us on Facebook!

www.facebook.com/goodteenreads

- Video Trailers
- Connect with your favorite authors
- Sneak peeks at new releases
- Giveaways
- Fun discussions
- And much more!